# BEYOND SANCTUARY

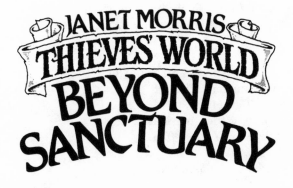

JANET MORRIS
THIEVES' WORLD
BEYOND
SANCTUARY

A BAEN BOOK
Distributed by Simon and Schuster
NEW YORK

BEYOND SANCTUARY

A Baen Book
Distributed by Simon and Schuster
Simon & Schuster Building
Rockefeller Center
1230 Avenue of the Americas
New York, New York 10020

Cover art by Douglas Beekman

1  3  5  7  9  10  8  6  4  2

ISBN: 0-671-55957-5

**Library of Congress Cataloging in Publication Data**

Morris, Janet, 1946–
  Beyond sanctuary.

  I. Title.
PS3563.087435B4   1985        813'.54        84-24441
ISBN 0-671-55957-5

Printed in U.S.A.

# DEDICATION

Beyond Sanctuary *is dedicated with respect and affection to Bob Asprin and Lynn Abbey.*
*And to the entire motley crew of* TW *writers: Long may we wave.*

# ACKNOWLEDGMENT

This novel evolved from a concept and characters developed within the framework of the collaborative THIEVES' WORLD anthologies edited by Robert Lynn Asprin. Without Bob's support, patience and enthusiasm, this project would not have been possible. Lynn Abbey provided invaluable assistance, not only in clarifying logistical considerations and geography, but by providing me with additional, unpublished material from the *Sanctuary* universe: her encouragement and inventiveness are much appreciated. Andrew Offutt and C.J. Cherryh read parts of the manuscript before publication and made valuable suggestions. Lastly, to all my fellow TW authors, I extend my heartfelt thanks: every writer who has entered the Sanctuary construct has enriched the whole.

# Book One:

# Wizard Weather

In the archmage's sumptuous purple bedroom, the woman astride him took two pins from her silver-shot hair. It was dark—his choice; and damp with cloying shadows—his romanticism. A conjured moon in a spell-bound sky was being swallowed by effigy-clouds where the vaulted roof indubitably yet arced, even as he shuddered under the tutored and inexorable attentions of the girl Lastel had brought to his party. She had refused to tell him her name because he would not give his, but had told him what she would do for him so eloquently with her eyes and her body that he'd spent the entire evening figuring out a way the two of them might slip up here unnoticed. Not that he feared her escort's jealousy—though the drug dealer might conceivably entertain such a sentiment—Lastel no longer had the courage (or the contractual protective wardings) to dare a reprisal against a Hazard-class mage.

Of all the enchanters in wizard-ridden Sanctuary, only

1

three were archmages, nameless adepts beyond summoning or responsibility, and this Hazard was one. In fact, he was the very strongest of those three. When he had been young, he had had a name, but he will forget it, and everything else, quite promptly. The domed and spired estuary of venality which is Sanctuary, nadir of the empire called Ranke; the unmitigated evil he had fielded for decades from his swamp-encircled mageguild fortress; the compromises he had made to hold sway over curmudgeon, courtesan and criminal (so audacious that even the bounds of magics and planeworlds had been eroded by his efforts, and his fellow adepts felled on occasion by demons roused from forbidden defiles to do his bidding here at the end of creation where no balance remains between logic and faith, law and nature, or heaven and hell); the disingenuous methods through which his will was worked, plan by tortuous plan, upon a town so hateful and immoral that both the flaunted gods and magicians' devils agreed that its inhabitants deserved no less dastardly a fate—all of this, and more, will fade from him in the time it takes a star to burn out, falling from the sky.

Now, the First Hazard glimpses her movement, though he is close to ejaculation, sputtering with sensations that for years he has assumed he had outgrown, or forgotten how to feel. Senility creeps upon the finest flesh when a body is maintained for millennia, and into the deepest mind, through thousands of years. He doesn't look his age, or tend to think of it. The years are his, mandated. Only a very special kind of enemy could defeat him, and those were few and far between. Simple death, morbidity or the spells of his brothers were like gnats he kept away by the perfume of his sweat: merely the proper diet, herbs and spells and consummated will, had long ago vanquished them as far as he was concerned.

So strange to lust, to desire a particular woman; he was amused, joyous; he had not felt so good in years. A tiny

thrill of caution had horripilated his nape early on, when
he noticed the silvering of her nightblack hair, but this
girl was not old enough to be—"Ah*hhh!*" Her premedi-
tated rippling takes him over passion's edge, and he is
falling, place and provenance forgotten, not a terrible
adept wrenching the world about to suit his whim and
comfort, but just a man.

In that instant, eyes defocused, he sees but does not
note the diamond sparkle of the rods poised above him;
his ears are filled with his own breathing; the song of
entrapment she sings softly has him before he thinks to
think, or thinks to fear, or thinks to move.

By then, the rods, their sharp fine points touching his
arched throat, owned him. He could not move; not his
body nor his soul responded; his mind could not control
his tongue. Thinking bitterly of the indignity of being
frozen like a rearing stallion, he hoped his flesh would
slump once life had fled. As he felt the points enter into
his skin and begin to suck at the thread binding him to
life, his mortification marshaled his talents: he cleared his
vision, forced his eyes to obey his mind's command. Though
he was a great sorcerer, he was not omnipotent: he couldn't
manage to make his lips frame a curse to cast upon her,
just watched the free agent Cime—who had slipped,
disguised, into so many mages' beds of late—sip the life
from him relishingly. So slow she was about it he had
time to be thankful she did not take him through his eyes.
The song she sings has cost her much to learn, and the
death she staves off will not be so kind as his. Could he
have spoken, then, resigned to it, he would have thanked
her: it is no shame to be brought down by an opponent so
worthy. They paid their prices to the same host. He set
about composing his exit, seeking his meadow, starshaped
and evergreen, where he did his work when meditation
whisked him into finer awarenesses than flesh could ever
share. If he could seat himself there, in his established

place of power, then his death was nothing, his flesh a fingernail, overlong and ready to be pared.

He did manage that. Cime saw to it that he had the time. It does not do to anger certain kinds of powers, the sort which, having dispensed with names, dispense with discorporation. Some awful day, she would face this one, and others whom she had guided out of life, in an afterlife which she had helped populate. Shades tended to be unforgiving.

When his chest neither rose nor fell, she slid off him and ceased singing. She licked the tips of her wands and wound them back up in her thick black hair. She soothed his body down, arranged it decorously, donned her party clothes, and kissed him once on the tip of his nose before heading, humming, back down the stairs to where Lastel and the party still waited. As she passed the bar, she snatched a piece of citrus and crushed it in her palms, dripping the juice upon her wrists, smearing it behind her ears and in the hollow of her throat. Some of these folk might be clumsy necromancers and thrice-cursed merchants with store-bought charms-to-ward-off-charms bleeding them dry of soul and purse, but there was nothing wrong with their noses.

Lastel's bald head and wrestler's shoulders, impeccable in customed silk velvet, were easy to spot. He didn't even glance down at her, but continued chatting with one of the prince/governor Kadakithis' functionaries, Molin Something-or-other, Vashanka's official priest. It was New Year's holiday, and the week was bursting with festivities which the Rankan overlords must observe, and seem to sanction: since (though they had conquered and subjugated Ilsig lands and Ilsig peoples so that some Rankans dared call Ilsigs "Wrigglies" to their faces) they had failed to suppress the worship of the god Ils and his self-begotten pantheon, word had come down from the emperor himself that Rankans must endure with grace the Wrigglies' celebration of Ils' creation of the world and renewal of the year. Now, especially, with Ranke pressed into a war of attrition in the north, was no time to allow dissension to develop on her flanks from so paltry a matter as the perquisites of obscure and weakling gods.

This uprising among the buffer states on Upper Ranke's northernmost frontier and the inflated rumors of slaughter coming back from Wizardwall's mountainous skirts all out of proportion to reasonable numbers dominated Molin's monologue: "And what say you, esteemed lady? Could it be that Nisibisi magicians have made their peace with Mygdon's barbarian lord, and found him a path through Wizardwall's fastness? You are well-traveled, it is obvious.... Could it be true that the border insurrection is Mygdonia's doing, and their hordes so fearsome as we have been led to believe? Or is it the Rankan treasury that is suffering, and a northern incursion the cure for our economic ills?"

Lastel flickered puffy lids down at her from ravaged cheeks and his turgid arm went around her waist. She smiled up at him reassuringly, then favored the priest: "Your Holiness, sadly I must confess that the Mygdonian threat is very real. I have studied realms and magics, in Ranke and beyond. If you wish a consultation, and Lastel permits—" she batted the thickest lashes in Sanctuary "—I shall gladly attend you, some day when we both are fit for 'solemn' discourse. But now I am too filled with wine and revel, and must interrupt you—your pardon please—that my escort bear me home to bed." She cast her glance upon the ballroom floor, demure and concentrating on her slippered feet poking out under amber skirts. "Lastel, I must have the night air, or faint away. Where is our host? We must thank him for a more complete hospitality than I'd thought to find...."

The habitually pompous priest was simpering with undisguised delight, causing Lastel to raise an eyebrow (though Cime tugged coquettishly at his sleeve) and inquire as to its source: "*Lord* Molin?"

"It is nothing, dear man, nothing. Just so long since I have heard court Rankene—and from the mouth of a *real* lady. . . ." The Rankan priest, knowing well that his wife's reputation bore no mitigation, chose to make sport of her, and of his town, before the foreign noblewoman did. And to make it more clear to Lastel that the joke was on them—the two Sanctuarites—and for the amusement of the voluptuous gray-eyed woman, he bowed low, and never did answer her genteel query as to the whereabouts of the First Hazard.

By the time he had promised to give their thanks and regards to the absent host when he saw him, the lady was gone, and Molin Torchholder was left wishing he knew what it was that she saw in Lastel. Certainly it was not the dogs he raised, or his fortune, which was modest, or his business . . . well, yes, it might have been just that . . . drugs. Some who knew said the best krrf—black and Caronne-stamped—came from Lastel's connections. Molin sighed, hearing his wife's twitter among the crowd's buzz. Where *was* that Hazard? The damn mageguild was getting too arrogant. No one could throw a bash as star-studded as this one and then walk away from it as if the luminaries in attendance were nonentities. He was glad he hadn't prevailed on the prince to come along. . . . *What* a woman! And what *was* her name? He had been told, he was sure, but just forgot. . . .

Outside, torchlit, their breath steaming white through cold-sharpened night air, waiting for their ivory-screened wagon, they giggled over the distinction between "serious" and "solemn": the First Hazard had been serious, Molin was solemn; Tempus the Hell Hound was serious, Prince Kadakithis, solemn; the destabilization campaign they were undertaking in Sanctuary under the auspices of a Mygdonian-funded Nisibisi witch (who had come to Lastel,

alias One-Thumb, in the guise of a comely caravan mistress hawking Caronne drugs) was serious; the threat of
northern invasion, downcountry at the Empire's anus,
was most solemn. As her laughter tinkled, he nuzzled her:
"Did you manage to. . .?"

"Oh, yes. I had a perfectly *lovely* time. What a wonderful idea of yours this was," she whispered, still speaking
court Rankene, a dialect she had been using exclusively in
public ever since the two of them—the Maze-dweller One-
Thumb and the escaped sorcerer-slayer Cime—had decided that the best cover for them was that which her
magic provided: they need not do more. Her brother Tempus knew that Lastel was actually One-Thumb, *and* that
she was with him, but he would hesitate to reveal them:
he had given his silence, if not his blessing, to their union.
Within reasonable limits, they considered themselves safe
to bargain lives and information to both sides in the
coming crisis. Even now, with the war barely under way,
they had already started. This night's work was her pleasure
and his profit. When they reached his modest east-side
estate, she showed him the portion of what she had done
to the first Hazard which he would like best—and most
probably survive, if his heart was strong. For her service,
she demanded a Rankan soldat's worth of black krrf, before the act. When he had paid her, and watched her melt
it with water over a flame, cool it, and bring it to him on
the bed, her fingers stirring the viscous liquid, he was
glad he hadn't argued about her price, or about her practice of always charging one.

Wizard weather blew in off the sea later that night as
quickly as one of the Sanctuary whores could blow a
client a kiss or a pair of Stepsons disperse an unruly
crowd. Everyone in the suddenly mist-enshrouded streets
of the Maze ran for cover; adepts huddled under beds
with their best warding spells wrapped tighter than blan-

kets around shivering shoulders; east-siders bade their
jesters perform and their musicians play louder; dogs
howled; cats yowled; horses screamed in the palace stables and tried to batter their stallboards down.

Some unlucky ones did not make it to safety before a
dry thunder roared and lightning flashed and in the streets,
the mist began to glitter, thicken, chill. It rolled head-high
along byway and alley, claws of ice scrabbling at shuttered windows, barred doors. Where it found life, it shredded bodies, lacerating limbs, stealing away warmth and
souls and leaving only flayed carcasses frozen in the streets.

A pair of Stepsons—mercenary special forces whom the
prince's marshal, Tempus, commanded—was caught out
in the storm, but it could not be said that the weather
killed one: the team had been investigating uncorrobo-
rated reports that a warehouse conveniently stituated at a
juncture of three major sewers was being used by an
alchemist to concoct and store incendiaries. The surviving
partner guessed that his teammate must have lit a torch,
despite the cautions of research: human wastes, flour,
sulphur and more had gone in through those now-non-
existent doors. Though the problem the team had been
dispatched to investigate was solved by a concussive fireball that threw the second Stepson, Nikodemos, through a
window into an intersection, singeing his beard and brows
and eyelashes, the young Sacred Band member relived
the circumstances leading to his partner's death repeatedly,
agonizing over the possibility that he was to blame throughout the night, alone in the pair's billet. So consumed was
he with grief at the death of his mate, he did not even
realize that his friend had saved his life: the fireball and
ensuing conflagration had blown back the mist and made
an oven of the wharfside; Wideway was freed from the
vicious fog for half its length. He had ridden at a devil's
pace out of Sanctuary home to the Stepsons' barracks,
which once had been a slaver's estate and thus had rooms

enough for Tempus to allow his hard-won mercenaries the luxury of privacy: ten pairs plus thirty single agents comprised the team's core group—until this evening past. . . .

Sun was trying to beat back the night, Niko could see it through his window. He had not even been able to return with a body. His beloved spirit-twin would be denied the honor of a hero's fiery bier. He couldn't cry; he simply sat, huddled, amputated, diminished and cold upon his bed, watching a sunray inch its way toward one of his sandaled feet.

Thus he did not see Tempus approaching with the first light of day haloing his just-bathed form as if he were some god's own avatar, which at times—despite his better judgment—his curse, and his battle with it, forced him to become. The tall, autumnal figure stooped and peered in the window, sun gilding his yarrow-honey hair and his vast bronze limbs where they were free of his army-issue woolen chiton. He wore no arms or armor, no cloak or shoes; furrows deepened on his brow, and a sere frown tightened his willful mouth. Sometimes, the expression in his long, slitted eyes grew readable: this was such a time. The pain he was about to face was a pain he had known too well, too often. It brought to features not brutal enough by half for their history or profession the slight, defensive smile which would empty out his eyes. When he could, he knocked. Hearing no reply, he called softly, "Niko?" And again. . . .

Having let himself in, he waited for the Stepson, who looked younger than the quarter-century he claimed, to raise his head. He met a gaze as blank as his own and bared his teeth.

The youth nodded slowly, made to rise, sank back when Tempus motioned "stay" and joined him on his wood-framed cot in blessed shadow. Both sat then, silent, as day filled up the room, stealing away their hiding place. Elbows on knees, Niko thanked him for coming. Tempus suggested that under the circumstances a bier could still be made, and funerary games would not be out of order. When he got no response, the mercenary's commander sighed rattlingly and allowed that he himself would be honored to perform the rites. He knew how the Sacred Banders who had adopted the war name "Stepsons" revered him. He didn't condone or encourage it, but since they had given him their love and were probably doomed to the man for it—even as their original leader, Stepson, called Abarsis, had been doomed—Tempus felt responsible for them. His instructions and his curse had sent the gelded warrior-priest Abarsis to his death, and such fighters as these could not offer loyalty to a lesser man, to a pompous prince or an abstract cause. Sacred Bands were the mercenaries' elite; this one's history under the Slaughter Priest's command was nearly mythical; Abarsis had brought his men to Tempus before committing suicide in a most honorable fashion, leaving them as his parting gift— and as his way of ensuring that Tempus could not just walk away from the god Vashanka's service: Abarsis had been Vashanka's priest.

Of all the mercenaries Rankan money had enabled Tempus to gather for Prince/Governor Kadakithis, this young recruit was the most singular. There was something remarkable about the finely made slate-haired fighter with his quiet hazel eyes and his understated manner, something that made it seem perfectly reasonable that this self-effacing youngster with his clean long limbs and his quick canny smile had been the right-side partner of a Syrese legend twice his age for nine years. Tempus would rather have been doing anything else than trying to give comfort to the bereaved Stepson Nikodemos. Choosing a language appropriate to philosophy and grief (for Niko was fluent in six tongues, ancient and modern), he asked the youth what was in his heart.

"Gloom," Niko responded in the mercenary-argot, which

admitted many tongues, but only the bolder emotions: pride, anger, insult, declaratives, imperatives, absolutes.

"Gloom," Tempus agreed in the same linguistic pastiche, yet ventured: "You'll survive it. We all do."

"Oh, Riddler . . . I know . . . You did, Abarsis did—twice," he took a shivering breath; "but it's not easy. I feel so naked. He was . . . always on my left, if you understand me—where you are now."

"Consider me here for the duration, then, Niko."

Niko raised too-bright eyes, slowly shaking his head. "In our spirits' place of comfort, where trees and men and life are one, he *is still there*. How can I rest, when my rest-place holds his ghost? There is no *maat* left for me . . . do you know the word?"

Tempus did: balance, equilibrium, the tendency of things to make a pattern, and that pattern to be discernible, and therefore revivifying. He thought for a moment, gravely— not about Niko's problem, but about a youthful mercenary who spoke offhandedly of adept's refreshments and archmagical meditations, who routinely transported his spirit into a mystical realm and was accustomed to meeting another spirit there. He said at last: "I don't read it ill that your friend waits there. Why is it bad, unless you make it so? *Maat*, if you have had it, you will find again. With him, you are bound in spirit, not just in flesh. He would be hurt to hurt you, and to see you afraid of what once you loved. His spirit will depart your place of relaxation when we put it formally to rest. Yet you must make a better peace with him and surmount your fear. It's well to have a friendly soul waiting at the gate when your time comes around. Surely you love him still?"

That broke the young Stepson, and Tempus left him curled up on his bed so that his sobs need not be silent and he could heal upon his own.

Outside, leaning against the doorjamb, the planked door carefully closed, Tempus put his fingers to the bridge of

his nose and rubbed his eyes. He had surprised himself as
well as the boy, offering Niko such far-reaching support.
He wasn't sure he dared to mean it, but he had said it.
Niko's team had functioned as the Stepsons' ad hoc liaisons,
coordinating (but more usually arbitrating disputes among)
the mercenaries and the Hell Hounds (the Rankan Imperial Elite Guards), the Ilsig regular army and the militia
Tempus was trying to covertly form out of some carefully-
chosen street urchins, slit purses, and sleeves—the real
rulers of this overblown slum and the only people who
ever knew what was going on in Sanctuary, a town which
just might become a strategic staging area if war did
come down from the north. As liaisons, both teammates
had come to him often for advice. Part of Niko's workload
had been the making of an adequate swordsman out of a
certain Ilsig thief named Hanse, to whom Tempus had
owed a debt he did not care to discharge personally. But
the young backstreeter, emboldened by his easy early
successes, had proved increasingly irascible and contentious when Niko—aware that Tempus was indebted to
Hanse and that Kadakithis inexplicably favored the thief—
endeavored to lead him far beyond slash-and-thrust infantry tactics into the subtleties of Niko's own expertise:
cavalry strategies, guerrilla tactics, western fighting forms
that dispensed with weaponry by accenting surprise,
precision, and meditation-honed instinct. Though the thief
recognized the value of what the Stepson offered, his pride
made him sneer: he couldn't admit his need to know,
would not chance being found wanting, and hid his fear of
failure behind anger. After three months of justifying the
value of methods and mechanics the Stepson felt to be
self-explanatory (black stomach blood, bright lung blood,
or pink foam from the ears indicates a mortal strike;
yarrow root shaved into a wound quells its pain; ginseng,
chewed, renews stamina; mandrake in an enemy's stewpot incapacitates a company, monkshood decimates one;

green or moldy hay downs every horse on your opponents'
line; cheese wire, the right handhold, or a knife from
behind obviates the need for passwords, protracted dissembling, or forged papers) Niko had turned to Tempus
for a decision as to whether instruction must continue:
Shadowspawn, called Hanse, was a natural bladesman, as
good as any man wishing to wield a sword for a living
needed to be—on the *ground*, Niko had said. As far as
horsemanship, he had added almost sadly, niceties could
not be taught to a cocky novice who spent more time
arguing that he'd never need to master them than practic-
ing what he was taught. Similarly, so far as tradecraft
went, Hanse's fear of being labelled a Stepson-in-training
or an apprentice Sacred Bander prevented him from fraternizing with the squadron during the long evenings when
shoptalk and exploits flowed freely, and every man found
much to learn. Niko had shrugged, spreading his hands to
indicate an end to his report. Throughout it (the longest
speech Tempus had ever heard the Stepson make), Tempus could not fail to mark the disgust so carefully masked,
the frustration and the unwillingness to admit defeat which
had hidden in Nikodemos' lowered eyes and blank face.
Tempus' decision to pronounce the student Shadowspawn
graduated, gift him with a horse, and go on to new business had elicited a subtle inclination of head—an agreement, nothing less—from the youthful and eerily com-
posed junior mercenary. Since then, he hadn't seen him.
And, upon seeing him, he had not asked any of the things
he had gone there to find out: not one question as to the
exact circumstances of his partner's death, or the nature
of the mist which had ravaged the Maze, had passed his
lips. Tempus blew out a noisy breath, grunted, then pushed
off from where he leaned against the whitewashed barracks wall. He would go out to see what headway the
band had made with the bier and the games, set for

sundown behind the walled estate. He did not need to question the boy further, only to listen to his own heart.

He wasn't unaware of the ominous events of the preceding evening: sleep was never his. He had made a midnight creep through the sewage tunnels into Kadakithis' most private apartments, demonstrating that the old palace was impossible to secure, in hopes that the boy-prince would stop prattling about "winter palace/summer palace" and move his retinue into the new fortress Tempus had built for him on the eminently defensible spit near the lighthouse with that very end in mind. So it was that he had heard firsthand from the prince (who all the while was making a valiant attempt not to bury his nose in a scented handkerchief he was holding almost casually but had fumbled desperately to find when first Tempus appeared, reeking of sewage, between two of his damask bedroom hangings) about the killer mist and the dozen lives it claimed. Tempus had let his silence agree that the mages must be right, such a thing was totally mystifying, though the "thunder without rain" and its results had explained itself to him quite clearly. Nothing is mysterious after three centuries and more of exploring life's riddles, except perhaps why gods allow men magic, or why sorcerers allow men gods.

Equally reticent was Tempus when Kadakithis, wringing his lacquer-nailed hands, told him of the First Hazard's unique demise, and wondered with dismal sarcasm if the adepts would again try to blame the fall of one of their number on Tempus' *alleged* sister (here he glanced sidelong up at Tempus from under his pale Imperial curls), the escaped mage-killer who, *he* was beginning to think, was a figment of sorcerers' nightmares: When they'd had this "person" in the pits, awaiting trial and sentence, no two witnesses could agree on the description of the woman they saw; when she had escaped, no one saw her go. It might be that the adepts were purging their Order again, and didn't want anyone to know, didn't Tempus agree? In the face of Kadakithis' carefully thought-out policy statement, meant to protect the prince from involvement and the soldier from implication, Tempus refrained from comment.

The First Hazard's death was a welcome surprise to Tempus, who indulged in an active, if surreptitious, bloodfeud with the mageguild. Sortilege of any nature he could not abide. He had explored and discarded it all: philosophy, systems of personal discipline such as Niko employed, magic, religion, the sort of eternal side-taking purveyed by the warrior-mages who wore the Blue Star. The man who in his youth had proclaimed that those things which could be touched and perceived were those which he preferred had not been changed by time, only hardened. Adepts and sorcery disgusted him. He had faced wizards of true power in his youth, and his sorties upon the bloody roads of life had been colored by those encounters: he yet bore the curse of one of their number, and his hatred of them was immortal. He had thought that even should he die, his despite would live on to harass them—he hoped that it were true. For to fight with enchanters of skill, the same skills were needed, and he eschewed those arts. The price was too high. He would never acknowledge power over freedom; eternal servitude of the spirit was too great a cost for mastery in life. Yet a man could not stand alone against witchfire hatred. To survive, he had been forced to make a pact with the Storm God, Vashanka. He had been brought to collar like a wild dog. He heeled to Vashanka, these days, at the god's command. But he didn't like it.

There were compensations, if such they could be called. He lived interminably, though he could not sleep at all; he was immune to simple, nasty war-magics; he had a sword which cut through spells like cheese and glowed when the god took an interest. In battle he was more than twice as fast as a mortal man—while they moved so slowly he could do as he willed upon a crowded field which was a melee to all but him and even extend his hyper speed to his mount, if the horse was of a certain strain and tough constitution. And wounds he took healed quickly—instantly if the god loved him that day, more slowly if they had been quarreling. Only once—when he and his god had had a serious falling-out over whether or not to rape his sister— had Vashanka truly deserted him. But even then, as if his body were simply accustomed to doing it, his regenerative abilities remained—much slowed, very painful, but *there*.

For these reasons, and many more, he had a mystique, but no charisma. Only among mercenaries could he look into eyes free from the glint of fear. He stayed much among his own, these days in Sanctuary. Abarsis' death had struck home harder than he cared to admit. It seemed, sometimes, that one more soul laying down its life for him and one more burden laid upon him would surpass his capacity and he would crack apart into the dessicated dust he doubtless was.

Crossing the whitewashed court, passing the stables, his Trôs horses stuck steel-gray muzzles over their half-doors and whickered. He stopped and stroked them, speaking soft words of comradeship and endearment, before he left to let himself out the back gate to the training ground, a natural amphitheatre between hillocks where the Stepsons drilled the few furtive Ilsigs wishing to qualify for the militia-reserves Kadakithis was funding.

He was thinking, as he closed the gate behind him and squinted out over the arena (counting heads and fitting names to them where men sat perched atop the fence or lounged against it or raked sand or counted off paces for sunset's funerary games), that it was a good thing no one had been able to determine the cause of the ranking Hazard's death. He would have to do something about his sister Cime, and soon—something substantive. He'd given her the latitude befitting a probable sibling and childhood passion, and she had exceeded his forbearance. He'd been willing to overlook the fact that he had been paying her debts with his soul ever since an archmage had cursed him on her account, but he was *not* willing to ignore the fact that she refused to abstain from taking down magicians. It might be her right, in general, to slay sorcerers, but it was not her right to do it here, where he was pinned tight between law and morality as it was. The whole conundrum of how he might successfully deal with Cime was something he did not want to contemplate. So he did not, just then, only walked, cold brown grass between his toes, to the near side of the chest-high wooden fence behind which, on happier days, his men schooled Ilsigs and each other. Today they were making a bier there, dragging dry branches from the brake beyond Vashanka's altar, a pile of stones topping a rise due east, where the charioteers worked their teams.

Sweat never stayed long enough to drip in the chill winter air, but breaths puffed white from noses and mouths in the taut pearly light, and grunts and taunts carried well on the crisp morning breeze. Tempus ducked his head and rubbed his mouth to hide his mirth as a stream of scatological invective sounded: one of the branch-draggers exhorting the loungers to get to work. Were curses soldats, the Stepsons would all be men of ease. The fence-sitters, counter-cursing the work-boss gamely, slipped to the ground; the loungers gave up their wall. In front of him, they pretended to be untouched by the ill-omen of accidental death. But he, too, was uneasy in the face of tragedy without reason, bereft of the glory of death in the field. All of them feared accident, mindless fortune's disfavor: they lived by luck, as much as by the god's favor. As the dozen men, more or less in a body, headed toward the altar and the brake beyond, Tempus felt the god rustling inside him and took time to upbraid Vashanka for wasting an adherent. They were not on the best of terms, the man and his god. His temper was hard-held these days, and the gloom of winter quartering was making him fey—not to mention reports of the Mygdonians' foul depredations to the far north, the quelling of which he was not free to join. . . .

First, he noticed that two people sauntering casually down the altar's hillock toward him were not familiar; and then, that none of his Stepsons were moving: each was stockstill. A cold overswept him, like a wind-driven wave, and rolled on toward the barracks. Above, the pale sky clouded over; a silky dusk swallowed the day. Black clouds gathered; over Vashanka's altar two luminous, red moons appeared high up in the inky air, as if some huge night-cat lurked on a lofty perch. Watching the pair approaching (through unmoving men who didn't even know they stood now in darkness), swathed in a pale nimbus which illuminated their path as the witch-cold had heralded their coming, Tempus muttered under his breath. His hand went to his hip, where no weapon lay, but only a knotted cord. Studying the strangers without looking at them straight-on, leaning back, his arms outstretched along the fencetop, he waited.

The red lights glowing above Vashanka's altar winked out. The ground shuddered; the altar stones tumbled to the ground. *Wonderful,* he thought. *Just great.* He let his eyes slide over his men, asleep between blinks, and wondered how far the spell extended, whether they were ensorceled in their bunks, or in the mess, or on their horses as they made their rounds in the country or the town.

*Well, Vashanka?* he tested. *It's your altar they took down.* But the god was silent.

Besides the two coming at measured pace across the ground rutted with chariot tracks, nothing moved. No bird cried or insect chittered, no Stepson so much as snored. The companion of the imposing man in the thick, fur mantle had him by the elbow. Who was helping whom, Tempus could not at first determine. He tried to think where he had seen that austere face—soul-shriveling eyes so sad, bones so fine and yet full of vitality beneath the black, silver-starred hair—and then blew out a sibilant breath when he realized what power approached over the rutted, Sanctuary ground. The companion, whose lithe musculature and bare, tanned skin were counterpointed by an enameled tunic of scale-armor and soft low boots, was either a female or the prettiest eunuch Tempus had ever seen—whichever, she/he was trouble, coming in from some nonphysical realm on the arm of the entelechy of a shadow lord, master of the once-in-a-while archipelago that bore his name: Aškelon, lord of dreams.

When they reached him, Tempus nodded carefully and said, very quietly in a noncommittal way that almost passed for deference, "Salutations, Ash. What brings you into so poor a realm?"

Aškelon's proud lips parted; the skin around them was too pale. It *was* a woman who held his arm; her health made him seem the more pallid, but when he spoke, his words were ringing basso profundo: "Life to you, Riddler. What are you called here?"

"Spare me your curses, mage." To such a power, the title alone was an insult. And the shadow lord knew it well.

Around his temples, stars of silver floated, stirred by a breeze. His colorless eyes grew darker, draining the angry clouds from the sky: "You have not answered me."

"Nor you, me."

The woman looked in disbelief upon Tempus. She opened her lips, but Aškelon touched them with a gloved hand. From the gauntlet's cuff a single drop of blood ran down his left arm to drip upon the sand. He looked at it somerly, then up at Tempus. "I seek your sister, what else? I will not harm her."

"But will you cause her to harm herself?"

The shadow lord whom Tempus had called Ash, so familiarly, rubbed the bloody trail from his elbow back up to his wrist. "Surely you do not think you can protect her from me? Have I not accomplished even this? Am I not real?" He held his gloved hands out, turned them over, let them flap abruptly down against his thighs. Niko, who had been roused from deep meditation in the barracks by the cold which had spread sleep over the waking, skidded to a halt and peered around the curve of the fence, his teeth gritted hard to stay their chatter.

"No." Tempus had replied to Aškelon's first question with that sensitive little smile which meant he was considering commencing some incredible slaughter; "Yes" to his second; "Yes, indeed" to the third.

"And would I be here," the dream lord continued, "in so ignominious a state if not for the havoc she has wrought?"

"I don't know what havoc she's wrought that could have touched you out there. But I take it that last night's deadly mist was your harbinger. Why come to me, Ash? I'm not involved with her in any way."

"You connived to release her from imprisonment, Tempus—it *is* Tempus, so the dreams of the Sanctuarites tell me. And they tell me other things, too. I am here, sleepless one, to warn you: though I cannot reach you through dreams, have no doubt: I *can* reach you. All of these, you consider yours. . . ." He waved his hand to encompass the still men, frozen unknowing upon the field. "They are mine now. I can claim them any time."

"What do you want, Ash?"

"I want you to refrain from interfering with me while I am here. I will see her, and settle a score with her, and if you are circumspect, when I leave, your vicious little band of cutthroats will be returned to you, unharmed, uncomprehending."

"All that, to make sure of me? I don't respond well to flattery. You will force me to a gesture by trying to prevent one. I don't care what you do about Cime—whatever you do, you will be doing me a favor. Release my people, and go about your quest."

"I cannot trust you not to interfere. By noon I shall be installed as temporary First Hazard of your local mage-guild—"

"Slumming? It's hardly your style."

"*Style?*" he thundered so that his companion shuddered and Niko started, dislodging a stone which clicked, rolled, then lay still. "*Style!* She came unto me with her evil and destroyed my peace." His other hand cradled his wrist. "I was lucky to receive a reprieve from damnation. I have only a limited dispensation: either I force her to renege on murdering me, or make her finish the job. And you of all men know what awaits a contractee such as myself when existence is over. What would you do in my place?"

"I didn't know how she got here, but now it comes clearer. She went to destroy you in your place, and was spat out into this world from there? But how is it she has not succeeded?"

The power, looking past Tempus with a squint, shrugged. "She was not certain, her will was not united with her heart. I have a chance, now, to remedy it . . . bring back restful dreaming in its place, and my domain with it. I will not let anything stop me. Be warned, my friend. You know what strengths I can bring to bear."

"Release my people, if you want her, and we will think about how to satisfy you over breakfast. From the look of you, you could use something warm to drink. You do drink, don't you? With the form come the functions, surely even here."

Aškelon sighed feelingly; his shoulders slumped. "Yes,

indeed, the entire package is mine to tend and lumber about in, some little while longer ... until after the mageguild's fête this evening, at the very least.... I am surprised, not to mention pleased, that you display some disposition to compromise. It is for everyone's benefit. This is Jihan." He inclined his head toward his companion. "Greet our host."

"It's my pleasure to wish that things go exceedingly well with you," the woman said, and Niko saw Tempus shiver, a subtle thing that went over him from head to toe—and almost bolted out to help, thinking some additional, debilitating spell was being cast. He wasn't fooled by those polite exchanges: bodies and timbres had been speaking more plainly of respectful opposition and cautious hostility. Distressed and overbalanced from long crouching without daring to lean or sit, he fell forward, catching himself too late to avoid making noise.

Niko heard Tempus remonstrate, "Let him be, Aškelon!" and felt a sudden ennui, his eyelids closing, a drift toward sleep he fought—then heard the dream lord reply: "I will take this one as my hostage, and leave Jihan with you, a fair trade. Then I will release these others, who remember nothing—for the interim. When I am done here, if you have behaved well, you may have them back permanently, free and unemcumbered. We will see how good your faith can be said to be."

Niko realized he could still hear, still see, still move.

"Come here, Nikodemos," Tempus summoned him.

He obeyed. His commander's mien implored Niko to take all this in his stride, as his voice sent him to see to breakfast for three. He was about to object that only by the accident of meditation had he been untouched by the spell—which sought out waking minds and could not find his in his rest-place, and thus the cook and all the menials must be spellbound, still—when men began to stir and finish sentences begun before Aškelon's arrival, and Tem-

pus waved him imperatively on his way. He left on the
double, ignoring the stares of those just coming out of
limbo, whistling to cover the wheeze of his fear.

So it was that the Sacred Bander Nikodemos accompanied Aškelon into Sanctuary on the young Stepson's two
best horses, his ears ringing with what he had heard and
his eyes aching from what he had seen and his heart
clandestinely taking cautious beats in a constricted chest.

Over breakfast, Aškelon had remarked to Tempus that it
must be hell for one of his temperament to languish under
curse and god. "I've gotten used to it." "I could grant you
mortality, so small a thing is still within my power." "I'll
limp along as I am, thanks, Ash. If my curse denys me
love, it gives me freedom." "It would be good for you to
have an ally." "Not one who will unleash a killing mist
merely to make an entrance," Tempus had rejoined, his
fingers steepled before him. "Sorcery is yet beneath your
contempt? You are hardly nonaligned in the conflict
brewing." "I have my philosophy." "Oh? And what is
that?" "A single axiom, these days, is sufficient to my
needs." "Which is?" " 'Grab reality by the balls and
squeeze.' " "We will see how well it serves you, when you
stand without your god." "Are you still afraid of me, Ash?
I have never given you cause, never vied with you for your
place." "Who do you think to impress, Riddler? The boy?
Your potential, and dangerous proclivities, speak for
themselves. I will grant no further concessions. . . ."

Riding with the dream lord into Sanctuary in broad
daylight was a relief after the tension of his commander's
dining table. Being dismissed by Aškelon before the high-
walled mageguild on the Street of Arcana was a reprieve
he hadn't dared to hope for, though the entelechy of the
seventh sphere decreed that Nikodemos must return to
the outer gates at sundown. He watched his best horse
disappear down that vine-hung way without even a twinge

of regret. If he never saw that particular horse and its rider again, it would be too soon.

And he had his orders, which, when he'd received them, he had despaired of successfully carrying out. When Aškelon had been absorbed in making his farewells to the woman whose fighting stature and muscle tone were so extraordinary, Tempus bade Niko warn certain parties to spread the word that a curfew must be kept, and some others not to attend the mageguild's fete this evening, and lastly find a way to go alone to the Vulgar Unicorn, tavern of consummate ill-repute in this scabrous town, and perform a detailed series of actions there.

Niko had never been to the Vulgar Unicorn, though he'd been by it many times during his tours in the Maze. The eastside taverns like the Alekeep at the juncture of Promise Park and Governor's Walk, and the Golden Oasis, outside the Maze, were more to his liking, and he stopped at both to fortify himself for a sortie into Ilsig filth and Ilsig poverty. At the Alekeep, he managed to warn the father of a girl he knew to keep his family home this evening lest the killing mist diminish his house should it come again; at the Oasis, he found a Hell Hound and the Ilsig captain Walegrin gaming intently over a white-bladed knife (a fine prize if it were the "hard steel" the blond-braided captain claimed it was, a metal only fabled to exist), and so had gotten his message off to both the palace and the garrison in good order.

Yet in the Maze, it seemed that his luck deserted him as precipitately as his sense of direction had fled. It should be easy to find the Serpentine—just head south by southwest . . . unless the entelechy Askelon had hexed him! He rode tight in his saddle under a soapy, scum-covered sky gone noncommittal, its sun nowhere to be seen, doubling back from Wideway and the gutted wharfside warehouses where serendipity had taken his partner's life as suddenly as their charred remains loomed before him out of a pearly fog so thick he could barely see his horse's ears twitch. Rolling in off the water, it was rank and fetid and his fingers slipped on his weeping reins. The chill it brought was numbing, and lest it penetrate to his very soul, he fled into a light meditation, clearing his mind and letting his body roll with his mount's gait while its hoofbeats and his own breathing grew loud and that mixed cadence lulled him.

In his expanded awareness, he could sense the folk behind their doors, just wisps of passion and subterfuge leaking out beyond the featureless mudbrick facades from inner courts and wizened hearts. When glances rested on him, he knew it, feeling the tightening of focus and disturbance of auras like roused bees or whispered insults. When his horse stopped with a disapproving snort at an intersection, he had been sensing a steady attention on him, a presence pacing him which knew him better than the occasional street-denizen who turned watchful at the sight of a mercenary riding through the Maze, or the whores half-hidden in doorways with their predatory/cautious/disappointed pinwheels of assessment and dismissal. Still thoroughly disoriented, he chose the leftward fork at random, as much to see whether the familiar pattern stalking him would follow along as in hopes that some landmark would pop up out of the fog to guide him—he didn't know the Maze as well as he should, and his meditation-sensitized peripheral perception could tell him only how close the nearest walls were and a bit about who lurked behind them: he was no adept, only a western-trained fighter. But, being one, he had shaken his fear and his foreboding, and waited to see if Shadowspawn, called Hanse, would announce himself: should Niko hail the thief prematurely, Hanse would almost certainly melt back into the alleys he commanded rather than own that Niko had perceived himself shadowed—and leave him lost among the hovels and the damned.

He'd learned patience waiting for gods to speak to him on wind-whipped precipices while heaving tides licked about his toes in anticipation. After a time, he began to see canopied stalls and hear muted haggling, and dismounted to lead his horse among the splintered crates and rotten fruit at the bazaar's edge.

"*Psst! Stealth!*" Hanse called him by his war name, and dropped, soundless as a phantom, from a shuttered balcony into his path. Startled, Niko's horse scrabbled backward, hind hooves kicking over crates and stanchions so that a row ensued with the stall's enraged proprietor. When that was done, the dark slumhawk still waited, eyes glittering with unsaid words sharper than any of the secreted blades he wore, a triumphant smile fierce as his scarlet sash fading to his more customary street-hauteur as he turned figs in his fingers, pronounced them unfit for human consumption, and eased Niko's way.

"I was out there this morning," Niko heard, bent down over his horse's left hind hoof, checking for splinters caught in its shoe; "heard your team lost a member, but not who. Pissass weird weather, these days. You know something *I* should know?"

"Possibly." Niko, putting down the hoof, brushed dust from his thighs and stood up. "Once when I was wandering around the backstreets of a coastal city—never mind which one—with an arrow in my gut and afraid to seek a surgeon's help there was weather like this. A man who took me in told me to *stay* off the streets at night until the weather'd been clear a full day—something to do with dead adepts and souls to pay their way out of purgatory. Tell your friends, if you've got any. And do me a favor, fair exchange?" He gathered up his reins and took a handful of mane, about to swing up on his horse, and thus he saw Hanse's fingers flicker: *state it.* So he did, admitting that he was lost, quite baldly, and asking the thief to guide him on his way.

When they had walked far enough that Shadowspawn's laughter no longer echoed, the thief said, "What's wrong? Like I said, I was out at the barracks. I've never seen *him* scared of anything, but he's scared of that girl he's got in his room. And he's meaner than normal—told me I couldn't stable my horse out there, and not to come around—" Shadowspawn broke off, having said what he did not want to say, and kicked a melon in their path, which burst open, showing the teeming maggots within.

"Maybe he'd like to keep you out of troubles that aren't any of your business. Or maybe he estimates his debt to you is paid in full—you can't keep coming around when it suits you and still be badmouthing us like any other Ilsig—"

A spurt of profanity contained some cogent directions to the Vulgar Unicorn, and some other suggestions impossible to follow. Niko didn't look up to see Hanse go. If he failed to take the warning to heart, then hurt feelings would keep him away from Niko and his commander for a while. It was enough.

Directions or no, it took him longer than it should have to find his way. Finally, when he was eyeing the sky doubtfully, trying to estimate the lateness of the hour, he spied the Unicorn's autoerotic sign creaking in the moist, stinking breeze blowing in off the harbor. Discounting Hanse, since Niko had entered the close and ramshackle despair of the shantytown he had seen not one friendly face. If he'd been jeered at once, he'd been cursed a score of times, aloud and with spit and glare and handsign, and he had had more than his fill of Sanctuary's infamous slum.

Within the Unicorn, the clientele did not look happy to see a Stepson. A silence as thick as Rankan ale descended as he entered and took more time to disperse than he liked. He crossed to the bar, scanning the room full of local brawlers, grateful he had neglected to shave since the previous morning. Perhaps he seemed more fearsome

than he felt as he turned his back to the sullen, hostile
crowd just resuming their drinking and scheming and
ordered a draught from the bartender. The big, overmuscled
man with a balding head slapped it down before him,
growling that it would be well if he drank up and left
before the crowd began to thicken, or the barkeep wouldn't
be responsible for the consequences, and Niko's "master"
would get a bill for any damage to the premises. The look
in the big man's eyes was decidedly unfriendly. "You're
the one they call Stealth, aren't you?" the barkeep accused him. "The one who told Shadowspawn that one of
the best kills is a knife from behind down beside the
collarbone and, with a sword, cut up between your
opponent's legs, and in general the object is never to have
to engage your enemy, but dispatch him before he has
seen your face?"

Niko stared at him, feeling anger chase the disquiet
from his limbs. "I know you Ilsigs don't like us," he said
quietly, "but I haven't time now to charm you into a
change of mind. Where's One-Thumb, barkeep? I have a
message for him that cannot wait."

"Right here," smirked the aproned mountain, tossing
his rag onto the barsink's chipped pottery rim. "What *is*
it, sonny?"

"*He* wants you to take me to the lady—you know the
one." Actually, Tempus had instructed Niko to tell One-
Thumb about Aškelon's intention to confront Cime, and
wait for word as to what the woman wanted Tempus to
do. But he was resentful, and he was late. "I have to be at
the mageguild by sundown. Let's move."

"You've got the wrong One-Thumb, and the wrong idea.
Who's this 'he'?"

"Bartender, I leave it on your conscience—" He pushed
his mug away and took a step back from the bar, then
realized he couldn't leave without discharging his duty,
and reached out to pick it up again.

The big bartender's thumbless hand curled around his wrist and jerked him against the bar. He prayed for patience. "And *he* didn't tell you *not* to come in here, bold as brass tassels on a witch-bitch whore? *He* is getting sloppy, or he's forgotten who his friends are. Why didn't you come round the back? What do you expect me to do, leave with you in the middle of the day? I—"

"I was lucky I found your pisshole at all, Wriggly. Let me go or you're going to lose the rest of those fingers, sure as Lord Storm's anger rocks even this god-ridden garbage heap of a peninsula—"

Someone stepped up to the bar and One-Thumb, with a wrench of wrist, went to serve him, meanwhile motioning close a girl whose breasts were mottled gray with dirt and pinkish white where she had sweated it away, saying to her that Niko was to be taken to the office.

In it, he watched the man called One-Thumb through a one-way mirror, and fidgeted. Eventually, though he saw no reason why it happened, a door he had thought to be a closet's opened behind him, and a woman stepped in, clad in Ilsig doeskin leggings. She said, "What word did my brother send to me?"

He told her, thinking, watching her, that her eyes were gray like Aškelon's, and her hair was arrestingly black and silver, and that she did not in any way resemble Tempus. When he was finished with his story and his warning that she not, under any circumstances, go out this evening—not, upon her life, attend the mageguild fete—she laughed, a sweet tinkle so inappropriate his spine chilled and he stiffened.

"Tell my brother not to be afraid. You mustn't know him well, to take his terror of the adepts so seriously." She moved close to him, and he drowned in her storm-cloud eyes while her hand went to his swordbelt and by it she pulled him close. "Have you money, Stepson? And some time to spend?"

Niko beat a hasty retreat with her mocking, throaty laughter chasing him down the stairs. She called after him that she only wanted to have him give her love to Tempus. As he made the landing near the bar, he heard the door at the stair's top slam shut. He was out of there like a torqued arrow—so fast he forgot to pay for his drink, and yet, when he remembered it, on the street where his horse waited, no one had come chasing him. Looking up at the sky, he estimated he could just make the mageguild in time, if he didn't get lost again.

Thinking back over the last ten months, Tempus realized he should have expected something like this. Vashanka was weakening steadily: *some*thing had removed the god's name from Kadakithis' palace dome; the state-cult's temple had proved unbuildable, its ground defiled and its priest a defiler; the ritual of the Tenslaying had been interrupted by Cime and her fire, and he and Vashanka had begotten a male child upon the First Consort which the god did not seem to want to claim; Abarsis had been allowed to throw his life away without regard to the fact that he had been Vashanka's premier warrior-priest. Now the field altar his mercenaries had built had been tumbled to the ground before his eyes by one of Abarsis' teachers, an entelechy chosen specifically to balance the berserker influence of the god. And he, Tempus, was imprisoned in his own quarters by a Froth Daughter in an all-too-human body intent on exacting from him recompense for what his sister had denied her.

Glumly he wondered if his god could be undergoing a midlife crisis, then if he, too, was, since Vashanka and he were linked by the Law of Consonance. Certainly, Jihan's proclamation of intended rape had taken him aback. He had not been taken aback by *any*thing in years. "Rapist, they call you, and with good reason," she had said, reaching up under the scale-armor corselet to wriggle out of her loinguard. "We will see how you like it, in receipt of what you're used to giving out." He couldn't stop her, or refrain from responding to her. Cime had interrupted Jihan's scheduled tryst with Aškelon, perhaps aborted it. The body which faced him had been chosen for a woman's retribution. Later she said to him, rubbing the imprint of her scale-armor from his loins with a high-veined hand: "Have you never heard of letting the lady win?"

"No," he replied, genuinely puzzled. "Jihan, are you saying I was unfair?"

"Only arcane, weighting the scales to your side. Love without feeling, mind-caress, spell-excitation. . . . I am new to flesh. I hope you are well-chastised and repentant," she giggled, just briefly, before his words found her ears: "I warn you, straight-out: those who love me, die of it, and those I favor are fated to spurn me."

"You are an arrogant man. You think I care? I should have struck you more viciously." Her flat hand slapped, more than playfully, down upon his belly. "He—" she meant Aškelon "—cannot spare me any of his substance. I do this for him, that he not look upon me hungry for a man and know shame. You saw his wrist, where she skewered him. . . ."

"I don't fancy a gift from him, convenient or no." He was going to pull her up beside him, where he might casually get his hands around her fine, muscular throat. But she sat back and retorted, "You think he would suggest this? Or even know of it? I take what I choose from men, and we do not discuss it. It is all I can do for him. And you owe me whatever price I care to name—your own sister took from me my husband before ever his lips touched mine. When my father chose me from my sisters to be sent to ease Aškelon's loneliness, I had a choice—yea or nay—and a year to make it. I studied him, and felt love enough to come to human flesh to claim it. To become human—you concede that I am, for argument's sake?"

He did that—her spectacular body, sheathed in muscle, taut and sensuous, was too powerful and yet too shapely to be mortal, but even so, he did not critique her.

"Then," she continued, rising up, hands on her impossibly slim waist, pacing as she spoke in a rustle of armor-scales, "consider my plight. To become human for the love of a demiurge, and then not to be able to claim him.... It is done, I have this form, I cannot undo it until its time is up. And since I cannot collect satisfaction from her—*he* has forbidden me that pleasure—all the powers on the twelfth plane agree: I may have what I wish from you. And what I wish, I have made quite plain." Her voice was deepening. She took a step toward him.

He objected, and she laughed, "You should see your face."

"I can imagine. You are a very attractive ... lady, and you come with impeccable credentials from an unimpeachable source. So if you are inexperienced in the ways of the world, brash and awkward and ineffective because of that, I suppose I must excuse you. Thus, I shall make allowances." His one hand raised, gestured, scooped up her loinguard and tossed it at her. "Get dressed, get out of here. Go back to your master, familiar, and tell him I do not any longer pay my sister's debts."

Then, finally, she came at him: "You mistake me. I am not asking you, I am telling you." She reached him, crouched down, thighs together, hands on her knees, knees on what had once been Jubal the Slaver's bed. "This is a real debt, in lieu of payment for which, my patron and the elementals will exact—"

He clipped her exactly behind her right ear, and she fell across him, senseless.

Other things she had said, earlier in passion, rang in his head: that should he in any way displease her, her duty would then be plain: he and Vashanka could both be disciplined by way of the child they had together begotten on one of Molin Torchholder's temple dancers.

He wasn't sure how he felt about that, as he was not sure how he felt about Aškelon's offer of mortality or Vashanka's cowardice, or the positives and negatives of his sister's self-engendered fate.

He gave the unconscious woman over to his Stepsons with instructions that made the three he had hailed grin widely. He couldn't estimate how long they would be able to hold her—however long they managed it, it had better be long enough. The Stepson who had come from seeking Niko in Sanctuary found him, garbed for business, saddling a Trôs horse in the stables.

"Stealth said," the gruff, sloe-eyed commando reported: " 'She said stay out of it, no need to fear.' He's staying with the archmage, or whatever it is. He's going to the mageguild party and suggests you try and drop by." A feral grin stole over the mercenary's face. He knew something was up. "Need anybody on your right for this, commander?"

Tempus almost said no, but changed his mind and told the Stepson to get a fresh horse and his best panoply and meet him at the mageguild's outer gate.

There was a little mist in the streets by the time Tempus headed his Trôs horse across the east side toward the mageguild—nothing daunting yet, just a fetlock-high steaminess as if the streets were cobbled with dry ice. He had had no luck intercepting his sister at Lastel's estate: a servant shouted through a grate, over the barking of dogs, that the master had already left for the fete. He'd stopped briefly at the mercenaries' hostel before going there, to burn a rag he had had for centuries in the common room's hearth: he no longer needed to be reminded not to argue with warlocks, or that love, for him, was always a losing game. With his sister's scarf, perhaps the problem of her would waft away, changed like the ancient linen to smoke upon the air.

Before the mageguild's outer wall, an imprudent crowd had gathered to watch the luminaries arriving in the ersatz-daylight of its ensorceled grounds. Pink clouds formed a glowing canopy to the wall's edge—a godly pavilion; elsewhere, it was night. Where dark met light, the Stepson Janni waited, one leg crooked over his saddlehorn, rolling a smoke, his best helmet dangling by his knee and his full-length dress-mantle draped over his horse's croup, while around his hips the ragged crowd thronged and his horse, ears flattened, snapped at Ilsigs who came too near.

Tempus' gray rumbled a greeting to the bay; the curly-headed mercenary straightened up in his saddle and saluted, grinning through his beard.

He wasn't smiling when the mageguild's ponderous doors enfolded them, and three junior functionaries escorted them to the "changing rooms" within the outer wall where they were expected to strip and hand over their armaments to the solicitously smirking mages-in-training before donning proferred "fête-clothes" (gray silk chitons and summer sandals) the wizards had thoughtfully provided. Aškelon wasn't taking any chances, Tempus thought but did not say, though Janni wondered aloud what use there was in checking their paltry swords and daggers when enchanters could not be made to check their spells.

Inside the mageguild's outer walls, it was summer. In its gardens—transformed from their usual dank fetidness by artful conjure into a wonderland of orchids and eucalyptus and willows weeping where before moss-hung swamp-giants had held sway over quickmires—Tempus saw Kadakithis, resolutely imperious in a black robe oversewn with gems into a map of Ranke-caught-in-the-web-of-the-world. The prince/governor's pregnant wife, a red gift-gown splendid over her child-belly, leaned heavily on his arm. Kittycat's approving glance was laced with commiseration: yes, he, too, found it hard to smile here, but both of them knew it prudent to observe the forms, especially with wizards. . . .

Tempus nodded and walked away.

Then he saw her, holding Lastel's hand, to which the prosthetic thumb of his disguise was firmly attached. A signal bade Janni await him; he didn't have to look back to know that the Stepson obeyed.

Cime was blond tonight, and golden-eyed, tall in her adept-chosen robe of iridescent green, but he saw through the illusion to her familiar self. And she knew it. "You come here without your beloved armaments or even the god's amulet? The man I used to know would have pulled rank and held on to his weapons."

"Nothing's going to happen here," he murmured, staring off over her head into the crowd looking for Niko; "unless the message I received was in error, and we do have a problem?"

"*We* have no problem—" glowered Lastel/One-Thumb.

"One-Thumb, disappear, or I'll have Janni, over there, teach you how to imitate your bar's sign." With a reproachful look that Tempus would utter his alias here, the man who did not like to be called One-Thumb outside the Maze lumbered off.

Then he had to look at her. Under the golden-eyed illusion, her char-and-smoke gaze accused him, as it had chased him across the centuries and made him content to be accursed and constrained from other loves. *God*, he thought, *I will never get through this without error*. It was the closest he had come to *asking* Vashanka to help him for ages. In the back of his skull, a distant whisper exhorted him to take his sister while he could . . . that bush on his right would be bower enough. But more than advice the god could not give: *"I have my own troubles, mortal, for which you are partly responsible."* With the echo of Vashanka's last word, Tempus knew the god was gone.

"Is Lastel telling the truth, Cime? Are you content to face Aškelon's wrath, and your peril, alone? Tell me how you came to *half*-kill a personage of that magnitude, and assure me that you can rectify your mistake without my help."

She reached up and touched his throat, running her finger along his jaw until it found his mouth. "Ssh, ssh. You are a bad liar, who proclaims he does not love me still. Have you not enough at risk, presently? Yes, I erred with Aškelon. He tricked me. I shall solve it, one way or the other. My heart saw him, and I could not then be the one who stood there watching him die. His world beguiled me, his form enthralled me. You know what punishment love could bring me. . . . He begged me leave him to die alone. And I *believed* him . . . because I feared for my life, should I come to love him while he died. We each bear our proper curse, that is sure."

"You think this disguise will fool him?"

She shook her head. "I need not; he will want a meeting. This," she ran her hands down over her illusory youth and beauty, "was for the magelings, those children at the gates. As for you, stay clear of this matter, my brother. There is no time for quailing or philosophical debates, now. You never were competent to simply *act*, unencumbered by judgment or conscience. Don't try to change, on my account. I will deal with the entelechy, and then I will drink even his name dry of meaning. Like that!" She snapped her fingers, twirled on her heel, and flounced off in a good imitation of a young woman offended by a forward soldier.

While he watched, Aškelon appeared from the crowd to bar her path, a golden coin held out before him like a wand or a warding charm.

That fast did he have her, too fast for Tempus to get between them, simply by the mechanism of invoking her curse: for pay, she must give herself to any comer. He

watched them flicker out of being with his stomach rolling and an ache in his throat. It was some little while
before he saw anything external, and then he saw Nikodemos showing off his gift-cuirass to Janni.

The two came up to him wondering why it was, when
everyone else's armaments had been taken from them,
Niko, who'd arrived in shabby duty-gear, had been given
better than ever he could afford. Tempus drew slowly
into his present, noting Molin Torchholder's overgaudy
figure nearby, and a kohl-eyed lady who might easily be
an infiltrator from the Mygdonian Alliance talking to Lastel.

He asked his Stepsons to make her acquaintance: "She
might just be smuggling drugs into Sanctuary with Lastel's
help, but don't arrest her for trifles. If she *is* a spy, perhaps she will try to recruit a Stepson disaffected enough
with his lot. Either of you—a single agent or half a broken
pair—could fit that description."

"At the least, we must plumb her body's secrets, Stealth,"
Janni rumbled to Niko as the two strutted her way, looking virile and predatory.

With a scowl of concern for the Stepson to whom he
was bound by ill-considered words, he sought out Torchholder, recalling, as he slid with murmured greetings and
apologies through socialites and Hazard-class adepts, Niko's
blank and steady eyes: the boy knew his danger, and
trusted Tempus, as a Sacred Bander must, to see him
through it. No remonstrance or doubt had shown in the
fighter called Stealth's open countenance, that Tempus
would come here against Aškelon's wishes, and risk a
Stepson's life. It was war, the boy's calm said, what they
both did and what they both knew. Later, perhaps there
would be explanations—or not. Tempus knew that Niko,
should he survive, would never broach the subject.

"Torchholder, I think you ought to go see to the First
Consort's baby," he said as his hand came down heavily
on the palace-priest's bebaubled shoulder. Torchholder

was already pulling on his beard, his mouth curled with anger, when he turned. Assessing Tempus' demeanor, his face did a dance which ended in a mien of knowing caution. "Ah, yes, I did mean to look in on Seylalha and her babe. Thank you for reminding me, Hell Hound."

*"Stay with her,"* Tempus whispered sotto voce as Molin sought to brush by him, *"or get them both to a safer place—"*

"We *got* your message, this afternoon, Hound," the privy priest hissed, and he was gone.

Tempest was just thinking that it was well Fête Week only came once yearly, when above him, in the pink, tented clouds, winter gloom began to spread; and beside him, a hand closed upon his left arm with a numbingly painful grip: Jihan had arrived.

Aškelon of Meridian, entelechy of the seventh sphere, lord of dream and shadow, faced his would-be assassin little strengthened. The Hazards of Sanctuary had given what they could of power to him, but mortal strength and mortals' magic could not replace what he had lost. His compassionate eyes had sunken deep under lined and arching brows; his skin was pallid; his cheeks hosted deep hollows like his colossus' where it guarded an unknown sea, so fierce that folk there who had never heard of Sanctuary swore that in those stony caverns demons raised their broods.

It had cost him much to take flesh and make chase. It cost him more to remove Cime to the mageguild's innermost sanctum before the disturbance broke out above the celebrants on the lawn. But he had done it.

He said to her, "Your intention, free agent, was not clear. Your resolve was not firm. I am neither dead nor alive, because of you. Release me from this torture. I saw in your eyes you did not truly wish my demise, nor the madness that must come upon the world entire from the destruction of the place of salving dreams. You have lived awhile, now, in a world where dreams cannot solve problems, or be used to chart the future, or to heal or renew. What say you? You can change it, bring sanity back among the planes, and love to your aching heart. I will make you lady of Meridian. Our quays will once again rise crystal, streets will glitter gold, and my people will finish the welcoming paean they were singing when you shattered my heart." As he spoke, he pulled from his vestments a kerchief and held it out, unfolded, in his right hand. There on snowy linen glittered the shards of the Heart of Aškelon, the obsidian talisman which her rods had destroyed when he wore it on his wrist.

She had them out by then, taken down from her hair, and she twirled them, blue-white and ominous, in her fingers.

He did not shrink from her, nor eye her weapons. He met her glance with his, and held, willing to take either outcome—anything but go on the way he was.

Then he heard the hardness of her laugh, and prepared himself to face the tithe-collectors who held the mortgage on his soul.

Her aspect of blond youthfulness fell away with her laughter, and she stepped near him, saying, "Love, you offer me? You know my curse, do you not?"

"I can lift it, if you but spend one year with me."

"*You can lift it?* Why should I believe you, father of magic? Not even gods must tell the truth, and you, I own, are beyond even the constraints of right and wrong which gods obey."

"Will you not help me, and help yourself? Your beauty will not fade; I can give youth unending, and heal your heart, if you but heal mine." His hand, outstretched to her, quivered. His eyes sparkled with unshed tears. "Shall you spend eternity as a murderer and a whore, *for no reason?* Take salvation, now it is offered. Take it for us both. Neither of us could claim such a boon from eternity again."

Cime shrugged, and the woman's eyes so much older than the three decades her body showed impaled him. "Some kill politicians, some generals, foot soldiers in the field. As for me, I think the mages are the problem, twisting times and worlds about like children play with string. And as for help, what makes you think either you or I deserve it? How many have you aided, without commensurate gain? When old Four-Eyes-Spitting-Fire-And-Four-Mouths-Spitting-Curses came after me, *no* one did *anything*, not my parents, or our priests or seers. They all just looked at their feet, as if the key to my salvation was written in Azehur's sand. *But it was not!* And oh, did I learn from *my* wizard! More than he thought to teach me, since he crumbled into dust on my account, and that is sure."

Yet, she stopped the rods twirling, and she did not start to sing.

They stared a time longer at each other, and while they saw themselves in one another, Cime began to cry, who had not wept in thrice a hundred years. And in time she turned her rods about, and butts first, she touched them to the shards of the obsidian he held in a trembling palm.

When the rods made contact, a blinding flare of blue commenced to shine in his hand, and she heard him say, "I will make things right with us," as the room in which they stood began to fade away, and she heard a lapping sea and singing children and finger cymbals tinkling while lutes were strummed and pipes began to play.

All hell breaking loose could not have caused more pandemonium than Jihan's father's blood-red orbs peering down through shredded clouds upon the mageguild's grounds. The fury of the father of a jilted bride was met by Vashanka in his full manifestation, so that folk thrown to the ground lay silent, staring up at the battle in the sky with their fingers dug deep into chilling, spongy earth.

Vashanka's two feet were widespread, one upon his temple, due west, one upon the mageguild's wall. His lightning bolts rocked the heavens, his golden locks whipped by his adversary's black winds. Howls from the foreign Stormbringer's cloudy throat pummeled eardrums; people rolled to their stomachs and buried their heads in their arms as the inconceivable cloud creature enveloped their god, and blackness reigned. Thunder bellowed; the black cloud pulsed spasmodically, lit from within.

In the tempest, Tempus shouted to Jihan, grabbed her arms in his hands: "Stop this; you can do it. Your pride, and his, are not worth so many lives." A lightning bolt struck earth beside his foot, so close a blue sparkling aftercharge nuzzled his leg.

She jerked away, palmed her hair back, stood glaring at him with red flecks in her eyes. She shouted something back, her lips curled in a flash of light, but the gods' roaring blotted out her words. Then she merely turned her back to him, raised her arms to heaven, and perhaps began to pray.

He had no more time for her; the god's war was his; he felt the claw-cold blows Stormbringer landed, felt Vashanka's substance leeching away. Yet he set off running, dodging cowerers upon the ground, adepts and nobles with their cloaks wrapped about their heads, seeking his Stepsons: he knew what he must do.

He did not stop for arms or horses, when he found Niko and Janni, but set off through the raging din toward the Avenue of Temples, where the child the man and god had begotten upon the First Consort was kept.

Handsigns got them through until speech was useful, when they had run west through the lawns and alleys, coming to Vashanka's temple grounds from the back. Inside the shrine's chancery, it was quieter, shielded from the sky that heaved with light and dark.

Niko shared his weapons, those Aškelon had given him: a dirk to Tempus, the sword to Janni. "But you have nothing left," Janni protested in the urgent undertone they were all employing in the shadowed corridors of their embattled god's earthly home. "I have this," Niko replied, and tapped his armored chest.

Whether he meant the cuirass Aškelon had given him, the heart underneath, or his mental skills, Tempus did not ask, just tossed the dirk contemptuously back, and dashed out into the murky temple hall.

They smelled sorcery before they saw the sick green light or felt the curdling cold. Outside the door under which wizardsign leaked like sulphur from a yellow spring, Janni muttered blackly. Niko's lips were drawn back in a grin: "After you, commander?"

Tempus wrenched the doors apart, once Janni had cut the leather strap where it had been drawn within to secure the latch, and beheld Molin Torchholder in the midst of witchfire, wrestling with more than Tempus would have thought he could handle, and holding his own.

On the floor in the corner a honey-haired northern dancer hugged a man-child to her breast, her mouth an "ooh" of relief, as if now that Tempus was here, she was surely saved.

He took time to grimace politely at the girl, who insisted on mistaking him for his god—his senses were speeding much faster than even the green, stinking whirlwind in the middle of the room. He wasn't so sure that anything was salvageable, here, or even if he cared if girl or priest or child or town . . . or *god* . . . were to be saved. But then he looked behind him, and saw his Stepsons, Niko on the left and Janni with sword drawn, both ready to advance on hell itself, would he but bid them, and he raised a hand and led them into the lightfight, eyes squinted nearly shut

and all his body tingling as his preternatural abilities
came into play.

Molin's ouster was uppermost in his mind; he picked
the glareblind priest up bodily and threw him, wrenching
the god's golden icon from his frozen fist. He heard a
grunt, a snapping-in of breath, behind, but did not look
around to see reality fade away. He was fighting by himself,
now, in a higher, colder place full of day held at bay and
Vashanka's potent breath in his right ear. *"It is well you
have come, manchild; I can use your help this day."* The
left is the place of attack in team battle; a shield-holding
line drifts right, each trying to protect his open side. He
had Vashanka on his right, to support him, and a shield,
full-length and awful, came to be upon his own left arm.
The thing he fought here, the Stormbringer's shape, was
part cat, part manlike, and its sword cut as hard as an
avalanche. Its claws chilled his breath away. Behind, black
and gray was split with sunrise colors, Vashanka's blazon
snapping on a flag of sky. He thrust at the clouds and was
parried with cold that ran up his sword and seared the
skin of his palm so that his sweat froze to ice and layers of
his flesh bonded to a sharkskin hilt.... That gave him
pause, for it was his own sword, come from wherever the
mages secreted it, which moved in his hand. Pink glowed
that blade, as always when his god sanctified His servant's
labor. His right was untenanted, suddenly, but Vashanka's
strength was in him, and it must be enough.

He fought it unto exhaustion, he fought it to a draw.
The adversaries stood in clouds, typhoon-breaths rasping,
both seeking strength to fight on. And then he had to say
it: "Let this slight go, Stormbringer. Vengeance is disap-
pointing, always. You soil yourself, having to care. Let her
stay where she is, Weather-Gods' Father; a mortal sojourn
will do her good. The parent is not responsible for the
errors of the child. Nor the child for the parent." And
deliberately, he put down the shield the god had given

him and peeled the sticky swordhilt from a skinless palm,
laying his weapon atop the shield. "Or surmount me, and
have done with it. I will not die of exhaustion for a god
too craven to fight by my side. And I will not stand aside
and let you have the babe. You see, it is me you must
punish, not my god. I led Aškelon to Cime, and disposed
her toward him. It is my transgression, not Vashanka's.
And I am not going to make it easy for you: you will have
to slaughter me, which I would much prefer to being the
puppet of yet another omnipotent force."

And with a growl that was long and seared his inner ear
and set his teeth on edge, the clouds began to dissolve
around him, and the darkness to fade away.

He blinked, and rubbed his eyes, which were smarting
with underworld cold, and when he took his hands away
he found himself standing in a seared circle of stinking
fumes with two coughing Stepsons, both of whom were
breathing heavily, but neither of whom looked to have
suffered any enduring harm. Janni was supporting Niko,
who had discarded the gift-cuirass, and it glowed as if
cooling from a forger's heat between his feet. The dirk and
sword, too, lay on the smudged flagstones, and Tempus'
sword atop the heap.

There passed an interval of soft exchanges, which did
not explain either where Tempus had disappeared to, or
why Niko's gear had turned white-hot against the Stormbringer's whirlpool cold, and of assessing damages (none,
beyond frostbite, blisters, scrapes and Tempus' flayed
swordhand) and suggestions as to where they might re-
coup their strength.

The tearful First Consort was calmed, and Torchholder's
people (no one could locate the priest) told to watch her
well.

Outside the temple, they saw that the mist had let go of
the streets; an easy night lay chill and brisk upon the
town. The three walked back to the mageguild at a lei-

surely pace, to reclaim their panoplies and their horses.
When they got there they found that the Second and
Third Hazards had claimed the evening's confrontation to
be of their making, a cosmological morality play, their
most humbly offered entertainment which the guests had
taken too much to heart. Did not Vashanka triumph? Was
not the cloud of evil vanquished? Had not the wondrous
tent of pink-and-lemon summer sky returned to illuminate the mageguild's fête?

Janni snarled and flushed with rage at the adepts'
dissembling, threatening to go turn Torchholder (who had
preceded them back among the celebrants, disheveled,
loudmouthed, but none the worse for wear) upside down
to see if any truth might fall out, but Niko cautioned him
to let fools believe what fools believe, and to make his
farewells brief and polite—whatever they felt about the
mages, they had to live with them.

When at last they rode out of the Street of Arcana
toward the Alekeep to quench their well-earned thirsts
where Niko could check on the faring of a girl who mattered to him, he was ponying the extra horse he had lent
Aškelon, since neither the dream lord nor his companion
Jihan had been anywhere to be found among guests
trying grimly to recapture at least a semblance of revelry.

For Niko, the slow ride through mercifully dark streets
was a godsend, the deep midnight sky a mask he desperately needed to keep between him and the world awhile.
In its cover, he could afford to let his composure, slipping
away inexorably of its own weight, fall from him altogether.
As it happened, because of the riderless horse, he was
bringing up the rear. That, too, suited him, as did their
tortuous progress through the ways and intersections
thronging intermittently with upper-class (if there was
such a distinction to be made here) Ilsigs ushering in the
new year. Personally, he didn't like the start of it: the
events of the last twenty-four hours he considered some-

what less than auspicious. He fingered the enameled cuirass with its twining snakes and glyphs which the entelechy Aškelon had given him, touched the dirk at his waist, the matching sword slung at his hip. The hilts of both were worked as befitted weapons bound for a son of the armies, with the lightning and the lions and the bulls which were, the world over, the signatures of its Storm Gods, the gods of war and death. But the workmanship was foreign, and the raised demons on both scabbards belonged to the primal deities of an earlier age, whose sway was misty, everywhere but among the western islands where Niko had gone to strive for initiation into his chosen mystery and mastery over body and soul. The most appropriate legends graced these opulent arms that a shadow lord had given him; in the old ways and the elder gods and in the disciplines of transcendent perception, Niko sought perfection, a mystic calm. The weapons were perfect, save for two blemishes: they were fashioned from precious metals, and made nearly priceless by the antiquity of their style; they were charmed, warm to the touch, capable of meeting infernal forces and doing damage upon icy whirlwinds sent from unnamed gods. Nikodemos favored unarmed kills, minimal effort, precision. He judged himself sloppy should it become necessary to parry an opponent's stroke more than once. The temple-dancing exhibitions of proud swordsmen who "tested each other's mettle" and had time to indulge in style and disputatious dialogue repelled him: one got in, made the kill, and got out, hopefully leaving the enemy unknowing; if not, confused.

He no more coveted blades that would bring acquisitive men down upon him hoping to acquire them in combat than he looked forward to needing ensorceled swords for battles that could not be joined in the way he liked. The cuirass he wore kept off supernal evil—should it prove impregnable to mortal arms, that knowledge would eat away at his self-discipline, perhaps erode his control, make him careless. In the lightfight, when Tempus had flickered out of being as completely as a doused torch, he had felt an inexplicable elation, leading point into Chaos with Janni steady on his right hand. He had imagined he was indomitable, fated, chosen by the gods and thus inviolate. The steadying fear that should have been there, in his mind, assessive and balancing, was missing . . . his *maat*, as he'd told Tempus in that moment of discomfitting candor, was gone from him. No trick panoply could replace it, no arrogance or battle-lust could substitute for it. Without equilibrium, the quiet heart he strove for could never be his. He was not like Tempus, preternatural, twice a man, living forever in extended anguish to which he had become accustomed. He did not aspire to more than what his studies whispered a man had right to claim. Seeing Tempus in action, he now believed what before, though he'd heard the tales, he had discounted. He thought hard about the Riddler, and the offer he had made him, and wondered if he was bound by it, and the weapons Aškelon had given him no more than omens fit for days to come. And he shivered, upon his horse, wishing his partner were there up ahead instead of Janni, and that his *maat* was within him, and that they rode Syrese byways or the Azehuran plain, where magic did not vie with gods for mortal allegiance, or take souls in tithe.

When they dismounted at the Alekeep, he'd come to a negotiated settlement within himself: he would wait to see if what Tempus said was true, if his *maat* would return to him once his teammate's spirit ascended to heaven on a pillar of flame. He was not unaware of the rhythmic nature of enlightenment through the precession of events. He had come to Ranke with his partner at Abarsis' urging: he remembered the Slaughter Priest from his early days of ritual and war, and had made his own decision, not followed blindly because his left-side leader wished to teach Rankans the glory of his name. When the elder fighter had put it to him, his friend had said that it might be time for Nikodemos to lead his own team—after Ranke, without doubt, the older man would lay down his sword. He had been dreaming, he'd said, of mother's milk and waving crops and snot-nosed brats with wooden shields, a sure sign a man is done with damp camps and bloody dead stripped in the field.

So it would have happened, this year, or the next, that he would be alone. He must come to terms with it; not whine silently like an abandoned child, or seek a new and stronger arm to lean on. Meditation should have helped him, though he recalled a parchment grin and a toothless mouth instructing him that what is needed is never to be had without price.

The price of the thick brown ale in which the Alekeep specialized was doubled for the holiday's night-long vigil, but they paid not one coin, drinking, instead, in a private room in back where the grateful owner led them: he'd heard about the manifestation at the mageguild, and had been glad he had taken Niko's advice and kept his girls inside. "Can I let them out, then?" he said with a twinkling eye. "Now that you are here? Would the Lord Marshal and his distinguished Stepsons care for some gentle companionship, this jolly eve?"

Tempus, flexing his open hand on which the clear serum glistened as it thickened into scabby skin, told him to keep his children locked up until dawn, and sent him away so brusquely Janni eyed Niko askance.

Their commander sat with his back against the wall opposite the door through which the tavern's owner had disappeared. "We were followed here. I'd like to think you both realized it on your own."

The placement of their seats, backs generously offered to any who might enter, spoke so clearly of their failure that neither said a word, only moved their chairs to the single table's narrow sides. When next the door swung open, One-Thumb, not their host, stood there, and Tempus chuckled hoarsely in the hulking wrestler's face. "Only you, Lastel? I own you had me worried."

"Where is she, Tempus? What have you done with her?" Lastel stomped forward, put both ham-hands flat upon the table, his thick neck thrust forward, bulging with veins.

"Are you tired of living, One-Thumb? Go back to your hidey-hole. Maybe she's there, maybe not. If not . . . easy come, easy go."

Lastel's face purpled; his words rode on a froth of spray so that Janni reached for his dagger and Niko had to kick him.

"Your sister's disappeared and you don't *care?*"

"I let Cime snuggle up with you in your thieves' shanty. If I had 'cared,' would I have done that? And *did* I care, I would have to say to you that you aspire beyond your station, with her. Stick to whoremistresses and street urchins, in future. Or go talk to the mageguild, or your gods if you have the ears of any. Perhaps you can reclaim her for some well-bartered treachery or a block of Caronne krrf. Meanwhile, you who are about to become 'No-Thumbs,' mark these two—" He gestured to either side, to Niko and Janni. "They'll be around to see you in the next few days, and I caution you to treat them with the utmost deference. They can be very temperamental. As for myself, I've had easier days, and so am willing to estimate for you your chances of walking out of here with all appendages yet attached and in working order, though your odds are lessening with every breath I have to watch you take. . . ." Tempus was rising as he spoke. Lastel gave back, his flushed face paling visibly as Tempus proposed a new repository for his prosthetic thumb, then retreated with surprising alacrity toward the half-open door in which the tavern's owner now stood uncertainly, now disappeared.

But Lastel was not fast enough; Tempus had him by the throat. Holding him off the ground, he made One-Thumb mouth civil farewells to both the Stepsons before he dropped him and let him dash away.

At sundown the next day (a perfectly natural sundown without a hint of wizard weather about it), Niko's partner's long-delayed funeral was held before the repiled stones of Vashanka's field altar, out behind the arena where once had been a slaver's girl-run. A hawk heading home flew over, right to left, most auspicious of bird omina, and when it had gone, the men swore, Abarsis' ghost materialized to guide the fallen mercenary's spirit up to heaven. These two favorable omens were attributed by most to the fact that Niko had sacrificed the enchanted cuirass Aškelon had given him to the fire of his left-man's bier.

Then Niko released Tempus from his vow of pairbond, demurring that Nikodemos himself had never accepted, explaining that it was time for him to be a left-side fighter, which, with Tempus, he could never be. And Janni stood close by, looking uncomfortable and sheepish, not realizing that in this way Tempus was freed from worrying that harm might come to Niko on account of Tempus' curse.

Seeing Abarsis' shade, wizard-haired and wise, tawny skin quite translucent yet upswept eyes the same, smiling out love upon the Stepsons and their commander, Tempus almost wept. Instead he raised his hand in greeting, and the elegant ghost blew him a kiss.

When the ceremony was done, he sent Niko and Janni into Sanctuary to make it clear to One-Thumb that the only way to protect his duel identity was to make himself very helpful in the increasingly difficult task of keeping track of Mygdonia's Nisibisi spies. As an immediate show of good faith, he was to begin helping Niko and Janni infiltrate them.

When the last of the men had wandered off to game or drink or duty, he had stayed at the shrine awhile, considering Vashanka and the god's habit of leaving him to fight both their battles as best he could.

So it was that he heard a soft sound, half hiccough and half sniffle, from the altar's far side, as the dusk cloaked him close.

When he went to see what it was, he saw Jihan, sitting slumped against a rough-hewn plinth, tearing brown grasses to shreds between her fingers. He squatted down there, to determine whether a Froth Daughter could shed human tears.

Dusk was his favorite time, when the sun had fled and the night was luminous with memory. Sometimes, his thoughts would follow the light, fading, and the man who never slept would find himself dozing, at rest.

This evening, it was not sleep he sought to chase in his private witching hour: he touched her scaled, enameled armor, its gray/green/copper pattern just dappled shadow in the deepening dark. "This does come off?" he asked her.

"Oh, yes. Like so."

"Come to think of it," he remarked after a strenuous but rewarding interval, "it's not so bad that you are stranded here. Your father's pique will ease eventually. Meanwhile, I have an extra Trôs horse. Having two of them to tend has been hard on me. You could take over the care of one. And, too, if you are going to wait the year out as a mortal, perhaps you would consider staying on in Sanctuary. We are sore in need of fighting women this season."

She clutched his arm; he winced. "Do not offer me a sinecure," she said. "And, consider: I will have you, too, should I stay."

Promise or threat, he was not certain, but he was reasonably sure that he could deal with her, either way.

# Book Two:

# *High Moon*

Just south of Caravan Square and the bridge over the White Foal River, the Nisibisi witch had settled in. She had leased the isolated complex—one three-storied "manor house" and its outbuildings—as much because its grounds extended to the White Foal's edge (rivers covered a multitude of disposal problems) as for its proximity to her business interests in the Wideway warehouse district and its convenience to her caravan master, who must visit the Square at all hours.

The caravan disguised their operations. The drugs they'd smuggled in were no more pertinent to her purposes than the dilapidated manor at the end of the bridge's south-running cart track or the goods her men bought and stored in Wideway's most pilferproof holds, though they lubricated her dealings with the locals and eased her troubled nights. It was all subterfuge, a web of lies, plausible lesser evils to which she could own if the Rankan army caught her or the palace marshal Tempus's Stepsons (mercenary

shock troops and "special agents") rousted her minions
and flunkies or even brought her up on charges.

Lately, a pair of Stepsons had been her particular
concern. And Jagat—her first lieutenant in espionage—was
no less worried. Even their Ilsig contact, the unflappable
Lastel who had lived a dozen years in Sanctuary, cesspool
of the Rankan empire into which all lesser sewers fed, and
managed all that time to keep his duel identity as east
side entrepeneur and Maze-dwelling barman uncomprom-
ised, was distressed by the attention the pair of Stepsons
were paying her.

She had thought her allies overcautious at first, when it
seemed she would be here only long enough to see to the
"death" of the Rankan war god, Vashanka. Discrediting
the state-cult's power icon was the purpose for which the
Nisibisi witch, Roxane, had come down from Wizardwall's
fastness, down from her shrouded keep of black marble on
its unscalable peak, down among the mortal and the
damned. They were all in this together: the mages of
Nisibis; Lacan Ajami (warlord of Mygdon and the known
world north of Wizardwall) with whom they had made pact;
and the whole Mygdonian Alliance which he controlled.

Or so her lord and lover had explained it when he decreed that Roxane must come. She had not argued—one
pays one's way among sorcerers; she had not worked hard
for a decade nor faced danger in twice as long. And if *one*
did not serve Mygdon—*only one*—all would suffer. The
Alliance was too strong to thwart. So she was here, drawn
here with others fit for better, as if some power more than
magical was whipping up a tropical storm to cleanse the
land and using them to gild its eye.

She should have been home by now; she would have
been, but for the hundred ships from Beysib which had
come to port and skewed all plans. Word had come from
Mygdon, capital of Mygdonia, through the Nisibisi network,
that she must stay.

And so it had become crucial that the Stepsons who sniffed round her skirts be kept at bay—or ensnared, or bought, or enslaved. Or, if not, destroyed. But carefully, so carefully. For Tempus, who had been her enemy three decades ago when he fought the Defender's wars on Wizardwall's steppes, was a dozen Storm Gods' avatar; no army he sanctified could know defeat; no war he fought could not be won. Combat was life to him; he fought like the gods themselves, like an entelechy from a higher sphere—and even had friends among those powers not corporeal or vulnerable to sortilege of the quotidian sort a human might employ.

And now it was being decreed in Mygdonia's tents that he must be removed from the field—taken out of play in this southern theater, maneuvered north where the warlocks could neutralize him. Such was the word her lover/lord had sent her: move him north, or make him impotent where he stayed. The god he served here had been easier to rout. But she doubted that would incapacitate him; there were other Storm Gods, and Tempus, who under a score of names had fought in more dimensions than she had ever visited, knew them all. Vashanka's denouement might scare the Rankans and give the Ilsigs hope, but more than rumors and manipulation of theomachy by even the finest witch would be needed to make Tempus fold his hand or bow his head. To make him run, then, was an impossibility. To *lure* him north, she hoped, was not. For this was no place for Roxane. Her nose was offended by the stench which blew east from Downwind and north from Fisherman's Row and west from the Maze and south from either the slaughterhouses or the palace— she'd not decided which.

So she had called a meeting, itself an audacious move, with her kind where they dwelled on Wizardwall's high peaks. When it was done, she was much weakened—it is no small feat to project one's soul so far—and unsatisfied.

But she had submitted her strategy and gotten approval, after a fashion, though it pained her to have to ask.

Having gotten it, she was about to set her plan in motion. To begin it, she had called upon Lastel/One-Thumb and cried foul: "Tempus's sister, Cime the free agent, was part of our bargain, Ilsig. If you cannot produce her, then she cannot aid me, and I am paying you far too much for a third-rate criminal's paltry talents."

The huge wrestler adjusted his deceptively soft gut. His east side house was commodious; dogs barked in their pens and favorite curs lounged about their feet, under the samovar, upon riotous silk prayer rugs, in the embrace of comely krrf-drugged slaves—not her idea of entertainment, but Lastel's, his sweating forehead and heavy breathing proclaimed as he watched the bestial event a dozen other guests found fetching.

The dusky Ilsigs saw nothing wrong in enslaving their own race. Nisibisi had more pride. It was well that these were comfortable with slavery—they would know it far more intimately, by and by.

But her words had jogged her host, and Lastel came up on one elbow, his cushions suddenly askew. He, too, had been partaking of krrf—not smoking it, as was the Ilsig custom, but mixing it with other drugs which made it sink into the blood directly through the skin. The effects were greater, and less predictable.

As she had hoped, her words had the power of krrf behind them. Fear showed in the jowled mountain's eyes. He knew what she was; the fear was her due. Any of these were helpless before her, should she decide a withered soul or two might amuse her. Their essences could lighten her load as krrf lightened theirs.

The gross man spoke quickly, a whine of excuses: the woman had "disappeared . . . taken by Aškelon, the very lord of dreams. All at the mageguild's fete where the god was vanquished saw it. You need not take my word—witnesses are legion."

She fixed him with her pale stare. Ilsigs were called Wrigglies, and Lastel's craven self was a good example why. She felt disgust and stared longer.

The man before her dropped his eyes, mumbling that their agreement had not hinged on the mage-killer Cime, that he was doing more than his share as it was, for little enough profit, that the risks were too high.

And to prove to her he was still her creature, he warned her again of the Stepsons: "That pair of Whoresons Tempus sicced on you should concern us, not money—which neither of us will be alive to spend if—" One of the slaves cried out, whether in pleasure or pain Roxane could not be certain; Lastel did not even look up, but continued: "—Tempus finds out we've thirty stone of krrf in—"

She interrupted him, not letting him name the hiding place. "Then do this that I ask of you, without question. We will be rid of the problem they cause, thereafter, and have our own sources who'll tell us what Tempus does and does not know."

A slave serving mulled wine approached, and both took electrum goblets. For Roxane, the liquor was an advantage: looking into its depths, she could see what few cogent thoughts ran through the fat drug dealer's mind.

He thought of her, and she saw her own beauty: wizard hair like ebony and wavy; her sanguine skin like velvet: he dreamed her naked, with his dogs. She cast a curse without word or effort, reflexively, giving him a social disease no Sanctuary mage or barber-surgeon could cure, complete with running sores upon lips and member, and a virus in control of it which buried itself in the brainstem and came out when it chose. She hardly took note of it; it was a small show of temper, like for like: let him exhibit the condition of his soul, she had decreed.

To banish her leggy nakedness from the surface of her

wine, she said straight out: "You know the other bar owners. The Alekeep's proprietor has a girl about to graduate from school. Arrange to host her party, let it be known that you will sell those children krrf—Tamzen is the child I mean. Then have your flunky lead her down to Shambles Cross. Leave them there—up to half a dozen youngsters, it may be—lost in the drug and the slum."

"*That* will tame two vicious Stepsons? You *do* know the men I mean? Janni? And Stealth? They bugger each other, Stepsons. Girls are beside the point. And Stealth—he's a *fuzz*buster—I've seen him with no woman old enough for breasts. Surely—"

"Surely," she cut in smoothly, "you don't want to know more than that—in case it goes awry. Protection in these matters lies in ignorance." She would not tell him more— not that Stealth, called Nikodemos, had come out of Azehur, where he'd earned his war name and worked his way toward Syr in search of a Trôs horse via Mygdonia, hiring on as a caravan guard and general roustabout, or that a dispute over a consignment lost to mountain bandits had made him bondservant for a year to a Nisibisi mage—her lover-lord. There was a string on Nikodemos, ready to be pulled.

And when he felt it, it would be too late, and she would be at the end of it.

Tempus had allowed Niko to breed his sorrel mare to his own Trôs stallion to quell mutters among knowledgeable Stepsons that assigning Niko and Janni to hazardous duty in the town was their commander's way of punishing the slate-haired fighter who had declined Tempus's offered pairbond in favor of Janni's and subsequently quit their ranks.

Now the mare was pregnant and Tempus was curious as to what kind of foal the union might produce, but rumors of foul play still abounded.

Critias, Tempus's second in command, had paused in his dour report and now stirred his posset of cooling wine and barley and goat's cheese with a finger, then wiped the finger on his bossed cuirass, burnished from years of use. They were meeting in the mercenaries' guild hostel, in its common room, dark as congealing blood and safe as a grave, where Tempus had bade the veteran mercenary lodge—an operations officer charged with secret actions could be no part of the Stepsons' barracks cohort. They met covertly, on occasion; most times, coded messages brought by unwitting couriers were enough.

Crit, too, it seemed, thought Tempus wrong in sending Janni, a guileless cavalryman, and Niko, the youngest of the Stepsons, to spy upon the witch: clandestine schemes were Crit's province, and Tempus had usurped, overstepped the bounds of their agreement. Tempus had allowed that Crit might take over management of the fielded team and Crit had grunted wryly, saying he'd run them but not take the blame if they lost both men to the witch's wiles.

Tempus had agreed with the pleasant-looking Syrese agent and they had gone on to other business: Prince/ Governor Kadakithis was insistent upon contacting Jubal, the slaver whose estate the Stepsons sacked and made their home. "But when we had the black bastard, you said to let him crawl away."

"Kadakithis expressed no interest." Tempus shrugged. "He has changed his mind, perhaps in light of the appearance of these mysterious death squads your people haven't been able to identify or apprehend. If your teams can't deliver Jubal or turn up a hawkmask who is in contact with him, I'll find another way."

"Ischade, the vampire woman who lives in Shambles Cross, is still our best hope. We've sent slave-bait to her and lost it. Like a canny carp, she takes the bait and leaves the hook." Crit's lips were pursed as if his wine had turned to vinegar; his patrician nose drew down with his frown. He ran a hand through his short, feathery hair. "And our joint venture with the Rankan garrison is impeding rather than aiding success. Army Intelligence is a contradiction in terms, like the Mygdonian Alliance or the Sanctuary pacification program. The cutthroats I've got on our payroll are sure the god is dead and all the Rankans soon to follow. The witch—or *some* witch—floats rumors of Mygdonian liberators and Ilsig freedom and the gullible believe. That snotty thief you befriended is either an enemy agent or a pawn of Nisibisi propaganda—telling everyone that *he's* been told by the Ilsig gods themselves that Vashanka was routed ... I'd like to silence him permanently." Crit's eyes met Tempus' then, and held.

"No," he replied, to all of it, then added: "Gods don't die; men die. Boys die in multitudes. The thief, Shadowspawn, is no threat to us, just misguided, semiliterate, and vain, like all boys. Bring me a conduit to Jubal, or the slaver himself. Contact Niko and have him report—if the witch needs a lesson, I myself will undertake to teach it. And keep your watch upon the fish-eyed folk from the ships—I'm not sure yet that they're as harmless as they seem."

Having given Crit enough to do to keep his mind off the rumors of the god Vashanka's troubles—and hence, his own—he rose to leave. "Some results, by week's end, would be welcome." The officer toasted him cynically as Tempus walked away.

Outside, his Trôs horse whinnied joyfully. He stroked its mist-dappled neck and felt the sweat there. The weather was close, an early heatwave as unwelcome as the late frosts which had frozen the winter crops a week before their harvest and killed the young sets just planted in anticipation of a bounteous fall.

He mounted up and headed south by the granaries toward the palace's north wall where a gate, nowhere as peopled or public as the Gate of the Gods, was set into the wall by the cisterns. He would talk to Prince Kittycat, then tour the Maze on his way home to the barracks.

But the prince wasn't receiving, and Tempus's mood was ill—just as well; he had been going to confront the young popinjay, as once or twice a month he was sure he must do, without courtesy or appropriate deference. If Kadakithis was holed up in conference with the blond-haired, fish-eyed folk from the ships and had not called upon him to join them, then it was not surprising: since the gods had battled in the sky above the mageguild, all things had become confused, worse had come to worst, and Tempus' curse had fallen on him once again with its full force.

Perhaps the god *was* dead—certainly, Vashanka's voice in his ear was absent. He'd gone out raping once or twice to see if the Lord of Pillage could be roused to take part in His favorite sport. But the god had not rustled around in his head since New Year's day; the resultant fear of harm to those who loved him by the curse that denied him love had made a solitary man withdraw even further into himself; only the Froth Daughter Jihan, hardly human, though woman in form, kept him company now.

And that, as much as anything, irked the Stepsons. Theirs was a closed fraternity, open only to the paired lovers of the Sacred Band and distinguished single merce-naries culled from a score of nations and diverted, by Tempus' service and Kittycat's gold, from the northern insurrection they'd drifted through Sanctuary en route to join.

He, too, ached to war, to fight a declared enemy, to lead his cohort north. But there was his word to a Rankan faction to do his best for a petty prince, and there was this thrice-cursed fleet of merchant warriors come to harbor talking "peaceful trade" while their vessels rode too low in the water to be filled with grain or cloth or spices—if not barter, his instinct told him, the Burek faction of Beysib would settle for conquest.

He was past caring; things in Sanctuary were too confuted for one man, even one near-immortal, god-ridden avatar of a man, to set aright. He would take Jihan and go north, with or without the Stepsons—his accursed presence among them and the love they bore him would kill them if he let it continue: if the god was truly gone, then he must follow. Beyond Sanctuary's borders, other Storm Gods held sway, other names were hallowed. The primal Lord Storm (Enlil) whom Niko venerated had heard a petition from Tempus for a clearing of his path and his heart: he wanted to know what status his life, his curse, and his god-bond had, these days. He awaited only a sign.

Once, long ago, when he went abroad as a philosopher and sought a calmer life in a calmer world, he had said that to gods all things are beautiful and good and just, but men have supposed some things to be unjust, others just. If the god had died, or been banished, though it didn't seem that this could be so, then it was meet that this occurred. But those who thought it so did not realize that one could not escape the intelligible light: the notice of that which never sets: the apprehension of the elder gods. So he had asked, and so he waited.

He had no doubt that the answer would be forthcoming, as he had no doubt that he would not mistake it when it came.

On his way to the Maze he brooded over his curse, which kept him unloved by the living and spurned by any he favored if they be mortal. In heaven he had a brace of lovers, ghosts like the original Stepson, Abarsis. But to heaven he could not repair: his flesh regenerated itself immemorially; to make sure this was still the case, last night he had gone to the river and slit both wrists. By the time he'd counted to fifty the blood had ceased to flow and healing had begun. That gift of healing—if gift it was—still remained his, and since it was god-given, some power more than mortal "loved" him still.

It was whim that made him stop by the weapons shop the mercenaries favored. Three horses tethered out front were known to him; one was Niko's stallion, a big black with points like rust and a jughead on thickening neck perpetually sweatbanded with sheepskin to keep its jowls modest. The horse, as mean as it was ugly, snorted a challenge to Tempus' Trôs—the black resented that the Trôs had climbed Niko's mare.

He tethered it at the far end of the line and went inside, among the crossbows, the flying wings, the steel and wooden quarrels and the swords.

Only a woman sat behind the counter, pulchritudinous and vain, her neck hung with a wealth of baubles, her flesh perfumed. She knew him, and in seconds his nose detected acrid, nervous sweat, and the defensive musk a woman can exude.

"Marc's out with the boys in back, sighting-in the high-torque bows. Shall I get him, Lord Marshal? Or may I help you? What's here's yours, my lord, on trial or as our gift—" Her arm spread wide, bangles tinkling, indicating the racked weapons.

"I'll take a look out back, madam, don't disturb yourself."

She settled back, not calm, but bidden to remain and obedient.

In the ochre-walled yard ten men were gathered behind the log fence that marked the range; a hundred yards away three oxhides had been fastened to the encircling wall, targets painted red upon them; between the hides, three cuirasses of four-ply hardened leather armored with bronze plates were propped and filled with straw.

The smith was down on his knees, a crossbow fixed in a vise with its owner hovering close by. The smith hammered the sights twice more, put down his file, grunted and said, "You try it, Straton; it should shoot true. I got a hand-breadth group with it this morning; it's your eye I've got to match. . . ."

The large-headed, raw-boned smith sporting a beard which evened a rough complexion rose with exaggerated effort and turned to another customer, just stepping up to the firing line. "No, Stealth, not like that, or, if you must, I'll change the tension—" Marc moved in, telling Niko to throw the bow up to his shoulder and fire from there, then saw Tempus and left the group, hands spreading on his apron.

Bolts spat and thunked from five shooters when the morning's range officer hollered "Clear" and "Fire," then "Hold," so that all could go to the wall to check their aim and the depths to which the shafts had sunk.

Shaking his head, the smith confided: "Straton's got a problem I can't solve. I've had it truly sighted—perfect for me—three times, but when he shoots, it's as if he's aiming two feet low."

"For the bow, the name is life, but the work is death. In combat it will shoot true for him; here, he's worried how they judge his prowess. He's not thinking enough of his weapon, too much of his friends."

The smith's keen eyes shifted; he rubbed his smile with a greasy hand. "Aye, and that's the truth. And for you, Lord Tempus? We've the new hard-steel, though why they're all so hot to pay twice the price when men're soft as clay and even wood will pierce the boldest belly, I can't say."

"No steel, just a case of iron-tipped short flights, when you can."

"I'll select them myself. Come and watch them, now? We'll see what their nerve's like, if you call score. . . ."

"A moment or two, Marc. Go back to your work, I'll sniff around on my own."

And so he approached Niko, on pretense of admiring the Stepson's new bow, and saw the shadowed eyes, blank as ever but veiled like the beginning beard that masked his jaw: "How goes it, Niko? Has your *maat* returned to you?"

"Not likely," the young fighter said, cranking the spring and lever so a bolt notched and triggered the quarrel which whispered straight and true to center his target. "Did Crit send you? I'm fine, commander. He worries too much. We can handle her, no matter how it seems. It's just time we need . . . she's suspicious, wants us to prove our faith. Shall I, by whatever means?"

"Another week on this is all I can give you. Use discretion, your judgment's fine with me. What you think she's worth, she's worth. If Critias questions that, your orders came from me and you may tell him so."

"I will, and with pleasure. I'm not his to wetnurse; he can't keep that in his head."

"And Janni?"

"It's hard on him, pretending to be . . . what we're pretending to be. The men talk to him about coming back out to the barracks, about forgetting what's past and resuming his duties. But we'll weather it. He's man enough."

Niko's hazel eyes flicked back and forth, judging the other men: who watched; who pretended he did not, but listened hard. He loosed another bolt, a third, and said quietly that he had to collect his flights. Tempus eased away, heard the range officer call "Clear" and watched Niko go retrieve his grouped quarrels.

If this one could not breach the witch's defenses, then she was unbreachable.

Content, he left then, and found Jihan, his de facto right-side partner, waiting astride his other Trôs horse, her more than human strength and beauty brightening Smith Street's ramshackle facade as if real gold lay beside fool's gold in a dusty pan.

Though one of the matters estranging him from his Stepsons was his pairing with this foreign "woman," only Niko knew her to be the daughter of a power who spawned all contentious gods and even the concept of divinity; he felt the cool her flesh gave off, cutting the midday heat like wind from a snowcapped peak.

"Life to you, Tempus." Her voice was thick as ale, and he realized he was thirsty. Promise Park and the Alekeep, an east side establishment considered upper class by those who could tell classes of Ilsigs, were right around the corner, a block up the Street of Gold from where they met. He proposed to take her there for lunch. She was delighted—all things mortal were new to her; the whole business of being in flesh and attending to it was yet novel. A novice at life, Jihan was hungry for the whole of it.

For him, she served a special purpose: her loveplay was rough and her constitution hardier than his Trôs horses—he could not couple gently; with her, he did not inflict permanent harm on his partner; she was born of violence inchoate and savored what would kill or cripple mortals.

At the Alekeep, they were welcome. In a back and private room, they talked of the god's absence and what could be made of it, and the owner served them himself, an avuncular sort still grateful that Tempus' men had kept his daughters safe when wizard weather roamed the streets. "My girl's graduating school today, Lord Marshal— my youngest. We've a fête set, and you and your companion would be most welcome guests."

Jihan touched his arm as he began to decline, her stormy eyes flecked red and glowing.

"... ah, perhaps we will drop by, then, if business permits."

But they didn't, having found pressing matters of lust to attend to, and all things that happened then might have been avoided if they hadn't been out of touch with the Stepsons, unreachable down by the creek that ran north of the barracks when sorcery met machination and all things went awry.

\*    \*    \*

On their way to work, Niko and Janni stopped at the
Vulgar Unicorn to wait for the moon to rise. The moon
would be full this evening, a blessing since anonymous
death squads roamed the town—whether they were Rankan
army regulars, Jubal's scattered hawkmasks, fish-eyed
Beysib spoilers, or Nisibisi assassins, none could say.

The one thing that could be said of them for certain was
that they weren't Stepsons or Sacred Banders or nonaligned mercenaries from the guild hostel. But there was
no convincing the terrorized populace of that.

And Niko and Janni—under the guise of disaffected mercenaries who had quit the Stepsons, been thrown out of
the guild hostel for unspeakable acts, and were currently
degenerating Sanctuary-style in the filthy streets of the
town—thought that they were close to identifying the
death squads' leader. Hopefully, this evening or the next,
they would be asked to join the murderers in their squalid
sport.

Not that murder was uncommon in Sanctuary, or
squalor. The Maze, now that Niko knew it like his horses'
needs or Janni's limits, was not the town's true nadir,
only the multi-tiered slum's upper echelon. Worse than
the Maze was Shambles Cross, filled with the weak and
the meek; worse than the Shambles was Downwind, where
nothing moved in the light of day and at night hellish
sounds rode the stench on the prevailing east wind across
the White Foal. A tri-level hell, then, filled with murderers,
sold souls and succubi, began here in the Maze.

If the death squads had confined themselves to Maze,
Shambles, and Downwind, no one would have known
about them. Bodies in those streets were nothing new;
neither Stepsons nor Rankan soldiers bothered counting
them; near the slaughterhouses cheap crematoriums
flourished; for those too poor even for that, there was the
White Foal, taking ambiguous dross to the sea without

complaint. But the squads ventured uptown, to the east side and the center of Sanctuary itself where the palace hierophants and the merchants lived and looked away from downtown, scented pomanders to their noses.

The Unicorn crowd no longer turned quiet when Niko and Janni entered; their scruffy faces and shabby gear and bleary eyes proclaimed them no threat to the mendicants or the whores. Competition, they were now considered, and it had been hard to float the legend, harder to live it. Or to live it down, since none of the Stepsons but their task force leader, Crit (who himself had never moved among the barracks ranks, proud and shining with oil and fine weapons and finer ideals) knew that they had not quit but only worked shrouded in subterfuge on Tempus' orders to flush the Nisibisi witch.

But the emergence of the death squads had raised the pitch, the ante, given the matter a new urgency. Some said it was because Shadowspawn, the thief, was right: the god Vashanka had died, and the Rankans would suffer their due. Their due or not, traders, politicians, and moneylenders—the "oppressors"—were nightly dragged out into the streets, whole families slaughtered or burned alive in their houses, or hacked to pieces in their festooned wagons.

The agents ordered draughts from One-Thumb's new girl and she came back, cowering but determined, saying that One-Thumb must see their money first. They had started this venture with the barman's help; he knew their provenance; they knew his secret.

"Let's kill the swillmonger, Stealth," Janni growled. They had little cash—a few soldats and some Machadi coppers—and couldn't draw their pay until their work was done.

"Steady, Janni. I'll talk to him. Girl, fetch two Rankan ales or you won't be able to close your legs for a week."

He pushed back his bench and strode to the bar, aware

that he was only half joking, that Sanctuary was rubbing
him raw. *Was* the god dead? *Was* Tempus in thrall to the
Froth Daughter who kept his company? *Was* Sanctuary
the honeypot of chaos? A hell from which no man emerged?
He pushed a threesome of young puds aside and whistled
piercingly when he reached the bar. The big bartender
looked around elaborately, raised a scar-crossed eyebrow,
and ignored him. Stealth counted to ten and then methodi-
cally began emptying other patrons' drinks onto the
counter. Men were few here; approximations cursed him
and backed away; one went for a beltknife but Stealth
had a dirk in hand that gave him pause. Niko's gear was
dirty, but better than any of these had. And he was ready
to clean his soiled blade in any one of them. They sensed
it; his peripheral perception read their moods, though he
couldn't read their minds. Where his *maat*—his balance—
once had been was a cold, sick anger. In Sanctuary he had
learned despair and futility, and these had introduced
him to fury. Options he once had considered last resorts,
off the battlefield, came easily to mind now. Son of the
armies, he was learning a different kind of war in Sanctuary, and learning to love the havoc his own right arm
could wreak. It was not a substitute for the equilibrium
he'd lost when his left-side leader died down by the docks,
but if his partner needed souls to buy a better place in
heaven, Niko would gladly send him double his comfort's
price.

The ploy brought One-Thumb down to stop him. "Stealth,
I've had enough of you." One-Thumb's mouth was swollen,
his upper lip crusted with sores, but his ponderous bulk
loomed large; from the corner of his eye Niko could see
the Unicorn's bouncer leave his post and Janni intercept
him.

Niko reached out and grabbed One-Thumb by the throat,
even as the man's paw reached under the bar, where a
weapon might lie. He pulled him close: "What you've had

isn't even a shadow of what you're going to get, Tum-Tum, if you don't mind your tongue. Turn back into the well-mannered little troll we both know and love, or you won't *have* a bar to hide behind by morning." Then, sotto voce: "What's up?"

"*She* wants you," the barkeep gasped, his face purpling, "to go to her place by the White Foal at high moon. If it's convenient, of course, my *lord*."

Niko let him go before his eyes popped out of his head. "You'll put this on our tab?"

"Just this one more time, beggar boy. Your Whoreson bugger-buddies won't lift a leg to help you; your threats are as empty as your purse."

"Care to bet on it?"

They carried on a bit more, for the crowd's benefit, Janni and the bouncer engaged in a staring match the while. "Call your cur off, then, and we'll forget about this—this once." Niko turned, neck aprickle, and headed back toward his seat, hoping that it wouldn't go any further. Not one of the four—bouncer, bar owner, Stepsons—was entirely playing to the crowd.

When he'd reached his door-facing table, Lastel/One-Thumb called his bruiser off, and Janni backed toward Niko, white-faced and trembling with eagerness: "Let me geld one of them, Stealth. It'll do our reputations no end of good."

"Save it for the witch-bitch."

Janni brightened, straddling his seat, both arms on the table, digging fiercely with his dirk into the wood: "You've got a rendezvous?"

"Tonight, high moon. Don't drink too much."

It wasn't the drink that skewed them, but the krrf they snorted, little piles poured into clenched fists where thumb muscles made a well. Still, the drug would keep them alert: it was a long time until high moon, and they had to patrol for marauders while seeming to be marauding themselves. It was almost more than Niko could bear. He'd infiltrated a score of camps, lines and palaces on reconnaissance sorties with his deceased partner, but those were cleaner, quicker actions than this protracted infiltration of Sanctuary, bunghole of the known world. If this evening made an end to it and he could wash and shave and stable his horses better, he'd make a sacrifice to Enlil which the god would not soon forget.

An hour later, mounted, they set off on their tour of the Maze, Niko thinking that not since the affair with the archmage Aškelon and Tempus's sister Cime had his gut rolled up into a ball with this feeling of unmitigated dread. The Nisibisi witch might know him—she might have known him all along. He'd been interrogated by Nisibisi before, and he would fall upon his sword rather than endure it again now, when his dead teammate's ghost still haunted his mental refuge and meditation could not offer him shelter as it once had.

A boy came running up calling his name, and his jughead black tossed its rust nose high and snorted, ears back, waiting for a command to kill or maim.

"By Vashanka's sulfurous balls, what now?" Janni wondered.

They sat their mounts in the narrow street; the moon was just rising over the shantytops; people slammed their shutters tight and bolted their doors. Niko could catch wisps of fear and loathing from behind the houses' facades; two mounted men in these streets meant trouble, no matter whose they were.

The youth trotted up, breathing hard. "Niko! Niko! The master's so upset. Thank Ils I've found you. . . ." The delicate eunuch's lisp identified him: a servant of the Alekeep's owner, one of the few men Niko thought of as a friend here.

"What's wrong, then?" He leaned down in his saddle.

The boy raised a hand, and the black snaked his head

around fast to bite it. Niko clouted the horse between the ears as the boy scrambled back out of range. "Come on, come here. He won't try it again. Now, what's your master's message?"

"Tamzen! Tamzen's gone out without her bodyguard, with—" The boy named six of the richest Sanctuary families' fast-living youngsters. "They said they'd be right back, but they didn't come. It's *her* party she's missing. The master's beside himself. He said if you can't help him, he'll have to call the Hell Hounds—the palace guard, or go out to the Stepsons' barracks. But there's no time, no time!" the frail eunuch wailed.

"Calm down, pud. We'll find her. Tell her father to send word to Tempus anyway; it can't hurt to alert the authorities. And say exactly this: that I'll help if I can, but he knows I'm not empowered to do more than any citizen. Say it back, now."

Once the eunuch had repeated the words and run off, Janni said: "How're you going to be in two places at once, Stealth? Why'd you tell him that? It's a job for the regulars, not for us. We can't miss this meet, not after all the bedbugs I've let chomp on me for this. . . ."

"*Seh!*" The word meant offal in the Nisi tongue. "We'll round her and her friends up in short order. They're just blowing off steam—it's the heat and school's end. Come on, let's start at Promise Park."

When they got there, the moon showed round and preternaturally large above the palace, and the wind had died. Thoughts of the witch he must meet still troubled Niko, and Janni's grousing buzzed in his ears: ". . . we should check in with Crit, let the girl meet her fate—ours will be worse if we're snared by enchantment and no backup alerted to where or how."

"We'll send word or stop by the Shambles drop, stop worrying." But Janni was not about to stop, and Niko's attempts to calm himself, to find transcendent perception in his rest-place and pick up the girl's trail by the heat-track she'd left and the things she'd said and done here were made more difficult by Janni's worries, which jarred him back to concerns he must put aside, and Janni's words, which startled him, over-loud and disruptive, every time he got himself calmed enough to sense Tamzen's energy trail among so many others like red/yellow/pink yarn twined among chiaroscuro trees.

Tamzen, thirteen and beautiful, pure and full of fun, who loved him with all her heart and had made him promise to "wait" for her: He'd had her, a thing he'd never meant to do, and had her with her father's knowledge, confronted by the concerned man one night when Niko, arm around the girl's waist, had walked her through the park. "Is this how you repay a friend's kindness, Stealth?" the father'd asked. "Better me than any of this trash, my friend. I'll do it right. She's ready, and it wouldn't be long, in any case," he'd replied while the girl looked between the soldier, twelve years older, and her father, with uncomprehending eyes. He had to find her.

Janni, as if in receipt of the perceptive spirit Niko tried now to reclaim, swore and mentioned that Niko'd had no business getting involved with her, a child.

"I'm not *your* type, and as for women, I drink from no other man's tainted cup." So Niko broached an uneasy subject: Janni was no Sacred Bander; his camaraderie had limits; Niko's need for touch and love the other man knew but could not fill; they had an attenuated pairbond, not complete as Sacred Banders knew it, and Janni was uncomfortable with the innuendo and assumptions of the other singles, and Niko's unsated needs as well.

The silence come between them then gave Stealth his chance to find the girl's red time-shadow, a hot ghost-trail to follow southwest through the Maze. . . .

As the moon climbed high its light shone brighter, giving Maze and then Shambles shape and teasing light;

color was almost present among the streets, so bright it shone, a reddish cast like blood upon its face, so that when common Sanctuary horrors lay revealed at intersections, they seemed worse even than they were. Janni saw two whores fight for a client; he saw blood run black in gutters from thugs and just incautious folk. Their horses' hoofbeats cleared their path, though, and Maze was left behind, as willing to let them go as they to leave it, although Janni muttered at every vile encounter their presence interrupted, wishing they could intervene.

Once he thought they'd glimpsed a death squad, and urged Stealth to come alert, but the strange young fighter shook his head and hushed him, slouched loose upon his horse as if entranced, following some trail that neither Janni nor any mortal man with God's good fear of magic should have seen. Janni's heart was troubled by this boy who was too good at craft, who had a charmed sword and dagger given him by the entelechy of dreams, yet left them in the barracks, decrying magic's price. But what was this, if not sorcery? Janni watched Niko watch the night and take them deep into shadowed alleys with all the confidence a mage would flout. The youth had offered to teach him "controls" of mind, to take him "up through the planes and get your guide and your twelfth-plane name." But Janni was no connoisseur of witchcraft; like boy-loving, he left it to the Sacred Banders and the priests. He'd gotten into this with Niko for worldly advantage; the youth ten years his junior was pure genius in a fight; he'd seen him work at Jubal's and marveled even in the melée of the sack. Niko's reputation for prowess in the field was matched only by Straton's, and the stories told of Niko's past. The boy had trained among Successors, the Nisibisi's bane, wild guerrillas, mountain commandos who let none through Wizardwall's defiles without gold or life in tithe, who'd sworn to reclaim their mountains from the mages and the warlocks and held out, outlaws, countering sorcery with swords. In a campaign such as the northern one coming, Niko's skills and languages and friends might prove invaluable. Janni, from Machad, had no love for Rankans, but it was said Niko served despite a blood hatred: Rankans had sacked his town nameless; his father had died fighting Rankan expansion when the boy was five. Yet he'd come south on Abarsis' venture, and stayed when Tempus inherited the band.

When they crossed the Street of Shingles and headed into Shambles Cross, the pragmatic Janni spoke a soldier's safe-conduct prayer and touched his warding charm. A confusion of turns within the ways high-grown with hovels which cut off view and sky, they heard commotion, shouting men and running feet.

They spurred their horses and careened round corners, forgetful of their pose as independent reavers, for they'd heard Stepsons calling maneuver codes. So it was that they came, sliding their horses down on haunches so hard sparks flew from iron-shod hooves, cutting off the retreat of three running on foot from Stepsons and vaulted down to the cobbles to lend a hand.

Niko's horse, itself, took it in its mind to help, and charged past them, reins dragging, head held high, to back a fugitive against a mudbrick wall. "*Seh!* Run, Vis!" they heard, and more in a tongue Janni thought might be Nisi, for the exclamation was.

By then Niko had one by the collar and two quarrels shot by close to Janni's ear. He hollered out his identity and called to the shooters to cease their fire before he was skewered like the second fugitive, pinned by two bolts against the wall. The third quarry struggled now between the two on-duty Stepsons, one of whom called out to Janni to hold the second. It was Straton's voice, Janni realized, and Straton's quarrels pinning the indigent by cape and crotch against the wall. Lucky for the delinquent it had been: Straton's bolts had pierced no vital spot, just clothing.

It was not till then that Janni realized that Niko was talking to the first fugitive, the one his horse had pinned, in Nisi, and the other answering back, fast and low, his eyes upon the vicious horse, quivering and covered with phosphorescent froth, who stood watchful by his master, hoping still that Niko would let him pound the quarry into gory mud.

Straton and his partner, dragging the third unfortunate between them, came up, full of thanks and victory: "... finally got one, alive. Janni, how's yours?"

The one he held at crossbow-point was quiet, submissive, a Sanctuarite, he thought, until Straton lit a torch. Then they saw a slave's face, dark and arch like Nisibisis were, and Straton's partner spoke for the first time: "That's Haught, the slave-bait." Critias moved forward, torch in hand. "Hello, pretty. We'd thought you'd run or died. We've lots to ask you, puppy, and nothing we'd rather do tonight...." As Crit moved in and Janni stepped back, Janni was conscious that Niko and his prisoner had fallen silent.

Then the slave, amazingly, straightened up and raised its head, reaching within its jerkin. Janni levered his bow, but the hand came out with a crumpled paper in it, and this he held forth, saying: "She freed me. She said this says so. Please ... I know nothing, but that she's freed me...."

Crit snatched the feathered parchment from him, held it squinting in the torch's light. "That's right, that's what it says here." He rubbed his jaw, then stepped forward. The slave flinched, his handsome face turned away. Crit pulled out the bolts that held him pinned, grunting; no blood followed; the slave crouched down, unscathed but incapacitated by his fear. "Come as a free man, then, and talk to us. We won't hurt you, boy. Talk and you can go."

Niko, then, intruded, his prisoner beside him, his horse following close behind. "Let them go, Crit."

"*What?* Niko, forget the game, tonight. They'll not live to tell you helped us. We've been needing this advantage too long—"

"Let them go, Crit." Beside him his prisoner cursed or hissed or intoned a spell, but did not break to run. Niko stepped close to his task force leader, whispering: "This one's an ex-commando, a fighter from Wizardwall come upon hard times. Do him a service, as I must, for services done."

"Nisibisi? More's the reason, then, to take them and break them—"

"No. He's on the other side from warlocks; he'll do us more good free in the streets. Won't you, Vis?"

The foreign-looking ruffian agreed, his voice thick with an accent detectable even in his three clipped syllables.

Niko nodded. "See, Crit? This is Vis. Vis, this is Crit. I'll be the contact for his reports. Go on, now. You, too, freedman, go. Run!"

And the two, taking Niko at his word, dashed away before Crit could object.

The third, in Straton's grasp, writhed wildly. This was a failed hawkmask, very likely, in Straton's estimation the prize of the three and one no word from Niko could make the mercenary loose.

Niko agreed that he'd not try to save any of Jubal's minions, and that was that ... almost. They had to keep their meeting brief; anyone could be peeking out from windowsill or shadowed door, but as they mounted up to ride away, Janni saw a cowled figure rising from a pool of darkness occluding the intersection. It stood, full up, momentarily, and moonrays struck its face. Janni shuddered; it was a face with hellish eyes, too far to be so big or so frightening, yet their met glance shocked him like icy water and made his limbs to shake.

"Stealth! Did you see that?"

"What?" Niko snapped, defensive over interfering in Crit's operation. "See what?"

"That—thing. . . ." Nothing was there, where he had seen it. "Nothing. . . . I'm seeing things." Crit and Straton had reached their horses; they heard hoofbeats receding in the night.

"Show me where, and tell me what."

Janni swung up on his mount and led the way; when they got there, they found a crumpled body, a youth with bloated tongue outstuck and rolled up eyes as if a fit had taken him, dead as Abarsis in the street. "Oh, no. . . ." Niko, dismounted, rolled the corpse. "It's one of Tamzen's friends." The silk-and-linened body came clearer as Janni's eyes accustomed themselves to moonlight after the glare of the torch. They heaved the corpse up upon Janni's horse who snorted to bear a dead thing but forbore to refuse outright. "Let's take it somewhere, Stealth. We can't carry it about all night." Only then did Janni remember they'd failed to report to Crit their evening's plan.

At his insistence, Niko agreed to ride by the Shambles Cross safe haven, caulked and shuttered in iron, where Stepsons and street men and Ilsig/Rankan garrison personnel, engaged in chasing hawkmasks and other covert enterprise, made their slum reports *in situ*.

They managed to leave the body there, but not to alert the task force leader; Crit had taken the hawkmask wherever he thought the catch would serve them best; nothing was in the room but the interrogation wheel and bags of lime to tie on unlucky noses and truncheons of sailcloth filled with gravel and iron filings to change the most steadfast heart. They left a note, carefully coded, and hurried back onto the street. Niko's brow was furrowed, and Janni, too, was in a hurry to see if they might find Tamzen and her friends as a living group, not one by one, cold corpses in the gutter.

\* \* \*

The witch Roxane had house snakes, a pair brought down from Nisibis, green and six feet long, each one. She brought them into her study and set their baskets by the hearth. Then, bowl of water by her side, she spoke the words that turned them into men. The facsimiles aped a pair of Stepsons; she got them clothes and sent them off. Then she took the water bowl and stirred it with her finger until a whirlpool sucked and writhed. This she spoke over, and out to sea beyond the harbor a like disturbance began to rage. She took from her table six carven ships with Beysib sails, small and filled with wax miniatures of men. These she launched into the basin with its whirlpool and spun and spun her finger round until the flagships of the fleet foundered, then were sunk and sucked to lie at last upon the bottom of the bowl. Even after she withdrew her finger the water raged awhile. The witch looked calmly into her maelstrom and nodded once, content. The diversion would be timely; the moon, outside her window, was nearly high, scant hours from its zenith.

Then it was time to take Jagat's report and send the death squads—or dead squads, for none of those who served in them had life of their own to lead—into town.

Tamzen's heart was pounding, her mouth dry and her lungs burning. They had run a long way. They were lost, and all six knew it; Phryne was weeping and her sister was shaking and crying she couldn't run, her knees wouldn't hold her; the three boys left were talking loud and telling all how they'd get home if they just stayed in a group— the girls had no need to fear. More krrf was shared, though it made things worse, not better, so that a toothless crone who tapped her stick and smacked her gums sent them flying through the streets.

No one talked about Mehta's fate; they'd seen him with the dark-clad whore, seen him mesmerized, seen him take her hand. They'd hid until the pair walked on, then followed—the group had sworn to stay together, wicked adventure on their minds; all were officially adults now; none could keep them from the forbidden pleasures of men and women—to see if Mehta would really lay the whore, thinking they'd regroup right after, and find out what fun he'd had.

They'd seen him fall, and gag, and die once he'd raised her skirts and had her, his buttocks thrusting hard as he pinned her to the alley wall. They'd seen her bend down over him and raise her head and the glowing twin hells there had sent them pell-mell, fleeing what they knew was no human whore.

Now they'd calmed, but they were deep in the Shambles, near its end where Caravan Square began. There was light there, from midnight merchants engaged in double dealing; it was not safe there, one of the boys said: slaves were made this way: children taken, sold north and never seen again.

"It's safe *here*, then?" Tamzen blurted, her teeth chattering but the krrf making her bold and angry. She strode ahead, not waiting to see them follow; they would; she knew this bunch better than their mothers. The thing to do, she was sure, was to stride bravely on until they came upon the Square and found the streets home, or came upon some Hell Hounds, palace soldiers, or Stepsons. Niko's friends would ride them home on horseback if they found some; Tamzen's acquaintance among the men of iron was her fondest prize.

Niko. . . . If *he* were here, she'd have no fear, nor need to pretend to valor. . . . Her eyes filled with tears, thinking what he'd say when he heard. She was never going to convince him she was grown if all her attempts to do so made her seem the more a child. A *child's* error, this, for sure . . . and one dead on her account. Her father would beat her rump to blue and he'd keep her in her room for a

month. She began to fret—the krrf's doing, though she
was too far gone in the drug's sway to tell—and saw an
alley from which torchlight shone. She took it; the others
followed, she heard them close behind. They had money
aplenty; they would hire an escort, perhaps with a wagon,
to take them home. All taverns had men looking for hire
in them; if they chanced Caravan Square, and fell afoul of
slavers, she'd never see her poppa or Niko or her room
filled with stuffed toys and ruffles again.

The inn was called the Sow's Ear, and it was foul. In its
doorway, one of the boys, panting, caught her arm and
jerked her back. "Show money in that place, and you'll
get all our throats slit quick."

He was right. They huddled in the street and sniffed
more krrf and shook and argued. Phryne began to wail
aloud and her sister stopped her mouth with a clapped
hand. Just as the two girls, terrified and defeated, crouched
down in the street and one of the boys, his bladder loosed
by fear, sought a corner wall, a woman appeared before
them, her hood thrown back, her face hidden by a trick of
light. But the voice was a gentlewoman's voice and the
words were compassionate. "Lost, children? There, there,
it's all right now, just come with me. We'll have mulled
wine and pastries and I'll have my man form an escort to
see you home. You're the Alekeep owner's daughter, if I'm
right? Ah, good, then; your father's a friend of my husband . . . surely you remember me?"

She gave a name and Tamzen, her sense swimming in
drugs and her heart filled with relief and the sweet taste
of salvation, lied and said she did. All six went along with
the woman, skirting the square until they came to a curious house behind a high gate, well lit and gardened and
full of chaotic splendor. At its rear, the rush of the White
Foal could be heard.

"Now sit, sit, little ones. Who needs to wash off the
street grime? Who needs a pot?" The rooms were shadowed,

no longer well lit; the woman's eyes were comforting, calming like sedative draughts for sleepless nights. They sat among the silks and the carven chairs and they drank what she offered and began to giggle. Phryne went and washed, and her sister and Tamzen followed. When they came back, the boys were nowhere in sight. Tamzen was just going to ask about that when the woman offered fruit, and somehow she forgot the words on her tongue-tip, and even that the boys had been there at all, so fine was the krrf the woman smoked with them. She knew she'd remember in a bit, though, whatever it was she'd forgot. . . .

When Crit and Straton arrived with the hawkmask they'd captured at the Foalside home of Ischade, the vampire woman, all its lights were on, it seemed, yet little of that radiance cut the gloom.

"By the god's four months, Crit, I still don't understand why you let those others go. And for Niko. What—?"

"Don't ask me, Straton, what his reasons are; I don't know. Something about the one being of that Successors band, revolutionaries who want Wizardwall back from the Nisibisi mages—there's more to Nisibis than the warlocks. If that Vis *was* one, then he's an outlaw as far as Nisibisi law goes, and maybe a fighter. So we let him go, do him a favor, see if maybe he'll come to us, do us a service in his turn. But as for the other—you saw Ischade's writ of freedom—we gave him to her and she let him go. If we want to use her . . . if she'll *ever* help us find Jubal— and she *does* know where he is; this freeing of the slave was a message: she's telling us we've got to up the ante— we've got to honor her wishes as far as this slave-bait goes."

"But this . . . coming here *ourselves?* You know what she can do to a man. . . ."

"Maybe we'll like it; maybe it's time to die. I don't know. I *do* know we can't leave it to the garrison—every time they find us a hawkmask he's too damaged to tell us anything. We'll never recruit what's left of them if the army keeps killing them slowly, and we take the blame. And also," Crit paused, dismounted his horse, pulled the trussed and gagged hawkmask he had slung over his saddle like a haunch of meat down after him, so that the prisoner fell heavily to the ground, "we've been told by the garrison's intelligence liaison that the army thinks Stepsons fear this woman."

"Anybody with a dram of common sense would." Straton, rubbing his eyes, dismounted also, notched crossbow held at the ready as soon as his feet touched the ground.

"They don't mean that. You know what they mean; they can't tell a Sacred Bander from a straight mercenary. They think we're all sodomizers and sneer at us for that."

"Let 'em. I'd rather be alive and misunderstood than dead and respected." Straton blinked, trying to clear his blurred vision. It was remarkable that Critias would undertake this action on his own; he wasn't supposed to take part in field actions, but command them. Tempus had been to see him, though, and since then the task force leader had been more taciturn and even more impatient than usual. Straton knew there was no use in arguing with Critias, but he was one of the few who could claim the privilege of voicing his opinion to the leader, even when they disagreed.

They'd interrogated the hawkmask briefly; it didn't take long; Straton was a specialist in exactly that. He was a pretty one, and substantively undamaged. The vampire was discerning, loved beauty; she'd taken to this one, the few bruises on him might well make him more attractive to a creature such as she: not only would she have him in her power but it would be in her power to save him from a much worse death than that she'd give. By the look of the tall, lithe hawkmask, by his clothes and his pinched face in which sensitive, liquid eyes roamed furtively, a pleasant death would be welcome. His ilk were hunted by more factions in Sanctuary than any but Nisibisi spies.

Crit said, "Ready, Strat?"

"I own I'm not, but I'll pretend if you do. If you get through this and I don't, my horses are yours."

"And mine, yours." Crit bared his teeth. "But I don't expect that to happen. She's reasonable, I'm wagering. She couldn't have turned that slave loose that way if she wasn't in control of her lust. And she's smart—smarter than Kadakithis' so-called 'intelligence staff,' or Hell Hounds, we've seen that for a fact."

So, despite sane cautions, they unlatched the gate, their horses drop-tied behind them, cut the hawkmask's ankle bonds and walked him to the door. His eyes went wide above his gag, pupils gigantic in the torchlight on her threshold, then squeezed shut as Ischade herself came to greet them when, after knocking thrice and waiting long, they were about to turn away, convinced she wasn't home after all.

She looked them up and down, her eyes half-lidded. Straton, for once, was grateful for the shimmer in his vision, the blur he couldn't blink away. The hawkmask shivered and lurched backward in their grasp as Crit spoke first:

"Good evening, madam. We thought the time had come to meet, face to face. We've brought you this gift, a token of our good will." He spoke blandly, matter-of-factly, letting her know they knew all about her and didn't really care what she did to the unwary or the unfortunate. Straton's mouth dried and his tongue stuck to the roof of it. None was colder than Crit, or more tenacious when work was under way.

The woman, Ischade, dusky-skinned but not the ruddy tone of Nisibis, an olive cast that made the whites of her teeth and eyes very bright, bade them enter. "Bring him in, then, and we'll see what can be seen."

"No, no. We'll leave him—an article of faith. We'd like to know what you hear of Jubal, or his band—whereabouts, that sort of thing. If you come to think of any such information, you can find me at the mercenaries' hostel."

"Or in your hidey-hole in Shambles Cross?"

"Sometimes." Crit stood firm. Straton, his relief a flood, now that he knew they weren't going *in* there, gave the hawkmask a shove. "Go on, boy, go to your mistress."

"A slave, then, is this one?" she asked Strat and that glance chilled his soul when it fixed on him. He'd seen butchers look at sheep like that. He half expected her to reach out and tweak his biceps.

He said: "What you wish, he is."

She said: "And you?"

Crit said: "Forbearance has its limits."

She replied: "Yours, perhaps, not mine. Take him with you; I want him not. What you Stepsons think of me, I shall not even ask. But cheap, I shall never come."

Crit loosed his hold on the youth, who wriggled then, but Straton held him, thinking that Ischade was without doubt the most beautiful woman he'd ever seen, and the hawkmask was luckier than most. If death was the gateway to heaven, she was the sort of gatekeep he'd like to admit him, when his time came.

She remarked, though he had not spoken aloud, that such could easily be arranged.

Crit, at that, looked between them, then shook his head. "Go wait with the horses, Straton. I thought I heard them, just now."

So Straton never did find out exactly what was—or was not—arranged between his task force leader and the vampire woman, but when he reached the horses, he had his hands full calming them, as if his own had scented Niko's black, whom his gray detested above all other studs. When they'd both been stabled in the same barn, the din had been terrible, and stallboards shattered as regularly as stalls were mucked, from those two trying to get at each other. Horses, like men, love and hate, and those two stallions wanted a piece of each other the way Strat wanted a chance at the garrison commander or Vashanka at the Wrigglies' Ils.

Soon after, Crit came sauntering down the walk, unscathed, alone, and silent.

Straton wanted to ask, but did not, what had been arranged: his leader's sour expression warned him off. And an hour later, at the Shambles Cross safe haven, when one of the street men came running in saying there was a disturbance and Tempus could not be found, so Crit would have to come, it was too late.

What they could do about waterspouts and whirlpools in the harbor was unclear.

When Straton and Crit had ridden away, Niko eased his black out from hiding. The spirit-track he'd followed had led them here; Tamzen and the others were inside. The spoor met up with the pale blue traces of the house's owner near the Sow's Ear and did not separate thereafter. Blue was no human's color, unless that human was an enchanter, a witch, accursed or charmed. Both Niko and Janni knew whose house this was, but what Crit and Straton were doing here, neither wanted to guess or say.

"We can't rush the place, Stealth. You know what she is."

"I know."

"Why didn't you let me hail them? Four would be better than two, for this problem's solving."

"Whatever they're doing here, I don't want to know about. And we've broken cover as it is tonight." Niko crooked a leg over his horse's neck, cavalry style. Janni rolled a smoke and offered him one; he took it and lit it with a flint from his belt pouch just as two men with a

wagon came driving up from Downwind, wheels and hooves
thundering across the White Foal's bridge.

"Too much traffic," Janni muttered, as they pulled their
horses back into shadows and watched the men stop their
team before the odd home's door; the wagon was screened
and curtained; if someone was within, it was impossible
to tell.

The men went in and when they came out they had
three smallish people with them swathed in robes and
hooded. These were put into the carriage, and it then
drove away, turning onto the cart-track leading south
from the bridge—there was nothing down there but swamp
and wasteland, and at the end of it, Fisherman's Row and
the sea . . . nothing, that is, but the witch Roxane's fortified estate.

"Do you think—Stealth, was that them?"

"Quiet, curse you; I'm trying to tell." It might have
been; his heart was far from quiet, and the passengers, he
sensed, were drugged and nearly somnambulent.

But from the house, he could no longer sense the girlish
trails which had been there, among the blue/archmagical/
anguished ones of its owner and those of men. Boys' auras
still remained there, he thought, but quiet, weaker, perhaps dying, maybe dead. It could be the fellow Crit had
left there, and not the young scions of east side homes.

The moon, above Niko's head, was near at zenith. Seeing
him look up, Janni anticipated what he was going to say:
"Well, Stealth, we've got to go down there anyway; let's
follow the wagon. Mayhap we'll catch it. Perchance we'll
find out whom they've got there, if we do. And we've little
time to lose—girls or no, we've a witch to attend to."

"Aye." Niko reined his horse around and set it at a lope
after the wagon, not fast enough to catch it too soon, but
fast enough to keep it in earshot. When Janni's horse came
up beside his, the other mercenary called: "Convenience
of this magnitude makes me nervous; you'd think the

witch sent that wagon, even snared those children, to be sure we'd have to come."

Janni was right; Niko said nothing; they were committed; there was nothing to do but follow; whatever was going to happen was well upon them, now.

A dozen riders materialized out of the wasteland near the swamp and surrounded the two Stepsons; none had faces; all had glowing pure-white eyes. They fought as best they could with mortal weapons, but ropes of spitting power came round them, and blue sparks bit them, and their flesh sizzled through their linen chitons, and, unhorsed, they were dragged along behind the riders until they no longer knew where they were or what was happening to them or even felt the pain. The last thing Niko remembered, before he awoke bound to a tree in some featureless grove, was the wagon ahead, stopping, and his horse, on its own trying to win the day. The big black had climbed the mount of the rider who dragged Niko on a tether, and he'd seen the valiant beast's thick jowls pierced through by arrows glowing blue with magic, seen his horse falter, jaws gaping, then fall as he was dragged away.

Now he struggled, helpless in his bonds, trying to clear his vision and will his pain away.

Before him he saw figures, a bonfire limning silhouettes. Among them, as consciousness came full upon him and he began to wish he'd never waked, was Tamzen, struggling in grisly embraces and wailing out his name, and the other girls, and Janni, spreadeagled, staked out on the ground, his mouth open, screaming at the sky.

"Ah," he heard, "Nikodemos. So kind of you to join us."

Then a woman's face swam before him, beautiful, though that just made it worse. It was the Nisibisi witch, and she was smiling, itself an awful sign. A score of minions ringed her, creatures roused from graves, and two with ophidian eyes and lipless mouths whose skins had a greenish cast.

She began to tell him softly the things she wished to know. For a time he only shook his head and closed his ears and tried to flee his flesh. If he could retire his mind to his rest-place, he could ignore it all; the pain, the screams which split the night; he would know none of what occurred here, and die without the shame of capitulation: she'd kill him anyway, when she was done. So he counted determinedly backward, eyes squeezed shut, envisioning the runes which would save him. But Tamzen's screams, her sobs to him for help, and Janni's animal anguish, kept interfering, and he could not reach the quiet place and stay: he kept being dragged back by the sounds.

Still, when she asked him questions, he only stared back at her in silence: Tempus' plans and state of mind were things he knew little of; he couldn't have stopped this if he'd wanted to; he didn't know enough. But when at length, knowing it, he closed his eyes again, she came up close and pried them open, impaling his lids with wooden splinters so that he would see what made Janni cry.

They had staked the Stepson over a wild creature's burrow—a badger, he later saw, when it had gnawed and clawed its way to freedom—and were smoking the rodent out by setting fire to its tunnel. When Janni's stomach began to show the outline of the animal within, Niko, capitulating, told all he knew and made up more besides.

By then the girls had long since been silenced.

All he heard was the witch's voice; all he remembered was the horror of her eyes and the message she bade him give to Tempus, and that when he had repeated it, she pulled the splinters from his lids. . . . The darkness she allowed him became complete, and he found a danker rest-place than meditation's quiet cave.

In Roxane's "manor house" commotion raged; slaves went running, and men cried orders, and in the court the caravan was being readied to make away.

She herself sat petulant and wroth, among the brocades of her study and the implements of her craft: water and fire and earth and air, and minerals and plants, and a globe sculpted from high peaks clay with precious stones inset.

A wave of hand would serve to load these in her wagon. The house spells' undoing would take much less than that—a finger's wave, a word unsaid, and all would be no more than it appeared: rickety and threadbare. But the evening's errors and all the work she'd done to amend them had drained her strength.

She sat, and Niko, in a corner, propped up but not awake, breathed raspingly: another error—those damn snakes took everything too literally, as well as being incapable of following simple orders to their completion.

The snakes she'd sent out, charmed to look like Stepsons, should have found the children in the streets; as Niko and Janni, their disguises were complete. But a vampire bitch, a cursed and accursed third-rater possessed of meager spells, had chanced upon the quarry and taken it home. Then she'd had to change all plans and make the wagon and send the snakes to retrieve the bait—the girls alone, the boys were expendable—and snakes were not up to fooling women grown and knowledgeable of spells. Ischade had given up her female prizes, rather than confront Nisibisi magic, pretending for her own sake that she believed the "Stepsons" who came to claim Tamzen and her friends.

Had Roxane not been leaving town this evening, she'd have had to wipe the vampire's soul—or at least her memory—away.

So she took the snakes out once more from their baskets and held their heads up to her face. Tongues darted out and reptilian eyes pled mercy, but Roxane had forgotten mercy long ago. And strength was what she needed, which in part these had helped to drain away. Holding them high she picked herself up and speaking words of power took them both and cast them in the blazing hearth. The flames roared up and snakes writhed in agony, and roasted. When they were done she fetched them out with silver tongs and ate their tails and heads.

Thus fortified, she turned to Niko, still hiding mind and soul in his precious mental refuge, a version of it she'd altered when her magic saw it. This place of peace and perfect relaxation, a cave behind the meadow of his mind, had a ghost in it, a friend who loved him. In its guise she'd spoken long to him and gained his spirit's trust. He was hers, now, as her lover-lord had promised; all things he learned she'd know as soon as he. None of it he'd remember, just go about his business of war and death. Through him she'd herd Tempus whither she willed, and through him she'd know the Riddler's every plan.

For Nikodemos, the Nisibisi bondservant, had never shed his brand or slipped his chains: though her lover had freed his body, deep within his soul a string was tied. Any time, her lord could pull it; and she, too, now, had it twined around her pinky.

He remembered none of what occurred after his interrogation in the grove; he recalled just what she pleased and nothing more. Oh, he'd think he'd dreamed delirious nightmares, as he sweated now to feel her touch.

She woke him with a tap upon his eyes and told him what he was: her pawn, her tool, even that he would not recall their little talk or coming here. And she warned him of undeads, and shriveled his soul when she showed him, in her mirror-eyes, what Tamzen and her friends could be, should he even remember what passed between them here.

Then she put her pleasure by and touched the bruised and battered face: one more thing she took from him, to show his spirit who was slave and who was master. She had him service her and took strength from his swollen mouth and then, with a laugh, made him forget it all.

Then she sent her servant forth, unwitting, the extra

satisfaction—gleaned from knowing that his spirit knew, and deep within him cried and struggled—giving the whole endeavor spice.

Jagat's men would see him to the road out near the Stepsons barracks; they took his sagging weight in brawny arms.

And Roxane, for a time, was free to quit this scrofulous town and wend her way northward: she might be back, but for the nonce the journey to her lord's embrace was all she craved. They'd leave a trail well marked in place and plane for Tempus; she'd lie in high-peaks splendor, with her lover-lord well pleased by what she'd brought him: some Stepsons, and a Froth Daughter, and a man the gods immortalized.

It took until nearly dawn to calm the fish-faces who'd lost their five best ships; "lucky" for everyone that the Burek faction's nobility had been enjoying Kadakithis's hospitality, ensconced in the summer palace on the lighthouse spit and not aboard when the ships snapped anchor and headed like creatures with wills of their own toward the maelstrom that had opened at the harbor's mouth.

Crit, through all, was taciturn; he was not supposed to surface; Tempus, when found, would not be pleased. But Kadakithis needed counsel badly; the young prince would give away his Imperial curls for "harmonious relations with our fellows from across the sea."

Nobody could prove that this was other than a natural disaster; an "act of gods" was the unfortunate turn of phrase.

When at last Crit and Strat had done with the dicey process of standing around looking inconsequential while in fact, by handsign and courier, they mitigated Kadakithis's bent to compromise (for which there was no need except in the Beysib matriarch's mind), they retired from the dockside.

Crit wanted to get drunk, as drunk as humanly possible: helping the mageguild defend its innocence, when like as not some mage or other had called the storm, was more than distasteful; it was counterproductive. As far as Critias was concerned, the newly elected First Hazard ought to step forward and take responsibility for his guild's malevolent mischief. When frogs fell from the sky, Straton prognosticated, such would be the case.

They'd done some good there: they'd conscripted Wrigglies and deputized fishermen and bullied the garrison duty officer into sending some of his men out with the long boats and Beysib dinghies and slave-powered tenders which searched shoals and coastline for survivors. But with the confusion of healers and thrill-seeking civilians and boat owners and Beysibs on the docks, they'd had to call in all the Stepsons and troops from road patrols and country posts in case the Beysibs took their loss too much to heart and turned upon the townsfolk.

On every corner, now, a mounted pair stood watch; beyond, the roads were desolate, unguarded. Crit worried that if diversion was some culprit's purpose, it had worked all too well: an army headed south would be upon them with no warning. If he'd not known that yesterday there'd been no sign of southward troop movement, he confided to Straton, he'd be sure some such evil was afoot.

To make things worse, when they found an open bar it was the Alekeep, and its owner was wringing his hands in a corner with five other upscale fathers. Their sons and daughters had been out all night; word to Tempus at the Stepsons' barracks had brought no answer; the skeleton crew at the garrison had more urgent things to do than attend to demands for search parties when manpower was suddenly at a premium; the fathers sat awaiting their own men's return and thus had kept the Alekeep's graveyard shift from closing.

They got out of there as soon as politic, weary as their horses and squinting in the lightening dark.

The only place where peace and quiet could be had now that the town was waking, Crit said sourly, was the Shambles drop. They rode there and fastened the iron shutters down against the dawn, thinking to get an hour or so of sleep, and found Niko's coded note.

"Why wouldn't the old barkeep have told us that he'd set them on his daughter's trail?" Strat sighed, rubbing his eyes with his palms.

"Niko's legend says he's defected to the slums, remember?" Crit was shrugging into his chiton, which he'd just tugged off and thrown upon the floor.

"We're not going back out."

"I am."

"To look for *Niko? Where?*"

"Niko and *Janni.* And I don't *know* where. But if that pair hasn't turned up those youngsters yet, it's no simple adolescent prank or graduation romp. Let's hope it's just that their meet with Roxane took precedence and it's inopportune for them to leave her." Crit stood.

Straton didn't.

"Coming?" Crit asked.

"Somebody should be where authority is expected to be found. You should be here or at the hostel, not chasing after someone who might be chasing after you."

So in the end, Straton won that battle and they went up to the hostel, stopping, since the sun had risen, at Marc's to pick up Straton's case of flights along the way.

The shop's door was ajar, though the opening hour painted on it hadn't come yet. Inside, the smith was hunched over a mug of tea, a crossbow's trigger mechanism dismantled before him on a split of suede, scowling at the crossbow's guts spread upon his counter as if at a recalcitrant child.

He looked up when they entered, wished them a better

morning than he'd had so far this day, and went to get Straton's case of flights.

Behind the counter an assortment of high-torque bows was hung.

When Marc returned with the wooden case, Straton pointed: "That's Niko's, isn't it—or are my eyes that bad?"

"I'm holding it for him, until he pays," explained the smith with the unflinching gaze.

"We'll pay for it now, and he can pick it up from me," Crit said.

"I don't know if he'd...." Marc, half into someone else's business, stepped back out of it with a nod of head: "All right, then, if you want. I'll tell him you've got it. That's four soldats, three ... I've done a lot of work on it for him. Shall I tell him to seek you at the guild hostel?"

"Thereabouts."

Taking it down from the wall, the smith wound and levered, then dry-fired the crossbow, its mechanism to his ear. A smile came over his face at what he heard. "Good enough, then," he declared and wrapped it in its case of padded hide.

This way, Straton realized, Niko would come direct to Crit and report when Marc told him what they'd done.

By the time dawn had cracked the world's egg, Tempus as well as Jihan was sated, even tired. For a man who chased sleep like other men chased power or women, it was wondrous that this was so. For a being only recently become woman, it was a triumph. They walked back toward the Stepsons' barracks, following the creekbed, all pink and gold in sunrise, content and even playful, his chuckle and her occasional laugh startling sleepy squirrels and flushing birds from their nests.

He'd been morose, but she'd cured it, convincing him that life might take a better turn, if he'd just let it. They'd spoken of her father, called Stormbringer in lieu of name, and arcane matters of their joint preoccupation: whether humanity had inherent value, whether gods could die or merely lie, whether Vashanka was hiding out somewhere, petulant in godhead, only waiting for generous sacrifices and heartfelt prayers to coax him back among his Rankan people—or, twelfth plane powers forfend, really "dead."

He'd spoken openly to her of his affliction, reminding her that those who loved him died by violence, and those he loved were bound to spurn him, and what that could mean in the case of his Stepsons, and herself, if Vashanka's power did not return to mitigate his curse. He'd told her of his plea to Enlil, an ancient deity of universal scope, and that he awaited godsign.

She'd been relieved at that, afraid, she admitted, that the lord of dreams might tempt him from her side. For when Aškelon the dream lord had come to take Tempus' sister off to his metaphysical kingdom of delights, he'd offered the brother the boon of mortality. Now that she'd just found him, Jihan had added throatily, she could not bear it if he chose to die.

And she'd spent that evening proving to Tempus that it might be well to stay alive with her, who loved life the more for having only just begun it, and yet could not succumb to mortal death or be placed in mortal danger by his curse, his strength, or whatever he might do.

The high moon had laved them, and her legs had embraced him, and her red-glowing eyes like her father's had transfixed him while her cool flesh enflamed him. Yes, with Jihan beside him, he'd swallow his pride and his pique and give even Sanctuary's Kadakithis the benefit of the doubt—he'd stay though his heart tugged him northward, although he'd thought, when he took her to their creekbed bower, to chase her away.

When they'd slipped into his barracks quarters from the back, he was no longer so certain. He heard from a lieutenant all about the waterspouts and whirlpools, thinking while the man talked that this was his godsign, however obscure its meaning, and then he regretted having made an accomodation with the Froth Daughter: all his angst came back upon him, and he wished he'd hugged his resolve firmly to his breast and driven Jihan hence.

But when the disturbance at the outer gates penetrated to the slaver's old apartments which he had made his own, rousting them out to seek its cause, he was glad enough she'd remained.

The two of them had to shoulder their way through the gathered crowd of Stepsons, astir with bitter mutters; no one made way for them; none had come to their commander's billet with news of what had been brought up to the gatehouse in the dawn.

He heard a harsh whisper from a Stepson too angry to be careful, wondering if Tempus had sent Janni's team deliberately to destruction because Stealth had rejected the Riddler's offered pairbond.

One who knew better answered sagely that this was a Mygdonian message, a Nisibisi warning of some antiquity, and *he* had heard it straight from Stealth's broken lips.

"What *did* that?" Jihan moaned, bending low over Janni's remains. Tempus did not answer her but said generally: "And Niko?" and followed a man who headed off toward the whitewashed barracks, hearing as he went a voice choked with grief explaining to Jihan what happens when you tie a man spreadeagled over an animal's burrow and smoke the creature out.

The Stepson guiding him to where Niko lay said that the man who'd brought them wished to speak to Tempus. "Let him wait for his reward," Tempus snapped, and questioned the mercenary about the Samaritan who'd delivered the two Stepsons home. But the Sacred Bander had gotten nothing from the stranger who'd rapped upon the gates and braved the angry sentries who almost killed him when they saw what burden he'd brought in. The stranger would say only that he must wait for Tempus.

The Stepsons' commander stood around helplessly with three others, friends of Niko's, until the barber-surgeon had finished with needle and gut, then chased them all away, shuttering windows, barring doors. Cup in hand, then, he gave the battered, beaten youth his painkilling draught in silence, only sitting and letting Niko sip while he assessed the Stepson's injuries and made black guesses as to how the boy had come by green and purple blood-filled bruises, rope burns at wrist and neck, and a face like doom.

Quite soon he heard from Nikodemos, concisely but through a slur that comes when teeth have been loosed or broken in a dislocated jaw, what had transpired: they had gone seeking the Alekeep owner's daughter, deep into Shambles where drug dens and cheap whores promise dreamless nights, found them at Ischade's, seen them hustled into a wagon and driven away toward Roxane's. Following, for they were due to see the witch at high moon in her lair in any case, they'd been accosted, surprised by a death squad armed with magic and visaged like the dead, roped and dragged from their horses. The next lucid interval Niko recalled was one of being propped against dense trees, tied to one while the Nisibisi witch used children's plights and spells and finally Janni's tortured drawn-out death to extract from him what little he knew of Tempus' intentions and Rankan strategies of defense for the lower land. "Was I wrong to try not to tell them?" Niko asked, eyes swollen half-shut but filled with hurt. "I thought they'd kill us all, whatever. Then I thought I could hold out . . . Tamzen and the other girls were past help . . . but Janni—" He shook his head. "Then they . . . thought I was lying, when I couldn't answer . . . questions they should have asked of *you*— Then I did lie, to please them, but she . . . the witch knew. . . ."

"Never mind. Was One-Thumb a party to this?"

A twitch of lips meant "no" or "I don't know."

Then Niko found the strength to add: "If I hadn't tried to keep my silence— I've been interrogated before by Nisibisi. . . . I hid in my rest-place . . . until Janni— They killed him to get to me."

Tempus saw bright tears threatening to spill and changed the subject: "Your rest-place? So your *maat* returned to you?"

He whispered, "After a fashion. . . . I don't care about that now. Going to need all my anger . . . no time for balance anymore."

Tempus blew out a breath and set down Niko's cup and looked between his legs at the packed clay floor. "I'm going north, tomorrow. I'll leave sortie assignments and schedules with Critias—he'll be in command here—and a rendezvous for those who want to join in the settling up. Did you recognize any Ilsigs in her company? A servant, a menial, anyone at all?"

"No, they all look alike. . . . Someone found us, got us to the gates. Some trainees of ours, maybe—they knew my name. The witch said come ahead and die upcountry. Each reprisal of ours, they'll match fourfold."

"Are you telling me not to go?"

Niko struggled to sit up, cursed, fell back with blood oozing from between his teeth. Tempus made no move to help him. They stared at each other until Stealth said, "It will seem that you've been driven from Sanctuary, that you've failed here. . . ."

"Let it seem so, it may well be true."

"Wait, then, until I can accompany—"

"You know better. I will leave instructions for you." He got up and left quickly, before his temper got the best of him where the boy could see.

The Samaritan who had brought their wounded and their dead was waiting outside Tempus' quarters. His

name was Vis, and though he looked Nisibisi he claimed
he had a message from Jubal. Because of his skin and his
accent Tempus almost took him prisoner, thinking to give
him to Straton, for whom all manner of men bared their
souls, but he marshaled his anger and sent the young man
away with a pocket full of soldats and instructions to
convey Jubal's message to Critias. Crit would be in charge
of the Stepsons henceforth; what Jubal and Crit might
arrange was up to them. The reward was for bringing
home the casualties, dead and living, a favor cheap at the
price.

Then Tempus went to find Jihan. When he did, he asked
her to put him in touch with Aškelon, dream lord, if she
could.

"So that you can punish yourself with mortality? This
is not your fault."

"A kind, if unsound, opinion. Mortality will break the
curse. Can you help me?"

"I will not, not now, when you are like this," she replied,
concern knitting her brows in the harsh morning light.
"But I will accompany you north. Perhaps another day,
when you are calmer. . . ."

He cursed her for acting like a woman and set about
scheduling sorties and sketching maps, so that each of his
men would have worked out his debt to Kadakithis and
be in good standing with the mercenaries' guild when and
if they joined him in Tyse, at the very foot of Wizardwall.

It took no longer to draft his resignation and Critias'
appointment in his stead and send them off to Kadakithis
than it took to clear his actions with the Rankan represen-
tatives of the mercenaries' guild: his task here (assessing
Kadakithis for a Rankan faction desirous of a change in
emperors) was accomplished; he could honestly say that
neither town or townspeople nor effete prince was worth
struggling to ennoble. For good measure he was willing to
throw into the stewpot of disgust boiling in him both

Vashanka and the child he had co-fathered with the god, by means of whom certain interests thought to hold him here: he disliked children, as a class, and even Vashanka had turned his back on this one.

Still, there were things he had to do. He went and found Crit in the guild hostel's common room and told him all that had transpired. If Crit had refused the appointment outright, Tempus would have had to tarry, but Critias only smiled cynically, saying that he'd be along with his best fighters as soon as matters here allowed. He left One-Thumb's case in Critias's hands; they both knew that Straton could determine the degree of the barkeep's complicity quickly enough.

Crit asked, as Tempus was leaving the dark and comforting common room for the last time, whether any children's bodies had been found—three girls and boys still were missing; one young corpse had turned up cold in Shambles Cross.

"No," Tempus said, and thought no more about it. "Life to you, Critias."

"And to you, Riddler. And everlasting glory."

Outside, Jihan was waiting on one Trôs horse, the other's reins in her hand.

They went first southwest to see if perhaps the witch or her agents might be found at home, but the manor house and its surrounds were deserted, the yard crisscrossed with cart-tracks from heavily laden wagons' wheels.

The caravan's track was easy to follow.

Riding north without a backward glance on his Trôs horse, Jihan swaying in her saddle on his right, he had one last impulse: he ripped the problematical Storm God's amulet from around his throat, dropped it into a quaggy marsh. Where he was going, Vashanka's name was meaningless. Other names were hallowed, and other attributes given to the weather gods.

When he was sure he had successfully cast it aside, and

the god's voice had not come ringing with awful laughter in his ear (for all gods are tricksters, and war gods worst of any), he relaxed in his saddle. The omens for this venture were good: they'd completed their preparations in half the time he'd anticipated, so that he could start it while the day was young.

Crit sat long at his customary table in the common room after Tempus had gone. By rights it should have been Straton or some Sacred Band pair who succeeded Tempus, someone ... anyone but him. After a time he pulled out his pouch and emptied its contents onto the plank table: three tiny metal figures, a fishhook made from an eagle's claw and abalone shell, a single die, an old field decoration won in Azehur while the Slaughter Priest led the original Sacred Band.

He scooped them up and threw them as a man might throw in wager: the little gold Storm God fell beneath the lead figurine of a fighter, propping the man upright; the fishhook embraced the die, which came to rest with one dot facing up—Strat's war name was Ace. The third figure, a silver rider mounted, sat square atop the field star—Abarsis had slipped it over his head so long ago the ribbon had crumbled away.

Content with the omens his private prognosticators gave, he collected them and put them away. He'd wanted Tempus to ask him to join him, not hand him fifty men's lives to yea or nay. He took such work too much to heart; it lay heavy on him, worse than the task force's weight had been, and he'd only just begun. But that was why Tempus picked him—he was conscientious to a fault.

He sighed and rose and quit the hostel, riding aimlessly through the fetid streets. Damned town was a pit, a bubo, a sore that wouldn't heal. He couldn't trust his task force to some subordinate, though how he was going to run them while stomping around vainly trying to fill Tempus' sandals, he couldn't say.

His horse, picking his route, took him by the Vulgar Unicorn where Straton would soon be "discussing sensitive matters" with One-Thumb.

By rights he should go up to the palace, pay a call on Kadakithis, "make nice" (as Straton said) to Vashanka's priest-of-record Molin, visit the mageguild.... He shook his head and spat over his horse's shoulder. He hated politics.

And what Tempus had told him about Niko's misfortune and Janni's death still rankled. He remembered the foreign fighter Niko had made him turn loose—Vis. Vis, who'd come to Tempus, bearing hurt and slain, with a message from Jubal. That, and what Straton had gotten from the hawkmask they'd given Ischade, plus the vampire woman's own hints, allowed him to triangulate Jubal's position like a sailor navigating by the stars. Vis was supposed to come to him, though. He'd wait. If his hunch was right, he could put Jubal and his hawkmasks to work for Kadakithis without either knowing—or at least having to admit—that was the case.

If so, he'd be free to take the band north—what they wanted, expected, and would now fret to do with Tempus gone. Only Tempus's mystique had kept them this long; Crit would have a mutiny, or empty barracks, if he couldn't meet their expectation of war to come. They weren't baby sitters, slum police, or palace praetorians; they collected exploits, not soldats. He began to form a plan, shape up a scenario, answer questions sure to be asked him later, rehearsing replies in his mind.

Unguided, his horse led him slumward—a barn-rat, it was taking the quickest, straightest way home. When he looked up and out, rather than down and in, he was almost through the Shambles, near White Foal Bridge and the vampire's house, quiet now, unprepossessing in the light of day. Did she sleep in the day? He didn't think she was that kind of vampire; there had been no bloodloss, no punctures on the boy stiff against the drop's back door when one of the street men found it. But what did she do, then, to her victims? He thought of Straton, the way he'd looked at the vampire, the exchange between the two he'd overheard and partly understood. He'd have to keep those two quite separate, even if Ischade was putatively willing to work with, rather than against, them. He spurred his horse on by.

Across the bridge, he rode southwest, skirting the thick of Downwind. When he sighted the Stepsons' barracks, he still didn't know if he could succeed in leading Stepsons. He rehearsed it wryly in his mind: "Life to all. Most of you don't know me but by reputation, but I'm here to ask you to bet your lives on me, not once, but as a matter of course over the next months. . . ."

Still, someone had to do it. And he'd have no trouble with the Sacred Band teams, who knew him in the old days, when he'd had a right-side partner, before that vulnerability was made painfully clear, and he gave up loving the death-seekers—or anything else which could disappoint him.

It mattered not a whit, he decided, if he won or if he lost, if they let him advise them or deserted post and duty to follow Tempus north, as he would have done if the sly old soldier hadn't bound him here with promise and responsibility.

He'd brought Niko's bow. The first thing he did—after leaving the stables, where he saw to his horse and checked on Niko's pregnant mare—was seek the wounded fighter.

The young officer peered at him through swollen, blackened eyes, saw the bow and nodded, unlaced its case and stroked the wood recurve when Critias laid it on the bed. Half a dozen men were there when he'd knocked and entered—three teams who'd come with Niko and his partner down to Ranke on Sacred Band business. They left, warning softly that Crit mustn't tire him—they'd just got him back.

"He's left me the command," Crit said, though he'd thought to talk of hawkmasks and death squads and Nisibisi—a witch and one named Vis.

"Gilgamesh sat by Enkidu seven days, until a maggot fell from his nose." It was the oldest legend the fighters shared, one from Enlil's time when the Lord Storm and Enki (Lord Earth) ruled the world, and a fighter and his friend roamed far.

Crit shrugged and ran a spread hand through feathery hair. "Enkidu was dead; you're not. Tempus has just gone ahead to prepare our way."

Niko rolled his head, propped against the whitewashed wall, until he could see Crit clearly: "He followed godsign; I know that look."

"Or witchsign." Crit squinted, though the light was good, three windows wide and afternoon sun raying the room. "Are you all right—beyond the obvious, I mean?"

"I lost two partners, too close in time. I'll mend."

*Let's hope,* Crit thought but didn't say, watching Niko's expressionless eyes. "I saw to your mare."

"My thanks. And for the bow. Janni's bier is set for morning. Will you help me with it? Say the words?"

Crit rose; the operator in him still couldn't bear to officiate in public, yet if he didn't, he'd never hold these men. "With pleasure. Life to you, Stepson."

"And to you, commander."

And that was that. His first test, passed; Niko and Tempus had shared a special bond.

That night, he called them out behind the barracks, ordering a feast to be served on the training field, a wooden ampitheatre of sorts. By then Straton had come out to join him, and Strat wasn't bashful with the mess staff or the hired help.

Maybe it would work out; maybe together they could make half a Tempus, which was the least this endeavor needed, though Crit would never pair again. . . .

He put it to them when all were well disposed from wine and roasted pig and lamb, standing and flatly telling them Tempus had left, putting them in his charge. There fell a silence and in it he could hear his heart pound. He'd been calmer ringed with Tysian hillmen, or alone, his partner slain, against a Rankan squadron.

"Now, we've got each other, and for good and fair, I say to you, the quicker we quit this cesspool for the clean air of high peaks war, the happier I'll be."

He could hardly see their faces in the dark with the torches snapping right before his face. But it didn't matter; they had to see him, not he them. Crit heard a raucous growl from fifty throats become assent, and then a cheer, and laughter, and Strat, beside and off a bit, gave him a soldier's sign: all's well.

He raised a hand, and they fell quiet; it was a power he'd never tried before: "But the only way to leave with honor is to work your tours out." They grumbled. He continued: "The Riddler's left busy-work sorties enough— hazardous duty actions, by guild book rules; I'll post a list—that we can work off our debt to Kittycat in a month or so."

Someone nay'd that. Someone else called: "Let him finish, then we'll have our say."

"It means naught to me, who deserts to follow. But to *us*, to cadre honor, it's a slur. So I've thought about it, since I'm hot to leave myself, and here's what I propose. All stay, or go. You take your vote. I'll wait. But Tempus wants no man on his right at Wizardwall who hasn't left in good standing with the guild."

When they'd voted, with Straton overseeing the count, to abide by the rules they'd lived to enforce, he said honestly that he was glad about the choice they'd made.

"Now I'm going to split you into units, and each unit has a choice: find a person, a mercenary not among us now, a warm body trained enough to hold a sword and fill your bed, and call him 'brother'—long enough to induct him in your stead. Then we'll leave the town yet guarded by 'Stepsons' and that name's enough, with what we've done here, to keep the peace. The guild has provisions for man-steading; we'll collect from each to fill a pot to hire them; they'll billet here, and we'll ride north a unit at a time and meet up in Tyse, next high moon, and surprise the Riddler."

So he put it to them, and so they agreed.

# Book Three:

# Mageblood

On Wizardwall, those he favored called the archmage Datan; the rest knew him as the Osprey. Under that war name and its aegis, he wreaked his havoc, soaring over high peaks, predator to all—the adepts, the lesser mages, "mighty" enchanters, lowly sorcerers and fey magicians; of the secular populace of Nisibis, he thought little, if at all.

Roxane knew his real name, though he'd gone to great pains to conceal it; she'd kept the fact from him as her insurance, should he ever play her foul. Mages hid their names in fear of retribution. Names are power; true ones tell the number of your soul. Her true name she'd not signed or spoken for a hundred years; she missed it not at all.

Flying, transmogrified, northward on black eagle's wings whose span was twice her human height, she left the caravan far behind. Jagat would bring the spoils home; he'd never failed before. And now he led the caravan, leaving a scented trail the Tempus-fox would follow of his own accord. Her beaked head turned right and left, seeking prey along her way. Being eagle always made her crave warm blood and quivering loin and fur upon her tongue.

In night flight, she was careful: mages fed upon mages; she was yet over Ranke, where a rival mageguild held vicious sway. Gods fought gods and magics, magics; she exulted, thinking there must be no finer time to be alive and abroad with power. She had no doubt who, when this was over, would have the final say.

Towns below showed pastoral fires; the roads here were dotted with convoy lanterns; Rankan cities sprawled not far away. She veered northeast to skirt the capital and soared still higher, thinking of Datan and what he would say to the news she brought of theomachy and flouted gods, of entelechies and Stormbringer and a problematical demigod called Tempus. Some intelligence she bore might not be welcome; favorable assessment of an enemy seldom was. But she had learned so much from Nikodemos—of Aškelon, lord of dreams; of Abarsis, the Slaughter Priest who was in heaven; of the twelfth-plane force called Stormbringer in unearthly league and immortal collusion with the Riddler, and thus the Rankan foe. . . .

Approaching the Wall, she spiraled low after touching the stars to clear its shimmering barrier. She noticed changes in his abode, in the Wall itself. She alighted on his very rampart, and as she did an arrow whickered past, the *whucka-whucka-whucka* of its trajectory whispering in her feathered ear. Her eagle-squawk turned to a howl of rage as she half-changed form, sighting a mortal guard, a man with crossbow drawn. Her human finger pointed; power words leaped from her tongue. His crossbow clattered to the stone and a mouse ran into one boot it had just worn as a man. Back again in her eagle form she took wing and swooped and grabbed the boot, upending it as

she bore it high. Then she dropped the shoe and caught
the mouse, so recently a man, in her claws as it fell
toward the ground far below. And, skewering it through
its heart, she bore it back to Datan's crenelated high peak
keep, and ate its innards upon his wall. As it died, it
turned back to soldier, and as she fed she became a girl.

Wiping her bloody mouth she paused just long enough to
conjure robes to clothe her nakedness, and then a second
guard came on the run.

She waved him sleep, and he crumpled as he ran, landing sprawled between the wall's stone teeth, his weapon
falling a thousand yards before it crashed.

By then she'd changed her mind, unmade the robes, and
soared: his palace was too crowded now with men and
warlike toys. Circling high, she beat away his warding
spells like cobwebs with her wings, and landed on his
tower's very sill.

Within the room, through colored panes of leaded glass,
she saw him with three human allies, Mygdonians: a swag-
gering man, a general by his uniform, proud, fair-haired,
festooned with arms and armor; a woman, pale and elegant;
a boy.

She pecked the lock and swung the windows inward at
their joint. All ceased their conversation. She saw Datan's
downdrawn frown and flickered out of view. What men
should see or know she left to Datan's judgment; he came
toward the windows, striding across in simple robes of
black.

She'd scrambled in, invisible, by the time he reached
out to close the windows; he spoke no word of greeting
but she saw his mouth twitch—he was amused.

She waited then, unseen by the three Mygdonians.

"What in hell was that?" the general growled, his dagger drawn though even he must know he drew in vain.
The woman, flaxen-haired and green-eyed, touched the
general's arm and hustled the boy away, her fingers trail-

ing from Datan's as the archmage kissed her hand. The tow-headed boy kept staring where she was, though no human could truly see her, his pale eyes wide and grayish as if he had a trace of Nisibisi blood.

She thought on that, until they'd gone: when warlock or witch mates with a mortal, the eyes give all away. The last high-blooded coupling they'd recorded was when the Defender took the witches' queen to wife, three decades past when last men were ascendant, and the Defender's forces with Tempus's sanction climbed up Wizardwall. They hadn't won, but they'd gotten farther than mortals should have, and the sibyl had wed to consummate a pact of peace. The Defender, unknowing, signed his own empire's eradication warrant when he spread the legs of magic's queen. Abarsis had been their issue, and treachery among the army had led the officers to conspire to the mother's murder, lest their commander be a pawn of witchcraft— dark vengeance had followed in good order, the destruction of his empire by Ranke, the gelding and enslavement of his son fair payment for the sibyl's life, once peace was declared and Tempus drifted away south to Ranke where war and blood could still be found.

When the door closed upon the Mygdonians, the general last to leave, the archmage turned and welcomed her with outstretched arms, his mighty hairless head inclined: he'd missed her, sensitive lips kissed her, long lashes brushed her cheek.

Datan's corpulence was apparent in any shape; his was a soul of appetites; his was a face of classic beauty, sensual amid the fat; his were hands to crush a world; his soul, if he still owned it, was second-mortgaged, loaned back to him by powers who could wait forever and pile up interest—but it was this weight of payment due which made his manner dark. He exacted all he could from life; he'd given up eternal peace for war and yet conquest could not sate him.

Their embrace had heated up and her robes fallen by her feet when the door was pounded from without: a sentry with news of breached ramparts; the general back again bearing the eviscerated body of an elder son.

It took a while to calm the father, clothes gory and already rent with Mygdonian grief. Datan hushed her when she would have stepped forward and claimed the kill— she'd been attacked, done nothing wrong by fighting back. She flushed, and when the man was gone, she sat with folded arms upon his bedroom table and pouted: "Are we afraid, these days, of puny human ire?"

"These are our allies, Roxane. Need I remind you?" Datan's tone, severe, caused her back to stiffen. Her robe, pulled round her hastily when the knock had come, fell open as she leaned back, stiff-armed. He glared at her and chilled her flesh: "As for fear, it has its place. I'd just as soon not contend with Mygdonian hordes screaming 'Lacan is great' and clambering over one another, dead and living, to be the next soul martyred in his cause. The time will come to trim his sails, but not yet; not 'til Ranke's a forgotten name. *One* clutch of gods and *one* of enemy mages is enough to deal with—at a time. Do I make myself understood?"

She nodded; one did not rile him. She smiled at him and commenced her report. He'd been immobile; now he paced: "Let me get this straight: your idea of neutralizing him was to lead him *here*? The Riddler? Witch, you've overstepped your mandate."

"Not so, my lord. I held a conference here, with all your deputies, who gave me leave to act. Destroying him in his place was impossible; you know what he is—"

"*I* do. You, it seems, do not. What warlock suggested luring him north for battle?"

She named his most trusted three. He pounded one fist upon the table, more angry than she'd ever seen him, and choked back a curse: from *his* lips, curses leaped to life

and served like soldiers. Roxane tried to recall exactly
what words had been given her as mandate: "To 'take
him out of play in the southern theater,' my lord, was an
impossibility. Let those who wish to try Tempus, one by
one, step up to fate's starting line. Neither you nor I must
face him."

"No? Let's hope you're right, Roxane. I own I wish
you'd abided there in Sanctuary as I commanded. I cannot leave these fools alone a week before they're stepping
in their own excrement. You *do* know that his sister's with
the dream lord? That Stormbringer's given him an own-
daughter for a mate? That Lord Storm claims him as a
true son? That under his aegis the Defender almost had
*me* on a skewer the last time? You'll forgive me if I don't
congratulate you on a job well done, or take you to my
bed for this *favor* you've done the Alliance?"

She had her pride: "Not until it turns out ill or well. I
expect nothing untoward to come of this, Datan. I've controls on him, and I've placed them well."

"How's that?" The archmage's lightless eyes rested full
upon her.

She shivered, but hid it well: "Nikodemos, the young
bondservant. I invoked his spirit's debt and took him as
my own. He'd be with Tempus now but for those damn
snakes of yours, who couldn't follow simple orders, but
beat him to a pulp. When he mends, he'll follow closely;
when he catches up, we'll have a check on Tempus and a
spy in his confidence. The Froth Daughter, Jihan, is helpless,
lovestruck, and far too inexperienced in human ways to
be a threat. And the Riddler himself is full of doubt: the
Rankans think their god is dead. For a Storm God's favorite,
this presents some few problems. Keep the god plane-
locked, and Tempus's curse will destroy him and all he
loves ... no problem, lord, have I brought you, but a
canny solution to all of ours."

"Ah, my snakes. How are they? They're worth a clutch of Rankan factions, and the teetering emperor as well."

She steered him from it: "The faction there that wanted to prop up Kadakithis enough to usurp the throne and depose the emperor, the same faction who hired Tempus in the first place and who petitioned the god to instruct the man to build a temple in the south, is losing heart. And, this the case, Tempus will never throw his weight behind the reigning Rankan lord—he knows the man's not worth a fart. Without the avatar's sanction, the Rankans war as men; men cannot stand against magic's—"

"I asked," her lover-lord broke in, "about my snakes. Where are they? Have you brought them? I sense a bit of them right here. . . ."

And then she had to tell him what part of them his magic recognized, and where their remains now lived: "Stupid snakes, not worth your concern, or mine . . . they almost aborted the venture in its most delicate phase. . . . No . . . No! *No!*"

But he wanted them back, and he would have them. And the way he called them from her belly caused her agony, indescribable pain. As it was just beginning, he froze her tongue so no curse could issue forth from it, then assured her that once he had them back, she'd have learned a lesson . . . and possibly, just possibly, survive it.

The archmage Datan, having looked without compassion on the suffering of the witch, determined that she would live and decreed further punishment: she would pit her strength against the enemy she'd summoned, Tempus, a bright son whose intelligence and powerful friends she and three of his most trusted warlocks had underestimated, when none of their persons had seemed at risk.

He sent them to their deaths, he suspected, but this did not faze him. He needed to test the Froth Daughter, assess the strength of his enemy, try the Riddler to see what time and tribulation had done to that once-uncompromising spirit. If necessary he would take the field himself, but not before the avatar was softened up by summoned demons; perhaps, if luck attended him, and he and Tempus did come face to face, by then the soul of the man would be cracked and rent; possibly magic's minions would have him bound in purgatory; mayhap they'd have harmed him through his men. One way or another, Datan *would* have him. One cannot conquer peoples without bringing down their heroes and making nightmares of their dreams.

To that end, he had other irons in his infernal fires. One of these was the child born to a Mygdonian general's wife in prudent preparation, eight years ago, for what his foresight told him soon would come to be. The boy was Datan's; the Mygdonian general, a prince, suspected but could not admit that an heir of Mygdon had wizard's blood; to do so, he'd have to proclaim himself a cuckold and slay his wife, then come to Datan in puny mortal battle: suicide was not the general's way.

This hold upon one of the ruling three of Mygdonia might prove more than useful, as long as it remained a mere suspicion, not a public slur upon the general's manhood. And the woman remembered nothing more than a coupling in her dreams, though Datan's memory was clear enough and the woman's inclination toward him, now, so strong a child could see. And that child saw more than ever he should, half man, half adept, tortured by what he could not admit to be. "Possessed," his parents feared the boy, and brought him here to Wizardwall for Datan to "lift the curse." It was the mother's skirts, a second time, he ached to lift, her legs and not the boy's "affliction" he sought to pry apart and plumb the depths beyond. But if the father left the boy with him, he'd have another card to play. And the child, disdainful-eyed when he looked upon his sire of record and knowing-eyed when he looked his blood-father in the face, was a prize. Not since Abarsis, son of the Defender, had a high adept spawned a "human" child. Abarsis, though, might have sired a line of counter-wizards, his father's mark too strong on him, his mother's evil not enough to compel him to archmagical despite. The gelding of Abarsis had been worth an entire war where wizardry howled round high peaks and thousands fought and died. Datan himself had overseen the campaigns which culminated in the Defender watching while Rankans made a eunuch-slave of his firstling, one of the "Unending Deaths" Rankan cruelty was proud to inflict upon its enemies. But no hint of the wizard's complicity ever leaked abroad; the Rankans were not allies, just pawns, their land a likely place to raise an empire for evil, their emperor so foul and mean he was useful as he was. Their flaccid mageguild had claimed the feat and triumphs as theirs; Datan had been glad to let them; he'd never wanted glory or recognition, just to stop the Defender in his tracks. And it had worked: even the name of the slain lord's empire had vanished; his seed was neutered before it could spread upon the land like an insidious stain.

One nagging doubt troubled the wizard as he changed his form and sought the general's wife in her husband's likeness while the soldier slept in mid-step high on the battlement wall: Tempus had gone up into Uraete and snatched baby Abarsis from his slavemaster and taken the boy west to grow into a priest; the Riddler could know of Datan's part in all this; the gods told the man what they felt he needed to know. If so, the man he sought might be seeking him, and in the end they'd have to meet.

But the woman was warm and the night was soft, and yet another wizardspawn among Mygdonians increased the odds fourfold in his favor. She'd have to forget, of course, and seduce her husband yet tonight. His sperm would by then have done its work; human semen was no match for warlock's, let alone adept's.

When he was done he climbed his tower, took to the air, and went summoning; he'd friends to recruit for this endeavor, fiends to find and skeins of time to bind in serviceable knots.

Behind he left a crazed, uneasy sky, aurora borealis, wizard-fire to climb the spires and turn the towers blue and green against a flaring, colored night. And everywhere in Mygdonia and Ranke, enchanters who read the weather mumbled wards and ran for charms and locked themselves in safety vaults, their loved ones in their arms.

Tempus and Jihan came upon the caravan three days and nights north of Sanctuary on what was generously called the "general's route," not the usual caravan's trek—northeast through the badlands or east, then north, following the coast—but then this was no usual caravan. Its speed was phenomenal and its endurance a match to even Tempus' Trôs horses.

He could have gone all night and day at full gallop to interdict them; Jihan's stamina had never been tested. But the horses were flesh and blood uncursed and nonmagical; though Trôsbreds had constitutions twice the strength of any other strain, for their sakes the pursuers rested four hours nightly.

It must have been that the caravan did not, Jihan said softly to Tempus' throat the first evening, camped out between the forests easterly and the beginnings of the southern range that became Wizardwall when it veered and joined the high peaks, ten days' ride at the pace they were making. They had a fire that first night, and it flickered in the Frosh Daughter's eyes: "I could call a cloud to take us; we could travel by it to their camp, or just beyond them on any road."

"No. No magic," he declined her offer, conscious of her fiery eyes and the coolness of her flesh no bonfire could warm.

"It's not magic, it's my birthright. I need to make no pact with nature; I am one of its expressions; no demons can offer me controls on earth I don't already have."

"No, I said." He seldom repeated himself; he was not used to being questioned, or brooking argument, or hearing out disparate views. He'd turned away and gotten up and gone out hunting with his bow. They'd eaten well, but from their stores; grouse or quail for morning would suit him. The moon was just past full on its way to third quarter and plenty bright for him. He didn't know if she slept—he still could not. Perhaps she'd learn respect as she got more experience of femininity, perhaps she'd never learn—human for a year was hardly human.

If she continued insisting on cloud-conveyance and such manipulations of order, he was going to lose her somewhere in these hills. He'd had too many close encounters with the comptrollers of unnatural advantage to take them lightly. His mouth was soured with the taste of her words: despite his resolve and best effort, he'd gotten involved with something, in Jihan, which could not be weighed on natural scales or assessed in the way he liked.

Pretense of hunting cast aside, he climbed a hill and sought the gods. When he'd daily been afflicted with the Rankan Storm God's presence, he'd longed to be without it. But he sought a sign, now, to ease confusion: wisdom seemed to have fled him as he fled his Stepsons and responsibilities in the town. He seethed with a craving for bloody vengeance such as he had not known for ages. It was not just Abarsis, Janni, or Niko—or Niko's prior deceased partner—but all he'd done in vain in Sanctuary, all the god had put him through and left. "Come forth, mighty Pillager! Show Yourself. Art Thou craven, coward's god? Art Thou weak, a mouse among deities? Where is Thine thunder and Thine lightnings, now?"

But the sky was silent; it flickered with colored light but thundered not. He shot three grouse when dawn was breaking to make things look aright and brought them back to camp. She'd kept the fire burning; if she'd slept, there was no sign of it. In her tricolor enamel armor, she blended into the terrain so that he saw her only when she turned her head and waved.

"Better, friend Riddler? Did the night's solitude ease you?" She was amused, and he was not. He threw the grouse at—not to—her and growled: "You can cook, I hope? It's an attribute of your chosen sex."

"Cook?" She shrugged and pulled the wings off one fat grouse to eat it raw. When he stalked fireward to do the work himself, he saw her lift her gaze and grace him with a gory grin. She loved to bait him, as at times she tried to rape him. Of all the things his extended memory recalled, she was the strangest that had ever happened to him. He might deserve her, fit punishment for all he had squeezed from life, but at times he did detest her, a power-child playing human for a year.

The next night, when they stopped and cooled the blowing horses, iron-black with sweat and thinning before his eyes, they talked long into the night about the seven spheres whose regents guided the course of time, and the twelve planes, from which both she and Aškelon, lord of dreams, had come, metaphysical realms barred to earthly beings while they dwelled in flesh and blood.

He determined that Jihan, herself, while in woman's form, could not flit back home at will, but not how Aškelon had bent the rules for Tempus' sister Cime, and whisked her away where Tempus could never follow: Aškelon's domain was dream, the archipelago named in his honor materialized only once in a great while.

Tempus wished that he could dream, then was glad that he did not, as Jihan tried to tell him what "life" was like as a Froth Daughter, a principle of tide and wave.

The third night they had settled into a truce of sorts, not talking of what could not be solved, not his sister nor

Jihan's husband-of-intent, the dream lord. They kept to mundane matters: warlocks and wizardry abroad in Ranke; of the time he'd spent upcountry in the buffer-states of empire; of what he knew of Mygdon's allies and satellites—Uraete, Sivis, Altoch and black Nisibis, abode of archmages of the most heinous sort.

"The witch will know we're coming," she said sensibly.

"Perhaps," he admitted. He had his sword, which sliced sorcery like eggs. She guessed his thought when his hand went to it, and pointed out that if he could bide an antimagical weapon, then he had no right to tell her she couldn't use her own.

And it was well that he agreed that, much as he disliked to admit it, this was so. For on the next evening the caravan's lights showed round a hill where the general's route veers west, zigging before it zagged due east through the great forest toward Ranke's very seat.

"Look! See?" she called, her muscular arm afire with sunset.

"Silence. Quiet, girl." He'd seen.

They waited until dark, then crawled up the hillock on their bellies before the moon rose, while behind them Trôs horses stamped and snorted (hobbled, blindfolded, their noses cased in feedbags lest the smell of sorcery spook them, or the witch try to enlist them). If he could, he'd have stopped their ears as well.

On the hillock's crest he notched a bolt and waited for something to move in the dell below. The lights were lit on wagon's tarps; beasts of burden seemed still hitched between their traces, but the light was tricky—what he saw, he thought, could not be so: skeleton drays and luminous bones of oxen standing tall between wagon poles, harnessed up and grazing.

It was a sight to foul the calmest stomach; Jihan shuddered, turned away to him. "The witch awaits," she whispered, drawing a handful of throwing stars, a western fighter's weapon gotten from Niko along with instruction in the form. "I'll come upon them from the rear; you take the front."

He knew her eager. Why? To please him? Compete with him? She was overqualified for slaying even witches, he thought. But though the words rang clear in his mind he could not speak them; they would not mount his tongue to be said. So he did not deny her a part in this, but sent her forth, a few simple handsignals and whistled calls determined between them.

Then, alone, as he liked to be, he sat chewing a sweet weed's stalk, waiting for her to flush whatever foe she might. She was hardly in need of *his* protection; that femininity of hers was a wily asset, no debility.

Yet he couldn't cease thinking about her as he'd think of a weak Rankan woman, a girl for raping, a lady for safekeeping, a child—which, in the ways of men, she was.

So he slithered down the hill, bow in left hand, sword drawn in right and hastily wiped in muddy dirt to hide its glitter as the moon began to rise.

Down on the flat of the dell, he heard a clatter, a raucous din which made him start. Then Jihan's voice called out: "There's nothing here but detritus: bones and empty wagons; these beasts of burden died upright; a breath will blow them over."

He followed her voice and heard the war cry of an eagle far above, odd at night but not impossible; he saw it cross the moon from right to left, an auspicious omen. Then he heard another, as he trotted among the wagons, calling Jihan's name as she did his, close at times but never finding one another, until he was running and she was cursing huskily, and shadows began appearing with bright flickering eyes among the skeletons and the wagon hulks.

A beat of wings warned him as clouds scudded across the moon and all went black; he heard a human-sounding cry and yelled, "Jihan, get out of here!" before talons raked him, and he engaged a feathered enemy, his sword slicing it in twain with a single spattering blow. And the blood that fell on him stung like spiders' bites and burned his skin so that it smoked. He dived aside as the corpse of the eagle, writhing, changing as it fell in two halves to earth, landed. He thought he saw human arms take shape amid the lamplit feathers as another screeched his way.

He went down under the second and tore talons from his throat, his bow discarded: its killing power was for mortals, only. As its beak snapped and clacked inches from his cheeks, he struck down toward his own face to impale the huge eagle from behind.

In the name of all the gods of war he cursed sorcery and its offenders as he felt his blood flow and the eagle jerk and flap, spitted on his blade.

This time the acid blood spilled in one eye, and as he used what strength he had to throw a woman's weight of wounded bird from his swordpoint, he saw it turn to something female, swearing unintelligibly as it tried to crawl away.

He chased it, throwing himself to the ground to follow under a wagon, but the wagon burst into flame, and he heard Jihan's scream. And as he scrambled out from under its axle, he caught a glimpse of a witch's face, contorted and streaked with blood from what should have been a mortal neck wound, looking back over its shoulder at him. He'd seen that face before, seen it beautiful, its eyes black with kohl and not these awful ringed shadows, at the mageguild fête. He locked eyes with it, saluted, his blade's point up, her blood upon it: "Another time, then."

It hissed and faded away.

Then, gaining his feet he went running, one eye useless, blood flowing thick and fast from his gored neck, to where he thought he heard Jihan's voice and saw her engaged with a man-shaped foe. Coming up from behind at it, he saw her break its hold and thrust it toward him, her arms outstretched. Halfway to him, where it would have impaled itself upon his blade, mist came around it and thickened and froze: between steps, the foe was encased completely in a solid block of ice.

She came toward him then, tearing matted hair from blazing eyes. "What sort of fight is this?"

'Yours," he said, looking at the vanquished, frozen enemy. "Don't do that to another; I want one that can tell me where he's been and what he thinks he's doing."

"Or she?"

"*Or* she. From now on, follow my directions—" He kicked the ice. "—so we can find each other."

"You were worried?"

"I'd as soon not have your father's wrath on top of all else to contend with," he lied, and went seeking a witch or warlock among the train.

But nothing magical came charging, beyond the odd event that skeletons turned to living dray beasts and wagons filled with merchandise and loot.

He found apparently human foes, dispatched two who wouldn't listen, took seven men hostage and went seeking one the others swore was their leader, called "Jagat."

He discovered the caravan's master snoring loud in the lead wagon, a krrf pipe by his head. He bound him, since he couldn't wake him, and sought Jihan, who'd used up all her throwing stars and had eight wounded coffled like newly consecrated slaves.

Off to the side, he said: "We need no prisoners."

"What, then? Slay them? They're human hirelings, mediocre fighters, anxious for a quick surrender, so it seems."

"So it seems. But they might be anything—traps of sorts, mages in disguise or canny demons. Kill whom you can; whoever won't die is of the other sort. I have the leader, he's all I want of this trash."

She scowled at him. "Such disrespect of life."

"Yes, well, I've heard all that before. You're welcome to

take your moral indignation elsewhere. Me, I've got a war to win."

He stalked away to dispatch his prisoners, not waiting to see what she'd do with hers.

Two hours later they left the burning wagons, corpses in their midst, the animals turned loose because he was softhearted. Any mage who knew him might well have taken bovine form to escape a confrontation by that means. But one cannot slay every living thing upon a battlefield: they can come as eagles and go as fleas, and fleas are hazardous to chase, near impossible to slay in the dark and open grass.

When they had the leader back at campside, he told Jihan to take a walk, go away. But the man, the witch's hireling, begged her please to stay: "Protect me, gracious lady." The creature whimpered, a one-eyed, stubbled face implored her as it began to sweat. Tempus' bloody, ravaged doom-face was not one from which mercy might be exhorted.

Tempus knew there was something wrong here, but hushed his inner voice and set about a polite, by Rankan standards, interrogation that lasted all that night.

In the morning, chilled by what he'd learned, he slew the man—if man it was—and admitted that he'd like to take Jihan up on her offer of cloud-conveyance. He needed to get to Tyse; there was an intelligence officer at the Tyse station named Grillo he must see.

But when the cloud separated itself from the natural clouds of sunrise and stretched itself their way like a telescopic glass extended, the horses balked at stepping in between the mists, beyond which could be seen the terraced outskirts of a once-great city, now contoured ruins crumbling into dirt.

"Come on, now, horse. Hark, you've done this once before." He'd gotten these two when Abarsis brought them down to Sanctuary this very way. But they wouldn't, or couldn't, remember—or the night's death had spooked them: the smell of roasted man still lingered along with oil and char upon the air.

At length, when ropes upon their rumps wouldn't goad them and his pushing from behind while Jihan tried to lead them forward wouldn't convince them, when his toes had been stepped on thrice and his yet-swollen eye and serum-sticky neck had been pelted with clods and dirt and dust, they blindfolded them both and led the snorting, dancing, froth-necked stallions through into the cloud whose mists let them out in Tyse, a mere dozen horses' lengths away.

Roxane almost spoke his true name when she caught Datan with the Mygdonian bitch headed up toward the ramparts for breakfast while she was coming down. She checked herself in time, though, and struck the woman blind instead: the rage in her was too great to be bottled long, and mortal eyes had no right to see her wounded, half a woman, half eagle yet, too weak from her wounds to change in full, her black-feathered bleeding wing dragging with a sussurrus upon the high peaks stones.

And her lover-lord, unmoved, looked upon her plight with lightless eyes and murmured that she must get some rest, must Roxane. He could have helped her, lent her strength to hasten her return to human form. But he forbore it, more concerned with the hysterical human mare swooning on his arm. If the sight of Roxane so distressed her, then it was best for her to see no more.

And he, with a mere "Control yourself, enchantress," would have gone upon his way, the blind woman mincing and moaning, her face gone white as the skull beneath her flesh.

But Roxane interposed herself in his path: "Ask, dear lord, of your second in command, sweet warlock gone to pay eternal price."

"I see you. I have no need to ask. Next time, witch, proceed with caution. And be successful, or your discomfort now will be a state you remember fondly, even crave. You boasted you could lure him, you could take him, stop him and rout him. Now do what you have said. Be gone. On your way."

"Her dark you shall not lift!" Roxane pointed to the woman, frail and groping, and then at last discerned the new life stirring under a well-tended belly flat and firm. "Not in this life."

"Then in the next," he answered calmly, a tiny frown auguring the end of his patience.

Hers was gone but for a shred. She brushed on past, the clack of one clawed foot and the brush of one wounded wing all that could be heard in the daystruck hall but for the blinded human's sobs. A warlock was dead, and Jagat and many minions who'd cost much to raise and more to field. There were two others, yet, to summon; help to find, strength to gain, a war to win. Then Datan, false beloved lord, would feel *her* wrath. Men, beguiling with their childish pride and lust for war, good for little more than raising castles and making laws and changing currency, cannot stand before feminine ire; straightforward thinking always fails before the convoluted passion of womankind. As in humans, threefold in mages. And Roxane was the strongest witch born in Nisibis in a thousand years.

She'd only just begun to fight. She'd win, and he'd know weakness against which Roxane's transitory debility would seem like virile strength. Once she'd been content to love him. Now, fury within, she sought to break him. No omen contravened her. She'd triumph. There was but time to pass till then.

Meanwhile, she'd play the servant. She lurched along the halls and came upon the general's boy, a child of sorcery, woman-spawned, and took him under her bleeding wing. He showed no fear, as a wiser one might have, but came along of his own accord. She'd find some use for this one, before the search for him was on. Or she'd place his lifeless body where the Mygdonian "father" might find it—prince and noble general, he'd expected to have his war and win with magic but never pay as others must.

For Roxane needed strength, and the child's soul was delectable and rare: half mage, thus worth a dozen mortals, he'd give her all she craved, slain or bound in service. And some soul must buy a murdered warlock peace. Datan cared not a whit about her colleague, lost this night, but Roxane did, and her rage was so fierce it clouded over the morning sky.

In her chamber she threw the bolt and seated the boy, all bright-eyed with excitement that finally a power of Wizardwall had acknowledged him, upon her feathered bed. She'd more in store for this one than he reckoned, but, calmer now, she meant to let him love her, initiate him, and make him the Mygdonian Alliance's foulest bane.

While he stripped, she judged him old enough for ritual copulation, and while he watched she summoned both the warlocks who remained alive who'd had a hand in the plot to lure the Riddler up to Wizardwall. And while they conferred, the boy stayed, privy, his hungry eyes upon her helping to turn her wing to arm and clawed foot human. And when they'd gone, to make themselves ready, she bade him bring her bowl all filled with water and showed him Nikodemos, enthralled and convalescing, and what a witch could do to change the fate of men.

It was the nights, not the days, spent in his billet recuperating, that Niko remembered most clearly. During the daytime, Sacred Banders sat with him in shifts, so that if he woke from delirium he would not be alone. By the third day, his nights of sweat-drenched dreams troubled all nine Sacred Band pairs, for the youngest of their number was obviously possessed. The second night, when none were with him, he'd been seen shuffling through the camp, bent rightward to ease his tight-bound ribs, collecting his effects and his equipment. In the morning, when the first team came bearing breakfast and determined smiles to hide their worry, he lay red-eyed and wrapped in sopping bedclothes, an enameled cuirass amid the sheets. And there was no doubt that it was the same arcane, enchanted armor the dream lord had given him (with its curling colored snakes and raised demons from Enlil's myths), which he had sacrificed upon his left-man's bier months before.

That day was Janni's pyre day; they couldn't wait another: they'd put it off twice. And, as if the reappearance of the charmed cuirass from out of nowhere was not enough, Abarsis's shade coalesced out of the smoke and flame and, before it took Janni's spirit up to heaven, walked across the space cleared of awed and retreating Stepsons to peer into Niko's battered face, where he stood supported by the senior Sacred Band team, and frown, and weep, and touch his cheek.

Critias came to see him, pacing back and forth the third night in his billet, for he'd heard that Niko was determined to leave in the morning:

"You can barely hobble about, Stealth. What's the hurry? Death's easy to find. If she wants you, you'll meet her here as well as anywhere."

Niko, standing to prove he could, one arm braced against the whitewashed wall, had spoken as strongly as he had the strength to: "I can't stay. All my ghosts are here. My rest-place is filled with strangers; my nights are battles. I don't expect you to understand. I don't.... I've got to go."

"Where?" Crit stalked up to him, fists balled as if he would strike him, but hit the wall beside his head instead. Niko didn't flinch. Crit sighed, then said: "You're my responsibility. *Tell* me where you're going, why you won't let a pair go with you—we've got four teams queued up to volunteer—or you'll go as a civilian."

"That's your choice. I don't have one. I've got to go, Tyse. Every night I feel it more strongly: I'll find the Riddler, my dreams tell me."

"Bugger your dreams, Stealth. Your thinking's addled; you've taken a blow to the head. This happens . . . men go down hard, they come back hard. Stay until you're well, at least."

"Nothing's going to happen to me," Niko said wearily. "I almost wish it would. Now, if you care about your responsibilities, you've discharged them. If you care about the Stepsons, let me go. You saw the omen at Janni's funeral. And they want me to pair again. I'm not strong enough to keep refusing if I stay . . . you don't know what it's like to lose two partners. . . ."

"Would that I didn't." Crit put thumb and forefinger to the bridge of his nose, massaging. "Go on then, stubborn bastard. Go. But leave an itinerary—you're still *putatively* under my command."

He did, but the dreams got no better. He'd stumbled around putting his packs together, saddling his pregnant sorrel mare while two Sacred Band pairs stood by, silent and unhappy, their offers of assistance refused, with crossed arms and helpless scowls. Despite his protestations, they'd ridden with him the first day—all Critias, concerned that his authority was being eroded, would allow.

He'd meant to go by the coast route—it would be easier on the mare, three months along, and on himself. He did, that first day, trying not to think about the half-Trôs foal she carried, though it wouldn't show until fall, and what the invasion of his rest-place by spirits known and unknown could mean. He couldn't talk to the Sacred Banders about it, so they talked about the unseasonably hot weather, about the substitutes to be hired so the Stepsons could go north, about where he'd meet them when they did. The coastal route was cool and the sea breeze welcome; he'd packed all his winter gear on the bay gelding he ponied—a gift from Janni, willed to him.

They'd camped by the shore and had a farewell dinner, the two pairs pledging to handle all Niko's affairs—the replacement who must be found, the obligation he felt to do something for Tamzen's father—and though the ocean breeze dried their summer sweat and eased their worry, he could see it in their eyes and in their auras.

After the meal, they rode due west back to town, and Niko was alone.

The relief he felt was monumental. If he'd known himself a plague carrier, he'd have been no more anxious to go a solitary route. He could let out his fear, his pain, wrestle with the horror he kept meeting in his rest-place.

He didn't understand why his place of peace had been invaded. Before his elder partner's death, it had been his sure refuge, his safe place where no evil penetrated, his shelter from all worldly storms.

He'd dealt with the visitations of his left-side leader as Tempus had suggested, banishing his own fear and making room for a soul who'd chosen to stay with the boy he'd spent near a decade protecting. He'd had discussions in his mind with his old friend, and, along with his *maat*, his poise and perspective, the soul of his left-side partner had seemed to fade away.

He was beyond worrying that he'd lost his nerve; if it had been that simple, if he could have owned to cowardice and returned to normal, he'd have written the damning sign upon his brow. But it was worse—it was real. He knew it, and he knew he didn't know enough, that he didn't understand what was happening to him. When the fire burned out he was too sore and weak and dizzy to see to it; he rolled slowly, cautiously over onto his back and, alone, he cried.

He should never have taken another partner after his

left-side leader perished, not when Aškelon, the very lord of dreams, had seen into Niko's future and known that charmed weapons would be needed. He'd brought the dirk and the sword, he wore them now, when before he'd arrogantly assumed he could decline the offer to enter a higher plane of battle. And the cuirass had come back like a flying wing, as real and substantial as it had been the day he threw it on his leader's bier.

He'd thought, before, that it was time for him to strike out on his own. Janni had come between him and the solitude that was his lot, and died of it. He knew he was marked; he didn't know how, or why, but the sword he fondled even as he lay with tears blurring the stars of the summer night above had been given him for just this purpose—whatever it was, whatever lay at this journey's end.

But alone, with no *maat* to guide or caution him and no comrade to share his doubts, he was particularly vulnerable. And he couldn't die with his mental mansion in such disarray. That was a death he couldn't face, one without the surety and comfort that Niko, born in war and orphaned by Ranke, had traveled far west and studied long in the Bandara Islands sanctuaries to claim. His studies told him eternal damnation awaited, and his chances of avoiding it lessened daily.

They'd made only a few miles that first day, Niko setting a slow pace because of the mare. He slept not at all that first night, afraid to sleep, and in the morning he saddled the mare and harnessed the bay and set off, so tired that he kept falling asleep in his saddle, one arm pressed firmly against his bound side for the comfort that brought, his puffy eyes closed against the hot summer sun.

He must have slept a long time, for when he awoke the sea was nowhere in sight and out of earshot, and sands were all around him, the sands of the young desert, not the shore. The mare must have veered off to join the caravan route; she'd been that way before. The sun was white-hot here and Niko couldn't even summon sufficent worry, just kept drifting in and out of consciousness, recollecting where he was, feeling a start of fear sharpen him transitorily, then sinking back into lethargy. And yet, when he woke in sunset, they'd made better time than ever he thought they could: before him, birds of prey, eagles or hawks, wheeled high in the pink and purple dusk; where they congregated, water was. He headed the mare toward it and found they'd made the first caravan oasis; perhaps he'd slept around the dial.

He didn't care. He slid from his mare and she nuzzled him. He reached up and slipped off her headstall, telling her to go eat and drink, and stretched out upon the oasis's cool lush grass beneath a pair of tree-high ferns, thinking he should unsaddle her and unburden the pack horse. But when next he woke, it was dark and all that was done: the horses tended, a fire burning, stew cooking in his single pot.

He hadn't dreamed at all, that he remembered. He felt stronger, and his vision was clear.

He ate his food and fondled his horses and went back to sleep, a blanket pulled over him against the desert night's chill. This time in his dreams he met Tamzen and the other girls, undead with pure white eyes, and they were throwing dice in his meadow. They waved gaily and called to him to join the game.

He was walking that way, reminding himself that he was dreaming, that his body was sick and hurriedly healing, that all this would pass, when the dream lord himself reared up before him, Tempus' sister on his arm.

They were so real he tried to run, then, but Aškelon stayed him with a gentle hand. He'd seen that hand drip the blood of eons in the real world; he'd seen that face, so calm, so compassionate, much paler and insubstantial in reality than in his dream it had become. The voice he

heard was the same, though, and the woman, Cime, grasped
him by the swordbelt as she had done in life.

"Am I dead?" he heard himself ask.

"Not yet, young fighter," she laughed. "When you see
my brother, tell him we will help him—give him courage
to act, make him strong when he is weak—but he must
call on us. We cannot interfere directly." She was weeping,
but talking as if she didn't know it, just the glistening
tears rolling unheeded down her fine cheeks.

"Why do you cry?" Niko asked, and Aškelon, not Cime,
answered: "You've a trial to endure, boy. What I've given
you should help you, but lose or cast aside any piece of it
again, and I will not be able to rearm you."

"Why does she cry?" he asked again, for Cime was
dissolving; he could see through her; then she was gone.

The dream lord shrugged, eyes gray like pack ice and
full of shadows. "She has much to cry for: what has
happened, and will happen. Don't add yourself to her
wealth of tears. Be strong. Control your mind. Heed your
dreams. Guard your soul."

"My dreams are frightful. I'm weak. I'm afraid. My
*maat* has deserted me. Help me—" Even in dreams that
was hard for Niko to ask. "—you're master of dreams. I
can't sleep at night, and in the day, I can't stay awake. . . ."

But the dream lord was going, shaking his head sadly,
his translucent, then transparent lips forming words a
wind whipped away.

When Niko woke he was soaked and shivering and his
mare was snuffling round him, her wet muzzle and moist
breath in his hair. He stroked her, then put his arms
around her neck and she helped him gain his feet by
raising her head. He stood a long time that way, an arm
over her withers, his face pressed to her neck. Already the
dream's message, if there had been one, was fading.

*     *     *

From the moment the cloud-conveyance deposited them on the outskirts of Tyse, whirling in on itself to disappear with an audible "pop," Tempus had been conscious of the change in his internal rhythms—the adjustment his body made to the smells and sights of war.

His pulse beat more determinedly; his energy, never low, was continually at peak; his recent wounds tingled as they rushed to heal, and all the nagging debilities he'd lived with for interminable peaceful years made themselves known by their absence: his back didn't ache; his muscles refused to knot with fatigue; his senses were sharpened, and his stomach and gut tingled with a low-key excitement he'd not realized was part of what he missed when he cursed the sluggish peace long abroad upon the land.

Jihan, craning her neck at Wizardwall, hulking over the town of Tyse dark and shimmering with sorcery which made a difficult climb nearly impossible, remarked upon its foreboding reaches.

The Trôs horses, nostrils distended to catch the messages the cool wind brought them high in the foothills, arched their necks and danced along.

They'd ridden only as far as the mercenaries' hostel that first day, where they checked in and secured clean box stalls for their mounts and requested the sort of accommodations reserved for Sacred Banders—a pair of rooms with a door between. The duty officer looked at Jihan quizzically, but made no objection to Tempus lodging her as his guest.

In the evening, they went sightseeing, Jihan's hand clamped upon his upper arm and her scale armor polished so that it glittered in the torchlit streets. To do so, they'd had to obtain passes they wore on armbands: Tyse was under martial law.

Jihan was distressed by what she saw: wars of attrition have a particular coloration and stench of slow death about them, and Tyse's plight (enmeshed in civil war fomented by Nisibisi agitators, her once-great central "contoured city" reduced to a mile-long, walled and crumbling refugee camp holding southward-fleeing deportees chased down from Mygdonia with an eye toward straining Ranke's ability to cope, both economically and militarily) was obvious to even her untrained, newly human eye.

He tried to explain to her that if not for the cause of Ilsig nationalism, then for the emancipation of the left-handed or equality of the obese or the hook-nosed would Mygdonia have come to the "aid" of the "oppressed" south, and that whether life for Tysians would be any better under elitist Mygdonian rule than totalitarian Rankan, no one here had leisure to consider: one cannot abstain from war on one's own flanks.

But as they walked the better neighborhoods, where the outreach satrapies maintained their missions and Rankan treaty cosignatories had their embassies and consulates, he realized that Upper Ranke could not long survive or absorb the influx of indigents, criminals, orphans and husbandless girls with fat child-bellies begging soldiers to let them sleep in doorways.

Normal police and Elite Guard stations were so outnumbered as to be useless. Jails were full. Hangmen were busy. Common graves were the order of the day.

On every street corner and byway army patrols were deployed. Sandbagged bunkers hosted infantry squadrons in Embassy Square; siege engines and "mountains" on wheels with men atop the towers and great slings to throw naphtha fireballs rivaled Wizardwall with their threatening profiles against the moonlit night sky.

The sewers were overtaxed, and the refuse stacked high, and the stench, even in the better quarters, far from the teeming refugee camp, was intolerable; people burned cedar and pennyroyal and walked with kerchiefs bound over their noses and mouths.

"But it's so terrible!" Jihan whispered, as he chuckled at her naiveté. "You told me Sanctuary was the nadir of the human condition!"

"It is. This is transitory, a condition imposed from without. In Sanctuary, the status quo is maintained by choice. Those who live there make the town what it is. As for terrible—I'm not sure it's terrible enough to have the desired effect."

"And what is that?" She turned her head to look at him in the torch- and moonlit street; he saw the red flecks stirring in her eyes: she was earnest, angry, or distressed.

"To stop insurrection here: containment. No one wants this to be the state of empire. Civil war—"

"No, no. What is *that?*" She pointed toward the intersection they were approaching, lighted on every side with panniers of oil borne by colossal lions of chocolate granite.

"Oh, that . . . the palace. There's a royal family in there somewhere, gnashing their teeth and picking at moth-eaten ceremonial brocades. Tyse's being administrated by a provisional military governor, invited in along with the Rankan army to reestablish order . . ." He thought better of explanations. He wasn't about to get into politics with Jihan.

Coming out onto the palace square of a once-sovereign city-state which was now a client and buffer-state of Imperial Ranke, Jihan asked innocently: "How long ago, sleepless one, was the army invited?" She had seen one permanent garrison; he had mentioned the other three. Despite the factions warring in the streets, order was being maintained from four Rankan garrisons—one at each compass point—which made sure that no street in town save in the central refugee camp was free from the tramp of Rankan boots.

"Invited? Nearly three years, but there's been a Rankan presence here ever since the treaties were signed—"

"And before?" She bared her teeth.

He did likewise: "How else would the treaties have been signed?"

The "free zone" was in the middle of the city; the refugees observed no curfew. Getting in through the gates wasn't difficult. Tempus hoped it would be as easy getting out again.

They were warned by a bored, fat sentry that they might lose their property, their identity, or even their lives, and that neither the provisional governor of Tyse nor the Rankan government would redress any grievances incurred within. When his rote speech was done, the portly sentry, who was posted right between two braces of torches flanking the entrance, removed his helmet to wipe a perspiring brow and offered to put them in touch with "various sources of hire or pleasure . . . for a fee."

Tempus asked pointblank if the sentry knew of any agents of the Successors in the camp, and the man held out his hand.

He followed the directions he'd bought for a Rankan soldat through a press of stinking humanity: the weak ones who could only survive on the outskirts, the beggars, the worst of the working women, cripples, handless thieves, sleeping drunks, lots filled with snoring mortal refuse so thick it seemed a flock of penned sheep slept there. Jihan hugged his arm to her breast and leaned her head against his shoulder as they made slow progress through the living dross of war.

"Successors?" she whispered, finally. "What success lies here?"

"Bashir's commandos recruit from streets like these." They were entering the "business" section, where tents and hovels had in common tightly-laced flaps or shuttered doors. He knew what to look for.

He'd left word at the hostel that he wanted to see Grillo. Wherever he was, he'd get Tempus's message. Going to the embassy asking for him might be the most harmful thing Tempus could do to the man whose help he sought. Meanwhile, other means must be explored.

The free zone's center was pocked with circular depressions once used as meeting places and temples when the walls around towered three stories high. Now the thatch-and-cane roofs had crumbled, and the felled trees which once supported them were but stumps protruding from mortared walls.

But the refugees had found their own use for the pits; even in this chaos, a social order existed: the powerful and the feared held the circular sunken theaters and the open spaces and the few defensible buildings which had once served as the Tysian city-state's administrative headquarters. It was toward these that Tempus guided Jihan, passing trading stalls and colored tents whose greasy flaps told that they'd been here for years; goats and sheep and the occasional pony were strung on tethers; men in brightly colored tatters made deals before their stalls; the smell of krrf and beer and wine going to vinegar mixed with garlic and pig and unwashed woman on the breeze.

They passed between a man selling boys and two boys selling their sisters and skirted a goatskin tent. Before them was the first of the great circular depressions, this one filled with makeshift altars raised to the glory of a dozen gods. Here incense burned and blew their way so that Tempus's sore eye stung. An ox bellowed and lunged on his tether while three men hacked at his neck with dull-edged axes.

Jihan turned her face against his shoulder and refused to descend the steps into the pit. He said something he'd been meaning not to say—that her father, Stormbringer, had wreaked such havoc and slaughter in Sanctuary that even the god Tempus served was vanquished, perhaps destroyed, and she had stood by unmoved, uncaring: he felt her despair at the human condition to be overblown, inappropriate, since her sort decreed the fates of men.

"You cannot know that my father had a hand in the god's disappearance! Perhaps He became despairing of *you*, which anyone might—"

And so they argued their way through innumerable makeshift alleys until a child, tow-headed and gasping, in headlong flight their way, crashed through pots and crates, colliding with Jihan, his arms going round her hips to stay both their falls, then struggling to get by while Tempus reached down and grabbed him by his filthy nape. "What's this, boy?"

The child, in torchlight flush-cheeked and better fed than most Tempus had seen here, writhed until Jihan grasped Tempus' arm: "Put him down," while the boy wriggled, lips pressed tight together, neck craned, and eyes darting back in the direction from which he'd come.

"God got your tongue?"

"He's afraid!"

"Are you, boy?"

"Let me go!" The boy's voice was imperious, his accent Mygdonian. Tempus held onto him.

Two men came careening around a corner, shouting to Tempus to hold the wretch, and there was a soldier in it for him.

Jihan stepped in front of Tempus and the child, who could be no more than eight or ten, her arms crossed and her flesh chilling the air.

"Jihan, don't do it! Perhaps they have good reason, perhaps he's a thief, a—"

"Then we shall pay his debt," Tempus heard her say as the boy, who had ceased struggling, fixed him with a gray-eyed gaze too fatalistic for his years.

He lowered the child so that his feet touched the ground. The urchin stood uncertainly for a moment, turned once full around, deciding which escape route might serve him, then bolted toward Jihan, burying his head against her mailed waist: "Help me, lady, they'll make a slave of me. Oh, help me. . . ."

"We'll help you, little one, never fear." She ruffled the tow-head's hair and Tempus almost left her then, to deal with complications of her own making.

But the men had slowed to a walk and approached, hands on their swords. Their cuirasses were scuffed and dirty; their boots were worn through and their smell preceded them. Yet there was something wrong about them— their shoulders were too straight, their backs unbowed, and their command of the dirt they strode through taken too much for granted.

Tempus came up beside Jihan and felt the boy's fingers clutch his belt. He pried them away, not looking down: "What's the trouble here?"

"You've a hold of it. That's our boy, there."

"He says not." Tempus didn't like their eyes—too calm, too steady for slavers'; too pale for Mygdonians'. . . . "My friend fancies him. I'd not argue with her, if I were you. A disputed person in the free zone is not uncommon—"

Their hands went to draw their swords, but Jihan was quicker: two throwing stars whispered through the air and stuck in two bearded throats. The men went down like sacks of flour, crumpling in place; then they began to smoke, or to crumble—he couldn't tell which. Like smoke, their substance diffused, leaving only clothing and weapons lying abandoned in an empty street.

A man or two muttered wards; most lingering by the stalls and tents roundabout merely turned away. "Come on, then—bring him," Tempus allowed, and out of the corner of his eye saw camp snipes scuttle out from shadows to fight over the swordbelts, cuirasses, and boots lying in the dirt.

The boy was weak, so Jihan hoisted him and bore him

on her hip, his head against her breast; Tempus could hear him choking back sobs as he thanked her and she promised him salvation Tempus doubted they could accord. His was not a family outing; she was becoming more trouble than she was worth.

Without her, he'd have gone down into the altar pit and supplicated Enlil for a sign; this was the ancient Storm God's territory. With her, and now the fleeing boy, in his company, he was constrained from it. He thought of turning back, taking her to the hostel and having her wait there for him, but the youth couldn't be boarded where mercenaries lodged: Tempus couldn't break the rules of his guild, not here.

So he strode onward toward the tent he sought, hoping they'd get lost or disappear. When he found it, he bade her wait outside, and this she was willing to do. The child had her full attention. At the time, he thought it a stroke of luck.

Within the tent a score of reavers lounged, and he asked for someone who could take a message to Bashir when two barred his way—nearly his height and looking older and more worn than three centuries had left him.

"Bashir? Why not? For a fee. . . . And then the gods, too . . . any you choose," one said, and his companion, then the others behind, all rising, laughed.

"Who wants him?" the second said, half-turning his head to make a signal behind his back that Tempus understood.

"A friend of his father's. From the old wars."

"The *long* wars? You're not old enough to remember them," a grizzled veteran with half his cheek gouged away and scars dragging the flesh tight and leftward above his eye said, pushing between and past the pair of sentries. The man had grayish-yellow hair and a trio of symbols etched into the shoulder of his cuirass where bronze plates met leather: he'd fought the Defender, one of the symbols proclaimed to all who could read them; he'd fought the Nisibisi, and fought them still; he'd fought Ranke. . . .

Tempus named Bashir's father, who'd formed the Successors, premier guerrilla fighters turned high-mountain bandits; he spoke a safe-passage code he hadn't had to use in twenty years. Had the man not been close to fifty, he wouldn't have remembered it.

As it was, the old fighter was suspicious: "At the mercenaries' hostel, you say? Rankan, are ye? Friendly calls by Rankans aren't welcome. The scumbag army regulars pay us too many of 'em. But we'll send someone with your message . . . fight *beside* us, you say? How many men?"

Tempus was careful not to give his name or divulge that those who followed him were Stepsons and Sacred Banders: "Enough to make a difference. Send word where I can meet him." He backed out of there and, when the tent flap fell, breathed a sigh of relief. He'd collect Jihan and pry her from the boy, who'd got his freedom, who'd be happy with some coin and an escort out of the free zone. Then he'd go back to the hostel and wait. . . .

She wasn't there. No Jihan, no boy. He looked around cursorily, then more thoroughly, searching first in anger (composing his scathing critique of her behavior) and then in earnest. But he couldn't find them. No one remembered seeing them and not even Rankan gold could jog their memories. Jihan was not easy to miss—her stature, her swagger, her expensive mail. He didn't like this turn of events one bit.

As the waning moon crawled across the sky, and he couldn't find her, he began to worry. The boy's gray eyes, wizard eyes, danced in his inner sight. Halfway around the perimeter of the camp, turning sleeping bodies and corpses too new to stink, a voice came out of the gloom behind him: "Riddler!"

"Grillo!"

"By the god's seething eye—I'd thought it was a poor joke. . . ." Grillo was tall, well set-up, a Rankan of the upper class. His hair was light brown, and his skin was pale, the bones under it well-formed, and the mind in that handsome head quick and cold; his kind always prided themselves on being able to blend into any population and anticipate the strategy and tactics of their enemies. But here, despite his ragged mantle and some artfully smeared dirt on his boots and soot on his brow, he stood out like a torchlit statue of the god.

And he knew it: "I shouldn't be in here; all perdition's breaking loose in town tonight. Come, let's get very drunk and—ah, you don't drink . . . well, I'll get drunk and you can watch and we'll talk things over. . . ." A hand on Tempus's arm, he guided him toward an ill-lit section of the perimeter wall. "I still don't believe it's you. . . ."

"It is, and it's not. I've fallen into disrepute. I'll drink my share. But I've lost my traveling companion . . ." He described Jihan.

Grillo chuckled. "That's what I heard, the description I got, all right. I didn't believe the report." He whistled piercingly through his teeth. A quartet of beggars who had been fighting over a refuse pile got to their feet; a pair of male prostitutes left potential customers with whom they'd been haggling and sauntered their way. "Gentlemen," Grillo said when the prostitutes accosted them, "this is a friend of mine, who's lost his girl." He described Jihan in more detail than Tempus had to him. "See what you can do. We'll be at my place."

The prostitutes swished their scarves and made kissing noises, and Grillo shouted at them to stay out of his way or they'd lose the tools of their trade.

As they headed toward the deepest of the wall's shadows, the four beggars followed. "Yours?" Tempus asked.

"Them? Sure, yes. And what of yours? Sacred Banders and such?"

"You know, then?"

"My business is hearing things. Believing them is another matter. We've trouble with the mercenary hordes—keeping them on our side and off the townspeople's necks. If you're going to be here awhile, perhaps we could work a trade—service for service, like the old days."

"This is a nice little staging area you've got here," Tempus remarked as they entered the blackest shadows, and out of them voices asked for passwords and, receiving them, suggested that they "step right this way, lords."

"Is that what I've got? Maybe I'll need it, with you here. What happened to your face?"

"A little disagreement with a witch or two. That's why I'm here. My people are coming upcountry a few at a time. We've a score to settle with Datan and his crew, witch taunts aside. One of my men—"

"I heard. This way." Grillo ducked through a postern gate, taking Tempus's hand and pressing it to the lintel which was so low they had to bend nearly double.

When they'd come through and out, they were beyond the free zone's curving wall of rubble faced with stone. "So, you were saying that your cohort is coming? . . ."

"A few at a time."

"Again, I could use them, and you. This way . . ."

Tempus paced the Rankan officer until they were out of the wall's shadows, and two men came up leading horses.

"Ride with me?"

Tempus mounted and Grillo pulled his horse up beside: "My house isn't safe for this sort of thing; no one's is. Damn wizards have spies everywhere. We'll just ride around until we're thirsty. You didn't answer—assist me, and I'll return the favor."

They rode until the specifics were ironed out: Tempus would help Grillo keep order among the unruly mercenary contingent, lend his Sacred Banders for special assignment; Grillo would help Tempus find Jihan, put him in touch with various special agents, but: "As far as the Successors go, I think your own Nikodemos, if it's the same Niko—ashy hair, good fighter, western-trained—is your best hope. He's fought with them. They don't like me, I can't imagine why." Teeth gleamed in the dark. "Unless it's that I can't pay them the way I used to be able to . . . this is one damnably expensive revolution. We're down to contingency funding; every six months Ranke evaluates us. One of these times, they're going to decide it's cheaper to turn Tyse over to the Mygdonians as an object lesson to Machad and the other buffer states. But, for the rest of it, I'll work with you. We'll share information; we'll find your friend; we'll get the Nisibisi warlord. To that end, I have what might be a pleasant surprise for you."

"Which is?"

"A Mygdonian general, Lacan Ajami's brother, no less. Came in tonight seeking asylum. Seems the Nisibisi warlord—Osprey, they call him—"

"Datan."

"Whoever . . . he had the general up in the high keeps; the man's eldest son died in mysterious circumstances while on guard duty; his wife went blind; his youngest son disappeared. He's had enough, so he says. Wants to help us convince Lacan he's got the wrong allies—get him to join with us and destroy the Nisibisi mages once and for all. Then, he thinks, a real treaty could be drafted."

"I'll talk to him."

"There's one problem." Grillo pulled up his horse.

Tempus followed suit. "What's that?"

"You. . . . You were working for that Rankan faction down in Sanctuary, the one that thinks Kadakithis might make a good puppet emperor—now, let me finish. I can't get involved in anything seditious. Assure me you're not here on their—"

"I'm not. I'm here to avenge, and to war. You don't trust me, after all these years?"

"I trust that if you're here, there's a good reason. Your word's enough for me. We'll make an end to the mages of Nisibis, and show Mygdonia where her salvation lies." He held out his hand.

Tempus clasped it. "We'll try, you mean."

"We'll do it. I don't put my hand or commit my men to what I don't expect to accomplish."

The general's name was Adrastus. Tempus didn't need more than a moment to ascertain that the man's grief was real: it went deeper than his rent garments and flamed hotter than his red-rimmed eyes. In Grillo's commodious quarters, an estate requisitioned by the army but still housing the Tysian widow whose property it was, they drank watered wine and the general, embittered and drunk, his mail cast aside and his linen undershirt hanging out over his belt, lamented at length the wages of complicity with warlocks.

"Adrastus means 'the inescapable,' does it not?" Tempus asked him in an infrequent pause when the general's cup was empty. The room in which they drank was small and windowless; Grillo had tacked sheepskins, fleece wallward, over every inch of it to decrease the possibility of eavesdropping. The hides still reeked of tanning.

"Does, yes. And I'd better be. Gods," he turned, "my wife—my sons— There's nothing those adepts won't do. They think they've got me by the balls, having my youngest in their power. But he's not—he's—He might be . . ." Adrastus swore and refilled his cup with a shaking hand; the wine spilled over onto his bare feet. "My wife's still up there." He gazed northward as if, through the roof, he could see the looming heights of Wizardwall. "It's better if they slay her. Blind as a bat."

"What does he look like, the youngster?"

"Tow-headed, like his mother. Funny eyes. Don't like to

dwell on where he might have got them—gray like dead winter sky. But they say he's gone . . . run off—"

"In the morning," Grillo interjected gently, "our general here is going back up there. The tale will be that he rode all night, seeking the boy, found nothing, but outrode his guilt, if not his grief. He'll go from there back to Lacan and we'll wait for word. . . . Agreed?"

General Adrastus Ajami agreed. Tempus thought about the boy Jihan had befriended in the free zone, and said nothing. When the patrols came in at dawn, no one had seen or heard from her. By then, he was sequestered in Grillo's chapel, lamenting his curse and waiting for the god to speak.

The silence which answered each of his increasingly impolite solicitations was eloquent; it occurred to him that he wanted just this—that he was beyond the point where gods or even entelechies could help him, that he'd managed to give new meaning to the term "irredeemable": if Jihan was gone—lost, wounded, hostage, defected, or merely distracted—it was a manifestation of his curse. All the lords of all the heavens pleading in unison couldn't have persuaded him that any cause was worth what would follow if Stormbringer's daughter were hurt on his account. And if she was simply *gone*—this, too, was his curse in action. If he'd come to care for her, much as he'd tried to avoid it, then acrimonious separation, at the very least, was their lot: she'd spurn him, disdain him. But that was better than her fate if she loved him.

He'd gone back to the mercenaries' hostel, on the off chance he'd find her there, and found that both Trôsbreds were gone. He'd thought again of the boy and sworn loudly enough to bring a stablehand running, who could recall no armored, muscled woman. But then, Tempus' voiced frustration had waked him—he was still rubbing sleep from dazed and bleary eyes.

So Tempus berated the gods, but refrained from calling Stormbringer—he'd as soon not bring the Weather Gods' father bad news ...

In the little chapel, he performed a lengthy ritual. It was a chapel to the war gods, the lords of death and conquest; on its altar were all things necessary to sharpen the tools of war and make weaponry's leathers supple. Intermittently snorting first-grade krrf that Grillo had pressed on him, he worked, on his knees, putting an edge to cut a groundward-floating hair upon his sharkskin-hilted sword.

While about his "prayers" he heard a sound, looked around to see the Tysian widow, whose grounds these were, sidle in. She was tawny, with brown hair and eyes, fine and purely human. Without thought to Grillo's claim on her or what their relationship might be, he bade her come to him. A woman in the Storm Lords' temple could only want one thing. And, whether she knew it or not, or wished it or not, he was glad to give it to her: if a sacrifice was needed to clear his path or change his fate or merely change his mind, and make him content to wield his power without blaming what he did on gods, he'd make it. In the streets he'd traveled here from the mercenaries' guild he'd seen three armed confrontations: one between two civilian factions, one between civilians and drunken soldiers, and one broken up with sure precision by a practiced squad of Grillo's "specials." He was, right then, content to stay awhile in Tyse.

For preparing to shed mageblood, nothing was better than a wench to sanctify all morose endeavor with her fear and lust and sweat.

Grillo had long known from his informants in the Tysian chapter of the Rankan mageguild that Tempus was intent on coming north; the adepts' network brought him news quicker than the fastest mounted relays. But that news was enchanter-edited and sorcerer-censored. Often he could not believe it; seldom was it free from the prejudice of Hazards and their kind.

But now the Riddler was here, and his cohort soon to follow. Riding that evening toward the Nisibisi border, alone, the Rankan officer who worked surreptitiously to further many diverse interests pondered the difficulties that Tempus had brought with him: black-market deals in krrf and drugs and slaves must be protected until the Riddler's purpose and allegiance were made clear. Double dealing must be more closely shrouded. The Riddler, after scant hours in town, had disdained the safe and well-to-do south side and drifted into the free zone, seeking Bashir. There was more than a chance that this was no coincidence, that Tempus knew more about Grillo's work at the foot of Wizardwall than Grillo about Tempus—curse, god, mystique, and all.

At the rock marker which signified the end of Tysian sovereignty, Grillo pulled up his horse in the twilight and whistled. A mournful jackal's laugh was his only answer. He kicked his horse's ribs and it picked its way across the stony black soil of Nisibis, soil that on his right and left for five miles across and nearly fifty miles northward was called "Free Nisibis" and controlled, with sword and fury, by Bashir's Successor militia.

A hundred feet into Free Nisibis, he halted, slid off his horse, got a wineskin from his saddlebag and settled down to wait in the dark with only the rising sliver of the last-quarter moon to illuminate his position.

When stone struck against stone to his left he clutched his swordhilt but sat unmoving, tracking by the sounds it made a furry form which rose up from behind a tumble of boulders.

As it came close enough for Grillo to see the soot-smeared limbs of a man under the pelt, three others with similar helmets of jackal heads and mantles of jackal fur slunk into view, crouched low, attentive shadows among the rocks.

Grillo's horse snorted at the smell of cured jackal hide and a blackened face well known to the Tyse station's chief intelligence officer split into a gleaming grin. A long-nailed hand stretched out and Grillo grasped it: "Bashir."

"Grillo." The fur-clad figure with the soft baritone voice which made Nisi sibilances sound like autumn winds rattling the trees squeezed his hand, pushing something into it, unclasped it, and folded into a squat.

Grillo put the lump of high-mountain pulcis, most rare and coveted of drugs, into his belt, thanked the Successors' leader in ritual fashion, and in his turn laid a hide-wrapped dagger in Bashir's palm. Gifts exchanged, Grillo broached the subject concerning him to Bashir: "You will meet with the Riddler?"

"My father's friend? How can I not?"

"By considering that if you sit with him, you sit with Rankans."

"I sit with you."

"I've proved my intentions. I can't vouch for his."

"You've proved a good friend, and I will consider your warning. How goes the battle for the town?"

"Well enough. The woman whose description I sent—have you seen her?"

"With a boy, yes? No, we saw none such. But we saw horses make the hard climb—up the trail of tears. If that was she, she's gone to the wizards' high keeps, and they smoothed her path—no unaided horse could make that climb."

"Thank you. That sounds about right." Grillo rose up, stiff-kneed. "About the Riddler—I'm uneasy."

"I, too. Niko is headed this way? Your message said this was so."

"So I'm told."

"Then we will wait and see what Niko has to say."

Bashir rose also and stepped close to him, so close Grillo could smell the onions on his breath and see, in the rising moon's light, Bashir's sardonic smile. The commando continued: "When and if we meet them, we will have forgotten your name."

"Good enough, then. Die on your feet, Bashir."

"And you, Grillo," Bashir replied, backing away without a sound. In the space of a dozen heartbeats, he was gone, melting into the night he commanded.

Grillo, mounting up, hurried. Since the Riddler's companion, Jihan, had disappeared, freak storms had pummeled Tyse. The wind, picking up as he headed his horse south toward the town, was wet and wild. He urged his horse into a lope. If hail or mistral came tonight, it would clear the streets. The death toll, since Tempus had arrived, had doubled—no direct fault of the man who served rapacious gods, but circumstances in keeping with his nature.

And Grillo, who feared few men and dared to dispute with mages who should live free and who should pay wizards' tithe, wished fervently (if he'd a god he trusted, he'd have prayed) that Tempus would just disappear, drift back the way he'd come, or on to one of the other beleaguered border states where Grillo had nothing at stake.

But the chances of that were less than of adepts forgetting how to change shape or how to fly. Tempus was here, and somehow Grillo was going to have to bring him into his confidence or compromise him so that efforts to aid the Successors need not be curtailed. If there was a hope alive in Upper Ranke to flout the mages and withstand Mygdonian expansion, it lay in the person of Bashir, not in the senile Rankan empire, or in hateful and self-serving gods.

Feral and thick as mageblood, a fog rolled down from the high peaks, turning the night pale like phosphorescent foam. In it, the Trôs horses picked their way slowly, and in it the boy, Shamshi, talked loudly of his mother and his brother at home and everything but his fear that they were lost.

Jihan knew the truth of it, and it troubled her. Her distress might have been the cause of the thick fog, called by the boy and the indigenous hillmen "whiteout" because naught could be seen through it, and sounds were misdirected by it, and most of humankind stayed still under it, afraid to stumble or become befuddled in it. But Jihan had been lost for a day and more, now, and her temper was roused, her pride piqued, and even, down deep, something very much like uneasiness stirred in her. Weather was her ally; water, her particular talisman. But the water in the fog was not helpful. They'd been lost since yesterday afternoon, and now another day was gone.

Shamshi swore they were traveling in circles; his gray eyes wide, and his lips blue with cold. When they stopped to eat, he'd gritted out his fears through chattering teeth, golden head to her breast while she stroked his hair.

He wanted his mother; she wished *she* were enough.

He wanted his warm Mygdonian bed—it was his bloodline that had convinced her that to help Tempus, to prove herself more than the overprivileged amateur he thought her to be, she had only to return this lost waif to his highborn Mygdonian family. Then, once she'd made a friend on the far side of Wizardwall, Tempus would see that she was worthy. She might solve all disputes for him, bring peace to the fragile, warring mortals whose only solution to their own suffering was to inflict the same upon others. She'd meant well.

She knew, though the boy did not believe her, that their recurving path was of unnatural design. She thought, taking another loop in the line that tethered the Trôs Shamshi roan to Tempus' so that they wouldn't become separated in the whiteout, that she should have trusted the Riddler, asked him to join her or left word of her intentions.

She considered calling upon her father, but that, too, was an admission of failure, of inadequacy, of the disaster she and the boy, in common, feared most of all: they wanted respect from their elders.

She wished the power obstructing her would show itself. In direct confrontation, face to face, no adept or even archmage could daunt her.

But they were too wise for that. No demon descended from the heavens, though occasionally an eagle cried or a wild hound bayed at the moon she couldn't see. And the Trôs horses, withers quivering with unspoken remonstrance, plodded determinedly onward, heads down, nostrils wide and snuffling to judge by smell alone that there was solid ground where they would next put their hooves.

When the great crenelated keep of black stone rose out of the opaque mists as if it had been fashioned by some god's hand at that very moment, Shamshi gave a little cry of relief and urged her toward it: "My mother; my father! You will meet my father, Jihan!"

And as he prattled his relief, all her doubts bled away. She was anxious to succeed, though the Trôs horses were not. They set their haunches and raised their heads and, smelling the sorcery she could feel like carnivorous gnats upon her skin, whinnied loudly in complaint when she urged them forward so that at length they had to dismount and lead them up and in across a narrow bridge over a precipitous defile filled with writhing smoke and deep with echoes from pebbles skittering down when Tempus' Trôs, which she led, balked halfway across. So, as she had seen the Riddler do, she tore a strip from her undershirt and blindfolded him, hurrying, as the boy implored, to her meeting with his sire.

Having nothing better to do, Tempus had taken to stalking with one of Grillo's six-man teams, the first night under their leader, to learn the ins and outs of Tysian

brigandry, thereafter as their leader. They broke up gath-
erings of more than three on any street and pulled
rabblerousers off their boxes; they chased down a pair of
Nisibisi agents and brought them in where Rankan mages
performed the equivalent of putting salt upon their tails—
binding them with holding spells so that when they returned to consciousness they couldn't change their shapes
and disappear, slipping the strongest temporal chains.

From that pair, information had come of a nest of spies,
southwest of the free zone, disguised as nobles holed up in
the Outbridge district in an estate hectares wide and walled
and fortified so that its inhabitants could hold off an army
for months, unaided.

The team was well-honed, three of them seasoned
mercenaries, the other three Rankan specialists in guerrilla warfare. They scaled the estate's walls in silence,
poisoning as many dogs as possible, first with meat thrown
over, and, all in blacks with weapons sheathed to hide
their glitter and every piece of metal which might clink or
jangle wrapped in dark cloth, they made their way toward the main house, crossbows drawn and quarrels tipped
with poison drawn from almond shells.

This night action didn't sate, but suited, a man in his
position. He'd cursed Jihan when he couldn't find her.
Like the gods, she had deserted him. He put her, six times
and more each day, firmly out of mind.

When he'd raped the widow Maldives, Grillo's mistress,
he'd learned a bit of Tysian lore and a few things Grillo
might prefer he didn't know, but he'd not enjoyed it as
once he would have.

She had, but that was beside the point. Women come in
as many varieties as horses, and this one was an activist,
a fierce sort who'd been born to the Tysian insurrection
and took his arrival as a sign that the Lord Storm, her
own patron, had sanctified their struggle for freedom, and

his willingness to strip her and split her as a sublime affirmation of her writ.

He'd felt manipulated, after, but gotten good information from her. And he'd made, despite his intentions, a friend who, if she could be believed, he could count on "as Grillo does, my lord."

He had enough troubles without a "friend" in Tyse, but he'd let it pass without a word. She was tough and she was knowledgeable of the environs. She might prove useful, or prove to be a gift of conciliation from gods who, for their own reasons, would not come to him or speak with him. He didn't expect her to live much longer, since she craved his company, but even that, he didn't say.

Out here, among the troops, he took revenge upon the town and even upon the gods—Enlil, who snubbed him; Vashanka, left behind but not forgotten—and on the mages whose forebears had bequeathed him his current plight.

The inner court, now that the team had reached it, was dotted with statuary bearing panniers filled with burning oil. They doused as many as they dared with sand, but left the balance, slinking along in shadows, skulking their way, weapons drawn and armored backs tight to walls, toward the stone manse in the estate's center.

Half a dozen outbuildings remained to be passed by when a tower guard thought he saw a movement and called down to unseen companions to "look sharp by the stables, there!" and someone whistled for the dogs.

He'd given orders for this contingency; they all split up and scattered. They'd meet at the back door of the house, where a root cellar used for covert meetings had its own wooden bulkhead. They'd brought naptha preparations and incendiaries made from a crude concoction rolled up in parchment: they meant to roast the Nisibisi agents where they huddled under ground.

A pair of greaves, ill oiled, squeaked as their owner tried to sneak, unheard, round a corner. Tempus met him with a sword which once glowed pink but now, bereft of godly sanction, merely killed.

Whether the armored chest he cleaved had magical protection, he could not tell for certain; the blue tinge he thought he saw was as faint as witchfire. The man dropped without a sound and Tempus stepped over, wrenching his blade from a chest reluctant to release it.

And then, from somewhere, barking split the night and shouts commenced—his men, letting others know they'd been discovered, and he moved to slide within a doorway and wait until the furor died.

But something four-legged, white teeth and spiked collar gleaming, leaped at him without a single sound. This "dog," who neither growled nor barked, was near his own weight, and its claws were sharp as daggers. He was bowled over by its charge and on the ground he wrestled it, his hands, despite the spikes, gripping its straining neck and, at last, snapping its spine.

Then he left, running, headed toward the sounds of battle: now that they were found out, the odds were hard against his team and he thought to even them.

Before him (as he dodged a whickering weapon, not looking up to see if spear or bolt or flying wing had sped by next to his cheek), for just a moment, two great red orbs like cat's eyes were visible and a bone-chilling snarl echoed inside his head, a snarl he remembered from his fight above the Sanctuary mageguild.

When he realized he had stopped stock still, he exhaled the group he hadn't known he was holding, rubbed his horripilated arms, and ran ahead.

What he saw when he reached the battleground was not a group of men who held two of his, or three, at bay, but three gray and stinking fiends, each with a soldier in its jaws or claws: one tearing out a living liver from a screaming man; one using a human head as a battering ram, running repeatedly against the high stone wall, the helpless soldier in his grip no longer conscious; one committing atrocities on a recumbent form, while over the proceedings a winged demon, copper-skinned and glowing in the night, hovered in mid air, urging the fiends to better sport.

And into this he charged, sword sheathed, crossbow aimed high at the demon, inhuman commander of nearly mindless fiends. He put three bolts into it in quick succession; one through each wing, one through a hellish eye.

And as he'd hoped, the demon fixed on him and, its flight erratic, its judgment of space and distance skewed because of the bolt which skewered its eye, gave a howl and came at him, flapping downward in drunken circles and calling out more of Tempus' names than any demon not sent to confront him could have known.

He'd stopped the fiends, though, who hesitated, without supervision, crouching down where they were to gorge themselves on the dead they had in hand, paying no attention to his three remaining men who had a chance now to fight the humans running to engage them. Tempus had just time enough to use his speed to their advantage (loosing four quarrels which reduced the odds by dropping three human guards and one immense wolflike dog who came careening round the corner, others, smaller, in its wake) before the demon closed with him in grappling battle, descending on him hard and fast and penetrating his mundane armor with sulpherous claws.

Its breath was stinking and corrosive; its undamaged eye was yellow, and as they fought and rolled there in the dirt it spoke to him of unearthly dooms and eternal service to a mage named Datan, and how long he would regret his impulse to save "useless, mortal fools" which had led him to sheath his able sword and use the crossbow when, if he'd any hope at all, the sword was it— residually "tainted" with supernal power.

He got a knee upon one wing, though its jaws clamped on his shoulder, and tried to roll them over. He heard the wing snap and rend, the demon howl around the mouthful of his flesh it had. He felt its fangs grate against his collarbone and its spittle, as demon's spittle will, begin to do its work, making him weak and woozy, forgetful of the need to fight.

As darkness closed in upon him, he made a gargantuan effort to draw his sword, got it partly out and then, only half pretending, went limp and lay quite still. He felt the demon shudder, he heard a voice from far above, calling the demon's name as hot drool fell upon his throat and its teeth clacked near to his jugular.

The voice, a mage's, commanding the demon: "Cease!" was the only chance he might ever have. Tempus wondered, briefly, in a shattered second, whether his slowed regeneration could save him if the demon bit out his throat, and then what sort of afterlife he'd earned, and whether the mage he heard could keep him from it.

Then, in one last effort, nauseous from loss of blood and dizzy and willing his eyes to focus, he lunged backward in the demon's grip and broke its hold.

His sword came out of his scabbard, and his eyes came open, and though he could hardly see for the sweat in his eyes and the blood stinging his face and the narcotizing demon spittle coursing his blood, he struck out at it with his sharkskin-hilted blade and connected with its neck, a crosscut that cleaved down from right to left, through the collarbone and spinal column, so that as he thrust it off and scrambled back, to gain his knees, he saw the ground round about begin to steam and smoke, then bubble like hot-springs' mud as the demon's blood ran upon it and beyond, he saw two manlike feet take retreating steps.

Pushing himself upright with his sword, he took three steps toward the human form swimming in his blurred vision, a huge and gross manform, hairless head and cloaked bulk all he could make out.

Its hand raised. Its finger pointed. Ball lightning jumped from the extended digit to run up the Riddler's sword and shock him numb and senseless.

He knew he was crumpling. He felt the dirt hit his knees and with an effort of will went down no further. He raised his head and blinked and tried to meet the eyes of the wizard, but the shape was fading away, going to mist, going to wisp, until only a voice was left: "You want your woman back, Riddler? Your superhuman female toy? Come to me and ask politely, if you live. And bring some souls to trade."

Then there was nothing there, and something like rain began to fall.

In a howling wind it came, blotting out the scant moon-light and dousing the oil fires on their plinths. It was a rain that stung and steamed and made the wounded cry and writhe where they lay in the dirt.

And then beneath the manse and to its rear an explosion roared, flames spewing skyward: one soldier, one of the mercenaries, had gotten through and carried out the plan. And the conflagration did battle with the caustic tempest from the heavens. In its light, Tempus, his hands above his head and his head to the earth, noticed that the rain yet falling was blood red.

It was some little time before he gathered enough strength to fight off the debilitating effects of the demon spittle in his system and the dizziness the loss of his own blood caused, and took stock of his wounds before trying with his one good arm, using his sword as a lever, to gain his feet.

Having done so, he stood weaving among the corpses of men and dogs, garish and horrid in the fire's light, and took slow, painful steps toward them to see if any of his lived yet.

Thus it was that, as his blood began to clot in the cauterizing heat from the fire and he wiped his brow with a sticky hand, he looked upward into the heavens (expecting to see dark clouds or eagles circling, more demons, the absent fiends—*anything* but what he saw) and met Jihan's father's blood-red eyes peering down at him.

He raised his sword to his brow then, knowing that it was Stormbringer's intervention which had dissuaded the Osprey from finishing him, capturing him, or further cursing him on the spot.

It was nice to know that Datan feared something.

"Stormbringer," he called, shouting loud above the roaring blaze, weaving, hardly a heroic figure at that moment, his torn flesh showing the shoulder bones beneath and his stance chancy, "my thanks."

By the time he'd finished speaking, the luminous eyes had faded from the sky and a soldier was trotting toward him, helmet held by its strap because of the ferocious heat, his weapons sheathed, stripping off his breastplate as he came.

The mercenary took one squinting look at Tempus, slowed, came the rest of the way with naked incredulity on his face as he surveyed the carnage and his task force leader.

"Need some help, there, commander?" He stopped, a few lengths away, his gaze fastened on wounds that should have been incapacitating, if not fatal. Some men don't know they're dead for an hour or so, commit feats of valor beyond reason in the field, then die when the fervor fades away. His expression said he thought Tempus in such a state, dead but just not aware of it, about to keel over in his tracks.

The Riddler indicated the men lying on the field, five of this one's comrades, a welter of guards and dogs. "See if any need help to live or die," he grated, and limped slowly and painfully over to the stable wall to watch the fire burn and the one remaining soldier he commanded do as he was bid.

After a time the mercenary came to him: one would live, one craved a quick death, the others had secured one.

And: "Fiends! Where are the accursed fiends? Or am I mad, or spell-bound? There *were* fiends . . . weren't there? And a winged thing? Copper colored? And some damn huge dog?"

"There were. As for where they are, be grateful they aren't here. Find some horses." From the stable, nervous pounding and a few whinnies of fear could be heard as the horses sensed and smelled the fire. "Make a litter for the wounded man and let's go home."

"Yes, m'lord!" The soldier's gratitude was heartfelt. He met Tempus' eyes, tearing his gaze from the left arm dangling uselessly, chewed and broken. He opened his mouth as if to say something more, closed it, shook his head, and trotted away, calling back: "I'll just see if our own horses aren't still around here, somewhere. . . ."

By the time he had a chance to question the young mercenary at length, Tempus was terribly cold, but he was able to determine that the Nisibisi agents they'd come here seeking had either slipped away or been incinerated. Whichever, he thought he could use this place to billet his cohort when it arrived, and gave orders to that effect.

Then he collapsed in the soldier's arms.

The moon was in its dark phase when Niko reined in his bay before a roadside inn called the Shepherd's Crook. Its torchlit sign proclaimed in incised gilded letters that it offered the "Last Bed And Board Before Tyse" and this was so: Tyse's suburbs were no more than two hours ride to the north east. Even from this vantage, as he dismounted and tied his among a dozen other horses, he could see Wizardwall's wards flickering, blue and intermittent, against the cleaner dark of the star-dusted night.

He hesitated before the inn's oak and fieldstone threshold, stroking his pregnant mare's muzzle, fiddling with the feedbag he slipped on it: he was feeding her oats and corn, twice what he gave the bay, but she was losing weight daily. He felt the now-familiar twinge of guilt. Whatever had possessed him to *ride* her out of Sanctuary?

He went around her, his hand sliding along her trail-sharpened croup, extracted his moneybelt from where he habitually secreted it between the bay's saddle and the sheepskin he used for a saddleblanket, trying not to think about Wizardwall glimmering against the sky or any of the old and painful memories these roads south of Tyse evoked. He was confronting as many ghosts here as he'd become used to meeting in his rest-place. But unlike Tamzen and her friends or his deceased left-side leader, these shades weren't friendly.

He'd smeared the cuirass Aškelon had given him with ashes and grease from his cookfires; now he struggled into it, fastened its buckles, took his helmet from the rosette on his saddle and, propping it under his arm, climbed the steps and pushed open the door.

The Shepherd's Crook had changed since last he'd come this way: whitewashed walls had been paneled over with weathered planks; weapons long past service hung over the fieldstone hearth which dominated the wall opposite the bar. There were tables now, a score or more, and chairs instead of benches. The floor's sawdust was clean, and he didn't recognize anyone—not the three serving wenches or the athletic, hatchet-faced man with shoulder-length black hair who presided behind the bar.

Niko let out a sigh of relief and approached the barkeep. Perhaps no one would recognize him, either. The face he'd seen in a pool of water yesterday bore only a passing resemblance to his old one: his broken nose and the bumps on his forehead and his left cheek were still puffy. Maybe it would be all right.

He scanned the crowd as he made his way among the tables: a threesome of Rankan garrison soldiers, noncommissioned officers by their devices; six in the unadorned leathers of hillborn fighters sporting the braided sidelocks of Free Nisibis, backs to the wall and watching him closely; three tables hosting two guild mercenaries each, talking

softly, their eclectic armor and weapons gleaming with
polish and oil in the flames from tapers in sconces above
on the walls; two men in civilian garb: one with the short
suede cloak and linen, ankle-length breeches of Tysian
style and one whose tunic was a dusty moiré silk—a merchant of some kind, plumed hat and all.

He positioned himself at the bar so he could study the
mercenaries' faces, ordered Tysian white wine, neat, paid
with a Rankan Imperial, and got more change than he'd
expected, commented, learned from the bartender that
the exchange rate these last weeks favored Ranke, and
listened, as he sipped, to the talk along the bar, where
three young brash farm boys and two inveterate drinkers
with wine-dark noses leaned precariously.

He'd almost decided not to eat here, not to pursue the
matter which had prompted him to stop in, when a girl
came from the kitchen bearing a tray on which bowls of
meat-and-dumpling stew steamed provocatively. "Any more
of that?" he asked the barman, and the big man in home-
spuns cocked his head and squinted before he answered,
"Yes, if m'guest will have a seat. And wouldya be wanting
bread with it, or rice or winter wheat?"

"Wheat." *Guest* in Tyse was a title which conferred
privilege: a guest, here, was protected like a family member.
Even an enemy, if he was accepted as a guest, was
succorded.

When he'd taken an empty table in a corner by a half-open
window paned with skin, and one of the girls came to
bring his order, he asked her if the owner was about. She
pointed to the bartender and replied in Rankene thick
with Tysian accent that "you're lookin' at 'im, sirrah."

The contemptuous form of address made him meet her
eyes, and these were gray and hollow-deep, familiar tunnels,
not the hopeless, tired eyes of a serving wench likely to be
one of the comforts the house extended to its boarders.
She thumped the bowl down before him and as she picked

up her tray he grabbed her wrist. "Do I know you?"

She looked down at his hand, tugged against his grip: "You'll not have the chance if you don't let me loose, sirrah. That's my husband there." She tossed her black-haired head, let the tray clatter to his table, crooked her finger at the bartender. The man, throwing down his rag, came out from behind the bar.

Niko released her and rubbed his eyes. "I'm—sorry, mistress. You reminded me of someone. . . ." She'd reminded him of the witch, of Roxane. He couldn't say that, and her husband was hulking now, both fists on Niko's table.

"Trouble? Wife? Guest?"

The woman was retreating, leaving Niko to answer to it, not saying a word, just her laughter sounding, transiently, in the suddenly quiet room—a light, trilling, tinkle, not the bray of an alehouse workwife. And he couldn't recall her face, just her eyes. . . .

"Well, guest?" The man leaned close.

"I came here—The man who owned this place before you was my mother's brother. I've been abroad for years, thought I'd stop in to visit. I don't have much family . . . not in the north, not in Ranke. Would you know where they've gone, him and his family?"

"To the gods, Nisibisi style. Bought the place at auction nine months back. What's this got to do with *her?*" His sharp chin jutted in the direction the woman had gone, through the swinging doors behind the bar.

"Nothing. . . . I thought she might be a cousin of mine, is all."

The man straightened up and the smell of garlic faded: "Sorry, not a chance of that. But since you expected a free meal and won't get one, take a flagon of wine on the house, guest."

Still *guest.* It was odd, but he accepted. He hadn't been close to his mother's brother—it had been his father's twin, a krrf dealer in Caronne, who'd bought him free and

sent him to Bandara when Niko had been taken as a serf
by a Rankan officer after the sack that had made him an
orphan. No other members of his immediate family had
been as lucky. This uncle had spared his loved ones by
going to his knees to kiss Rankan boots.

Rankans, Nisibisi, Mygdonians or the sea-raiding Beysibs—there was no choice among them: all sides are evil if
you're not on them.

He ate, paid, and got out of there, the food making him
tired, and the wine making him depressed. As he was tightening the bay's girth and preparing to mount, the sound of
sandals slapping stone made him turn, hand on hilt. The
group of six mercenaries was descending the stairs. He heard
the name "Tempus" and the word "hostel", and then they
saw him watching them. Their conversation ceased.

Silently, the men who had been talking in the multilin-
gual patois of guild mercenaries approached their horses;
as they did so, he found himself surrounded: two mounted
men behind him, one on either side of his own two horses,
and two who came up to the rail and leaned on it.

One said, "Life to you, brother," in Machadi, cautiously
but firmly. They weren't curious on a whim, Niko realized.
They were going to roust him, ask for his papers (he
carried none) or of his business here, or—"These horses
have been a long way, fighter. Where from? Where to?"

He didn't want trouble. He thought of the crossbow in
the bay's saddlebag, wrapped in hide, too well hidden and
protected to be accessible quickly enough to help him. But
he didn't want to announce himself. Not yet. He'd heard
the Riddler's name from one of these; he wished he'd
heard the context.

"From the south. To the hostel. Looking for hire," he
responded in the same tongue.

"Plenty of your sort, boy," the second said. "Your face
says you haven't been faring too well in your warring. No
room for youngsters in this battle. Go home and practice

another few years. It's *seniors only* at the guild hostel, if that's where you're headed. And seniority's something you're not likely to have."

Niko shrugged, "It's a big war," and swung up on his bay, the mare's tether in hand. He wrapped it twice around his saddlehorn, simultaneously telling the bay: "Back, back," in Rankene.

But the second—a portly, grizzled veteran—grabbed the bay's bridle, and the two mounted men behind closed in, blocking his retreat. The two others, one on his left and the sixth on the mare's far side, crowded him. One of these said, "Let's take him home and see what headquarters makes of him. He'll work for some damn faction or other, if he's not already, once he finds out what we've said is true."

Niko let his reins drop, spread his empty hands where all could see. "Life to all, so the saying goes. Let's observe it— and guild courtesy, if there's any of that this far north. Or ride with me to the hostel, *if* you're not afraid to show your faces there.... As for mine, it got this way winning, not losing."

It was not the right thing to say, but he didn't want to start explaining.

"There's a curfew, child. You'll not make it that far without kissing Rankan asses." This was from the first, who'd come out from behind the rail and had drawn his sword. "Get down now. Let's have a better look at you."

"And at what's in these fat bags on the mommy horse. No professional takes a mare in foal on as long a haul as she's showing. Slit his throat for cruelty to animals and I'll report him to the guild for impersonating a grown man."

He just didn't have the patience for this sort of thing. Without conscious decision, his booted foot kicked up and caught the man at his saddle under the chin. He heard the neck snap back but not the succeeding thud. From his belt came throwing stars; with his left hand he cast two: one at the closest mounted mercenary, on his right, one at the grizzled companion of the fallen man. By then the sword Aškelon had given him was drawn in his right, the two remaining stars moved into throwing position. "Anyone else?"

The man he'd kicked was moaning. The two he'd cast at, both throws meant only to wound, were clutching thigh and arm, where only the slimmest point of each star protruded. One was cursing; the other, the mounted man, was trying to pull the star out of his thigh.

The men at his rear had their crossbows cocked, however. He'd known this wasn't a good idea, but he turned in his saddle: "I've got two of these left, gentlemen. You want to play or you want to ride away? If I'd meant it, those two would be dead. You'll get me, maybe, but you won't live long enough to boast about it."

"Who in the god's name *are* you?" one of the two mounted riders asked intently, face screwed up, peering through his crossbow's peep sight, not yet decided.

"Someone who doesn't want to introduce himself to the wrong people," the other mounted man hazarded.

"That's right. Now get out of my way. Unless these friends of yours get those stars out in the next few moments, the poison will kill them before they bleed to death." There was no poison on the stars, but Niko wanted to be away.

The men backed off, muttering among themselves. Niko saw the one he'd kicked make an effort to gain his knees, fall back. No casualties, then.

As he maneuvered his horses between the two who still held him at crossbow's point, he could hear one exhort the other: they couldn't just let him *go*.

The second was dismounting: "Then go with him, man. I'll stay with these. Wait until Grillo hears about this— four men of first tier hire downed by a single teenage delinquent. That is, if he'll *allow* you to accompany him."

The one still mounted gestured with his bow. "All right with you, fighter? We'll just check your credentials, and then if you're bracketed halfway where your skills should put you, we'll see the commanders. You really want hire, you'll get it."

"Good enough." Niko, taking a chance, sheathed his sword. The bowman's slitted eyes were still on his stars as Niko carefully backed his horses the rest of the way and the rider came abreast of him.

"I'm Ari," the mounted man, flipping the lever back to safety-lock his bow, held out his right hand. His eyes, in the torchlight, weren't angry; his tone held just a trace of laughter. "And this is—or was—my team. That's Haram, there—team leader of the sortie unit known as—"

"Ari, don't tell him your life story. Find out his. Go on, before these three forget their wounds enough to object and we've got to kill him."

"Life to you, then, leader. And everlasting glory," Niko called softly as he kicked the bay into a dispirited lope, still looking back at the man who'd lost a team on his account. It wasn't a good beginning, he was certain.

"My ass to you," he thought he heard the man called Haram retort, but he could not be sure over the sound of his own blowing horses and creaking gear and the words of the fighter riding beside him: "Where'd you pick that up—those things you threw? The speed of it. . . ."

"West."

"How many have you?"

"Enough."

"All poisoned?"

"None," Niko lied. On his left hip, six poison-tipped stars rode, undisturbed.

The other chuckled, then laughed aloud. "Left up here, at this fork. What kind of hire did you want?"

"I can't say yet. I'll see what's offered." The left fork wasn't the quickest way to the mercenaries' hostel, which was southeast of town, but he went with his escort. The curfew sounded real enough; he didn't want to explain himself to any Rankan garrison sergeant.

"I think there'll be something for you, when I tell 'em what I just saw back there. Teach me that? The 'stars,' I mean?"

"Gladly."

They rode awhile in silence. Then Ari said: "West? Machad? I never saw anything like that there. You speak Machadi."

"Not Machad."

"I don't mean to pry. . . . Maybe we could use you in our own unit . . . we'll have a vacancy or two—temporarily, anyhow."

"Paired fighters, isn't it?"

"Some are. You?"

"Once. No more."

"Real communicative, aren't you?"

"I don't know you."

"You're going to need a friend, someone to speak for you—you just put down three men, any of whom makes more in a month than you've seen this whole season."

"Then they're overpaid."

Again, Ari laughed. "Have you a name, guildbrother? By the gods, I hope you're at least *that*. If you're not in good standing, dues paid up and all, we'll have to do something about all this. . . ."

"Stealth. And I'm up to date."

"Good enough, then, Stealth."

They rode on, west of town, never getting close enough for Niko to see more than the brownish haze of lights and smoke that hovered over it. He recognized the Outbridge quarter as their destination long before they rode among the upscale estates and the vinehung inns. When they came to cobbled ways he asked Ari to slow their pace, saving his horses' hooves.

They had been riding along a two-story masonry wall topped with outward-curving spikes for a while when Ari gestured toward it: "This is it. Gates ahead. If there's some reason you can't give your *whole* name in there, to our field commander or the intelligence chief, you'd better run for your freedom now. Inside, there's no chance of it."

Niko thought seriously about that. If Tempus was this man's quarry, for some reason, and not one of the "commanders" then Niko was in serious trouble.

It was his last chance; the other fighter was right.

Niko said, "This isn't the hostel."

"We're specials; we don't work out of the hostel."

They approached the gate, and sentries appeared from the shadows. Ari gave a password and some scatological banter was exchanged. Both peltasts looked at Niko but neither questioned him. They called within, and a creak and whine of heavy timber over metal sounded. The gate was drawn back, revealing a stone corridor through which they must pass single file. In it, they were subject to further scrutiny and possible execution through staggered slits in the high walls behind which bowmen and spearmen were posted.

But nothing untoward occurred, and the farther gate was opened.

Men came running to take their horses in an inner courtyard bright with statuary-borne flames. Niko hesitated there: "I'll stay with my horses. Whoever I have to see can come this far. I've come far enough."

Ari gave him a reproving look and wondered aloud where he'd gotten away with this sort of behavior, but jogged off to "bring somebody back to see you."

Waiting, Niko slipped from the bay and walked his horses in slow circles, cooling them. He thought about loosening their girths: he couldn't get out of here if anyone decided to try to prevent him. Walls were guarded; he could see the glitter of flame off spearpoints. There had been a fire here recently; the stones beneath his feet were blackened and the air about still smelled of it; charred wood was piled in a corner. The whole situation reminded him of the early days of the Stepsons out at Jubal's. *Specials*, Ari had said. Well, it could have been worse—it could have been that he'd run into an army patrol. And everything Ari had said—so far as Niko could tell by ear and eye and what use he'd been able to make of his peripheral perception—had been true.

He sensed that the sentries and guardpost personnel were edgy; he was careful to make no sudden moves.

After a time he heard voices; discipline was bowstring-taut here, so it wasn't the guards or the sentries. Soon three men came into view. One was Ari; one was in civilian clothes; and one was in spartan field armor of unadorned leather and tarnished mail but had no helmet. Both the civilian and the officer wore blades.

Niko stopped his horses and waited, telling them "stay" and dropping the bay's reins and his mare's tether.

When the three came up to him, Ari a little behind the other two, the civilian stepped forward and offered his hand: "Stealth, is it? I'm Grillo."

Niko clasped and released it; it had been dry, strong, hard with calluses only swordplay can raise. "I remember you, my lord." He met eyes crinkled with amusement and relaxed a bit. This man had been a friend of Niko's left-side leader.

"This is our esteemed Tysian guild representative, Vasili. Vasili, this is Stealth, called Nikodemos."

The guild official saluted him. Niko returned the gesture, not liking the grim countenance of the uniformed man.

"Ari tells us you've put the lie tonight to some of our most overblown reputations," Grillo said easily. "I knew we were paying that lot more than they were worth."

Vasili said: "They were worth it. They still are, Grillo, and you know it. This one here," he pointed at Niko, "has a lot of tricky Bandaran moves. We've heard you and your cohort from the south are not going to be easily assimilated, Nikodemos. You should have gone straight to the guild hostel and taken what assignment we offered."

"I would have. Ari persuaded me otherwise."

"And your tour in Sanc—"

Grillo elbowed the guild representative in the ribs.

Vasili was undaunted: "—your *previous* commission? We don't like the way your squadron fulfilled its obligation."

"By the rules, my lord. We *did* it by the rules."

"But not the spirit. That's the thing, isn't it? Enough. Grillo, you want him, you've got him. We'll work out a pay scale for this crew now that the first of them is here. But don't come to me if they slay more within your walls than beyond them. Sacred Bands and elite squadrons aren't what the mercenaries' guild is about. Field them at your peril."

"Fine with me," Grillo said, and the guild representative stalked away. "Well, Niko, I suppose you'd like to see the Riddler before you and I have our talk?"

Not waiting for a reply, Grillo headed off. Niko looked after him, at his horses, at Ari. Ari waved him on: "I'll watch them."

Niko signed his thanks and caught up with Grillo, aware that this could be some elaborate trap: Grillo was a canny double-dealer who took ten per cent of everything that passed under his nose and whose Rankan allegiance was perfunctory at best.

Niko could be "seeing" Tempus in a dungeon built for two or a mass grave awaiting more bodies to fill it. He tried not to be impressed by the massive masonry of the grounds; he saw further evidence of fiery sack: this place had changed hands recently, or withstood an attempt to cause it to do so.

Grillo asked him casual questions; he answered in non sequiturs until the other man volunteered the information that Tempus had sent a message to Bashir, received no reply, and thus would be doubly glad to see him: "Both he and I think your old acquaintance with the Successors might be the most valuable weapon in our arsenal right now."

They were climbing wide granite steps; Niko ventured: "So it's 'we'?"

At the top of them, Grillo answered, "It is. This way."

Beyond an oak door, reinforced with wrought iron and

guarded, was a second, inner court where the sack hadn't reached. They entered the low stone building centering it, trod the corridors and stairs. Then Grillo stopped: "I'll wait here." He lifted a latch and pushed a door inward. "The next door on your right is his . . . and, Niko?"

"My lord?"

"Our condolences on the death of—"

"Thank you." He didn't want to talk about it. He turned his back on Grillo and knocked where he'd been told to.

"Come," he heard; the Riddler's gravelly voice was unmistakable.

The door was unlocked. He pushed it open and paused, shocked by the infirmity of the man on the bed. He'd thought Tempus to be indestructible. The man he saw was bristle-chinned and sweating, arm in a sling. Around the sharp, long eyes dark shadows hovered.

"Close it. Sit. You're a fortnight early. Tell me how that is."

Niko did as he was bid, pulling a chair up beside the bed. On a nightstand was a pitcher, two goblets standing on their rims, one on its base with wine in it. Tempus picked up that one, bade Niko serve himself.

Sipping watered wine, he tried to explain what he himself didn't understand: "Short cuts. I was delirious part of the time. The mare—I brought her, couldn't leave her . . . She picked the route. Everyone's coming. Critias ruled that each must find a substitute first to satisfy the guild." He knew he was rattling on, but all he could think of was the Riddler's obvious wounds and what could have made them.

"It's all right, Niko. You can relax."

He saw Tempus's mouth twitch, half a smile dance there. "I had a run-in with some Nisibisi-fielded demons and fiends. I'll be well enough in another week or two. Meanwhile. . . ." The Riddler pushed himself up on one stiff arm, and Niko was reminded of last full moon in Sanctuary, when their positions were reversed. ". . . I'm pleased you're here. Jihan's gone, disappeared."

Niko held the other's gaze, unspeaking.

"She took both Trôs horses."

*"What?"*

"We suspect foul play. Nisibisi magic, possibly."

*"Where? How?"*

"Those are questions I'd like your help answering. Until the other Stepsons come, you are the single man I can trust. You know Grillo's background?"

Niko nodded.

"Then I don't have to explain. These men here, as well as this place, are ours. Mix among them and take their measure, but carefully."

"I will."

"Too, if you are up to it, I'd ask special favors . . ."

"Command me."

"Bashir. I have to meet with him. Personally. You know the free zone?"

"I knew it once. Better than I'd have liked."

"Little's changed, I wager. Vouch for me with the Successors."

Niko smiled at that, shaking his head slightly, a hand gesturing: "Surely there's no need. But if you wish? . . ."

"As in Sanctuary, I'd like you to work apart from these others at first, construct what rationale you please; let me know what you need in the way of support and verification. Check in at the guild hostel; infiltrate the free zone; find Bashir and convince him to meet with me; come back then and tell me where and how."

"But Grillo will know. He said the same to me."

"If we can't fool him, we'll have to trust him. You had trouble with some of his specials, he told me. You've a reputation for temper. We'll say your price was too high, and Sanctuary soured you—with the loss of two partners, it sounds likely enough."

"I'm not sure, commander . . ." He was tired, suddenly. He'd thought he'd get a different welcome. He wondered if the Riddler was trying to keep him out of the avenging obviously under way.

"Sure of what?"

"That I can ..." Half into a complaint that he, too, could use a few nights' rest where sleep was secure and danger minimal, Niko backed away from it. Before Tempus, he could not show weakness. "... convince Grillo that we've come to a parting of the ways."

"Just a temporary dispute over wage and accommodation. The guild will rate you below what you're worth."

Squinting at him, Tempus reached under his mattress, pulled forth a pouch, shook it. "Tysian currency. Work money, not pay." He tossed it, and Niko caught it in his hand, hefting it.

"I'd like to leave my mare here, Commander, where's she's safe."

"Take any of mine, then. I'll give orders. And be sure you get a curfew pass before you leave."

The audience was over, Niko thought. He rose, trying to stand straight, not to look disappointed, not to show his hurt. Perhaps Janni and some few others had been right: perhaps the Riddler still resented Niko declining his offer of pairbond. He almost offered himself once more to Tempus as a right-side fighter, but his commander's next words saved him from it:

"Has your *maat* not returned? Are your dreams still troubled?"

"No. Yes."

"I see. We have the same sort of problem with death squads up here that we had in Sanctuary. Is that going to bother you?"

"Undeads? Love 'em. Got a few of my own who claim to be taking special care of me. If that's all? ..." He backed toward the door.

"Stepson . . . you don't have to accept this . . . I can send you elsewhere, put you in here. If you're not able, say the word."

"I'm fine, Commander. Life to you." He loosened the
latch's leather strap and pulled open the door, not waiting
to hear Tempus respond in kind, not looking back to see
his commander salute him as an equal. The loss of the
Trôs horses was a terrible one; from his commander's condition, enemies here were as formidable as he remembered.

And Tempus was sending him, alone, across the Nisibisi
border.

He wished, securing the door and leaning against it, eyes
closing of their own accord as he rested for a moment before
going to seek out Grillo, that he'd been able to refuse.

But there was nothing else for him to do. Tempus knew
it. He couldn't strut around inside these barracks walls and
play politics with status-conscious sellswords. He shouldn't
resent his commander making best use of him. And yet *something* inside him wanted to stay with the Riddler.

He pushed off and headed for the door where he'd last
seen Grillo. His own thoughts made no sense to him. He'd
always maintained that a man's primary obligation was to
think clearly; ever since his encounter with the witch,
he'd been second-guessing himself.

There *was* nothing else for him. He was a fighter; it was
what he did and what he knew, what had kept him alive
all these years. In the Sacred Band, code of honor was the
only reality Niko understood—harsh, but life was harsh.
Here in Tyse, where he had been enslaved, where he'd
promised himself that freedom, should he ever regain it,
was something he'd never lose again, he had a chance to
avenge not only Janni, and the treatment he'd suffered at
the witch's hands, but all the hell his childhood had been.
He didn't understand why he wasn't eager to begin it,
unless his fear of the mages had eaten through and hol-
lowed out his heart.

The mercenaries' hostel sat upon Tyse's southeast
boundary, its front door in Tysian jurisdiction, its sleep-

ing quarters, rear exits, postern gates and stables beyond Tyse's city limits and thus free from curfew or any other law the local police or Elite Guard might wish to enforce.

The hamlet in whose jurisdiction the balance of the hostel sat was called Peace Falls; there Peace River cascaded down three hundred feet of cliffs and wound about the farms like a lady's holiday girdle. On the river, Roxane had long maintained a home.

But tonight she was at the back door of the hostel, on a Peace Falls street dotted with other ladies whose skirts were shorter and faces painted brighter as they loitered, snaring mercenaries to take inside the red-lit houses of ill repute which intermingled with custom weaponers and taverns and gaming houses there to serve the mercenaries. The street was called Commerce Avenue and it was wide and busy day and night. Nowhere in Tyse were caravaners so free with contraband. Drug dens specializing in krrf or opiates advertised their wares along with others offering more arcane substances to flood the mind with psychedelic dreams and give more personal glimpses of the future than abutting psychics' shops or card-readers could offer. On Commerce you could have your fortune told by presenting head or hand or foot or more private parts, or choosing a painted turtle or a cup of tea—as long as copper coins accompanied your choice.

The fortune Roxane meant to tell was Niko's. She'd made a fine disguise he'd never penetrate, as he had almost done when she'd served him rehabilitating stew at the Shepherd's Crook, where she'd merely cohabited with a barmaid in a shabby body. This time she'd made a whole persona, that of a young and comely virgin girl of the sort that Niko liked.

She waited till she sensed him on the street and cued the snakes, disguised as drugged south-siders of the well-heeled sort that played at debauch here and paid for pleasures they'd never dare demand from their wives or indulge in at their homes. The snakes accosted her loudly, looking like Tysian popinjays, merchants' sons or politicians' spawn of the ilk that buy freedom from conscription by sending serfs to war in their stead.

Like a well-bred and frightened girl, as she heard Niko's horses, she tried to fend off the snakes. And like the fool he was, he vaulted down from his bay to intervene.

The snakes ran as they'd been told to; she swooned and Niko had to catch her. She'd been angry when he hadn't stayed with the Riddler, but Tempus was simply a more crafty quarry than others Roxane had sought. She'd lost two more minions fielding Adrastus' "son," Shamshi. She and Datan had already lost two warlocks to the Riddler in fair battle, and a hapless demon besides. Nisibis had not counted casualties of that magnitude in a century. These mortals would have much to answer for, by and by.

In Niko's arms she played the girl, calling herself "Cybele" and hesitating when he offered to buy her drink and dinner, as would any runaway from good family origins who was out of money but yet had pride.

Thus she lured him into an establishment known as Brother Bomba's, which served first-class food in front and offered anything a man might name behind a back door.

"Now tell me what you're doing on a street like this, Cybele," Niko prodded, drinking tea because she'd refused even watered wine as they broke bread together.

Her hair was fair, and her eyes were green, and her clothes were once noble, but layered with dust. She could see in his eyes that he was taken; she could feel in his mind his concern; Niko, whose youth had been a horror, would always save a young one what he could. She said, "It shames me, my lord. I cannot." She covered her eyes with her hands.

"Niko," he reminded her. "I'm *not* your lord. Where are your parents, Cybele?"

Still hiding her face behind her hands, she shook her

head, using the time to put the suggestion in his mind that he give her money to find an apartment, that he shelter her and succor her, and perhaps . . .

He began to broach the subject, explaining carefully that his intentions were honorable, offering to use his guild connections to contact her relatives, if she had any.

Then she put down her hands and took one of his in both of hers, and kissed its rough, scarred back. By tomorrow she'd have him where she wanted him—at her river house; she'd be his confidant, perhaps his lover.

Datan faced his son, Shamshi, whose shoulders were squared and eyes shining brighter than the candelabras in the archmage's inner sanctum.

"She sleeps," said the boy, bursting with pride at a job well done.

Datan, too, was proud. A son such as this one could not be supplicated from the masters of the four elements or even the underworld. Luck had played a part. "Well done," he replied, and hugged the boy to him. It was the first time they had ever embraced. Once he'd realized that the boy had been with Roxane, lain in carnal embrace and ritual copulation with Wizardwall's finest witch, everything began to change between them: there was no need for further subterfuge.

Now he regretted the years his child had struggled to hide his light among Mygdonians. It must have been like living in with wolves, being educated by chimpanzees or fraternizing with pigs. "Come and tell me all about it— your sojurn in the free zone, your trip here."

He tousled the boy's pale hair and led him to a table in which a map of the known world was incised. A snap of fingers sufficed to bring food and drink from the kitchens: pheasant stuffed with almonds and grapes, watered wine, pastries he'd had prepared specially to please a child. He didn't need to hear Shamshi's account of his venture into

Tyse; he'd overseen it personally, changing shape as circumstance required, always ready to intervene. Once waked by Roxane's premature caresses, the mageblood in this child could not be put back to sleep. He must be taught, he must be trained.

Listening, Datan nodded in the appropriate places; when the boy would falter, he asked the right questions. He'd not chastised Shamshi for lying with Roxane, as he'd made little of it with the witch. Enchantresses of such power often dreamed of dominance, and Roxane's nature was vengeful and mean. It was best to turn her devisive efforts to his benefit—for what benefited Datan benefited Wizardwall. So he'd sent her out to tend to Nikodemos and the Riddler in person, away from more disastrous pursuits.

When the boy hesitated, then trebled that his story was done, Datan broached a difficult and painful subject: his son must continue what he'd started, keep Jihan intrigued, even ride with her up into Mygdonia—*if* the Froth Daughter could be persuaded. Jihan had sworn to return Shamshi to his parents and safety; the blindstruck mother was in her husband's keeping, halfway to Mygdon by now.

The boy blinked hard, hiding tears his upbringing as a prince had made him too proud to shed. Before Shamshi could frame the words to ask how he'd failed, that Datan would so punish him when all he wanted was to stay here with his sire and learn to be as he, the Osprey explained as much as he dared—enough to soothe, not enough to be injurious should inexperience or Tempus pry the truth from that young, tender mouth.

Then, when the child's appetite assured Datan that the boy was content with the offered explanation, he went to greet his guest.

He'd kept her sleeping long, a thing one so new at life and so long in the company of the untiring Riddler would think entirely natural. He'd had things to do, an avatar to test, a witch's self-serving mechinations to contravene.

Nothing he'd seen in Roxane's errors or intentional misinterpretation of his orders troubled him as much as the Stormbringer's blood red orbs appearing on the field of battle over Tempus as Datan and the Riddler stood face to face.

And yet, he was sure the Froth Daughter's father would not interpose Himself directly so long as the daughter was not threatened physically. No father's meddling is welcome when a child tries its independence.

He knocked upon her door and as he did so snapped the slumber spell, and she came to greet him, her scale armor corselet glimmering in the soft hall light, her magnificent figure limned enticingly in the open door.

"I trust you slept well, my lady Jihan," he said smoothly, not a hint of the impact her human form's animal magnetism had on him sounding in his words. A vision is one thing, a mental impression another, but a meeting in the flesh with Jihan made Datan almost forget whose daughter she was and whose lover she'd become. "I'm Shamshi's—"

"Father. He told me. I'll keep your secret, Osprey." Jihan stepped forward, out of the shadowed doorway. Datan spread his arms to embrace her in thanks as was Nisibisi custom. She caught his right hand as it swept by and shook it so firmly he thought he heard his bones complain.

" 'Protector,' I like to call myself. His mother would be executed, his father-of-record shamed unnecessarily, if his lineage were known." As she loosed her grip, he turned her hand in his and led her down the corridor.

"Not to mention the boy's inheritance . . . the power, the position . . . these too, I wager, would be lost to him— and you."

"Ah, I hear in your tone that you've accepted all the evil things said of me with not even the tiniest doubt. All men

hate their enemies, and anyone the slightest bit smarter
or more able. Surely you've seen this for yourself, even in
so short a time among—"

"So you know my provenance?"

Datan couldn't stop looking at her; every inch of him
longed to press against her; he headed them toward his
seraglio, a plan forming in his mind. "It makes us even.
And it should ease your mind: your father is respected
here, as everywhere He is known. As long as you wish it,
you are my honored guest. And I hope it will be long
enough to let me plead my case, mayhap to change your
opinion of me. Though you walk among men you needn't
share their prejudices—your intelligence offers you so much
more in insight. . . ."

"I promised the boy to accompany him to safety—home
to his mother. She's not here, your staff says. She had
some sort of accident? . . ."

"Yes, unfortunately. She went north with her husband.
What you and Shamshi have agreed is between you two,
but I swear he's safe here and you may leave him—"
Pausing, he pushed open the door at the hall's end and he
heard Jihan's breath catch in her throat at the splendor of
illusory vistas upon the walls and hanging silks and forgotten works of art from age-old cultures. The last of the
seraglio's women, alerted by his unspoken signal, hurried
out by the chamber's back door. "Leave him with me," he
continued, leading her to the right where a room those
women seldom entered could be found—if one could de-
materialize a section of travertine wall.

The wall dissolved; Datan bowed low: "After you, Jihan."
She passed through the portal, her fine high buttocks
making her scale armor slither like a sea serpent's coils.
He followed, hearing her reply that she'd keep her word
and see Shamshi home to Mygdonia since his mother
wasn't here.

"He'll need a few days' rest."

*"More?* We've been here—"

"He's just a boy, my lady. And one who's had adventures arduous for a child his age."

"My . . . friends will be worried. I must send a message, then."

"Your friends? Or is it one in particular, who pretends to friendship, but in reality is an enemy of mine with thought for little else but bloodshed and. . . ."

"I'll hear no ill word spoken of him." Her eyes flashed red as she turned about in the ante room, staring at him, her muscular arms crossed.

"Such loyalty. You've heard tomes of evil said of me, no doubt, without complaint. Let me make my case, dear lady. An intelligence such as yours should gather all the facts it can before choosing sides."

A smile danced in the corners of her mouth; her arms unfolded. She was looking beyond him now, where the doorway he had made was once more a solid marble wall. "You'd woo me, O fearsome, vilified archmage?"

"You loved an 'archmage' enough to take that form, or so my sources tell me. I wish only justice, a hearing, august Froth Daughter. And to prove it, I'll conjure the Riddler forth for you, and facilitate any message you choose to send him."

"You can do this?"

"Assuredly." He had her, then. He escorted her around the conrner and into the vaulted chamber he used for summoning, and on a single daybed bade her sit. Then he went and spun the globe within its mosaic circle which stood in the very center of the room, starlight spewing on it from the roof's skylight. And as the gem-encrusted globe spun round, the light it caught flickered along the walls and streaked, and when he stopped it with an outstretched hand and then stepped back, the light coalesced, and where the globe had been a man took form, lying on his back with a woman riding high atop him. His eyes were closed, and one hand on her buttocks, and as these two began to thicken into flesh Datan heard Jihan's harsh indrawn breath and stayed the process: "Yes, my lady? It seems we've chosen an inopportune time to interrupt him."

"That's right," she snapped. "And I've changed my mind about the message: I'll let him worry."

And so Datan let the lifelike image of Tempus, his arm in a sling and his needs being tended by the widow Maldives, fade away.

Luck, this night, was doubly on Datan's side.

# Book Four:

# *Peace Falls*

Niko hadn't liked what he'd seen in the free zone. The specials he'd fallen in with—Ari and his left-side leader, Haram—called the refugees "Maggots" and couldn't tell a civilian from a Successor. To deem the situation in Tyse "explosive" was an understatement: among the half-dozen citizen militias and as many private armies, Elite Guards and Rankan garrisons and mercenary hordes who fought among themselves, casualties were a daily occurrence.

Niko had remarked to Ari that he should have been given a tally sheet along with the armband that let him pass where he willed and allowed him to ignore the curfew.

The wisest thing to do in such environs was to harden one's heart to the pathos, close one's ears to the fanatics of the factions, forget words like justice and mercy, and do one's job.

To that end, he'd come up here, northeast of town, to seek out Bashir in Free Nisibis. He'd tried convincing the Successors in the free zone to have Bashir come down to meet him, but his armband and pale skin spoke against him. He couldn't blame them: Tyse was little more than a baited trap or an open grave for a man who let his caution slip.

And he couldn't send a message which might be intercepted, couldn't divulge what it was he wanted. Tempus had straightforwardly asked Bashir for a meeting and been ignored.

He let Janni's bay pick its way through the new moon night. It was raining, and he'd been waiting for a night like this for nearly a week now. No scent or track would be left behind him; the sound of the rain would mask his movement. He'd be able to rate Bashir's security when he saw him. Over his shoulders he pulled the oilcloth mantle he'd been issued when he was inducted into Grillo's special forces. The sight of its yellow lining was enough to send honest men running for cover and criminals fumbling for bribe or weapon. The repute of his profession had fallen, in these lands where he'd been born, to an all-time low. But the lining kept the rain off, and the color kept the curious away, and Niko, who couldn't trust himself, bereft of *maat* and partner, to steer a middle course or negotiate a fair solution as once he'd done, valued it for these reasons. In the hostel, where he was billeted, he didn't rest easy. In Cybele's rented house down by Peace River he'd found a refuge which he guarded jealously, kept secret from the specials who thought themselves his friends here. He'd given up making friends. The pretense of it he kept up under orders: Tempus wanted these fighters' measure taken. Niko, to do that, was keeping company with men whose natures and entertainments (save for Ari, who simply mimicked his left-side leader) were reprehensible to him. If the elite among the mercenaries had been skimmed off to form the Stepsons, then its opposite was stationed here in Tyse, like the sediment at the bottom of a cheap wine jug.

Some might have said that what Niko was doing was less than honorable, but none of that sort resided here at the foot of Wizardwall.

Crossing the Nisibisi border he could feel the difference, as if the wards still lingering here from former times were cobwebs jeweled with rain which wrapped themselves about his limbs. He wasn't worried; the wards were ancient wraiths of lost power: this was Successor country, and Wizardwall little more than an evil shadow on the horizon. Enlil's priesthood ruled here, warrior-priests who fought in the lines like Abarsis and blessed swords to cut through charms and eyes to pierce illusion.

After his release from servitude on Wizardwall, he'd spent a pleasant year here—or memory had made it seem better than it was.

He reined his horse to the right at a fork and soon saw haloed lights of a farm or tiny village up the road. He thought of stopping to secure a meal—guesting was taken seriously here where everyone had the sorcerous enemy in common—and was about to head his horse across a field when he heard a scuttling in the tall corn planted by the roadside.

He set the bay after the sound: anyone who ran away, time had taught him, should be chased and caught and questioned.

Between the rows of saddle-high corn over squishing, muddy ground his horse cantered slowly, ears pricked forward, nostrils wide—then leaped ahead suddenly and veered sharply left, and ran the skulker down, trampling its vestments, heavy with mud, so that as the figure fell it sobbed a bit, too winded to scream.

He knew it was a woman as he backed the horse and slid down into ankle-high mud; he didn't realize it was a pregnant girl until he tried to turn the curled-up form and was bitten on the wrist and clawed. He couldn't risk a torch; he couldn't wrest an answer from the pale, thin face smeared with mud or make the frightened eyes meet his own. But the child was near her term and hardly older than he had been when he came out of Bandara. He'd hurt her, too. Cursing his horse and his luck he hoisted her up on his saddle and led the bay through the field until, one hand holding the girl in place and the other on his reins, he came up to the farmhouse's back door.

But the people who wouldn't open it swore they didn't know her; they refused to guest a "Rankan barbarian and your filthy slut."

Back on the road, he swung up behind her, wondering if it was blood or rain that ran down her legs, and whether she spoke any language at all. She responded to none of his six.

A few miles farther on he saw a jut of table rock he remembered. There was a cave there. He'd leave her with a blanket, his full wineskin, and make her a fire; she wasn't his problem; she wouldn't talk to him or acknowledge him though her buttocks were pressed against him as they rode double—she might, he thought, be feeble-minded.

He kept hearing a wolf howl, plaintive whines and occasional sneezes off in the pines that grew thickly on either side. It could be a pack. If the girl was bleeding, not just wet, the smell would have drawn them. When he urged the horse off the road and up an incline to where the cave he recalled still gaped, he could hear wet pine needles rustling and water cascading down from low branches.

He pulled her off the horse and carried her into the cave and put her down. The whole time she said nothing, didn't even stiffen, just endured him.

He ducked back out to get a blanket and his flint and an oil-soaked torch to light inside while he looked for dry dung or branches to make the fire. His horse, drop-tied, was snorting and rolling its eyes, dancing in place: the wolves. He calmed it and got what he wanted from its saddlebags, slipping off its headstall so that if it had to fight, it would be at no disadvantage.

He was just turning to go back inside when once more he heard a sneeze, followed by a whine. And there above the cave, upon the rock, its eyes luminous, was a timber wolf, sparse moonlight glinting off its wet fur.

It sprang down to the flat ground before the cave and Niko stepped back reflexively, drawing the sword Askelon had given him, its hilt warm in his hand. Magic was about—the wolf, perhaps.

"Come on then, wolf. Come try your luck." Before the cave's mouth, the beast bristled, its ruff thickening. It whined. It sneezed. It shook itself all over. It sat on its haunches and rubbed its nose and then its eyes with one paw.

And as he watched, it began to change, to shimmer and to grow until, as he circled to get a better look and his hackles rose and his mouth dried and he blinked to try to pierce illusion, a naked man—a youth, nearly hairless— crouched there.

It sneezed again, then grabbed up a leaf and blew its nose and waved its hand before it where a pile of clothes and an oil lamp came to be.

"What in Enlil's—?" Niko began to close.

Sniffling loudly, the apparition raised its head and said thickly, as if it couldn't breathe through its nose: "Stealth, called Nikodemos? Let's not curse in any Names here." Its n's sounded like d's and its h's were silent.

Niko lowered his sword and crouched down to indicate a truce.

The manform was struggling into its clothes now. In the light of the oil lamp at its feet, dressed and sopping, red-nosed and teary of eye, it looked like a badly-set table in its Rankan mageguild formal wear: the girdle, lacy and embroidered with the devices of its rank, proclaimed it a Hazard-class magician, junior grade.

It said: "I'm Randal. Of the Tysian branch of the Rankan mage—"

"—guild, I see. What do you want of me, Hazard?"

An explosive sneeze wracked it: "Begging your pardon, Stealth. I'm allergic to animals, fur most of all. Every time I have to do this," he bent down, fumbled in the diminished pile before him, came up with an embroidered handkerchief and blew his nose, "it brings on an attack. I hate animal forms. That's why I'm still a junior. . . . Drink?"

The Hazard waved a hand and a canopy materialized above them, a great metal bathtub on silver bulls' backs in the midst of it, a fire beneath to keep the water hot. Beside this was a table set with victuals fit for a mageguild fete. "Don't look at me like that, fighter. It's not catching. It's just the hair . . . it gets in my nose."

Niko's horse had scrambled back a hundred yards when the striped pavilion had appeared from nowhere. He said: "I've got to see to my horse," and backed out of the light.

As Niko watched from what he hoped was a safe distance, the mage hiked up his robes, tucked them in his girdle, poured himself a goblet of wine mulling so that its spices, wafting on the dank and drizzly wind, reminded Niko how cold and tired he was, then climbed up to seat himself on the bathtub's curving rim, his feet in the steaming water up to his knees. *"That's* more like it. By the Writ, I hate these field excursions. Aaah . . ."

Niko, at his horse's head, spoke soothing words and filled the bay's feedbag. To do so, he had to sheath the sword. Then he had no more excuses (except the girl in the cave beyond) not to deal with this enchanter, who had gone to so much trouble to seem benign. But they never were. Promising himself not to eat or drink or believe anything offered him by the shape-changer, he approached and stood just beyond the canopy's shelter.

"Come join me?" There was a whiney tone to the

Hazard's voice. Niko remembered the wolf-sounds which had accompanied him for the last few miles.

"You've been following me. What do you want?"

"Randal. My name is Randal." The mage snuffled as he reminded Niko of this. And: "Would you hand me that other handkerchief there? Steam's best for this. But then my nose runs worse . . ."

Trying not to chuckle, Niko brought it over. The warmth of the water was no illusion. The steam and the heat were enticing. He said: *"Were* you following me, Randal? If so, why?"

"*Why?* Because you haven't had the grace to check in with the mageguild. Don't you people ever collect your messages?"

"Messages? I have no friends who'd—"

"*Every*one who's *any*one sends messages north and south through the mageguild network."

"Fine. What's the word you've brought? And from whom?" The mage had prodigious ears and a long, swanlike neck. It was hard to fear him, but Hazard-class status was not easily reached. Even a junior had power.

"Word? Well, it's not *exactly* words . . . it's a dream . . . this dream I had."

"Go on."

"I'm *tell*ing you. The dream lord—Aškelon—came to me in my sleep, and that's why I'm here. I wasn't going to do this. I refused. Very brave of me . . . after all, he's not *our* archmage. But then I . . . changed my mind."

"There's a pregnant girl in that cave who's injured. Can you do anything for her?"

"Aren't you going to rape her and kill her? I don't want to interfere. I'll just give you your message and depart. . . ."

"If you can do all this, you can take her with you. I'll pick her up when I get back to Tyse."

"*If* you do. We'll strike a bargain, then—"

"I don't bargain with warlocks."

"Then she'll die, with or without rape and torture. Your message from the dream lord is as follows: you're supposed to tell Tempus that he must call on Aškelon and . . . ah, some woman or other (I've left my notes behind) . . . if he wants their assistance. And on a personal note—this I can quote: 'Be strong. Control your mind. Heed your dreams. Guard your soul.' That ring any bells?"

Niko shook his head mutely.

Randal looked at him askance. "Well, it's something you forgot, it seems—something the entelechy was quite anxious that you remember." The mage's watery eyes were narrowed on him now. "Doesn't sound quite like you'll be riding back to Tyse this evening, does it?"

Niko's sword rasped out. When its point touched the young mage's Adam's apple, its hilt, always warm, heated perceptibly in his grasp as it had when he fought sorcery in Vashanka's temple. "I'll be fine. Don't worry about me. Now here's the 'bargain': take the girl and disappear, or I'll send your soul with hers to buy her a better death than the life she's had."

The sword, touching the mage's flesh, would anchor him as long as contact was maintained.

Snapping his fingers to no avail, the Hazard found this out. Then he said, "Agreed," Niko lowered his weapon, and mage and pavilion and bathtub and lamp—and girl, he found when he went to check—were gone. All that was left was the wine, mulling in its bowl, to prove he hadn't dreamed it—and the message, which sounded so familiar.

Grillo had suggested to Tempus that he look in on one of Niko's "skirts," a girl-child named Cybele who lived down by Peace River in higher style than most refugees could afford. The Rankan officer hadn't made a point of it, but mentioned it offhandedly—that was Grillo's way. What prompted the suggestion, Tempus still wasn't sure as he backed a big roan war-horse of no particular breeding out of its stall to curry and saddle it. He'd chosen the gelding from Grillo's string, as he'd chosen the squadron billeted at Outbridge from Grillo's pool of specials, based on Niko's recommendations and Grillo's advice. Like the horse, the men would do for the nonce.

Across the barn, Niko's pregnant mare stuck her blazed head over her stall's door and whickered at him. He left the roan cross-tied and went to stroke her. She missed Niko, but the foal she carried was nearly priceless now, with both the Trôs stallions gone. He felt the loss of his Trôs horses more sharply than that of Jihan: she might have deserted him of her own accord, and Datan's taunt might be no more than opportunistic lies on the archmage's part, but the horses would never have left him willingly. He wanted them back.

The manifestation of Stormbringer during the Outbridge sack lent credibility to the claims of Wizardwall's warlock, though. One way or the other, he'd soon find out the truth of it. Rear echelon checkpoints had sent word that the first of the Stepsons' units was within a day or two of Tyse. An advance pair of Sacred Banders had come in shortly after Niko had gone north to arrange the meeting with Bashir. Everything was proceeding apace, despite Bashir's recalcitrance and Grillo's reluctance to share information.

Yet the meeting he'd had with the advance pair was troubling: they'd nearly killed their horses trying to catch up with Niko on the trail. But it wasn't only their failure to do so which prompted their distress. Hesitantly they confided that it was possible that Niko was possessed. Even under the circumstances they described—Abarsis's manifestation at Janni's funeral, the reappearance of the enchanted cuirass among Niko's other effects, Niko's manic insistence on leaving alone long before he was fit to travel— they had been reluctant to put a label on what they'd seen. But love had won out over honor, and the pair who had left early at Crit's behest to "follow close enough to help if he needs you but not so close that he can see you if he does not" had confided in Tempus: Niko couldn't have outdistanced them so thoroughly without supernatural aid; even had *he* been in perfect health, the pace should have killed the mare. It hadn't. Tempus had merely nodded and assured them he would respect their confidence and take care of the matter in whatever fashion seemed appropriate. Their relief had been palpable. He'd assigned Ari to show them around, after warning them that discipline among the Outbridge mercenaries and the quality of these fighters in general was less than what the Stepsons were used to, and left them to their own devices.

When the entire cadre was in Outbridge, all his personnel problems would shake out without him having to exacerbate rivalries by giving disciplinary orders or seeming to favor one unit over another: Critias wouldn't tolerate the sort of laxity that Haram, Grillo's ranking task force leader, permitted.

He led the saddled roan out into the cloudy night. The rain had abated, though thunderheads still masked the sky to the north. The moon was setting. Riding through the double gates with a wave to the sentries, he considered what he'd learned. There was some truth behind the Sacred Band pair's worries. Niko should have mentioned the return of the cuirass; though the young mercenary was retiring by nature, he wasn't secretive. And yet, thinking back to their reunion in Tempus' quarters, it was clear to him that the youth had been wearing the very panoply in question. Niko had been exhausted, and Tempus consumed with the feat of healing—it could have been just an oversight, after all. Possession was a serious accusation, nothing to be taken lightly. Often, one so afflicted could be cured only by death. He hoped that this would not be so in Niko's case.

It was late to be abroad in Tyse; he met only garrison

soldiers, a team of Grillo's covert actors, and two of his own three-man patrols on his way to Peace Falls.

Commerce Avenue, when he crossed the border and turned onto it, was thronged even this late.

On a whim he stopped to buy some krrf at Brother Bomba's, a full-service establishment of the sort for which Commerce Avenue was famous, and spent a pleasant interval trading rumor and innuendo with Bomba's statuesque wife, a canny woman who had been a camp follower and then a mercenary barber-surgeon in her younger days, and thus had guild standing and a second income as an information monger of unparalleled expertise. Too, because of her unusual history and the breadth of her travels and experience, her black-market connections were as singular as her informants, and she pressed on him a little satin pouch of pulcis, with a twinkling eye, saying it had come straight from hell via a famous krrf dealer in Caronne whom she named. And: "You know, don't you, sleepless one, that the man's the uncle of one of your sellswords? Stealth, his war name is. Get the boy to send his uncle a note and we'll be up to our buttocks in pulcis, and share the profits." Madame Bomba's drug-reddened eyes glittered in a weathered face which had once been beautiful. Pulcis, which took the mind on out-of-body excursions and was as thoroughly habit-forming as indescribable ecstasy tended to be, incapacitated its users only evanescently, leaving a residue which made of men supermen and of women seeresses and sexual athletes for up to a week following a single dose. But it was rare and costly.

Still, Tempus sensed a different purpose: "So coy with me, Mistress Bomba? If not for your husband, whose good will I'll keep, I'd rape the truth from you. As it is, you've earned a tweak." He reached for her under the table.

She sighed at his touch, then cowered in mocking, girlish fear. They played this game at every meeting. She was a woman he respected, and that respect had been earned over years of servive to the armies. Not for her the cosmetic spell or cheap jewels of the aging wench. She traded on her acumen and was delectable for her wisdom. They'd often joked of murdering Bomba and running Peace Falls in tandem.

But now she took a lock of hip-length, gray-streaked hair and twirled it round her long fingers, whose skin was crinkling but whose bones still bespoke fine breeding, strength and skill. She was a fraction of his age, yet looked a decade older. "My guest, dear friend, tales are told . . . many of them unwelcome. You love your Stepsons. Will you hear a bad word of one?"

"I'll hear you."

"Stealth brought a girl in here we don't think suits a son of the armies."

"Niko keeps strings of girls like other men keep horses. But they are children, mere fuzz . . . What's he done, deflowered one of yours?"

She chuckled heartily, stabbed over her shoulder toward a curtained door behind which boys and girls took lovers for the enrichment of the house. "Mine? I've none intact right now, and that's how he likes 'em. But I've a barmaid who swells up all over with hives when she's close to a Nisibisi witch or warlock—bought the charm from one of the mageguild Hazards and had it put on her myself."

"So?"

"So, when she was serving them, she began to itch. She must be new hereabouts—the one he escorted in, that is—no one knows her. But talk to Randal at the mageguild local, if you don't believe the spell's well cast. It's never yet been in error." As she spoke, she apportioned krrf for them, and they both partook while Tempus thought that over.

"You haven't told this tale about? To Grillo, perhaps?"

She feigned insult. "You *are* turning into a filthy Rankan

barbarian, friend, to think such a thing of me. *Is* he Grillo's, then? Or still yours?"

"Some think he's one of Grillo's specials. . . ."

"I'm not one who believes that lions follow jackals' orders, Riddler. I'm not like the widow Maldives, who runs to Grillo with every morsel of intimacy you slip her . . ." Fist to her nose, she snorted loudly, smacked her lips as she swallowed the krrf that ran down the back of her throat. "Do take care, love. We value thee, thy custom and thy trade."

He nodded, paid his bill, and took his leave of her, nothing learned there he hadn't suspected.

On the avenue, where the roan was tethered, an unfamiliar voice hailed him. He turned around and there in Brother Bomba's shadowed doorway spied its source as he mounted up.

He'd had enough conversation; he backed his horse into the street, not acknowledging the other, but the man left the porch and came after him, so he stayed the roan to let the stranger have his say: "What is it, man? I'm late for an appointment."

"My name is Randal," said the short-haired, large-eared stranger, whose neck was long and clothes wet and streaked with mud. "I believe my name was taken in vain in there . . ." The slight man in mageguild robes stepped closer. Tempus's knees counseled his mount to back a pace. The mage kept up, saying: "I know how you feel, but please don't make me shout."

"Speak, then, mageling."

The junior Hazard stiffened perceptibly, his flush evident even in the street's torchlight. "I've been on an errand for powers concerned with you. Don't ask me who. And I've come back bearing a burden your Nikodemos pressed on me—a pregnant child who'll give birth before dawn: her water's broken. Now, do you want him to collect it at the mageguild, or shall I deposit it at the Outbridge station?"

"I don't like my men involved with mage—"

"Not his fault or mine. I'm stretching matters, coming here. The least you can do—" the mage sneezed, wiped his nose on his sleeve, backed a half-step, cursing Tempus's horse under his breath but without invoking any names "—is listen. Will you?"

"Best hurry, boy," Tempus suggested. "My patience with your kind's worn thin through the ages."

"When Niko returns, be sure he remembers to tell you what I had to remind him he forgot." The mage stepped back then, quickly.

"That's it? The whole reason for this interview?"

"The pregnant girl," the mage called back. "Remember? Your place or mine? It matters not to me." Randal was plainly exasperated.

"Keep it. If he wants it, he'll collect it." *Pregnant girl?*

He wheeled his horse and rode away, wondering if he had patience enough left in him for baby Hazards and mistakes such as Niko seemed continually to be making lately.

Roxane, a/k/a Cybele, cursed so that the snakes, once again in her service, rushed for cover as soon as they'd slithered into her study to announce that Tempus was at the front door.

She wasn't prepared for him; she wasn't about to try him in battle, her magic against his deific mandate. All the tests she and Datan had undertaken suggested that the Storm Gods still favored him.

And anyway, she meant to use him to destroy Datan, not let Datan use him to destroy her. Having to apologize for what she'd done with Shamshi, and to stand by while Datan had taken the boy out of her hands in mid-adventure, had only hardened her resolve. And she knew Datan was watching her closely; he'd bade her come down here and work openly, doubtless expecting her to come up short against this dangerous "mortal" called Tempus. She didn't intend to let that happen.

She'd been busy, this evening, collecting souls and farming out murder to the death squads. The warlock who'd burned to death in the root cellar during Tempus's sack of the Outbridge headquarters was a restless, tortured spirit still—Datan hadn't lifted a wand to help him.

Roxane, long established in Tyse in the guise of a human revolutionary, knew all the death squad leaders of the insurgency, and fielded *dead* squads besides. This evening, the undeads had brought her three fat and dissipated souls stained with sin: she'd just been consigning them to a demon who would send them in coffle down to weigh against the slain warlock's soul. She'd wanted to wait and watch to make sure the scales balanced. The dead adept was a friend and confidant; he'd the right to expect her help.

Now she had to put her scrying bowl aside. A little water slopped out as she did so. She ran a finger through it and used its charm to hasten and strengthen her change into the "Cybele" persona, a body devoid of sorcerous indicators, unsullied and virginal so that even Niko's enchanted panoply didn't react to it. This and her presence in Stealth's confused mind were her most potent weapons at the moment.

She'd use them, she decided, and went to let the Riddler in, changing her home's decor as she strode through rooms, adding dust and scratches and creaking floorboards and moth-chewed holes in velvet drapes. Tempus must see what he'd expect, if she was to prevail. Too rich and fine a home would not do at all.

Nervous as the girl she seemed, she lifted the latch and loosened the thong and pulled the door back just a crack. Yes?" she quavered, smoothing down a wrinkled, high-necked robe she'd conjured. It was ecru and modest and spotlessly clean, threadbare at one elbow, but just the sort of bedclothes a noble child, chased homeless down from Vandor or Machad, might wear.

As a final precaution, she sent the snakes a wordless command which propelled them tumbling out the back door into the night. They were Datan's spies as well as useful thralls: she couldn't quite forgive them for the pain they'd caused her when the Osprey called them from her belly. Stupid snakes might misinterpret what she said or what she did. . . .

"I'm looking for a maid called Cybele," came Tempus's hoarse and raspy voice. Through the crack she could see him, towering, helmet under arm; his face, lit by the oil lamp on the doorpost, arranged—nonthreatening, noncommittal. "I'm a friend of Niko's," he added when she did not respond or open up the door, as if that explained it all.

She thought quickly, then exclaimed: "Niko? He's not *hurt?* You're of the army? Please!" She jerked back the heavy door with an artful, flustered stumbled. "Tell me he's not slain! Oh. . . . In, come in, kind sir. Tell me it's not bad news you bring!"

He stepped within, shoulders blocking the hall, leather and armor creaking, the smell of horse and whetstone and man and rain coming with him. She'd never thought to be this close. She backed away with mincing steps, a girl whose fingers shook as they covered her lips, who had obviously had experiences with soldiers come bearing tidings of loss and mourning, but who stood up straight and gave back glance for glance through wide and gentle eyes.

And he surmised what she'd hoped he would, assuring her that Niko was "on a mission . . . for me. I just thought to stop by and let you know whom to call on should you need anything while he's away."

She slumped at the "good news" and he reached out to catch her by the elbow. This was the test: she would see whether his flesh could contact hers without him sensing anything amiss—that she was no more or less than what she seemed. She mumbled her relief and welcomed him: "There's not much here . . . a bit of beer he's left, some young potato wine. He'd want you to have it, sir. . . . Are you Grillo, then? He's said that name to me. . . ." Making girlish guesses, prattling on, she led him into the front sitting room, more modest than it had been moments before, and fetched pottery cups and a wine jug from the sideboard, asking questions the Riddler wouldn't want to answer—about where Niko was and why and how long he'd be away.

"We can't say, I'm sure he told you. Has he left you enough money? Don't hesitate to say if he has not."

She tossed back tawny hair and demurred bravely that Niko had provided for her, then hesitated: "—as best he could." And she let her face show caution, then, and a pretense of dissembling he'd see right through: "And I have my own means, my inheritance . . ." Then, a trace of fear to spice it: "I shouldn't be talking with you this way. You haven't even said your name. How can I be sure you are a friend of his, and not an enemy? How can I know I'm not endangering him?" She rose. "You'd better go!" She saw to it that he noticed how her hands, wringing one another, trembled.

He chuckled, an odd laugh with gravel in it, and cocked his head at her: "Grillo's name's on many tongues hereabouts. You've not broken any confidence by using it to me. But I wouldn't tell anyone else who might come by that Niko's even gone. Do you understand me? A girl your age in a house like this . . . alone . . . you'd want to give the impression that he'll be back at any time." He put down the ceramic cup he was holding and stood up: "I'll be going, as you've asked. If you come to think you need protection, or find you're short of funds if he's gone longer than he expected—or if you worry and need news of him, send word to the mercenaries' hostel or the Outbridge station by any soldier with crossed lightning bolts or bulls upon his armband. Or call at Brother Bomba's and tell Madame Bomba you need a loan. Security in my name— Tempus. She'll give you what you need."

She thanked him and rushed toward him, grasping his hand and pressing it to her cheek. She hoped she hadn't overdone it. But her success had emboldened her; she'd try to enlarge upon this contact, see him again. "I've been so worried, so lonely," she blurted out. "I feel much better now you've come. I'm afraid to go out, and since the dog died I'm afraid in the night. . . ."

Until he'd crossed her threshold and donned his helmet and mounted, she stood watching. Except for his odd little smile and the alertness in his eyes, she'd have been sure that she had fooled him. As it was, she'd gained the promise of a watchdog, courtesy of the armies, and even a way to insinuate herself into the Riddler's very company, should she dare or need to try.

When he'd gone, she conjured guests for a celebration: three undeads, friends of Niko's, who might just be drafted into service before too long.

It was time to pull tight Niko's string; pregnant girls and magelings bearing messages from the dream lord were no part of Roxane's plan. Niko mustn't get back with word to Tempus; or he must forget again. Or she must find some way to use the meddling of the entelechy of the seventh sphere to her advantage: if Tempus sought out Datan and made an end to him, not Roxane or any other witch or adept of Wizardwall would scour the hills for souls to buy him peace. He'd not lifted a finger for any of them. And each time she did what Datan should have done, for spirits languishing in immemorial recompense for the favors they'd enjoyed in life, she made sure that each shade in question knew that it was she, *not he*, who bought them out of purgatory.

Thunderbolts clashed in the sky over Tyse and along the Nisibisi border lightning furrowed the earth in rows as if the gods had turned to farming, though gods had no hand in calling the tempest raging overhead: the wizards of Nisibis were testing the Tysian mageguild's strength.

Now and again a canny bolt came to ground in Tyse, unparried. One had struck the old stones of the palace; whether any had survived within, none could say. One had struck the altar pits within the free zone, crawling blue and bright along the ground until every god's abode was singed and blackened. One had struck the northern garrison, lighting fires which touched off magazines of corn and wheat and naphtha: the entire northern quadrant was ablaze.

At midday, the black smoke from the north on the black wind from Nisibis under the black clouds above made the staunchest man doubt his senses: those without knotted ropes which burned away the hours soon lost all track of night and day.

In Peace Falls, mercenaries stayed close by their horses; some slept with favorites in their stalls, in wetted straw with blindfolds near and wineskins filled with bubbling water mixed with soda to soak kerchiefs for their noses if they had to fight their way through noxious smoke; some gamed and argued in the tackrooms over whether the Tysian mageguild could hold its own; others simply waited for the change of ad hoc shifts: twenty men here had drawn straws for the early watch over more than sixty horses. No one groused or shirked this duty: without their mounts, any cavalry such as the newly-arrived Stepsons were next to useless.

Entering Brother Bomba's with three Sacred Band pairs

in their wake, Critias and Straton were offered hot towels
to wipe the ash and trail dust from face and hands by a
yet-comely matron who introduced herself as Madame
Bomba: "By the god, are ye Sacred Banders or chimney-
sweeps? If you've reservations, it's our pleasure to serve
ye? Come now, lieutenant, I didn't catch the name? . . ."

Pulling out a slate, she pursed her lips, detaining them
in the foyer so that Straton looked about for hidden traps
or hostiles crowding in behind the six Stepsons in the
narrow, darkened hall.

Crit slapped the towel down into the woman's hand.
"Critias, I'm called, if it's any of your concern. Either let
us in or turn us out. We're eight and we're not in the
mood—"

"There, there, Critias. Yes, I've your name right here.
And these others? . . ." To Crit's surprise, she named each
of his men, nodding at the end: "That's it, then. The whole
lot, present and accounted for. Come this way, gentlemen."

And she led them in, around a blind corner to a smoke-
filled, taper-lit dining room with linen on the tables and
clean, well-dressed women at the bar. "The Riddler wants
you all to make yourselves at home here," she confided,
taking Critias by the arm, "where a man can do as he
might please without being misunderstood. In there—"
she pointed to a curtained arch with filigree at its apex
"—you'll find an upstairs and a downstairs . . . *up*stairs is
for what upstairs is always for—rest and matress sports;
*down*stairs we've smoking rooms and substances of many
sorts."

"Just food, a little wine. We were told we'd meet with
our—"

"I *know* why you're here. We'll send word to the Riddler,
as we've done with your mates. You've a full twenty-four
hours entertainment here, by Tempus' decree and mine.
So enjoy, gentlemen . . . it's on the house."

And she left Critias by a window table in the room's far

corner, set for four, though only he and Strat sat there.
The others, when he looked about, were scattered throughout the room—deployed, he admitted, as well as he could
have done it, so that every entrance was covered and yet
no one sat alone—and he hadn't had to ask, as he usually
did, in a place like this, to be seated against a wall.

"What do you think?" Strat asked him. "Or have you
fallen in love?"

"Half," Crit smiled bleakly. And: "This *is* where we
were told to report. If there's a trick to it, we'll deal with
it when it comes."

What came was a peaches-and-cream serving wench
with a bosom modestly covered in lace to her throat, who
gave a recitation of the menu and recommendations as to
what was best, then lemon-chicken soup and crown of
lamb in quick succession, with a light white wine to wash
it down and asparagus and rice with onions on the side.

"Am I dreaming?" Straton wondered, wiping his bearded
lips. "This is hardly the 'three hots and a flop' I'm accustomed to."

"The poison hasn't hit yet; dream on." Crit wasn't entirely joking. He'd let the girl choose their menu but
waited until she'd seen Straton clear half his plate before
partaking of what surely must be black-market delicacies.
There was quite a bit wrong about this place, so calm and
sedately mannered when magewar raged outside. Every
now and then the floorboards shook, or a flare of lightning
brightened convivial dimness, reminding him of where he
was, and why. But Tempus's orders had been specific:
they were to rendezvous here even before they talked to
any officials at the hostel. And that hadn't been easy to
do.

When Tempus appeared in the curtained archway, Crit
had just decided to find the Bomba woman again and
have a heart-to-heart.

"That's the biggest dog I've ever seen," Straton remarked

as Tempus, in sooty corselet and cloak, and the huge black dog with the ferocious demeanor came their way.

"Well met, Critias. And just in time." Tempus sat, and the dog—or wolf, for it was that big and strong—crawled under the table from where emanated a sneeze and a growl which made Straton tilt his chair back, one foot up on its rung. "Straton, life to you."

Straton saluted Tempus, eyes on the tablecloth's hem.

"It is with great relief and pleasure that I return your band to you," Crit said, only a sidelong glance at Straton revealing his wish to make his report privately.

But Strat knew him; the fighter was already getting up. "I'm ready to see what lies beyond those curtains. *If* you won't be needing me, commander?" He grinned mischievously.

"In an hour, come back down." Tempus smiled a tiny smile all Stepsons knew well: some action or other was in the offing, blood about to be shed, fur to fly: it was in the Riddler's noncommittal, glittery eyes.

"With pleasure, my lord. The trip's been dull, long and too full of boring reminiscences I've heard before. May I assume we'll be—?"

"Strat, you've got an hour," Crit broke in.

"Right." And he was gone.

"I regret I'll have to cut your recreation short . . . you've seen the state of things, Critias."

"What I can do about it? I don't know, but I expect you'll tell me. The woman here, Bomba, knows more about us than I'd think prudent."

"She's a good friend. You'll billet here, with this last six of yours. Objections?"

"None. Everyone else in all right? The advance pair? The balance? She said we're 'all accounted for'."

"Stepsons, yes. But Jihan's gone, and both Trôs horses. Niko is out seeking Bashir—we've much to cover, and no time to spare." And Tempus proceeded to debrief him concerning the state of affairs he'd left in Sanctuary, the replacement Stepsons, what had been done for Tamzen's father, whether the bodies of the children had been found, matters of covert enterprise concerning the Beysibs, Jubal's hawkmasks, One-Thumb and the vampire who lived in Shambles Cross.

Though he had some successes to report, Crit had thought to leave those stones unturned—Sanctuary's problems were in essence insoluble; they would keep until the avenging was done and glory won in battle. If not for the fact that he'd left the town in the care of guttersnipes and slit-purses who were free to maraud in the name of Stepsons, he'd not have given the blighted south a second thought, he admitted. The wise and the prudent fled Sanctuary by the score, like fleas departing a dead Downwind dog.

Tempus nodded matter-of-factly, looked around, leaned closer and said, "Speaking of dogs, this one's to go to a house on Peace River, a mile downstream from the falls. I want you to deliver it to a young woman who calls herself Cybele, one of Niko's girls. The house is large, and the girl is suspect, and you're to tell her it must have its krrf three times daily—this much." Tempus pulled a silver box from his belt and apportioned enough of the drug for a long evening's revel into a packet, then held it out. Crit took it.

"Suspect?"

"Niko's having problems. Possession is a serious charge. We need to confirm the allegations or dismiss the charges. The dog will do that."

Crit knew better than to ask how the dog could help: "Possession? He's still not right? I'm sorry. But about the woman—anything we should know?"

"You and Straton shouldn't have any trouble. She's expecting the dog and swears she lives alone. Tell her you've come from me and you're a friend of Niko's, but don't be forthcoming. I'll brief you thoroughly when you return, but right now . . . what you don't know, she can't find out."

"A witch, then?"

"Maybe. Maybe just a girl. He's been picking up strays. There's another at the mageguild, a girl of thirteen who has just given birth to a son—"

"Not even Niko works that fast."

Under the table, the dog whined. Tempus shook more krrf into his palm and stuck his hand under the table. The dog, in its haste to have its treat, made the table shudder and the wine cups teeter.

Crit did some mental addition: *Trôs horses gone; Jihan missing; billet here instead of the hostel or Outbridge.* "Well at least you've got some interesting work for me. I won't pretend I liked mollycoddling that bunch of ersatz swordsmen we left behind any more than chaperoning this lot up here." Crit's eyes shifted to one of the Sacred Band pairs just disappearing beyond the curtain.

"When you finish with the dog, go familiarize yourself with Grillo's specials—Haram's their task force leader; insert a team as close to Grillo as you can without seeming obvious—set up your own network, use whomever you like, reassemble your old task force . . . whatever you think the situation requires. But watch Grillo—he's one for playing angles. Stay away from the guild representative, Vasili, as much as possible, or he'll read you the rulebook. We'll be writing our own rulebook for this one."

"Just what I hoped you'd say."

Riding through the ashen streets with Critias toward the house where they were supposed to deliver the huge, black wolf of a dog that Tempus had entrusted to them, Straton waxed uneasy. A krrf-sniffing dog was in itself an oddity; this one, trotting docilely beside them, spooked the horses for no apparent reason.

Crit had come from his meeting with Tempus cranky

and self-absorbed—worried, he admitted when Straton
pressed him, that sorcery was involved in this endeavor,
no matter how straightforward it seemed. Deliver the dog
to Niko's girl, make sure she understood that it must have
its krrf, and get out of there without any additional
conversation.

What business Niko had setting up a girl in noble fashion in a private house a mile downstream from the falls so
that white water murmured by its back door and the
small sounds a guerrilla fighter counts upon to warn him
in moments of danger were masked, Crit couldn't, or
wouldn't, say.

Niko was north on assignment; a mercenary's women
weren't usually his commander's concern. And this whole
set of circumstances reminded Strat so much of Ischade
and the house by the White Foal in Sanctuary that he was
anxious to be done with it: Ischade's beautiful, inky-eyed
face haunted him still. Crit had made a point of keeping
Straton well out of whatever arrangements he might have
made with her. It hurt Straton's pride to see Critias go to
such lengths to protect him; it hurt worse to feel that Crit
was right: he'd been bewitched by the vampire woman.
This chink in his armor still rankled.

"There it is." Crit pulled up his horse and wiped a sooty
wrist across his brow. Purple thunderheads looming to
the north were underlit by the fires yet blazing so that it
seemed they rode in perpetual sunset, though it was only
midafternoon.

The dog, uncanny and weird, sat down on its haunches,
its tongue lolling. It sneezed, rolled its eyes, and bayed as
if at the moon. Somehow, it sounded distinctly frustrated.

Lightning flared; thunder followed; his horse shivered,
tossing its head. "I wish it would *rain*." Straton's nose
was stuffy from the grit he'd been inhaling; the sky
threatened, but never made good.

"We'll just drop off the dog and leave. No long talks.

She may be a friend of Niko's, but I got the impression that the Riddler wants to to be discreet."

"Send it with a note on its collar, then. It's smarter than some Stepsons I've met." The reference to the recruits they'd found for the Sanctuary unit made Crit turn.

"Don't start. At least we haven't got that whole crew of sellswords to wetnurse. A task force is more my size. I'd say we ought to count our blessings."

"Count 'em after we've walked away from this one. Do you think there's a special reason *we're* making this delivery?" Not for the first time Straton wondered why he always ended up in these covert enterprises, rather than facing ⌐ clean and mortal enemy on a nice, daybright field of batٟle.

"He'll tell us, later. Or not. It's not our job to speculate." Critias spurred his horse forward. He called back: "Come *on*, Straton. Or stay behind. I want to get this over with."

Straton wasn't going to stay behind. There had been altogether too much of that lately. He loosed his horse's reins, and it leaped to catch up, sharing his own feelings about hanging back.

Cybele's house, once they'd ridden up an overgrown path to its front door, loomed forbiddingly in the gloom. Lightning flashed, blue-white, and it looked worse: once a noble building, it had fallen into disrepair. Ivy crawled over its two stories, loosening stones and blocking windows; high shade trees scraped its roof. Its windows gaped blackly.

Tethering their horses and walking up to an overhung, trellised door with the dog between them, Straton wondered again what interest the Riddler had in Niko's love life, and whether the dog had some significance—watchdogs were just not that rare, that Tempus would choose a special one—and whether Niko had finally pushed his luck too far.

Just as Crit was about to knock, the door opened.

He called the dog to heel, slapping his thigh, and announced to the face behind the latch-strap (wide and blue-eyed and decidedly unmagical looking): "Mistress Cybele? We've come from Tempus with the dog he promised."

The door closed in their faces, then opened wide.

Straton saw a girl of the sort Niko liked—young and fair and barely budding.

Her voice was cultured: "Oh, he's beautiful! Bring him in, please . . . come in."

"We've just got time to give you his feeding regimen and special instructions." Crit held out a piece of parchment. "You do read Rankene?"

"Oh, certainly, yes; I do." She was innocently fetching. She stared behind at the sanguine sky and shivered: "It's upon us, now, the war? I'm all alone and *he's* not home . . . I can't say how much this means." Stuffing the parchment in her belt she knelt down and cooed to the dog: "Come here, big boy, come on, come . . ."

The dog's fur bristled; his lip curled; he growled, backed up two steps, went forward three.

"That's a good puppy." She let him sniff her hand, then scratched his head. "What's his name?"

"He hasn't got one. You shouldn't make a pet of a watchdog. And he's high as he can be on krrf." As Cybele pulled her hand away and looked at them accusingly, Crit explained: "That's how they're best; he'll tear any intruder limb from limb, and he won't eat a poisoned treat put out to down him. You have to give him krrf three times a day." He held out a pouch of krrf worth a week's pay. "Else he'll get lethargic, seem to have a cold or worse, and maybe bite you in your sleep. Got that?"

"What's your name?"

Strat spoke: "We've got to go, soldier. We're late."

"Wait, oh please. Are you two friends of Niko's? Have you word of him—how long he'll be away? Your master said I could ask anyone wearing armbands like yours—?"

"We don't have a 'master,' girl." Straton jostled Crit;

the dog trotted inside the house. "Lock your door. Don't be so forward. Anyone could say they knew your friend and take this place right over, you're so anxious for company. If you were smart, you'd move into town. This is no place for a child."

Hurt showed in her eyes, and the door shut thereafter, leaving Critias shaking his head as they both walked away.

"Thank you, Ace."

"For what?" Strat asked.

"I don't know why, but I really wanted to go in there. Poor little thing, alone like that, Niko gone ... *And I know better.*"

Inside the house, the Stepsons gone, Randal was having second thoughts. Doing this for Tempus—infiltrating the abode of an alleged witch in the guise of a watchdog—hadn't been Randal's idea. Tempus had arranged it with the First Hazard, who in turn had come to him and put it in a way Randal couldn't refuse: a temporary truce between Tempus and the mageguild might lead to a permanent alliance; even if it didn't, joining forces to defeat Datan was in itself a worthy endeavor. And Randal, with the aid of correlative spells from the finest sorcerers in Tyse, would surely fool the witch. Nisibisi or not, she was basically no more powerful than the whole Tysian mageguild. Wizardwall's pretensions, of a master race and superior bloodlines born to enchantment, were nothing more than propaganda.

For himself, Randal would gain a grade—he'd be a junior no more, when this was over. All he had to do was perform this minor treachery with his guild behind him, and he'd be a full-fledged member of the Hazard class. He hoped Niko wasn't this witch's willing accomplice; that was treachery too foul. He didn't want to run home telling tales of venal Stepsons. Tempus had abrogated a long-standing rule of his by joining forces with enchanters;

every mage involved knew his Order to be on trial. If Niko was in feckless thrall, then all Randal had to do was figure out how to save him. He looked up at the Nisibisi witch and wagged his tail.

She called him: "Here, doggie."

He slunk over, stifling a sneeze and reciting in his mind a warding spell.

The krrf he had eaten should help maintain the spell and his courage, keep his allergies in check.

"Good dog, that's the boy," she crooned, and he strove to penetrate illusion, find the witch beneath the innocent facade. Her hands were soft and long, their touch on his ears and fur immensely pleasurable. If he hadn't smelled the sorcery—charm and ward and ophidian dankness—he'd think the Riddler might be wrong.

His eyes half closed reflexively; he knew his tongue lolled: one could not be an animal only in name. He opened them, an act of will, and saw her changing form before him, murmuring: "It's all right, hound puppy, see? I still smell—and *am*—the same."

From head to toe a dark shimmer cloaked the witch, descending, leaving a jet-haired, pale-eyed beauty where a comely child had been before. Her face was heart-shaped, arch and in essence ageless.

Despite himself, Randal whined and shivered and felt his belly touch the floor: this was not just *any* Nisibisi witch, but fearsome, fabled Roxane, bane of the Tysian mageguild, adept assassin, queen of undeads, "Death's Queen" in Nisibisi lore.

He almost howled; he froze, instead, in panic, hoping he could hold his form, not break and run as man or mouse or flea. He thought of all there was at stake: Niko's tortured soul, Tempus and an end to a bloodfeud with his brother mages which had gone on for centuries, his own life should Roxane see through his dog-disguise and all the krrf and brother mages he'd used to reinforce it.

Then he smelled snake so strong and close he almost gagged, and the witch rose up, taller now, and shedding a blue afterglow of power which lit the shadowed room, now more opulent and gracious in appointments than it had been before or any Peace Falls dwelling had the right to be, and told him "Stay," and disappeared through the farther doorway.

With Roxane gone, he calmed his heart and tried to think, but snake odor still assailed him, and he snuffled around the edges of the room to find its source. As he reached the doorway, he heard low sounds of conversation. His canine ears detected words, a man's: "Vasili's death won't—" and Roxane's: "Use this. It will tell the tale we need to spread, incriminate the Successors."

And then, as Randal sat quite still, his head cocked, something hissed close by, and a basket up against the wall began to teeter. He backed a step, then used his nose: therefrom, the smell of snake.

House snakes, writhing, tipped their basket over, then slithered out to arch up on their coils and hiss at him. The closest one, its tongue protruding, swayed back and forth, and the dog in him took over: he'd bounded in and fastened his powerful jaws on its neck, behind its head, before he knew it.

A cry, quite human, anguished, long, came forth from somewhere. Snakes have no vocal cords. He didn't pay attention. The instinct of his change-form had taken over: he shook it in his jaws and ground his teeth on its neck; it hardly struggled; its writhing soon ceased. He was chewing on it, its lifeless body stretched between his paws, when human feet appeared before him, and fearful curses rang out above.

Then: "Bad dog! Get back! Away!"

It was Roxane, and around her neck the second house snake curled, its tongue aflicker.

He'd done something wrong; he cowered, whined, sat

back and lay down flat, his expression as mournful as he could make it, his head between his paws.

He sensed her wrath, its smell, its fury. Then the rage darkening her complexion came visibly under control as three men in Tysian dress rushed in to see what the trouble was.

"Nothing, gentle sirs. My dog . . . he's new . . . he ate a house snake. Poor dog, he did what any dog would do." Her voice was tremulous. She herded the men back the way they'd come, and just in time: the house snake he'd been eating was beginning to take other shapes, in death mimicking every form its life had ever known.

Among the refugees in the free zone, Niko and Bashir moved easily, their horses left beyond the crumbling wall where the Successors' tunnel came up to ground level in a burned out, abandoned barn.

There was drizzle, now, and fog—an extra blessing. The fact that they were healthier than most, with all their teeth and limbs, well armed beneath their rags, was doubly-hid by weather. As for the rest—they reeked of garlic, or Niko did, from using fresh cloves of it to disinfect a long, deep scrape upon his arm he'd gotten in the tunnel; they were reeling slightly, tipsy from the blood wine Successors favored; and Bashir, morose and bellicose as he moved among the "Maggots," was ranting under his breath about "heartless Rankan overlords" and "Nisibisi witches" and "Mygdonian oppression" soon to come—in short, the Successors' leader was looking for a fight.

"You promised we'd not get drunk on this." Niko slapped the empty wineskin at his hip, grabbed Bashir's arm and steered him around a tumble of poke-ribbed children eating garbage in the street and ready to defend their pile of rotting rinds and suet and slop with sharpened sticks and jagged teeth.

"*I* am not drunk," Bashir replied thickly, shrugging Niko's hand away and walking an elaborately careful straight line for six steps before his arms shot out to balance him and he tottered.

Niko put out a hand to save Bashir from a fall, pretending he was steadying his own uncertain progress. "You're not. I am. And I can't show up like this. . . . We've your reputation to protect, if—"

"Excuse me." Bashir stopped, retched between two low black tents, then straightened, fumbling in his pouch.

"Here." He handed Niko a sprig of mint and a small packet of krrf mixed four-to-one with pulcis. "Chew the mint, snort the powder, and we'll be sober as foxes, sweet-smelling as farm maids, yes?"

Niko sniffed the clay-colored powder, the mint in his mouth, and everything around became preternaturally clear.

He handed the packet back to Bashir, who did likewise. "Shrivel me, that's better. Now, Stealth, escort me to your mighty, much-vaunted immortal. Let us steal upon him out of shadows, though, break through his perimeter as you did mine; it befits my mood to descent upon this meeting place from the rear."

"Anything is possible."

But when they got to the tent Tempus had designated as a meeting place, things looked less than hopeful: despite the need for secrecy, here in the free zone, a dozen operatives were stationed around the tent in varying degrees of disguise, their posture and their swagger belying darned mantles and three-day beards. One was off by himself, interrogating a prisoner lashed to a wagon's wheel, and that prisoner had the braided sidelocks of a Successor of Free Nisibis.

"Is this the kind of talk your commander thinks to have with me? Even for you, Niko, I'll not chance it." Bashir moved closer to him, dark eyes troubled in his oval, bearded face, his skin pallid in the foggy twilight, his broad forehead etched with worry lines.

"I know how it looks, what you're thinking," Niko whispered. "Stay here, out of sight. Be quiet. I'll give the jackal call, then come back *myself* to get you. If it's not me who comes looking, or you hear no call, then I'll be dead, and you'll be on your own. As for your man, there must be some good reason, but I'll see what I can do."

"Success, then."

"And to you." Niko slipped away, backtracked, crossed the dirt track and approached the tent and wagon from the upwind side.

A beggar/sentry rose and fell in behind him; a rug merchant left his stall and showed Niko his blade, saying, "Hold!"

"Hold yourself, Ari. You're about as subtle as a siege engine. What's afoot? Why is that Successor strung up there?"

The beggar behind backed off; Niko heard him grunt as he resumed his seat.

Ari pulled him by the elbow to his stall. "Afoot? Have you not heard? Vasili's been murdered . . . shot. The arrow in his neck was made in Free Nisibis—helical fletching, it's their handiwork, all right. And don't go marching over there to tell him his business . . . that one's the task force leader's boyfriend, some interrogation specialist . . . very nasty. It's nothing much to worry about—"

"Nothing *much*. . . . Does Tempus know of this? Where's Grillo?"

"In the tent, there. But no one's allowed inside . . . Niko? *Niko?*"

But Niko was already striding away, toward the tent. Halfway there, he was stopped by two men he didn't know and told the same: no admittance.

He considered mayhem, remembered Bashir, watching, and approached the interrogator instead.

"Turn this man loose." He clapped his hand on the interrogator's shoulder and spun him around: "Straton!"

The mud-specked, dirty face which had been scowling began to smirk. "Niko! I don't think you can save this one, but I warned Crit you'd want to try. Have you *seen* Crit? Or Tempus? You haven't, yet? They're waiting for you. This one'll keep. Come on, I'll take you in."

But Niko didn't move. "Let that man go. I can't bring Bashir in here with you torturing one of his people before his eyes . . ." He stopped before he made it worse. Straton was no one to offend.

"They killed the guild representative, Vasili," Straton shrugged. "Or at least that's what the evidence seems to indicate. I can't confirm it from any I've interviewed. But I'll wait on this one, until you've seen the Riddler. *Now* come with me."

Within the tent, Grillo, Critias and Tempus fell silent as the flap was raised and Straton ushered Niko through. "Niko has voiced some strong objections to the interrogation in progess. He thinks, with Bashir watching, it might not be a good idea."

Grillo's handsome head came up: "Bashir? Here?"

Crit, back to Niko, sitting crosslegged before a low map table, twisted in his seat. "That's something, anyway." In his hand he had an arrow with helical fletching. "Take a look at this." He bared his teeth. "And welcome back."

Niko, eyes locked eyes with Tempus, then examined the arrow and handed it back. "Plenty of men didn't like Vasili, myself included. And helically-fletched arrows can be had six for a soldat right here in the free zone. I brought someone important to you," he said to Tempus, "for reasons you said were sufficient. I can't believe you'd throw three weeks work and more away to find a scapegoat."

"*Do* you have him?" Grillo demanded.

"He got him," Crit said quietly, looking Niko up and

down, "he's just not sure that we deserve him. Let's prove we do: Straton, go turn that Successor loose with our apologies and some money."

"Gladly," said Strat, in a tone that said he'd expected exactly this result, and ducked through the flap.

"That suit you, Stealth? That's twice I've let a prisoner loose at your request. Sit down, and we'll debrief you before you bring Bashir in."

He refused: "I'm not bringing him in here. He's a friend of mine. He'll meet with the Riddler . . . alone."

Grillo's head snapped around, and he examined Niko, for the first time looking the Stepson in the eye.

Crit remarked that it wasn't only Grillo's specials who needed discipline. Stooped over in the low tent, Tempus came to stand beside Niko and said, very low: "Are you unwell?"

Then: "Come with me, we'll get some air, Niko. You two, try solving this murder mystery of yours another way. Niko's right: anyone can buy a Nisibisi arrow."

Niko followed the Riddler out into the twilight, and the light suited his mood. "Grillo's running weaponry and supplies to the Successors in exchange for drugs and security. I'm not supposed to know and I didn't tell you."

"Good. Now, Niko . . . do you have a message for me . . . something you forgot?"

"Forgot? I—" He froze, words stillborn on his tongue, remembering a wolf who spoke and a note he'd written to himself and put carefully away so that he would remember . . . and then forgot. He found himself on the verge of tears, unable to look Tempus in the face. Fumbling in his belt pouch, he found the bit of parchment and held it out. His hands were shaking. "Here. I . . . I'm sorry, sir. I don't know what's the matter with me."

Tempus took the grimy, wrinkled piece of parchment, read the text, nodded, and told Niko not to worry, that he understood Niko's problem, and was working on a solution.

For his part, Niko must only have faith and not question others' motives: the Sacred Band took care of its own. And: "Now, where's Bashir?"

"I can't tell you until you promise me he'll not be harmed. Not interrogated. Not detained."

"Done. Now, where is he?"

Niko told him, and Tempus nodded. "And signals? Have you any? Give them."

Niko explained about the jackal call.

"Take me to him. Introduce us and take your leave. I'll guarantee his safety. There's a girl waiting for you at the mageguild, I've been told, who's had a son. And other things to attend to, I'm sure. Take a few days rest. We'll call you when we need you."

They were walking circuitously toward Bashir's hiding place. "Bashir . . . we've both had too much blood wine and too much krrf and pulcis. You'd best explain about that Successor very clearly. And I know he wants to stay with me. We've arranged it. Down by the river, I've a friend with a house."

"Do you? All right. I'll see to it he discovers Brother Bomba's, and you can meet him there and take him with you, if he wishes. But he should stay at Outbridge, where we can offer him protection. I'll have to tell him that."

They skirted a pile of refuse. "And Niko? Your *maat*?"

Niko chuckled mirthlessly. "I can't even find my rest-place, anymore." He thought he should have lied, said that he was fine, but it wasn't true and he was sure that Tempus saw it.

At the proper distance, Niko gave forth a jackal call and heard an answer. They came up to the spot where Niko and Bashir had parted company; the Successor was no-where to be seen. "Bashir? *Bashir?*" he whispered, pulse pounding in his throat.

"Here."

Behind them, Bashir rose up from shapeless shadows, a

blade glinting in the lowering dark. "And who is this, Stealth?" He kept his distance, his weapon drawn but not threatening.

"My commander, the man we spoke of. Bashir, Tempus; Tempus—"

"I knew your father. He died on his feet, eyes uplifted," Tempus interrupted. "As you've seen, this is not a propitious time or place for meeting. Will you come with me to Outbridge? There I can offer you information, safe food and drink, and a bargain I think your father would have liked."

"Niko? What say you? Shall we trust him?" Bashir's upslanted eyes glittered in his broad face; his gaze went beyond them, to where the empty interrogation wheel was; his mobile mouth drew wide: he was teasing.

"Aye."

"Stealth has another assignment, he can't go with us. We've arranged for you two to meet later. Now, I must talk with you . . . alone."

Bashir grinned, a flash of teeth, and agreed, saying he knew that if anything *else* unforseen happened, Niko would take word home to the Successors. It was the most veiled of warnings.

"Nothing," Tempus promised, "is going to happen to you, Bashir, while you are my guest. Niko, you'd better hurry."

Dismissed, Niko wandered off alone through the havoc of the free zone, his eyes narrowed against the squalor in the streets, uncertain and uneasy. If Tempus was lying, if harm came to Bashir, then it was on Niko's head, a heavy debt to repay, an insupportable error. His mantle thrown wide to the night chill, its yellow lining keeping the refugees away, his armband turned round so that the Sacred Band bulls-and-lightning showed clearly, he passed through the gates and out into Tyse unchallenged by civilian or sentry.

Tempus knew about the girl his horse had injured north of the Nisibisi border. The mage Randal, then, must have kept his word. But somehow the Riddler had found out that Niko had made a bargain with the junior Hazard. Perhaps that was why he was being banished, dismissed like a picket and told to take "a few days rest."

Whatever Bashir and Tempus were going to talk about, Niko's commander did not want Niko to know.

Feeling pestilential and ill-used, he sought out the barn in which they'd left their horses and, ponying Bashir's, rode down to Peace Falls, downhearted and sick from the drugs and drink, dreading he knew not what: the undeads who had shown themselves in Free Nisibis wouldn't dare plague him here. He'd finished the krrf-and-pulcis mixture by the time he reached Cybele's river house. He was hungry and tired. He'd stopped in briefly at Bomba's to see if any of the Sacred Banders were there and had gotten so cool a reception from two of them that he'd left straightaway. It could be that all of them knew he'd had dealings with a Tysian magician; it could be that the loss of two partners had made him a pariah among those he loved the best.

When the bay was curried and went down on his knees with a whicker of pleasure to roll around in knee-deep fresh straw in his stall, and Bashir's horse was fed and watered, he went up to the house and found he had to knock; the leather latch-strap was drawn in, the door bolted securely. But there was light in the windows.

A dog barked furiously. Claws scrabbled against the door. He heard her voice and leaned his head against the doorjamb. At least Cybele would be glad to see him.

And she was, once she'd cautiously demanded to know who was there, pulling open the door and flying into his arms, her soft blond hair perfumed and silken against his stubbled cheek so that, laughing, he had to push her away.

But it was too late: the grime which had obscured the twining snakes and the glyphs of power on his cuirass had soiled her dress.

"No matter," she said, pulling him inside. "We'll clean your gear and put you in hot water—a bath; one for me, too." She giggled and he shut the door.

"That's a big dog." It curled its lip at him, cocked its head and sneezed. It was black, huge and formidable. Yet its tail thumped the floorboards, wagging, and it had not attacked him when he stepped inside.

"A gift from your commander. Oh, Niko, he came to *see* me while you were away, to see if I needed anything, and I said I was frightened, alone, so he sent me the dog. . . . You are frowning. You're angry? Why? He didn't mind."

Niko bent down and put out his hand. The dog offered its paw. He shook it gravely. "Some watchdog, this."

But she was already headed down the hall, calling back that she'd start his dinner and their bath at once, but that he must bathe before he ate.

In her tub, his panoply cleaned and hung upon a rack and his undershirt and breech burning in the oven (too filthy to be saved, she'd said), she joined him, laughing and teasing him, her nimble fingers rubbing the fatigue from his cramped muscles as if by magic. Grouse roasting and potatoes baking filled the whole kitchen with a wonderful aroma.

"I don't know how you do all this," he remarked, his head back, eyes closed, content to let her sponge the hot water over him, one hand upon her supple thigh.

"For you, I can do anything. Now you must tell me how you got so dirty, and what reason was good enough to keep you away from me so long." As she spoke, her smooth leg slid along him and the water, a perfect temperature, lapped against his chest.

"What's this?" She'd found the long scrape on his arm he'd gotten in the tunnel and she scrubbed at the garlickly scab there: "Primitive! Garlic does nothing for wounds, no more than for warding off magic. Only love heals." And she kissed him, touching him, then eased atop him so that his eyes opened to see her hair, golden with jewels of water drops in it, spread out upon his chest as her lips caressed him.

"Cybele!" He pulled her head up. "You cannot wait? You'll drown!"

"I have waited long enough for you," she pouted and one of the candles guttered, then another. In one of the other rooms, the dog began to howl.

He touched her breast and a sigh came out of her. "I've got to go out later. I'm so tired . . . if we make love now, I'll surely fall asleep."

"Good, then. Sleep is what you need. Why should *you* have to go back on duty?"

"No." He hoisted himself gently up and out of the tub. She followed, water shining on her skin, no petulance about her, to get him toweled dry.

"Sit!" she commanded, pointing to the kitchen table. She dried his hair and held his head between her breasts. He couldn't refrain from touching them, each in turn, or from kissing the water from her skin. She'd been a virgin when he took her off the street; she was a virgin yet. With young girls he'd found it best to let them wait until they couldn't wait a moment longer; then they had a good beginning, came to a man's arms slick and hot and free from doubt.

In the past, he'd let her mouth him, slept hard against her, nothing more till now. But tonight he couldn't hold back with her, or even wait to carry her upstairs to the soft feather bed he'd bought. He had all he could handle to raise her head from between his thighs and lift her young hips up and keep in mind that he had to breach her physical defenses gently. Once he felt her shield give way, he rolled them over, and while she gasped he had her

there on the kitchen table, stopping now and again to
make sure he wasn't hurting her, that her teeth, sunk in
his arm, were clenched from pleasure, not from pain.

She cried out that she loved him, and he'd made her
wait too long, and rose up under him and wrapped her
legs around him so that he had to get his shoulders under
her knees to gain control. And what he felt when she
began to quiver, he'd never felt in a new girl before, or in
his own response to one.

He said so: "Usually, it's not like this for me until later
. . . till a girl's experienced."

"I love you," she muttered thickly from underneath his
arm. "You'll need no other girls, just me. I'll make you
happy. You won't want—"

He chuckled, sliding out and off of her. That, at least,
was normal.

Then she sat bolt upright. "The potatoes! Oh, devils
save me; I've burned them." And naked, off she ran to
salvage his homecoming meal.

Somehow, she'd cleaned his gear and fed him and found
time to cuddle up against him and even fall asleep. He
held her in the crook of his arm before the hearth and
wondered if he had the strength to go out again tonight."
He mustn't keep Bashir waiting. . . .

He looked up, and the black dog was hovering near. He
thought at first it wanted scraps, to lick their plates, but it
stared at him and stared at him and sneezed and scraped
its nose.

Strangely, it seemed familiar. But no, it couldn't be. . . .
He put thoughts of wolves and mages from his mind and
set about dressing to go out; the first part (slipping out of
Cybele's embrace without waking her) was the most
difficult.

When he put his weight against the heavy door to open
it soundlessly upon its hinges, the black dog lunged past
him and out into the night.

\* \* \*

For the Stepsons' use, the Outbridge station now had a chapel dedicated to the gods of the armies and filled with implements of war. In Enlil's vault, Tempus met at length with Bashir of the Successors, deep below ground among the weapons and the dead.

This warrior-priest of Free Nisibis made Tempus uneasy: his upswept eyes which saw for gods and sometimes turned within, unseeing, to take Their counsel, reminded Tempus of Abarsis; in all other ways—from wide, flat face to broad, thick limbs—he was his father's son, long on guile and comfortable in the company of death-dealing, vengeful gods.

It was easier to enlist Bashir's aid in the assault on Wizardwall than to warn him of Niko's plight. A sortie upcountry with a warrior-priest of Enlil meant advancing upon warlocks with the god's sanction; the Successors' leader knew the crags and craved to pray atop them; to consecrate a temple to the Storm God where the Osprey's keep now affronted piety was Bashir's fondest dream.

But to explain why Niko's hospitality must be shunned, Tempus had to admit that he himself had entered into an accomodation with Tyse's mageguild. Even for Niko's soul's sake, this was hard to justify. Only Critias, of all the Stepsons, knew the full extent of the Riddler's involvement with the mageguild; even Tempus was distressed at having to join forces with the Hazards. Not in all the wars he'd fought had he ever warred in tandem with magicians; if Niko's predicament had not been his commander's fault, Tempus would have shunned them yet, and let the boy meet his damned and heinous end.

Revealing all to Bashir had been no part of Tempus's plan. A little bit, he'd thought to tell, enough to enlist the priest and pacify the gods who listened through his ears.

Then Crit came trotting down the stairs, smiling his most cynical smile: "Randal's here. I thought you'd want

to see him. He hasn't got much time." Crit's sharp eyes
assessed the progress of negotiations: the incense burnt,
the food spread out on polished stones, the wine jugs
spent by Bashir's unshod, propped-up feet. "I'll stay and
go over maps and some logistical considerations with
Bashir, if it pleases my lords? ... Also, Grillo's sent a
copy of a message from Adrastus Ajami, saying that Machad
will be Mygdonian by month's end; it's already under
siege."

Crit's forthcoming speech was for Bashir's benefit, to
let the priest know just how efficient and formidable a
network he was being inducted into, and where Critias
stood in Tempus's estimation—it was Crit with whom
Bashir would have to come to terms on a workaday basis,
since he was second in command.

"Bring him down, Critias. And I'll want you here. When
we're through with this, we'll all be going to Bomba's.
Arrange to be free for the rest of the evening."

Crit left to get the junior Hazard, and Bashir sat up
among his cushions: "I'm not sure this is the proper place
for meeting wizards, or that I should dignify this aberra-
tion by my presence ..."

Tempus merely stared at him until Bashir continued:
"But I've seen for myself that Niko's troubled; the gods
have turned away from him; Enlil has forgotten his name.
He spoke of going back to Bandara, the western sanctuaries,
when his tour with you is done, to try to solve his problems with the secular adepts. He's never been a man for
gods; I'd thought, since he was with *you*, perhaps this too
might change."

"Gods, these days, don't speak to me."

"Ah, but they look over your shoulder. Your Rankan
Storm God's penned by magic. Defeat Datan, and you
might loose the Pillager again. If He were not merely out
of play, Enlil would love to have you, but one god may not

vie with another for adherents. Jealousy among the planes causes havoc in the world of men."

"So my curse falls on innocents like Niko, and even the Nameless One's daughter—Jihan, from the loins of the Stormbringer Himself—is bound up in its evil."

Bashir picked his teeth with a thin, long blade that resided in his bracer. "There are other friends of yours . . . entelechies, lords of upper planes, one who rules the seventh sphere of dream and shadow. . . . Things, revered Riddler, are not so bad as you make them seem. We will rout the Osprey, reclaim your wondrous horses, free my friend's soul . . . like *that*." He snapped his fingers. "All Successors will rally to such a just and—"

"Six. I want just six of yours, and your own presence as upcountry avatar and spiritual guide. Until I'm cleansed of this taint of magic . . ."

By the time Critias brought Randal down, they'd finalized their pact and were on to specifics of the plan: Bashir would guide the Stepsons north, up Wizardwall's high peaks, if the gods allowed; Wizardwall and all its riches beyond what loot each Stepson could carry down would be Bashir's; the Successors would have their homeland, rule in their beloved mountains with no obligation to Ranke, Mygdonia, or even to the Riddler himself.

But Randal's report almost caused the newborn alliance to belly-up before it learned to swim: the junior Hazard, puffing hard and wild-eyed, was nearly addled from all the krrf he'd had to take to keep his allergies in check and his courage resolute, and the burden his new knowledge placed upon him:

"Riddler, my lords. . . . It's *Roxane* . . . not just *any* witch, but Roxane who's got Niko. He's nearly beyond salvage, enthralled for good. And her undeads . . . I heard her plotting with insurgents to use her minions to kill the mercenaries' representative, Vasili . . . use a Successor arrow, and thus set the mercs against the free men of

Nisibis. And there's her snakes—I killed one, couldn't help myself—but they're *not* snakes . . . I mean, they're *house* snakes, but they're minions . . . like Niko will be, if we can't—"

"*Slow down!*" Critias exploded. "Sit, light somewhere!"

Randal circled around in place as if still the dog he'd so recently been, sighed deeply, and squatted down where he was: "Sirs . . . lords . . . you don't under*stand*. . . . If I'm going back, I've got to leave here straightaway. Anything that Niko knows, Roxane knows also . . . she's inside him all the time, eating up his soul. And she's sharing him with Datan, as far as I can tell . . . that's the archmage—"

"We *know* who he is," Crit interrupted. "Now what's this about her being inside him? Are you positive? How can we free him?"

Bashir shifted restlessly, his gaze averted, apparently studying the maps before him; Tempus heard a god's name muttered, saw fingers work in invocation.

"*Free* him?" Randal repeated. "You can't. Death won't even do it. Burn the witch . . . it's not certain, just a start. Or *buy* him back from Datan, who could make her loose him. A trade . . . we've done that before. . . ."

"No!" Bashir's voice rang out. "No deals with magelings or their devils."

"No?" Randal looked from Tempus to Critias. "Who's this? Look here, my lords, I've got to go . . . if you want me to get back in there. . . ." He started to rise.

Crit strode over, put a hand upon his shoulder. "Tempus?"

"He's right, a trade won't do. Randal, come with me. Critias, confer with our guest about personnel and troop strength. If Mygdonia is entering Machad, we haven't got much time. We have to secure the peaks before they reach Tyse's borders, or all this will be in vain. Meet us at Bomba's in an hour or so."

And, to Bashir: "Son of my brother, work well."

"Gods go with you," Bashir replied, and blessed him

openly so that Randal scrambled up and, shuddering, backed across the room to bolt up the stairs and Tempus had to chase him.

At the stairs' head, he caught the mage. "Be calm, mageling. He won't hurt you."

"Who *was* that? Nisibisi sidelocks . . . was it? . . . No, you wouldn't. It couldn't be . . . one of the murder-god's lovers. . . . *Could* it?"

"Randal, you've a lot to learn about expediency and war. The real constitution of things is accustomed to hide itself. That is, an unapparent connection is stronger than an apparent. Those factions whom I join together in this venture are all expressions of the same force, like wind and water, fire and ether, the wet and the dry, which feed upon their opposites. Do you understand me?"

"No. Without gods there is the order of magic; with gods, there is the chaos of emotion. Magic is logic; gods are illogic . . ."

"Exactly. There, you do comprehend. Nothing exists without its opposite. To triumph in this matter, we will bring opposites to bear. How would you like to become a Stepson?"

"*What?* A *fighter?* You jest. I'm not cut out for—"

"Your bravery is proven. Most of your sort would have fled when they learned the identity of the witch. Your weapons will be those with which you are familiar: spells and so forth; we'll not have time to make you a man at arms. But I'm asking you to become Niko's right-side partner in the action brewing, to climb with us up Wizardwall and do battle with your hereditary enemies, every one of Datan's clutch of evil beings—from demon to witch."

"Why don't you just *make* me do it; go over my head and have the First Hazard give the order? No, I'm being unfair. I . . . like Niko too."

"Is that an answer? Have you volunteered?"

"We'll need the Hazard's permission. And, I mean . . . do I get a horse? I don't have to *be* fourfooted, do I?"

Tempus chuckled. "I'll give you one of mine."

"Does this mean I don't have to go back to Roxane's . . . Cybele's that is?"

"Are you endangered there?"

"No more than Niko is." The mageling squared his shoulders: "A Stepson . . . who'd have thought it? All right, given the mageguild's assent, I'm yours to command for the duration . . . master."

"Stepsons have no master. I'm their commander, Critias is my second, Straton is next in line."

"What of Grillo?"

"An advisor, a co-worker. Don't pass him any information; he gets too much through the mageguild network as it is."

"He's very . . . *close* . . . to you-know-who—the priest down there."

"We've gathered that. It's none of our affair. Now, back to work, Stepson. I'll expect to hear from you in three days' time. If Niko doesn't return home tonight, we'll have lured him out here or to the mageguild, where I hope to get a second opinion on his condition. Do you think he favors that girl you brought in for him enough to pay a visit there?"

"Niko? He likes his ladies. You might get him there . . . but the witch will know, and the girl and child may be in jeopardy. . . . Oh, I see: you want to lure Roxane forth, is that it?"

"Go on, now, Randal. If Straton doesn't come to the Peace River house looking for Niko, stay in place. If he does, that's your signal to get out of there as fast as you can and come straight here. Understood?"

The mageling held out a sweaty hand.

He'd be sufficient to his tasks, Tempus realized, as the youngster strode away.

Then he had to face his own responsibilities: no reason left to delay, no way to put it off.

Niko's note had been quite plain; all Tempus had to do, to begin unraveling this mess he'd made, was humble himself before the lord of dreams and call his sister, his heart's bane, down from her sojourn among the planes.

He really didn't want to do this. But too many fates had become entangled with his own.

In the stable, saddling up to ride out among the mists and the intermittent lightning of the mages' feints which made late autumn out of summer skies, he nearly said a prayer for Niko, but managed to refrain. He shouldn't let himself feel so much for these youngsters, or love his Stepsons the way he did. But without the god to occupy his mind, his curse owned him fully. Having Cime back would put things in perspective, if Aškelon listened to his plea and let her come.

Without her, he had a feeling all his plans would come to naught—Niko die with soul enthralled, consigned to deep damnation; Bashir would learn that gods were not so omnipotent or omniscient as they claimed and bury Successors rather than pylons deep in the high peaks earth; and himself—well, if Datan wanted battle-won souls to do his bidding, an old one such as his might be the prize of all the ages.

He would have to wait and see, he thought, stopping only long enough to stroke Niko's pregnant mare and promise her he'd have him back home soon, safe and sound and soul intact.

She whinnied softly, reassured.

When the last sounds of Niko's horses had faded and she was sure that he was well away, Roxane cast aside her Cybele-form, made a scullery maid of her one remaining snake and oversaw the clean-up of the kitchen. She could have willed the mess away, but the snake, its sibling gone, was being punished. Stupid snake must learn enough to stay out of the watchdog's way. Impulsive and foolhardy, the snake her dog had chewed the life from deserved its fate thrice over. But its death presented problems—she hadn't used her water bowl to report to Datan or sent her soul on high in person because when she did she'd have to say one snake was dead.

And she'd nothing crucial to report yet; when Niko came back from this meet with Tempus and his Stepsons, she hoped to know more; she hoped he'd bring Bashir back here, where "natural causes" would soon end the Successor's life.

In the kitchen she picked up Niko's cuirass gingerly, as if it were offal, not metal, then changed her mind and left it with sword and dirk upon its drying rack. She'd had to prompt him not to take it with him; he'd gone out in dark shirt and hillman's trousers, not giving it a second thought. She'd find a way to claim it lost or stolen; it cramped her style. To keep it cool she'd needed to take extra care with her disguise and never once let hostility to Niko overwhelm her: it was magic hostile to the wearer which energized the dirk and sword and cuirass into action.

This loving Niko was not difficult; it was too easy. So long inside his mind had taught her to appreciate qualities she'd never understood: kindness, youth, naiveté. She spoke a curse which froze the snake in horror, and it dropped a stoneware plate. Would that Datan, lover-lord, had half the sense of duty to which this child adhered so willingly, a heavy burden proudly toted that gave meaning to a life of struggle no Nisibisi warlock would endure.

She sighed and wiped her brow and sat up on the kitchen table where so recently they'd "made love," as Niko said. She'd never for a moment had to feign her passion; she'd almost let her Cybele-face slip away when first he came inside her, so transported by ecstasy was she.

Once she'd thought to murder him and nibble on his sweet young soul a morsel at a time; she might make it last a year. Now she thought of saving him intact, keeping him a minion in delectable servitude—alive, a willing servant who would give her pleasure year by year.

And this complicated simple measures: she could not send the snake with a few undeads to slay him as he rode home with Bashir. She told herself that she yet needed him to spy on Tempus, though the crafty Riddler gave out precious little information to any man, somehow thwarting her at every turn as if by accident, though she knew no "fate" or "luck" was so consistent.

She'd failed to turn Bashir away with the undeads sent in Niko's wake to daunt the priest and cast a shadow over their reunion. She'd take the soul of Enlil's priest instead, though she felt with Niko every pain and shared his sadness and his troubles. If she could, she'd have whisked her Stepson up to Wizardwall tonight and kept him there; she'd soon make him a willing captive of the pleasure she longed to share with him.

But Datan waited, and war was nigh, and witches never failed. She knew that half of what she felt was the taint of Niko's suffering; sometimes she wanted to give him back his *maat* and let him find his rest-place and be Cybele for him forever . . .

She laughed a harsh and angry laugh, and her snake, its work done, scuttled away.

She'd have him spurn the slut he had waiting for him in the mageguild, the one Tempus kept reminding him to see. That whole encounter with the wolf-mage had been inauspicious; much energy had gone into making Nikodemos forget, and then the Riddler had found a way to get the dream lord's message from him. She'd done the best she could; she couldn't chance destroying Niko's mind completely; he was too useful.

But she needed something favorable, a triumph to report to Datan, not merely a listing of aborted possibilities, a chronicle of little failures.

And he'd let the dog out; she heard it scratching at the door right now. Almost, she arose to let it in, but Niko was even then approaching Brother Bomba's and the dog would learn a lesson: let it wait all night upon her stoop, at least till Niko and Bashir came home.

She deepened her trance and, leaning back, closed her eyes so that she could see through his.

And because of her preoccupation with Nikodemos and her scheming, it never once occurred to Roxane to wonder why Tempus had refrained from mentioning to Niko anything about the Riddler's trip to see her or that he'd given her the dog, but only remarked, "Do you?" when Niko said that he'd a friend down by the river, and there Bashir had agreed to lodge.

When Niko arrived at Brother Bomba's, Bashir's horse in tow and his crossbow in his hand, Madame Bomba herself showed him through the crowd and down the stairs to where Crit and Bashir sucked on bubbly pipes awaiting Tempus.

"Now, Stealth," she said, "don't think I'm being forward, but I've a proposition for you . . . your uncle in Caronne, you see . . . he's a man I crave an introduction to."

"It's been years—"

"He loves you, kin and all. Just a note from you; I'd like to be his client. I'll make you wealthy, you won't have to do a thing." She let go of his arm, stepped back. "Here we are. They're right in here. What say you? Do an old woman of the armies a favor, soldier?"

She was a friend of Tempus', he knew. Still, he never traded on that family relationship; he owed his uncle far too much . . . and he'd refused to come into the family business; they'd parted on uneasy terms. But then, life was full of obligations: "A note, you say? Give me paper and I'll write it. But as a favor, Madame; you're a good friend to the Stepsons. Show the Sacred Band your usual generosity; help the Riddler. I don't want anything more for this. It's nothing much to write a letter." As he spoke, with the quill and paper she pulled out of her voluminously pocketed apron, he wrote his uncle; Madame Bomba would have her contraband at half the going price.

"May I read it?" Eager as a child, she scanned the lines, then stood on tiptoe and kissed his cheek. He grinned at her and shook his head; he saw the child within her: what a wench she must once have been.

Then she slid aside the thin partition and Bashir rose up to embrace him; their lips met in northern greeting, and he heard a derisive snicker come from somewhere among the dozen men within the smoke-filled chamber. Whether it was at his expense, he couldn't say. Half these men stretched out on mats with pipes and blown-glass jars before them were Stepsons, Sacred Banders; the rest were specials and a pair of side-locked free men of Nisibis; none of them had the right to smirk. But upstairs as Madame Bomba brought him through he'd seen others of his squadron and got no more in greeting than a wave or nod of head. From the two who'd ridden with him out of Sanctuary he'd asked for more—some indication that their promises to act in his behalf had been fulfilled. Distant stares and taut mouths were what he'd gotten; no one wanted him too close, that much was clear.

Bashir's hug was fierce and lingered: "Are you all right, my friend? Where's your gear?"

Niko saw Crit's hawk eyes watching. He tugged on Bashir's laden belt and slipped free of him, replying, "There are weapons at hand here if I need them. I had to sneak away without waking a certain lady." He hoped he'd hidden the uneasiness he felt as he squatted down between his task force leader and Bashir. He'd worn that panoply too long; he was glad to be free of it. In his belt he had his stars and blossoms and a hunting knife, single-edged with serrations on the curve from point to flat of blade. The only difference between a hunting knife and a combat knife was what you stuck it in. He laid the crossbow by his knee: "Expecting trouble, are we?"

"Not unless you brought it with you," Crit said, his eye-whites red from sucking on the waterpipe, whose mouthpiece he held out.

Thinking that he'd never be at ease socializing with his task force leader, Niko dragged deeply and sought to pass the mouthpiece on. This time Bashir spoke up: "Smoke on, we're well ahead of you." And as he did he thought that in this room where those he loved the best lay about, relaxing, he felt totally alone. The Stepsons stepping wide of him he'd half expected, tried to understand. But Bashir, too, was acting strange, and this was sudden. Bashir was not one to criticize or worry; Enlil granted the warriors he favored a calm heart and far-seeing eye. And Bashir knew Niko's skill with Death Touch and found objects; together in the old days they'd thought and fought their way out of many a tight spot against ridiculous odds. He coughed, then drank the wine his old friend proffered and put speculation by. It was his lot to be alone, he'd had omen after omen of it.

When Straton and Tempus came in together, every man upon the floor sat up or raised his head or straightened shoulders, but the Riddler waved them back and put them at their ease.

By then Niko's head was spinning and voices loud and colors brighter than they should have been and he found it difficult to speak.

Tempus said, "I'm late. Your pardon, fighters. Sometimes it takes longer than expected to prove oneself a total fool," and sat where Bashir and Crit moved over to make room for him with Straton on his right.

"Commander?" Critias asked his meaning.

"Never mind. It doesn't matter." The Riddler's eyes were on him so that Niko shifted, pulling on his tunic.

The pipe was passed and talk turned, as talk will, to women, and then to the girl Niko'd found north of the border, and Strat suggested that they go take a look at her: "You can't leave her in the mageguild forever, Stealth. They've few provisions for women there. We don't need to be beholden to those sorcerous ants. And, too, if you don't want her, you could give her to a friend. . . ."

He thought he'd say no, decline, explain he had no interest beyond preventing an innocent's death. But somehow they all got up and staggered out of there, headed for the mageguild, Niko wondering if he were dreaming this: one didn't go reeling through hostile streets in the middle of the night carousing with one's commander and one's task force leader. Neither Critias nor Tempus were known as public revelers; having them on either side like drinking buddies of the rank and file was disconcerting; he couldn't decide whether it was for good or ill, whether he was being accorded some due privilege, or just there to ease Bashir.

If not for all he'd smoked and drunk too much wine, he would have balked outside the mageguild. He expected Bashir to do it for him, to the extent that he could anticipate or think out anything at all.

He never should have let himself indulge in drug and drink so carelessly; he concentrated on walking upright; when his eyes left his feet he saw the Tysian mageguild's colonnaded front. By then he was leaning on Straton's shoulder, and he could hear voices behind him: Bashir's, and Tempus', and Critias in occasional monosyllabic comment, all speaking Nisi low and fast, trouble riding whispered sibilances and urgency in their tenses and their tone. But the sense of their discussion was beyond his befuddled capacity to fathom and, next he knew, Straton was telling him: "That's it, Stealth, just one more flight."

Then there were nightmarish halls thick with shadows and incense so sweet he gagged when he breathed. He'd never in his most tortured dreams thought to set foot inside a mageguild. To be there with the Riddler, who disdained all power arts—including gods, of late—and with Bashir, who was on the other side from mages, and be there barely under his own power, leaning on Straton, most superstitious and cautious of all the Stepsons . . . he must be dreaming: passed out safe in Brother Bomba's, hearing their voices through his stupor, letting their presence spark the nature of his dream.

But then Strat said, "There you go, Stealth," and, "Sit right there, don't move. We'll be back to get you," and all familiar voices ceased.

He was propped against a wall, and his eyelids were weighted closed. He struggled to get them open and when he did he closed them straightaway against what he saw.

He was in a long, narrow chamber with lofty ceiling and painted walls depicting ceremonies of adepts working classified acts of magic; at its end was a raised and shrouded dais with a shriveled mage upon its throne.

The eyes he'd seen in that brief glimpse were cavernous and ancient; the head was barren of hair and the mouth pleated and open: the words that came out of it danced in fiery letters before Niko's eyes and then turned to ropes which bound themselves about his limbs. He had time to think it consummately sad that those he'd trusted most and loved the best had betrayed him. Then the invocation of the wizened creature took over his spirit and he could not think at all.

"I'm sorry," the archmage of Tyse said, shaking his bald and ancient head as he came out of a room only Straton had been allowed to enter, just long enough to seat Niko there.

"You'd better be more than sorry," Critias warned,

stopped still where he'd been pacing; "you'd better have a good idea about what we can do to help him. We didn't bring him here to—"

"That's enough, Critias." Tempus left Bashir's side, where he had been trying to ease a warrior-priest forced by circumstance and love to enter into the citadel of his soul's enemy: Bashir subvocalized a curse upon sorcerers and their kind, which made the aged little archmage cast a blazing look his way. "Venerable magician," Tempus began, trying his best not to let his own despite leak through, "there must be *some*thing we can do. We have no intention of giving up on Nikodemos."

"You'd best do it quickly, then, my children."

Bashir growled a wordless threat, and Tempus heard the rustle of his armor as he quit the wall and he and Crit conferred. Moving close to the archmage, Tempus lowered his voice: "There's no hope?"

"Burn the witch, and you've her infernal lord to deal with. Let her go on feeding on that boy, and your problem will solve itself in a month or so. He'll expire. Rid of him, you'll be better off. He's a spy in Wizardwall's interest. Willing or not is hardly germane. Or slay him yourself; it's kinder and your sort is inured to murder, we've all seen."

"To what end? Will he die a peaceful death? Find the afterlife he's earned?"

"You know that answer, soldier." The burning coals which served this wraithlike mage for eyes met Tempus' and held them. "You're older than I, Riddler. Why aren't you wiser? Haven't you learned yet that mortal-lovers consign themselves to recurrent, hopeless pain? Let him meet his fate and wreak your vengeance on the Osprey. Revenge, I know, you understand. Now, what about this waif, the girl we've been keeping for him?"

"We'll take her and her child to Outbridge," Tempus heard himself growl, trying to keep his temper. His fingers itched and twitched to get themselves around that scrawny neck.

The mage felt it. "Well, you asked for my opinion. You've had it. Let that one—" A wavering, gnarled finger pointed to Straton. "—go in and bring the accursed forth. We'd prefer not to be implicated; if he regains his senses, the witch will know he's been here. We've all our aggressors engaged—"

"You keep him there. Keep him safe. You *can* do that, magician?" Tempus smiled as he spoke but eyed the archmage bleakly. "We'll oust the witch and then come back."

Straton's sigh of relief sounded in the antechamber fallen silent.

"We've put one mage at risk for you, sleepless one—"

"Do this, or Bashir and I will take it ill."

Crit muttered: "It's about time."

Straton said: "Then I don't have to go back in there?"

Bashir said: "Hark to him, old man. The Riddler speaks for me and the god speaks through me. You don't yet know the meaning of 'damned.' Keep him, and keep him well, or all the devils you feed from that foul hand of yours won't save you."

"Enough!" Tempus silenced them. "Archmage, yea or nay?"

The ancient waved a hand and Straton flinched. "It falls within the bounds of our agreement, I suppose. But don't blame me if boy or girl or babe dies of this mortal foolishness. Now go! Get out! Your priest," he glared at Bashir, "disturbs our wards and right now you need them to protect this sold soul you think still yours. Go make fools of yourselves and fail as you must. Then we'll hear a different tone. But don't think to sacrifice my Hazard, young Randal whom I loaned you, for this soldier—"

Tempus got them out of there. The details of his bargain

with the Tysian mageguild were nothing he wanted spelled out for Straton or Bashir.

Crit took his arm when they'd made it down the steps and whispered: "Where were you, before? What did you mean about making a fool of your—"

"Niko's message, when I got it, suggested that I might call upon the dream lord for a certain kind of aid. I tried it. It didn't work. So perhaps it was a diversion prepared by Roxane. So I thought, at any rate, and half expected to find you all in pieces or ensorceled when I returned."

"Ha! That day's still a long way off. What say we go rout this witch now?"

"Nothing else for it," Tempus agreed and added, slowly: "We may be doing Niko more harm than good."

"We must do something to let them know we won't give him up without a fight."

"I know, Critias." Tempus smiled again, just slightly, knowing that Critias was ready then to stand and war with demons from a brace of hells if it would bring Niko's spirit back. "Try to get that panoply. She's succeeded if she's wrested it from him."

Straton came up: "You'd better explain things to Bashir. Me, I don't care *whose* aid you've got or what you've paid, but if I listen to the warrior-priest much longer, telling me where and how long I'm going to burn for this, I'll trade my war-horses in for oxen and my weapons in for sheep."

"Done. But one thing, Straton," Tempus told him; "you've got to go in first, walk up to Roxane's door, knock, and ask for Niko."

"By Vashanka's third and ghostly ball, *why?*"

"*Strat!*" Crit snapped. "We take orders, we don't—"

"He has a right to ask. Because that's Randal's signal to get out of there. Try to keep her talking long enough for him to slip by, out the door."

"Randal?"

"The *dog*, fool! He's the *dog*, remember? Black and large and—"

"Oh. That's different, then. Consider it done, Riddler."

Straton had never, in Tempus's memory, called him that before. He fell into a discussion of strategy and tactics then with both Stepsons, forgetting Bashir until the warrior-priest joined them, saying that Niko was his bond brother and whatever could be done to save him, Bashir must help to do, mages or no mages: "Enlil will sanctify us, and his fire will purify those grounds as war without a god's clean flame could never do. Anyway," the priest grinned, "I do love roasting the occasional witch. And this time, it's in a cause that's more than just." The grin faded as he glanced back over his shoulder at the mageguild, and when he turned, his countenance was filled with unmitigated hate. "If I left Nikodemos in there, trusting you, the least I can do is hasten the moment we can get him out again."

"He's never to know of this," Tempus warned. "Not that we know the witch is in him, even when it's over. I won't leave him there later than morning, Bashir. You and I have an aversion to these necromancers in common. Now, when we get him back, we'll admit to taking him there to claim the girl and her child, that's all. For the rest, he's had too much to smoke and too much to drink. And never, if we all get old together, are any of you to tell another person what we've learned. He has troubles enough without being outcast, shunned and suspect."

"You said, 'never,'" Bashir remarked. "What if none of this avails us?"

"Then we take him back among us, keep his secret, let him spend what time he has with those who love him best."

"How?" Crit objected. "When everything he knows, *she* knows? And probably the Osprey, too?"

"An information conduit flows both ways. We'll use him

to affect old Datan's judgment; bad information, given as
truth from an impeccable source, can hurt the wizard's
planning."

"In a fight?" Strat wondered.

"Randal. He'll be a temporary Stepson; I'll assign him
to Niko's right. It's up to you both," he looked at Critias
and Straton, "to see that the squadron accepts him, and
that no one knows what kind of fighter Randal really is."

"No problem," Critias nodded, his intelligent stare letting Tempus know he'd made the leap to comprehension.
With a score just like him Tempus could have scoured the
known world clean of evil.

And as Tempus walked toward the horses with Crit
beside him, he heard Bashir explaining quietly to Straton
just what kind of weapons a mage such as Randal could
bring to bear, and why they both must put aside rightful
prejudice, even lie and misrepresent themselves and others,
promising Straton that this once the gods would make
allowances.

Tempus hoped he was right.

Critias sent Strat on ahead, almost too busy for mis-
givings. But he'd had to say, "Take care, Ace; don't tarry
with her; remember how she nearly charmed me last
time," and clap his friend upon the back, and even hand
over his eagle-claw fish hook for Strat to carry. "It will
bring you luck."

"Luck? Let's hope I don't need it." Strat was glum, but
resigned. He stuffed the fish hook in his pouch and strode
up the winding drive which led to Roxane's with only one
puzzled, backward look.

After he'd gone, Crit cursed himself for letting Strat
know how worried he was. He should have kept silent. He
remembered that night six weeks ago when he'd cast his
personal prognosticators in Sanctuary's hostel, sitting in

the common room after Tempus had saddled him with the welfare of all the Stepsons.

He'd done well enough by the single fighters and the paired; all a man could do, he'd done in accordance with custom and regulation as well as in the spirit of the honor-bond that elevated Sacred Bands. Watching Straton walk, lightly armed and with that swinging gait of his, up to the vine-enshrouded house in the early hours of the morning, he knew he'd been fooling himself in thinking pairbond was a problem he no longer had. Undeclared or not, his nature had found its mate in Straton's; his heart went with his friend up to the witch's door.

Men were sneaking round the sides and bush by bush up close with incendiaries hastily concocted from kitchen staples; when Bashir gave his jackal howl, they'd place them strategically around the old manse's foundations; by the time dawn dared to break the whole place would be in flames. He took an instant to thank the gods that Roxane had no high wall to be scaled. An arrogant witch, she shunned mundane defenses. He hoped she didn't know better than he, that what seemed an advantage to his side would turn out to really be one.

Above the masking sound Peace River made rushing behind her house, he could hear Bashir's low baritone, intoning prayers and blessing commandos while overhead a godly cloud began to mass.

Wishing he could see the door from where he crouched among the bushes, he crawled back to join the other Stepsons gathered to receive Enlil's blessing. It couldn't hurt. He bowed his head.

Then a dog's bark, ending in a whine (low, then louder) broke his concentration and he almost sprinted up the drive.

Bashir caught him by the arm, intervening: "It's in the god's hands."

"Hug my crack. Every man's in his own hands, with a little help from his brothers. Let me go."

"Wait and see." Bashir held on tight.

"Too much rides on this."

He couldn't argue with Bashir in front of Sacred Banders. He was glad the majority of them were deployed around the house. He'd have to talk to Tempus about which of them should command this task force when both had fighters in it: half the men behind the house were side-locked Nisibisi. For the moment, he merely wrenched his arm free and walked away without another word.

Back at his bush, he could see a little light spill forth among the trees as if the door had opened, and then something black and panting came careening into him, all teeth and tongue and wet-nosed, its tail between its legs and trembling.

"*Randal?* Get changed, I've got to know what happened. Where's Strat?"

Then he heard Bashir give the jackal call, and Randal howled along with it in some eerie duet, and Critias had to get his bow and quarrels and form his men and call firstline codes for "ready."

A fire Bashir had made with pungent charcoals that burned green was now uncovered; those with bows of Nisibisi style had wrapped their points in cloth soaked with Enlil's holy oil; those with crossbows didn't wait in line, but began scuttling through the undergrowth.

When Crit looked away from the blacker shadow of the house against the purpling night, Randal was darkly clad and crouched beside him.

"Strat?" Crit whispered.

"I'm not sure. I'm sorry." Randal spread pale hands, then obeyed Crit's order and put on his gloves.

"Come on, then, Stepson, let's go roast this witch-bitch." *Strat*, Crit thought, *this one's for you*, and disobeyed his own instructions to wait until the house erupted into flames to sneak up closer.

But as he came within the house's shadow, charges flared and pieces of stone and wood and gouts of flame erupted; he covered his face with his arm as concussions reverberated around him, counting off the seconds between blasts, feeling the heat sear the hair on his arms and warm his helmet and sweat begin to run down his neck, along his backbone, as his battle-sharpened sense dilated moments. The charges should have gone off simultaneously; some men were better at this than others; he'd have to weed them out so that this sort of thing didn't happen again. A stone dwelling is hard to raze.

He looked up before he should have, afraid the house would have its walls intact and they'd have to go in there fighting, room to room, with demons or undeads or whatever minions Roxane had. A soldier such as Critias avoided, when he could, such sorties round blind corners, in unfamiliar passageways where others of your team could accidentally kill you; he hated close-in fighting, being penned by walls and prey to unexpected trap doors or floors and roofs which might give way. . . .

And what he saw when he looked up was a roof and climbing vines and windows all ablaze and figures limned in firelight through burned-out doors and crashing timbers and then, from above, a lightning bolt zagged down from clouds and wrapped itself around the house entire, a blue and awful net of power. Stone by stone, the old manse came apart and showered men and trees and road with pebbles; chunks and even blocks like hell-sent hail came flying forth from the inferno, so bright his eyes teared and stung.

Something hit his helm and he saw a tiny constellation of new stars all his own; then the ground came up to meet him, and he had all he could do to get up on his hands and knees, to shake away the dizziness, to rise and run. . . .

Into smoke thick and cloying and sweet with the tang of roasting meat he fought his way, hearing whoops and cries and warriors' curses, but seeing no one else, so much sulphurous smoke did the old manse belch—or what was left of it.

He'd reached what should have been its doorway, and there was nothing there but a fall of stones, some smoking timbers, an afterglow of whitehot nails and, he thought, something quivering among the billows of greasy vapors. He heard a voice beside him: "Don't go in there yet!"

Randal's voice, it was. Well, at least the mageling was no coward, to have come this far. Crit stepped across the threshold and suddenly was halted by an awful keening, a sound which grated teeth and inner ear like all the devils up from every hell might make, if they all sang out in chorus. Then something dark and crackling with stinking arms or wings and crimson eyes brushed past him, opening his flesh where its blighting extremities touched his unprotected arm.

He wheeled and took a shot, crossbow on his hip, firing blind, by instinct, and heard a far worse cry than what he'd just heard. Then Randal shouted *"Aaiieee!"* and something beat the air about his head with hellish wings so that Critias dove to ground, hot stones and nails and smoking earth beneath him; rolling over onto his back, he levered and nocked and fired arrows as fast and best he might.

First crawling, then lunging through the ruins, he came upon what must once have been the house's kitchen, just as one Successor and a pair of Sacred Banders were scrambling in the other way.

And there, coughing and choking in the steaming wreckage, he paused and waved the three back. On a drying rack, gleaming through the smoke, bright despite the greasy pall on everything about it, was Niko's panoply— cuirass with raised enameled snakes and glyphs, the sword with

demons from elder myths, the dirk with stormbolts and
fabled beasts on its scabbard, hanging there from leather
straps.

He walked cautiously forward, feeling his way among
the turning stones and charred boards beneath him, mind-
ful that there might be a cellar under, and the whole floor
give way to bury him below. "If I go down, don't try to get
me out yourselves. Get Bashir and plenty of others."

"Whatever you say," said the leftman and crossed his
arms to wait and see. "We did it, looks like."

"You saw a witch's corpse?" he asked absently, hooking
his crossbow on his belt so that he'd have both hands free
to grab for safety or keep his balance.

"No, but I saw a form or two aflame in here, and
nothing could have survived—"

"Strat? Did you see Strat?" He was almost there.

"Straton? No. We thought he was with you."

The Successor, crouching down, said a prayer of thanks
in Nisi, picked up some pulverized debris and let it trickle
slowly through his fingers, an oblation to the gods.

Two good strides remained between Crit and the panoply.
If this was some witch's trap, then he was about to fall
into it. He gave up caution and strode the distance, his
hands outstretched to grab the gear and flee.

When he touched the breastplate, a cry escaped him. He
felt his skin sear and pulled his hands away. He should
have taken his own advice and put on gloves. He fumbled
for them and, wincing, eased them over palms burned
white, and was just reaching out again when Randal's call
came:

"Stop! I'll do that."

The pain he was ignoring made Crit snap sharply: "*You?*
Why not? It's something you can manage." Then he looked
around.

The little mage's face was scored with long, parallel
cuts, as if his cheek were flayed or plowed. One eye was

swollen shut and, as he walked, he staggered, mumbling charms or spells or simply cursing off his pain—Crit could make no sense of the dialect.

But the mage came across the rubble and said, "Hold onto me." So Crit grasped Randal's belt and the junior Hazard lifted the cuirass gingerly from the rack, his good eye narrowed, talking to the piece of armor as he did: "There's a good thing. Niko wants you back. You've got to let me have you," and so forth as he did the same with sword and dirk, then held them out to Crit.

Crit let him go and held up hands to forfend that burden: "Not me. That stuff likes you better. I've got the blisters to prove it. You carry it back to Niko, he's your left-side leader, I've been told. It's your privilege and duty." His voice was thick, and he wanted to be alone: Down beside the drying rack he had seen a piece of abalone glitter. "Would you get that little fish hook there for me? Right there. My thanks, Randal." And, the fish hook in his fingers, he turned and walked as fast as prudent out of the house and off among the bushes, to sit and let his grief run its course where no one would have to see.

He wanted to put his head between his hands, but they hurt too much. He bound his lacerated forearm and lay on his back, watching the smoke disperse and the red tinge of sunrise eat up the night, praying he wasn't going to cry for Straton, who deserved better than a death or *un*death, alone, while trying to save a junior Hazard who wasn't worth saving.

Most of all, he didn't want to face the possibility that they might have a second Niko on their hands; there was not a single bone or corpse or even a piece of Straton's panoply visible in the kitchen; in fact, he hadn't seen a casualty anywhere within the chaotic ruin which once had been a house. The wreck-and-rescue crew would go over what remained, of course, as soon as they could be pulled away from their current labors at the palace, where they still searched desultorily for royal remains under collapsed tons of stone.

But Straton ... Crit held the fish hook up before his eyes and it was blurry in his sight.

One of the men approached, stood over him; the silhouette looked down; Crit started to get up.

"You *found* it!" Straton said. "Gods' balls, I'm glad of that. I—"

"Strat, you bastard! *Where were* you?" Crit was on his feet, clasping Straton close. Then, embarassed, he pulled away. "Can't you *ever* follow orders? I want a full report, right now." Crit crossed his arms.

"Report? I don't know ... I knocked, she opened the door, I asked for Niko, she said he wasn't there, and that was that. No dog came out, though, so I asked her how it was doing, and she said it had gotten out earlier and was outside somewhere, maybe I'd look for it for her, so I had to look around ... then," Strat shrugged, "I was around the back and the call came so I took cover. That's all."

"That's all? I thought you were dead. You were supposed to report back to me."

"Crit, what's the matter?"

"How did this get in her kitchen, then?"

"I don't know. I dropped it, I told you." Straton stepped back a pace, uncertain, scrutinizing Critias. "I do believe," he said slowly, "that you were worried."

"Just a little. Between Bashir and Randal and not knowing whether we won this one or lost it. . . ." He couldn't keep this up: there was no reason to suspect foul play or witchery just because Straton had dropped a fish hook, or to pretend he was angry when in fact he was tremendously relieved. He said as much, made amends in his own terse fashion, and went one step further, so that when they got down to overseeing the clean-up and regrouping, they did it as an acknowledged pair, full and sharing partners.

\*     \*     \*

Tempus reclaimed Niko from the mageguild before the sun came up. He had never been far from him, choosing to stay close at hand in case the witch attacked Niko in the Tysian archmage's stronghold, as the old adept thought she might, rather than take part in the assault. If Critias and Bashir together couldn't raze the place, it couldn't be brought down.

He'd left his ailing Stepson only long enough to meet with Grillo, who had to be summoned and informed: certain of his specials were involved.

As Tempus had requested, Grillo had brought a wagon in which to carry Niko's girl and her newborn boy to the Outbridge estate; it was driven, as Tempus had specified, by the single survivor of the Outbridge sack, the special into whose arms Tempus had collapsed that night, and his favorite among Grillo's men, one he'd had transferred to him.

With the girl in safe hands and on her way, tended en route by the window Maldives, to whose skill at healing Tempus could attest, he was free to turn his thoughts to other matters: the archmage of Tyse was unabashedly eager to be rid of Niko; Tempus almost pointed out that it could be said that his Stepson's troubles were of this mageguild's manufacture: if they were not so impertinent and vain, they might have contained this magewar long ago, before it overflowed into precincts where it didn't belong and embroiled human empires and secular allies—mages should war with mages, men with men.

But he had said it all before in former times and other empires; he himself had become accursed because an archmage lusted after his sister, Cime. So it went: gods mixed in and sorcerers meddled, and puny mortals were the ones who suffered.

Having taken his spellbound, semiconscious Stepson from the mageguild amid the solicitous stares and lugubrious looks of portentous, self-important wizards gathered to gawk and prognosticate and teach their apprentices and impress each other as he half-carried, half-dragged Niko through the halls, he boosted the boy up on his horse and headed them west, sunrise at their backs: Niko's head would clear now that the sleeping draught and hypnotic spells they'd slipped him were wearing off.

The sky was dark overhead and red along the horizon; he was late; all this had taken much too long. He had hoped to have the Stepson safe and sound at Outbridge before the task force razed the witch's keep.

As it was, he had to hurry; he didn't need Niko looking back toward Peace River and the witch's house and seeing smoke and flame; he hadn't yet decided what he was going to tell the youth who wavered in his saddle but followed him without complaint. The archmage had made sure Niko would remember only meeting with his girl there; the spell was truly cast, for Niko asked him thickly if Tempus were sure it was all right: "—billeting her out at the barracks, I mean?" Then: "Commander, did you see that?"

He'd seen. To the west, above a brightening horizon, shooting stars came arcing down from heaven, a shower of green-tailed arrows from the bows of the gods.

"Make a wish, Stepson," he advised the youth, and they rode awhile in silence as darkness waned, and sunrise sought to defeat a mass of roiling clouds.

They'd stopped to relieve themselves before he broached it: "Niko, you'll be billeted at Outbridge yourself from this day on. We're moving north in a week or two."

The youngster turned around to face him, arranging himself within his loinguard, unspoken questions in his shadowed, deep-sunk eyes. Tempus saw those questions fade and Niko's customary control take over, and recalled when the boy's facade had been uncracked, when equanimity had seemed as much a part of Nikodemos as breathing, and realized fully how much it bothered him that this particular fighter suffered in his stead.

"Niko, I'm going to tell you something else. We sacked that Peace River house of yours this morning."

"You ... *what? Cybele!* I—" Niko squatted down in place and, eyes lowered, pulled up grass and earth. Then he twisted around and looked behind him, where an echo of sunrise might have glowed in the southeast, then back. He blew out a breath, then straightened up and threw down a chunk of sod. "Thank you for telling me." A Sacred Bander wouldn't question authority or demand an explanation; he was still completely that.

But Tempus volunteered: "Death squad leaders and a number of insurgents have been seen meeting there. It was the only decision we could take."

"You are sure, of course. I'm sorry you thought that I couldn't be trusted to know beforehand, but it's not surprising." Niko's glance was level, his hazel eyes blank and cold. "Everyone's been avoiding me as if I had the plague. If that stops, now, it's almost worth it." He looked away: "Cybele ... it's hard to believe ... she was just a child. I hope this doesn't mean you'll never trust me, henceforth, commander. I'm—" He fell silent, went to his horse and vaulted up on it, then sat stroking its neck, his shoulders slumped, his grief for a girl he yet thought might be an innocent barely checked.

Tempus mounted up and kicked the roan; he drew alongside.

"No chance that she'll survive and end up in Straton's hands?"

"None whatsoever," Tempus assured him and heard Niko's sigh of relief. "I have another piece of news: in the assault on Wizardwall, if you'll take a man I choose as your right-side partner for the action, I'll let you have the point."

"The point? I'd endure Haram's company for that chance, sir."

So much, then, for the youth's fears of being considered untrustworthy. But he had to chuckle. "It's not that bad—it's not Haram. But it may seem odd—your rightman will be Randal, the junior Hazard. I believe you've met."

Whatever Niko would have said beyond repeating "Randal?" was lost, because the boy could see past him. "Commander, you're not expecting an escort, are you? One rider, one extra horse?"

Tempus turned in his saddle. The rider came cross-country, from the direction in which lay Outbridge, and where the shooting stars had seemed to fall.

Niko was levering his crossbow; Tempus saw, out of the corner of his eye, the boy's hand go to his hip where the sword he had been given by Aškelon should have been, heard him curse, remembering where he'd left it, then spoke up, telling Niko to wait right there, and spurred the roan out to meet the silhouetted rider who was plainly bent on interception.

As he closed at a moderate lope, the dark rider got no lighter; it was helmed, and that helmet had a flowing pair of horse-tail crests like hair streaming down its back. Its mount and the riderless horse it led were sable, like its mail and arms. Soon he could see that its helmet had a full visor drawn down; below, a pale jaw showed between cheek pieces.

He reined in his own horse, told it "Stand," and waited. Other than the pale triangle of mouth, no light patch showed on rider or either horse, and both of these were Trôs-large, with arching crests and barrel chests and hooves that thundered when they touched the ground.

Horses worth a fight, worth slaying for, was his first thought as the rider slowed them to a walk and raised one gloved hand in casual greeting.

A few lengths away, he still had not placed the armor

style or the point of origin of tack or horses. They were of no breed he had ever seen before, with dished faces, tiny wide-set ears, and as great a breadth between their eyes proportionately as had their mighty chests. The armor seemed to be a sort of tiny-scaled corselet; no smith Tempus had knowledge of could work in such diminutive fashion. In truth, when the horses danced up close as if they were on springs, he saw that the rider was quite small as well.

Then a ray of sunlight struck its helm; it raised its hands and pushed the visor up, its mount suddenly stock still.

"Cime!"

"Greetings, brother. You called?"

"I . . . received a message that if I wished . . ."

"That's your Nikodemos, there, who has his crossbow trained on me? I'd tell him to put it by, were I you." She took her helmet off and hung it on her saddle.

Still stunned by the proximity of his sister, he turned and waved a signal; Niko was to put his weapon down and ride up. Then he faced her: "What took so long, sister?"

"I might ask that of you." She smiled, gray eyes like smoke lying lightly on him, yet he saw that they were puffy and red-rimmed, as if she'd been weeping long and hard. "We tried to reach you," she said; "used that boy. How is he?"

"You tell me."

She looked past him and on impulse he fumbled in his pouch and came up with a Rankan gold Imperial. When she turned back to him, he held it out as so long ago he had seen the dream lord do.

Her eyebrow raised. Her hand stretched out. She had to take it. She'd have to stay, now, until she'd given service. He could hold her thus as long as he could fend her off and not succumb to the urge, rising in him even now, which had started all their troubles centuries ago.

Then she answered the question he'd forgotten that he'd asked: "You've hurt Nikodemos more than helped him, brother. As usual, you rush in where you don't belong. The witch yet lives; his soul's all tangled up. You should have waited for me. *I* could have freed him with a wave of hand." She smiled at him pityingly. "But we'll save him, if it can still be done. Aškelon craves him as a mortal instrument, if you have not already guessed."

He'd thought as much, but discounted it as wishful thinking. "Then why let him suffer so?"

"We don't *own* him; he's human. He has free choice. He has his fate. And he's not ready to make a pact with even the most benign of powers. Now hush, he comes."

"Not quite yet. Why are you here?"

"To fight beside you, weakling brother. I've a dispensation from Aškelon himself. It's clear you'll never triumph on your own. But there are forms to be observed. We could not interpose ourselves without your invitation. Quite frankly, I was bored to tears with him; there's naught to do there."

"We have a clutch of mages sore in need of killing."

And Cime took her wands out and shook her hair down so that it floated, black and silver, in an errant breeze. The wands refracted sunlight like a pair of prisms, and all around them rainbows shivered into being. She sighed; she pocketed the coin he'd given her, which would bind her to him. She said, "I was beginning to fear you'd never ask. There's no shame in humbling oneself before such a lord as Aškelon— Ah, Nikodemos, I believe we've met before."

She held out a delicate hand and Niko leaned forward on his horse to take it, then brushed it with his lips, one eye on Tempus, his expression guarded. "That's right," he said. "At the Vulgar Unicorn, it was."

"You've been a careless boy, leaving the dream lord's gift unguarded. But we forgive you."

"*We?*" It was to Tempus Niko looked, his lips drawn tight.

Tempus scratched his neck and said uncomfortably, "My sister hobnobs with the plane lord."

"That's right," she said. "And he's sent you a token of remembrance and esteem, Nikodemos. Use it well and *remember* where you got it." From her saddle she unwound the second sable horse's tether and held it out.

Niko's bay backed three paces quickly; the fighter said, "I can't . . . take *that* . . . *him*"—he squinted at the magnificent horse trapped in exotic leathers— "from you. I hardly *know* you; I can't. My allegiance is already given. Commander, maybe you'll explain? . . ."

Tempus was at a loss for words; jealousy was an emotion he seldom had to deal with; he didn't know what to say.

But the sable horse raised up its head and curled its lips back and gave an ear-splitting call—half challenge, half welcome—so that Niko's bay gelding lowered its head and shivered.

"You take it, sir," Niko whispered.

"It's for you," Cime chuckled throatily. "Every time we meet, Nikodemos, I get the distinct impression you are afraid of me. Now take this horse; it's bad manners to refuse a gift from an entelechy; few men have the honor to receive one." She dropped its tether and the sable horse, his head high, minced over beside the cowering bay gelding and butted Niko with a fine, intelligent head. Niko looked at it askance, then with an uncertain, soft laugh and one last glance at Tempus, stroked its muzzle. The big stallion closed its eyes and stuck out its tongue.

Cime laughed again: "Don't look so crestfallen, brother. This one's for you; I've no need of *this* much help. We wish to make amends for the discomfort that we've caused you both, and the loss of the Trôs horses—"

"Loss?"

"Temporary, brother, temporary. Now, swap mounts with me and we'll talk about setting things aright while we ride out to your barracks—you *will* make accomodations for me?"

Dismounting with unconcealed eagerness, he knew he was accepting her too soon, without enough close questioning or making it clear to her that he wasn't about to get involved with her so deeply that he might not ever extricate himself or even have the sense to know he should. . . . Then he thought about the heinous bargain he'd made with the Tysian mageguild, and Niko's ensorcelment, and all the trials before them on their way up Wizardwall, and he too laughed: "My pleasure, sister. But you'll keep your place: not whore among my men or slay wantonly while among them. Not men *or* mages," he added, recalling Randal while he ran his hand down the sable mare's flank and Cime slipped a leg over to dismount.

As she slid down, he caught her in his arms.

"A welcome kiss, brother? Or has the Froth Daughter completely turned your head?"

He knew he shouldn't; he felt the Stepson watching; but his lips met hers and sibling considerations were no part of the welcome that she gave him.

He had to remind himself that the chances were good that they had no blood relationship, then force himself to disengage.

"So, my dear and most faithful lover, you *do* remember me."

Riding into the Outbridge station on the big sable mare bred on the archipelago of dreams with Cime beside him and Niko bringing up the rear, he wished he didn't remember quite so well all the harm and anguish she had caused him over so many years. But he was so deep into unsavory pacts with agents of sorcery and magic that a mage-killer like Cime might be exactly what he needed. He hoped so. She usually created repercussions worse than the problems she solved. He wondered if the dream lord had found this out and was glad to foist her off on him. But she wouldn't answer questions of that nature.

Crit, Bashir, Randal and Straton came riding in soon after, with Niko's panoply and a report of mixed success.

Cime demanded to see Crit's forearm, and when he had unwound the bandage and she'd fingered the dry, seared cuts, she said: "No doubt of it. The witch escaped."

"Who's this?" Critias had whispered to Niko when the four were first ushered into Tempus's quarters where they expected to report. *"His* sister," Niko had whispered back, and turned away to answer Straton's questions about the two new horses drawing an admiring crowd outside, then offered to take Strat out right then and let him try Niko's.

Since then, Critias had watched and waited without a word, his demeanor saying he wasn't about to speak freely with a woman—*any* woman—there.

Yet when she touched first his palm and then his arm with the butts of the diamond rods taken down from her hair, he covered her fingers with his own: "That's much better; it feels fine now. Thank you." His voice was very soft.

She said: "Cime. My name is Cime."

"I'm Critias, Tempus's second in command. And this is Straton, my right-side partner."

"Sacred Banders, are you?" Still her hand rested under his.

Tempus hadn't heard the rest; Bashir had pulled him off to one side to confirm what the priest suspected: that this was the famed and deadly sorcerer-slayer of legend. "What about *Randal?* Even for you, Riddler, this is a dangerous, convoluted game."

"The way up and down is one and the same."

"Meaning it is worth the risk?"

"Meaning if it *weren't*, we'd still have to accomodate her. Don't you have relatives, Bashir?"

"It seems to me she's going to be accomodating Critias."

"Did you see the horse she brought for Niko?"

"And one for you. Let's hope you don't need them to trek to hell together."

"With *you* here to watch over all our souls? Come, Bashir; let us see whether a priest of Enlil can drink an old soldier under the table."

And they left, with Randal trailing after, his eyes wide and his witch-scored face pale and wonder in his voice: "She says she's here to *help* us, Rid—commander. And she wants to confer, alone, with *me?*"

"Keep your belt tight, mageling, and you should survive it."

Already, she'd brought more troubles than he thought he could handle. But Bashir was as anxious as he to start the ascent to the high peaks keeps; after that, he wouldn't need her.

Niko had his cuirass back, if not his soul, and the sorrow in the Stepson's eyes was partly eased by the magnificent gift Aškelon had sent him; they'd not lost a single man to Roxane during the attack on the Peace River house; Bashir was committed and even Grillo seemed to be keeping his place. Whatever doubts the ranks had had were assuaged by the luminaries convening for this mission.

He heard Sacred Banders talking quick and easy victory as they headed for the mess; what with Enlil's priest and a successful night's work behind them, and the omen of gift horses from the entelechy of dreams, they could even fight hand to jowl with mages, against mages. It was almost as if they had Abarsis back again, so high were spirits in the camp.

Every one of them was spoiling for a fight, and Tempus knew one thing for certain: they were going to join the battle of their lives, sweat the blood of legends, and perform feats of valor the like of which they'd never know again.

# Book Five:

# Up Wizardwall

Around Wizardwall the wards snapped tight and rockfalls glowed bright blue. Nothing over fifty pounds in weight could pass through unnoticed or unscathed or by dint of force alone: the perimeter wards turned unwary insects into exploding fireflies, roasted rabbits in an instant, charred birds' feathers as they hit the high-strung fence of power wound about the citadel like ritual wool.

And down from the high peaks winter blew, and wizard weather vanquished summer: not one of the adepts gathered on the heights expected an easy rout, but all agreed a verdant carpet of flowered earth was not a proper welcome for the Riddler, his murderous sister Cime, Bashir of Free Nisibis who brought Enlil into the war, and Grillo, representative of Ranke under whose aegis even the Tysian mageguild had sent a young adept along to fight.

Nisibisi warlocks had never been so busy: already they were engaging the Machadi enemy side by side with Mygdon as the Mygdonian Alliance's most fearful weapon.

Most of the blood-hungry and the high-spirited warlocks had joined Lacan Ajami's rear echelon retinue; those remaining up on Wizardwall didn't dirty their hands with mortals or mix among the puny or the damned. A wealth of tender spirits and newly unconsecrated dead were delivered up to them by the lesser mages; the greater burped and lazed and fed, not really troubled by the distant, raging war or even sixty-six guerilla fighters climbing up with dogged determination to bring the war to them.

To teach Tyse a lesson long past due, blizzard weather was sent down. After camouflaging the high peaks routes and filling crevasses with treacherous drifts of white, it rolled on down the mountainsides, dispatching the summer with its blighting breath that bit off limbs and whispered harshly in reddened ears of famine soon to come.

Exploratory lightning bolts had been parried by Tyse's overweening mageguild; fair warning was ignored. Mere Hazards were not up to battling weather. Terror waxed among the townsfolk as their treasured prestidigitators bowed their heads and warmed their hands over sputtering hearths and tried in vain to call the banished summer back.

Priests pontificated over pious congregations larger than they had ever been before; armies drilled through slushy streets, a show of pretended force; mothers wrapped coughing children close and bought draughts that didn't cure them from overworked physicians; coins changed hands on Commerce Avenue for forecasts of fate and weather meant to make the frightened brave; whores warmed the bellies of unending clients who had fields full of frozen cattle to forget; girls wrapped in skins queued up before the mageguild to buy prophylactic spells and aborting preparations, but those who'd gone through times like these before just accepted that a baby boom was on the way.

In Brother Bomba's, the owner's wife was uncharacteristically glum: the place was full up night and day, reservations in advance were needed, and the storage magazines beneath would hold for a month or more while everything shot up in price and a mug of warming wine well-mulled or a barley posset was worth what a girl's night used to cost. But Madame Bomba's "soldier boys" were out mountain climbing in foul weather and this, her confidants agreed, was what was wrong: only good news down from the high peaks or word from one of Grillo's specials made her smile; a Sacred Bander, when one came down with a horse gone lame, was treated as her guest of honor; all others, rich or well connected or even intimately known as was her husband, were virtually ignored.

And high above the town the archmage Datan, in his preoccupation with the Froth Daughter snoring in his seraglio, could not be shaken to his senses or even spoken with, most days.

Since Roxane had flown up to heal her wounds and gird for battle, she'd hardly seen him. And when, chancing upon him in onyx, private halls, she'd tried to apprise him of his peril, he'd called her "stupid, short-sighted, and inept."

She'd left him with his belly shaking as he laughed at her and all his chins aquiver, certain then that she'd been right to deem him due for toppling. When this war was over, all of Wizardwall and the northern range would be hers, and hers alone.

Thus she didn't have to explain her own behavior: not how the snakes had died (though she'd been ready to blame it on the surprise attack by Stepsons) or even why they'd caught her unawares. She didn't have to justify the fact that she'd spared the young fighter Nikodemos for more spying despite the dream lord's cuirass or His alleged interest in the youth.

So she rehearsed the moment when she'd triumph and planned the fates she'd mete out to enchanters, high and low, to Enlil's priest and to the Riddler and his rightly-accursed sister, whom Roxane had hated at first sight in Sanctuary when One-Thumb introduced them.

As the Stepsons and Successors and specials of the army trudged on through snow and sleet she found those witches and warlocks she wanted for her faction, and prepared the oaths of fealty they must swear to earn salvation.

She was meeting with a chosen few when Datan called her to war council; the enemy had passed through the warding spells unharmed. It was Bashir, Enlil's foul priest, who'd facilitated this with sacreligious prayers sent on high, when from Wizardwall all worship was directed downward. Certain demons were incensed. The priest, it was decided, would be first to die.

The snow was deep, the shadows purple. Above them, as night fell, it seemed a man could touch the stars if only he reached out with lance or sword.

Tempus had split the force once Bashir was sure that sorcerous ramparts were well and truly breached: Niko had already taken his mixed group of Stepsons and Successors northeast; Grillo would have the western face to scale with Sacred Banders and his specials; Critias and Straton were to drift off in the morning with five pairs they had chosen for surreptitious entry and undisclosed diversionary action; Cime and he would stay with the main contingent and Bashir.

There had been some little wrangling. Critias had wanted Niko in his squadron: they were off to do what Niko liked and did the best. But Tempus had prevailed, citing Randal's presence as one reason to count against it. The witch's oversight through Niko's eyes he didn't mention until Critias and he had crunched knee-deep in snow to a spot near the horse lines where Tempus could be certain they were quite alone: "I want her thinking he *is* the main threat, that where Niko goes and what he penetrates should be the wizards' primary concern." He'd sent Niko's team off first, then given out further orders. The young Stepson thought the balance of the incursion force would follow close behind his advance, that he and Randal were the shock troop leaders on which all else depended.

Critias spat into the snow. "You'll likely lose him."

"By standards such as you or I employ, we've already lost him. He's got the mage close on his right; if he comes through this, it will be a combination of his luck and Randal's skill, not anything more or less, that saves him. He's got a witch upon his back, her collar round his neck." To no one else would Tempus have explained himself at length. But Crit's usefulness was enhanced the more he knew; he saw and understood too much to be kept ignorant, allowed to draw his own conclusions, which might be wrong. "And Cime's been over all possible contingencies with Randal. You've seen for yourself that my sister is unparalleled at strategy with men."

Crit looked at him sidelong: "Have you objections to my spending time with her? She's your sister, after all . . . perhaps I should have asked. I'm not serious, not in love—just. . . ." He stopped and frowned: "That's not how I meant to say this . . . I mean, it's a war, commander. Men bunk in where and how they can."

Tempus chuckled at his task force leader's discomfort: Critias was seldom at a loss for words; Tempus couldn't remember him ever being obviously nonplussed. "As long as you're paying her what she asks, it's not my business—"

"You know about that?"

"Would that I did not."

"So? . . . It's all right, then? You've no objections?"

"Would it matter if I did? No, I'm sorry, Crit. It's hardly a case where you need to ask or I want to give permission. She's ten times your age, you know, surely old enough to choose her bedmates on her own. I'm not her father, nor will I give my blessing to any union she makes for the occasional coin. . . . She has a long, infernal history of

which, if you're smart, you'll stay in blessed ignorance."
He knew he had been too sharp, that Crit might misunder-
stand, and uneasiness between them was one thing he
could not afford. Yet he didn't like her bedding his best
officer, the one man on whom he must be able to depend.
Twice in the same evening, he found himself wishing
Critias were a trifle less perceptive.

"Listen, Fox," Tempus used Crit's war name; the sound
of it brought his second in command up short. "She's my
sister but she's not. . . ." He couldn't explain it. He said
instead: "Be careful of her, she's not a belly-warmer. And
she belongs to Aškelon, lord of dreams, not to men. It's
sport for her, and if it's sport for you, that's fine. But I
need your head, unturned, and your eyes full sharp, and
your mind on business. I can't have you leading men into
battle half asleep."

That lightened the mood, and Crit's cynical grin flashed
white as the snow about. The moon was rising, gibbous
and bright. "Now you sound like Straton. I promise I'll
pace myself. It's not a full time occupation of mine, pleas-
ing women. I've a right-side partner now, you know. . . ."

And on firmer ground they left the subject, talking of
the Successors' trick of pushing off from crags, their body-
weight guiding silken-strutted winglike kites, and whether
they could use it; and checking mules and asses among
the horses on the lines, and trying to evaluate without
prejudice Grillo's men and Grillo's motives—a difficult
task when both wondered where the Rankan really stood
to profit most, for that was where Grillo's interest always
lay. Neither had expected him to volunteer to make the
trip. Critias was just venturing that it must be because of
Bashir when a commotion among the low, black goatshair
tents sent them at full tilt, running in wide-paced strides
through the snowdrifts.

They followed sounds of horses screaming, growls and
howls and men shouting curses until they came upon a

crowd milling uncertainly about a collapsed tent with thrashing shapes beneath it.

"What's happening here? Who's in there?" Crit collared a Nisibisi fighter with arrow nocked and pulled him off his knees.

"Let me go! My lord's in there . . . and Grillo, too . . . and something . . . something *else!*"

"You can't shoot what you can't see, man. Come on." And Crit was running, pointing and yelling names and codes and gathering a group to lift the tent, another with ready arms, spear and bow and sword, to slay whatever was growling and howling under it when they got the cover off.

As ten men moved in to lift the tent, a wind began to gust. Snow rose up in blinding eddies off the ground and clouds attacked the moon. An unearthly whine came from the wind that blew the snow into their eyes and men snapped down their visors or held up arms to keep their lashes from freezing as they blinked and cursed, but Critias and Tempus, with his own sword drawn, wouldn't let them back away.

When they'd gotten it halfway up, the torches at intervals around all guttered, but Tempus had seen something furred and feral, a glimpse of glowing greenish eyes, and dived under, into the tent's confines.

"Bashir? Grillo?"

"Aye, my brother. I'm still here," Bashir replied, but faintly.

"Tempus? What took so long?" Grillo sounded stronger, closer. "You feel anything. See anything? Let's not hack each other to bits in here, my friends. All hold!"

And, pausing, his sword fouled in something—tent or beast, he couldn't say—Tempus listened. He strained his ears. He waited for jaws to close on him. He heard Grillo's breathing on his left, and Bashir's, too ragged, somewhat farther away. "I think you're right, Grillo; it's gone, what-ever it was—or wasn't. Let's help them lift this up."

Grillo answered; Bashir did not.

And when, with much straining and pulling and push-ing from within, they got the tent (which like a great bat with a will of its own seemed to want to smother them) pulled up and cast aside, and someone brought a torch Tempus hardly needed in the light from a moon come clear in a starry night with no traces of wind or snow to mar it, all could see the black blood running from Bashir's gut around the hand he held to his groin.

He was curled up, and Tempus called: "Get Cime," refusing to let Successors, pushing back the others to get close to their wounded leader, move him.

Bashir's eyes were open wide, and Tempus could see the shock in them. If he started flailing, he would surely die. So Tempus sat down in the snow and talked quietly but insistently to the warrior-priest, who had bubbles at the corners of his mouth, about what had happened and de-manded a description of the attacker.

Bashir was trying to get his words out clearly, willing himself to ignore the pain. Men crouched silent, close, and bit their lips; from farther back, Tempus could hear curses and prayers begin to sound.

"Make way, here. Let us through. *Move*, hillman!" It was Straton's voice. Then Tempus heard Critias, talking fast and low to Cime about getting her anything she needed and what it was going to mean to the endeavor if Bashir died now and his men, a superstitious lot, deserted, leav-ing them not much better than lost among the crags covered with snow.

"Crit, not now. Cime, look at this."

Then his sister was beside him; Bashir's grip tightened on his hand. The priest shook his head: *no*, he didn't want that kind of help. But he hadn't spoken aloud and Tempus leaned down, whispering, "This is no time for scruples, fighter. Unless you're a coward and seek an easy death."

That put life into Bashir's brown eyes, and Cime bent over him, diamond rods aglow.

As she worked, Bashir, against his will, gave one soft cry and sucked in breath; when she straightened up, she ran one bloody hand through her hair and said, "I cannot say for sure if this avails him." Then, louder: "Successors! That blood wine of yours is what he needs right now. All you've got, and hurry! Get it!"

"Straton!" she continued. "He needs a litter, a dry, warm tent—mine will do. Lots of furs, painkillers; get all the drugs together and someone to tell me about each one you've got. And start some soup—we need clear broth."

"Soup? Woman, with a wound like that? You'll kill him," Grillo objected.

Tempus was about to intervene; with all Bashir's Successors listening, the last thing he needed was dissension, open questioning of Cime's healing skills.

But she said: "The *wound* is closed. It's the blood he's lost which concerns me. And the pain he's in. Now, get back. Where's Straton? Brother, move these men and speed this up. He'll be on his way to Enlil's hands if he lies much longer in this snow."

When she'd used that same snow to wash away his blood from the angry, closing wound, she called her brother close: "Put your hand right here, and keep it there."

"I thought you said it's healed? . . ."

"In deep, it is. We've got to squeeze the fluids up and out; if it were to heal over poison, or his own wastes, we'd lose him. Just hold it closed and don't ask questions." He did as he was told, noticing that Bashir had quite passed out.

Later, within her tent, they traded guesses as to what had made the wound and whether Bashir would have to be left behind.

"One place is as bad as another. The trip up won't kill him more surely than the trip down. Leave him? And if it attacks again? We've got to take him, brother. The god loves him; if it's Enlil's will, he'll mend."

Grillo sneered that gods had nothing to do with this, that it was a werewolf, probably planted among the men.

"Oh yes? That's your guess? Then go out and find him, Rankan. Use this." From her belt Cime pulled a little dart, silvery and very thin at its tip.

Once the flap had closed behind Grillo, her mocking laugh rang out. "I keep wondering when these fools will grow up, but the answer is that they will not."

"There's no werewolf, then?" Straton asked.

"Not unless it's you, Stepson. Or Critias. I keep those stickers to pick my teeth."

Straton shuddered, made a face, and scrambled up to see if the broth was ready.

That left just Critias, Tempus, and Cime, her cheeks smeared with blood like rouge, a lock of hair hanging down before her eyes. She pursed her lips and blew it back: "Well, beloved sirs, what think you? His color's better."

"We'll take him," Tempus decided. "Critias, go spread the word among his men and see what you can do to ease their fears—the whole camp will be sitting up on doubled watch after this, and we cannot afford to let fear of magic waste their strength."

"I'll tell them," Crit said wryly and slipped away, touching Cime's neck as he passed by: "You can heal me any time."

"Now, brother, don't say anything," she warned when Crit was gone.

"I was going to remind you that *I* have first claim on your services," he replied.

"Which ones?" she rejoined wickedly, but as she did,

Bashir groaned and tried to rise up on his elbows, then thrashed as some men will in delayed shock, and they had their hands full trying to hold him still.

Three days after being bitten by a hell-spawned demon, Enlil's priest still lived. This troubled Datan greatly; watching Jihan sleep in his seraglio, his massive head propped upon one fist, his other hand on the tow-headed boy who cuddled by his knee, he brooded. The poison in Bashir's wound had failed to do its work; the priest had too much aid from higher realms: his own pious soul, the god Himself, and Aškelon's mage-destroying bitch, sicced on Datan straight from the archipelago of dreams.

The improbable was fast becoming likelihood, the unthinkable now had to be considered: he was about to find his fortress under siege. Every adept and lesser mage and first-class sorcerer and warlock who'd lounged about under Datan's wards for eons knew it. Some were packing up belongings; some were making safety vaults secure; some struck further bargains with the loan officers of hell to whom they'd one day be consigned; some even came to him with urgent pleas to underwrite a slim chance of Wizardwall's survival by surrendering up the boy and Jihan to these grim soldiers of the gods who ignored their mortal fears and smiled in death's foul face.

But these forgot that death, to god-fearing armies, was but a well-earned rest, an end to a life as full of terrors as death was to those who'd forfeited eternal peace and given up their souls. The Riddler's troops sought only death with honor, their places in the finest afterlife a man could claim were well assured. And so the fear Datan had once thought to strike into hardened commando hearts had boomeranged, come back upon his subjects like a flying wing to demoralize the high peaks' lords with doubts. Only Roxane and a handful of her cronies huddled hatching counterschemes, and those might do more harm than good.

He'd thought long on the fate of Jihan, and his feeling was that the risk he took by keeping her asleep, unwitting hostage, in order to forefend her father's mixing in, was well worth taking. Otherwise, if he'd sent her with the boy as once he'd thought to do, Stormbringer might be tempted to join the fray. And that chance, Datan couldn't take.

It was ironic that the supersitious fear he'd thought to foster in the hard young men who braved his spells and curses had come back to settle at his own hearth. But he'd not lived so long or gained so much to lose it to a motley crew of mercenaries led by a pair of accursed siblings and an all-too-human priest.

He was glad now that he'd kept the boy; he saw a different kind of salvation in those wide-set, worshipful eyes. He tousled the flaxen hair beneath his hand and told the boy, "Rise up. Quietly now, we mustn't wake her." To hold Jihan thus, he needed to let her wake awhile every day or so, and then Shamshi was necessary to make fast the illusion Datan fostered in her that both the Froth Daughter and the prince of Mygdon were still resting up to leave—that only days, not weeks, had passed since they'd come into his care. And when she woke he wooed her, and put into her impressionable head resentment toward the Riddler.

With her, he'd made good progress; as with the boy, he'd already won what mattered: the child was his, heart, soul and mind, as Jihan soon would be. Let the legion of the damned who clambered up his mountain come; let them clamor for revenge and even tear down his venerable citadel stone by stone. In child and more-than-human Froth Daughter he had aces yet to play.

"Where now, father?" young Shamski asked, once they'd left the sleeping Jihan and were out among the wenches of the seraglio and, behind, the wall of stone which came and went at Datan's bidding entombed her once again, its faceless, unmarked expanse giving no hint that Froth Daughter or room of summoning or anything at all but solid rock was there.

"We'll have a bit of sport with some of these," his father said, indicating the herd of fawning women, "then go seek out our friend Roxane. All adepts must help one another now that our hour of crisis has begun."

He saw young Shamshi's eyes go wide with wonder and excitement mixed in just the right proportion.

And he smiled down at his son. He might win this yet, on the larger scale eternals used to weigh their work. Let Enlil melt his snow and dissolve his demons and fend off his fiends, it didn't matter. All that mattered was the outcome—just survival, and the leave of those he served to "live" to fight again.

Crit could see the peak now, the ramparts black and craggy as if just natural rock scratched at the dusky sky. "See? There?"

Straton blinked and rubbed his eyes and cursed the blurriness through which he saw the world: "If you say it's there, I'll take your word, Crit, but it's just rocks to me."

Twisting in his saddle, Crit said to Cime, "Strat's vision, my lady. I'd take it as a favor if you could do anything for him."

Her tinkling laugh was gentle: "One victory at a time, Stepson. Now, let's firm this up: leave Straton with the men to secure the horses and plant the charges and take positions, or not— But one way or the other, I am going in there. With you or without you."

"I don't know . . ." Crit had five pairs of Sacred Banders to take care of; he couldn't seem to make her understand the gravity of that responsibility.

"Now you sound like Tempus. Decide, soldier, or muddle through alone." She slipped off the big roan the Riddler had loaned her and handed Straton its reins. She was wraithlike in the fading light; brown-armored with her crested helm, she might have been a man. But Critias knew from sweat-drenched nights that Cime was all woman, and enough more that she made him uncomfortable whenever she wasn't making him more comfortable than he'd dreamed a man could be.

This whole operation was a mess: she should have stayed with Tempus, attended to Bashir. "I'm not a nurse," she'd said, and invited herself along once Bashir had regained his hold on life, and the poison he fought off was no longer an imminent threat. When Bashir was well enough to begin supplicating Enlil to melt the snow, she'd proclaimed him healed, and that was that.

They'd spent one day slogging through the mud and slush Enlil's bright sun and warm winds had made of Datan's snow, the whole main contingent kept together by Tempus's order because, he said, the men should see their priest surmount his plight and gain their spirit back by watching gods make light of hostile magic. This extra day spent altogether put Niko's squadron far ahead and sore at risk. Critias didn't understand why neither Tempus or Bashir nor Cime were concerned with that. The Riddler simply refused to discuss sending a man or god-facilitated message to warn Niko to lay back another day. Cime had laughed at Crit's concern that timing and coordination were crucial to the venture, saying only: "I have conferred, dear lover, with Randal. All contingencies have been covered. Now come here and kiss me. . . ."

He had a feeling that Tempus was piqued, withdrawing from his sister and Critias so as not to tacitly sanction their affair. But when he'd tried again to either talk it out or simply shake off his infatuation, first brother and then sister had merely smiled at him.

And now she was all but calling him a coward. He

handed his own reins to Strat; their strategy was so precisely planned that either left- or right-side partner could recite it in his sleep. Beyond the point where strategy or planning would apply, every man was on his own in any case. The attack was set for dawn. He slipped an arm around her waist and said, "I'm a fool, but I'm coming with you. Just tell me what the point is; I've got to have a sufficient reason to leave my men."

Straton muttered a farewell blessing and reined the horses back. They stood before a deep defile across which they'd just come, every horse and man intact under Cime's aegis: she'd made a bridge of cloud where empty air had been before. They'd planned to leave their mounts on its far side when they'd gone over the terrain in the Outbridge maproom with Bashir. But Cime changed everything, every rule of every game—he'd been warned, but had chosen not to listen.

He turned on his heel to give his friend more than a cursory godspeed, but Straton waved him off in genuine disgust. That, too, he'd have to solve soon. Cime was disruptive, a passionate influence, just as Tempus said. Yet his own instinct told him that the opportunities she offered, in more than just the sphere of lust, might never come again. And if the dream lord took offense, or even Tempus . . . well, then, that was life.

"We'll be in and out of there and back among your fighters, leader, before they have time to miss you. We'll like as not have slain the archmage or his favorite witch; we'll surely reconnoiter unseen halls, maybe open up the doors. Enough 'point' for you, soldier?"

"Just tell me how," he insisted, uncomfortable, and let her go, squatting down on turf that felt like permafrost, so cold it numbed him through his boots. They'd suffered from this weather, horse and man alike.

"Disguises, soldier. We'll look like familiar mages, like friends of whomsoever we chance to meet."

"How? By magic? No thanks, lady. It's against my religion."

She raised her visor, studied him. "Yes," she sighed, "I suppose it is. Well, I shouldn't be surprised that you are all alike. You, my brother, all these men. It's a wonder any of you live to regret your prejudices. I thought you'd do, but I was wrong. Stay here, then, soldier. And may your god protect you. I cannot."

He put out a hand to object, opened his mouth to explain, but as he closed his fist where her shoulder just had been, there was nothing there but air.

The mage-killer Cime was gone, winked out of existence as if she'd never been.

Feeling foolish, but relieved, he headed back toward his men and his horses.

Straton had never been so glad, he said, to see him as when he came back from the edge of that deep defile alone.

Niko and Randal weren't getting on as paired fighters should. But then, Randal wasn't Niko's sort of fighter. When they'd used the Successors' tactic of soaring across chasms so deep even wizards' snow couldn't hide them, depending on natural updrafts and the favor of the gods to guide them to a safe landing, higher up, on the far side, Randal had balked at using the "flimsy" kites and come across some other way.

No one among Niko's squadron wanted to dwell on how. Having a magician with you when you're out to slay magicians might have benefits, but it had debits: the tough talk fighters used to up their courage and fan their hatred offended the young adept; outlandish boasts of what Nisibisi commandos did to Nisibisi mages when they caught them made Randal's ears turn red and wards drip from his lips, and oftentimes he blanched.

But now, a thousand yards from the high keep's sprawling blackness, whose sentries seemed so tiny atop the gargantuan blocks of stone piled high, everyone could see how labyrinthine the fortress, was and men had begun to watch their tongues.

"Why do you think they let us get so far?" Ari wondered through teeth clenched against a sharper, less natural cold than that which had made them leave their horses in a Successor-guarded cave where they'd spent the day and regained their strength and eaten from stores protected by Enlil's talismans.

Men were caring for their weapons, checking springs on crossbows, pulleys on Nisibisi double-strung bows which used helically-fletched arrows instead of bolts or short flights, putting poison on their tips with careful fingers. Each bowman had brought up "first line" ammunition: ninety bolts or feathered shafts apiece. The archers' concern was rain, which would make the fletched shafts go wide and some go useless; the swordsmen just talked low of prior exploits hand-to-hand and what they'd do when, ramparts breached, at last they were free to "mix it up" with an enemy so long vilified and so hard to convince to stand and fight. This time, all were sure, they'd have to; Niko never could remember men so eager for a fight. All the years of being polite to foul enchanters and enduring their excesses as if Sacred Banders were a lower class made the Stepsons just as passionate to shed mages' blood as were the men of Free Nisibis.

Of all his men, only Ari was reluctant. Niko had requested him because he had liked what he'd seen when they first met, and taken Ari's measure while schooling him with blossoms and throwing stars. But Haram hadn't liked that, and Tempus' decree was all that came between Niko and Haram settling the matter with naked blades.

Now Niko heard Randal whispering to Ari, who had dared to ask a question no one wanted to consider: this whole, easy ascent could have been a trap. The snow might have slowed them but it didn't stop them; surely the feared wizardry of Nisibis could wreak more havoc than this. Niko crouched and scuttled toward them, keeping low. The lights were lit above them in the magicians' fortress; guardians of the ramparts could be seen, in torchlight, to be not quite human.

Reaching Randal and Ari, Niko broke in: "Randal, nobody really *cares* why they 'let' us get so far, or *if* they did. Just hold your tongue. Supposition has no place on a battle line." And he pulled the junior Hazard away from the omen-conscious special when the mage was succeeding in scaring half to death by answering his question in ways a soldier didn't want to hear.

"Gods, Randal, can't you keep shut? Why I ever brought a pud like you upcountry, I don't know. If you live through this, maybe you'll become a man, but if you open your mouth again to one of mine with this portentous drivel, I'm going to shut it permanently, on the spot, myself. Clear?"

Niko would have given the panoply he wore—charmed cuirass, dagger, sword, the lot—to have his old left-side leader back, or Janni instead of Randal on his right. This was his first sortie as a unit commander; he *had* to do it right.

The mournful look on Randal's face made him try to exlain just a little of what it meant to be a professional soldier, what a leftman expected from his right, and what commanding fighters like these demanded in the way of white lies and the exercise of common sense. He took the mage off alone: ". . . so you see, you don't *advise* them of purported dangers they can't see, you don't tell them to beware what they don't know how to fight. We've got to stir them up and help them face this thing as if we're engaging an enemy who's equal; let them clutch at winning, not convince them that they don't know how to meet this enemy. By Enlil's—"

"*Don't* invoke any of your doting deities to me, Nikodemos. I've got enough problems. I'm cold and wet and I'm not fool enough to believe we'll live to face the battle in the morning. If you haven't realized it, your beloved Riddler sent us out ahead as diversionary fodder, to take the warlocks' attention from the *real* incursion force. We're *dead*, you just don't know it yet—" Randal's voice was a rising wail.

Niko slapped him, backhanded, across the cheek without even thinking. "Lies. Didn't Cime 'contact' you in some mysterious way and tell you to tell me to pull back a day and wait?"

"Yes, yes, but that's just what I mean—"

They were arguing in low and urgent tones, walking upright now behind a shielding tumble of high boulders through which not even Wizardwall's best could see, when suddenly Niko heard his name whispered, and Randal his, and both men stopped.

"Oh, by the Writ, we've done it now," the Hazard said, and clutched at Niko: "Go on, soldier. Run. Flee. Your men can't do without you . . . I'll handle—"

But then the whisperers came into view, and Randal's hissing voice was stilled.

Undeads with pure white eyes shuffled through the snow with hands outstretched and smiling faces: Tamzen, his beloved Tamzen, in the lead. And each child was weeping, begging Niko to help them, please, to free them and to comfort them and to take them home. They missed their mothers and their fathers and they missed their home, and they were damned because of him.

"Don't listen. Draw your weapons, fighter," Randal urged, his own fingers weaving blue-tinged wards before his face.

There were six undeads, Tamzen, her girlfriends, and other children Niko wished he didn't know: youngsters slain in battles long ago, in sacks of towns, or afterwards, when those who can't be saved must be dispatched; one even from the slavepits where he'd been incarcerated, a boy who'd died beside him of soldiers' rape in chains.

Randal's voice was distant, indistinct. Tamzen's face implored him. He'd seen it in too many dreams to let the white eyes frighten him. He was used to her; his soul cried for her; he thought they'd come to take him off to play their games amid the grass and summer of his rest-place. He had to touch her, to hold, console her; he had to make amends. . . .

He was walking toward her, arms spread wide, when Randal tripped him and he fell face down into the snow. The cold of it upon his cheeks and in his mouth helped to bring him to his senses—that and the way his cuirass was heating up. It steamed where it touched the snow and he heard: "Draw your blade, idiot. Or you'll be wandering around like them for eternity!" but the voice was muffled.

Niko rolled, confused, onto his back and saw Randal with three undeads hanging on his arms and pulling at his clothing, their teeth bared and their mouths open wide, and they were chanting awful, low sounds interspersed with clacks of snapping jaws. He could see the mage's popping eyes, his fearful struggles.

"Hold on, Randal!" He vaulted up, cross-drawing sword and dirk as he gained his feet and leaped toward the struggling Hazard, being pulled down into the snow.

He remembered wondering why the mage's magic couldn't help him, and hearing Tamzen tell him it could, he needn't worry, just come with her; and then, slipping in the melting snow, he reached the embattled mage upon his knees and swung his sword in a downward arc meant to sever undead necks.

But as his sword went through the first, head and torso disappeared, and when his continuing swing touched the shoulder of the second, it howled and fell apart; and the third, Randal's blood running from its mouth, scrambled back, its hands outstretched, calling: "Niko, Niko, don't! We're friends. You can't slay *me!*" But the dirk in his left hand, with a will of its own, shot forward out of his grip and impaled itself in the neck of the boy he'd watch die so long ago upon a slaver's chain.

"Niko! Niko! Stop!" It was Tamzen's voice, this time, tremulous and full of fear, and as he wheeled to face her specter, something jumped upon him from behind, its clammy hands locked around his neck, its childish legs clamped to his sides. Then it screamed as its limbs made contact with the cuirass, and burst into flame and threw itself back to sputter and flare in the snow.

Tamzen and her best friend advanced upon him, and he could barely see them for his tears. Tamzen's sobs were soft and low: "Hold me, Niko; hold me, I'm so cold."

He lowered his sword uncertainly, an instant, and in that instant both undeads sprang, their fingers crooked like claws.

Years of training prompted him; he didn't have to think; he stepped in, not out, and the blade so hot and shining now with ruddy light was like a living being in his grip, slicing down into the breast of a girl he'd introduced to love and been at pains, always, to protect. The blade went through as if through cheese and continued, the momentum of its arc catching the other girl beneath her ribs and opening her from side to side.

But they didn't fall into lifeless puddles right away; they didn't disappear; they both stood a moment, fingers with long, long nails spread over the wounds he'd made— which would have killed them if they'd only been alive. And Tamzen cocked her head, and nodded, said: "Niko. I knew you'd come," and tears streamed from her eyes, no longer white-on-white, but human eyes, dark like velvet, as they'd been in life. She tottered, turning to her friend, saying: "See, I told you Niko'd save us!" and then both she and the other girl disintegrated in a gust of wind. There was a puff of fetid dust which blew his way, then nothing, only Randal scrambling, panting, through the snow, holding a wound that bled profusely at his neck, his breath rasping:

"Bless you, Niko, bless you. By the Writ, that was as close to damned as I ever want to come."

Niko backed away. "Your neck. You're wounded. Are you now undead yourself? Or worse?"

The mageling managed a facsimile of a chuckle: "You've been listening to too many fireside tales spun by your gullible comrades. A little snow to clean the wound, a healing draught to give me strength, and I'll be fit and well again." Randal held out his free hand. In it was the dirk Aškelon had given Niko. "Take it. It's still hot, but then . . . you're used to that. And don't talk to *me* about proscribed methods or magic in the future, fighter, not with weaponry like this."

And Randal clapped him on the back, so that Niko had to shrug him off and tell the mage that he'd join him back at camp when he was ready, and Randal should precede him: "Don't say *any*thing about this to them, no matter how proud you are of not dying on the spot from fear or whatever kind of omen you think you've made of this, or for any other reason. *Understood?*"

"Yes, com*man*der," Randal aped a cringe of terror and hurried off with exaggerated stealth.

Niko was so sick at heart from what he'd seen, he didn't even have the will to correct the mageling: one doesn't call one's leftman "commander."

He knelt down in the snow where Tamzen had been and felt around for something—bone, or jewel, or piece of cloth—anything. But there was nothing there. And a part of him was glad for that: physical undead or vicious apparition, he was fairly certain that her spirit, by the grace of the sword bestowed on him by the entelechy of dreams, had found its destined rest.

The assault on the high peaks keep came with dawn; pink-tipped arrows raced a hundred yards straight up, glowing with Enlil's sanction, almost invisible in the tricky light of sunrise, to fell human thralls and fiends upon the ramparts. Ghouls yowled; undeads sparked and flared and burst apart when the god-sent arrows pierced them; demons crashed from dizzying heights to splatter on the rocks below.

And as the sun banished night with lavender and pink and lemon light, the very foundations of the citadel began to tremble and to shake, and warlocks to quake where they girded for battle.

Women wailed; wizards paled; *someone* cleared the wards from gates and high doors, front and back, and the enemy poured in where men were never meant to tread.

Datan's remaining minions and the bravest of the sorcerers had been on the southern rampart, trying to rout the tiny men below and stop the rain of quarrels whispering death as they whistled over walls magic should have kept secure, when flames licked the ancient rock which by some trick of Enlil's began to burn like tinder. The defenders begged for mercy as they roasted, but eager underworld claws and grasping hands from other planes reached out to take them. The very heavens split asunder, and specters of eternal retribution strode atop the battlements to claim shriveled souls they'd long been promised.

By the time it was clear that the attack on the keep's southern flank was just diversion, charges shook the towers, and stones began to rumble and tumble, and Nisibisi warlocks ran sobbing through its halls. The guardians of their fate knew who was due for death this day and weren't content to wait. They brought their deeper darkness along, cold and dank with death, to trap adepts and wrap up prized and damned witches who'd traded all they had and now could only weep and cower when their spells died unsaid upon their lips and eternity beckoned all to begin to pay a price that suddenly seemed too great. But it was too late for everyone who'd lived too long and fed on hapless, weaker souls. They shrieked; they threw themselves off towers and sought to gulp down poisoned draughts or fall upon cursed swords. But it *was* too late; the reckoning was here. Even repentance, tried by some, availed them not; they had bargained away their final option of salvation for power, long ago. The gods they supplicated had lost scores of followers to sorcery, and met wizards' pleas with lists of unspeakable sins whose payment had come due.

Roxane closed her ears to rumbling stones and cringing women's cries and ran, her hands above her head to ward off the ancient mortar and pulverized stone falling all about. Whoever had opened up the doors had to pay for treachery; she sought the coward among her own, but there were too many: she couldn't tell.

She skidded round a corner and saw Tempus' Stepsons thronging hallowed halls, every javelin and drawn sword and flying wing and crossbow bolt glowing pink with sanction from the god. She stopped. She estimated forces and chances. She turned and fled the other way, pushing aside other, lesser witches frozen in confusion or dashing aimlessly about, seeking protection in places where it could not be found.

Datan's fault, all this. She'd known it would go ill when he'd come to her with his princeling wide-eyed by his side, fresh from debauching with the boy, and demanded she sic her most precious undeads upon Niko and his Hazard friend, young Randal. It wouldn't work; it was too soon, she had objected. But Datan was still her ruler; she'd not chanced confronting him right then. So she'd lost her personal protection, given up Tamzen and her playmates to try to make an end to Randal without killing Niko—even in these straits, she'd wanted Stealth alive, somehow to save him while putting his team of fighters out of action. But Randal, more selfless than she'd thought a mage could be, had put his person's safety by and striven to save Niko—in the end, she'd lost her best undeads.

And Niko's unit hadn't run off, daunted by the specters she had sent to freeze them in their tracks with fear, but hunted witches now within these very halls, every accursed god who loved the armies with them in spirit and in strength.

She'd seen enough; she turned again and fled toward the inner sanctums, where a witch might make away or make a stand and pass from life with honor.

On her way, she cursed the soul of Datan, who was nowhere to be found, hearing Critias and Tempus shouting maneuver codes behind her as they fought their way upward, stair by stair. Stopping long enough to peer out a high tower's embrasure, she saw in the courtyard far below such carnage as made even one so inured to horror as Roxane close her eyes.

Datan, she knew, could stop this. Tempus would call a halt to war to face him, hand to hand. Heart pounding, she dashed through the seraglio's carpet of weeping women swooning on the floor and eunuchs of the blood huddled in the corner, seeking Wizardwall's master where he hid.

Behind the faceless wall of stone which barred the summoning chamber from the lesser mages and the sight of men, she found him, with the sleeping Froth Daughter and his boy. In the center of his power glyphs he stood, his huge bulk somehow smaller. And, beyond, the globe he used to concentrate his power spun, colors from its inset stones making kaleidoscopic patterns on the walls.

"Hold, Datan! Stand and fight! This slaughter doesn't have to be. Go face the Riddler! This is your doing! Undo it and save those adherents whom you may!" She strode over warming stones and stopped the globe, bitting her lip at the sizzling pain she felt when she touched it with her hand.

Then the soulless eyes of the Osprey fixed on her, and as he whispered, "No," and shook his head, his arm raised up and a finger pointed at her.

She was going to speak his true name—it was only fair, for this fat and loathsome creature whom she'd served had betrayed every single one of them.

But Datan's spell worked faster. From his finger a bolt of royal blue shot out and caught her by the throat. Struck dumb, she reeled and stumbled backward, hit the wall and slid down it, nearly senseless, crumpled in a heap.

The little boy let out a cry and ran to her. Shamshi's eyes were filled with tears. He looked up at his sire, and back to her, murmuring, "Roxane, oh Roxane, can you hear? Speak to me! *Speak to me!*"

She struggled to put out her hand and then she touched him, stroked his hair. Her vision cleared, and with what strength she yet had, she took his hand in hers. And into the boy she poured herself, taking over mind and tongue.

Datan wouldn't strike his own child dead or dumb, she knew. And as she opened Shamshi's mouth to use his vocal cords and lungs to speak the Osprey's true name and consign him to the hell he'd earned, Datan realized what it was she had in mind, and that great hulk of a creature wheeled with more speed than she'd thought he had, and even began to run, casting behind him another agonizing spell that made all things fade away: the chamber of summoning, the princely child who'd not hurt anyone or anything, the glyphs and globe—everything dissolved in pain and fractured, rainbow lights.

When next she thought at all, she thought she heard Jihan, awake. She looked up, blinking, trying to focus over the head of the boy who hugged her close and sobbed her name. Jihan stood there, though beyond she saw a sleeping form upon the couch where Jihan had long been snoring, insensible, at rest.

This Jihan, however, leaned down over her and touched her throat, demanding to know the proper word, the true nature of Datan's secret name.

And with what strength she still possessed, she whispered it, told the Froth Daughter what to say, and lost sight of everything once again.

Half the outer wall was crumbled; debris and bodies were everywhere. Tempus' eyes were smarting from the sulfurous fumes and the stench of rot that set in once these ancient foes met death. His sword glowed pink and dripped with acid blood and wherever he stepped ichor, in grainy puddles, ate into the paving stones.

He'd seen Critias, Straton too. They were bloodied but their teeth were bared and their eyes glittered with the shine of men engaging a worthy enemy in an honest fight.

Bashir he'd left long since, protected by his god and twenty men. The priest was still weakened from the demon spittle in his blood, but his god was not, and Enlil's blessing had helped to win the day.

He ran through halls where wizards sought surrender and met their deaths instead. Small young demons flapped their wings above, and with his last three quarrels he dispatched them. His twice-human speed and his flickering, shark-hilted sword made him the avatar of death, and he meted it out with impunity to all he met.

There was neither time for nor use in taking captives here, where every foe had more-than-human guile and none knew mortal restraint. He had seen Stepsons go down with their throats torn out; he'd pulled fiends off friends of his who'd had legs or arms bitten through so that jagged bones peeked out. The fury he'd once thought was lent him by a god raged inside him; now he knew it was his own. The last time he had met inhuman foes, he'd taken far too long to heal. Yet he'd lived to fight at least this one more time and if indeed he met his death here seeking Datan, his heart's sworn enemy, the mage he hated most of mages, an archmage he'd cursed throughout the ages, then he'd be content with that. One head and one alone he longed to sever. Once he'd seen Datan to his eternal unrest, Tempus would have avenged the spirit of Abarsis, Niko's suffering, and even crippled magic's rule upon a land so fraught with troubles that the meddling of enchanters was a wretched, godless expression of evil and excess.

A clawlike, warty appendage snatched at him from a foggy shadow: some demon lying in wait. He slashed with sword and the hand fell twitching; a demon cursed his name. He shrugged it off: accursed so thoroughly as he'd been through the eons, one more ill-wisher meant little to his fate.

He'd taken cuts; his naked arms bled freely; his right cheek was abraded. But his stamina was undimished.

He stalked Datan through every corridor and at last, on the highest rampart against an inappropriately delicate and lovely morning sky all blue and gold and fleeced with clouds, he found him.

The archmage had both arms lifted, and dark turbulence was beginning to mass far in the west.

"Datan! Turn and fight, arch-enemy of old."

The massive head turned but words no man should ever hear in a tongue which was the native speech of hell burned Tempus's ears and made them ring as if he'd been struck hard upon the head.

He staggered back, forcing his knees to lock to keep from falling: he'd never missed his patron god so much, and Enlil would not fight upon his right. It was archmage and ancient warrior of heaven, face to face.

And as he longed for battle, hand to hand, he forced his

limbs to move, though dark assailed him, dark from Datan's eyes. He'd have him, or be had *by* this prince of horror. Either way, he'd win. Death was no stranger to a man who'd fought so many wars; sometimes he thought they had an understanding, he and the reaper whom Tempus had served so well, bringing multitudes to their fate.

Doggedly, he closed, though dark winds wailed around him and cold bit at his flesh.

He heard hell's hounds howl and sirens sing and then, as he was struggling to come the last few yards, old Datan laughed a gusting laugh that blew the pink glow of salvation from Tempus's sword and thrust him back as if from a parrying blow. But then the world, instead of fading into blackness, grew bright:

Jihan stood there, her scale armor afire, her arms outstretched . . . not to him, but to the archmage.

And for an instant Datan's eyes left his, where they'd been locked in awful battle, and Tempus, the archmage's hold on his senses broken, stumbled forward as if physical bonds had been cut away, his sword arcing down and singing through the air.

But the copper-scaled woman was quicker still: Jihan stepped close, then closer, to the archmage, saying, "Thy name is Uomo, thy fate is agony unending. Go thee to the reward thine awful life has earned, and *stay!* I banish thee!" She shot her hands forward and Datan, his mouth open wide and hands up to shield his ears, his soulless eyes tight shut, stumbled back, and back, and as he did so, the crenelated wall behind him crumbled away and a black rent in Nature's fabric took its place.

From it horrid devils leaped and grabbed him with talons so hot that his skin smoked and crackled, and Datan, the Osprey, Uomo and archmage of all Wizardwall, let go a cry of terror so loud and horrible and ringing that everywhere fighting had been raging, men stopped still, demons dropped their prey and fled, fiends went to ground, and all about, a silence thick as sleep came over them.

Datan's wailing, kicking struggles as hell's coils closed about him soon diminished, and then the black tunnel into hell had swallowed him, and began to shrink and spin in upon itself, and it too soon was gone.

Tempus sank down where he was, his breath coming hard and his knees weak and shaking, glad for rock beneath his feet and gods above, after what he'd glimpsed beyond that dark maw where Datan was well and truly bound.

"Jihan," Tempus said, "thanks the gods you're safe. We've found you—"

A tinkling laugh made him look up and then sit upon the stone, his sword clattering to the flags where it steamed and cooled. What had been Jihan in tri-color scale armor was changing shape, shimmering and wriggling.

He wasn't sure he had the strength to fight another foe. He merely watched the transformation under way, and then lay back flat: it was Cime, his benighted sister, who stood there laughing at him gently in her brown-black armor, and her blacker humor chilled him.

"Jihan," she mimicked, "thank the gods . . . thank *me*, brother. Without me to save you, you'd have had the seat next to Datan's in some musty hell. It's a good thing I *was* here to help, that's sure, or you'd have let your men be slaughtered for no better reason than—"

"Cime, can't you hold your tongue?" He was staring up at the fine blue sky where white clouds lazed and brightness reigned. "Or am I cursed with you forever?"

"Not quite forever, brother. But nearly so." Her voice was close; she leaned down over him. "Now, are we going to be mature about matters, and let me heal thee? Or is suffering so beloved in your sight that you'll take extra, more even than your due?"

He was full of demon's poison, exhausted and weak. He

couldn't find the strength or make up excuses not to let her help him. And so, with words and deeds, Cime managed one more time to bleed the joy from triumph, to belittle him even in what might have been his finest moment. He closed his eyes and let her tend him, a submission he was loath to make.

Afterwards, he and she together went seeking Jihan behind a solid-looking wall his sister waved away as if it were a curtain.

And there he found the sleeping Froth Daughter and a weeping tow-headed boy named Shamshi, son of Adrastus Ajami, the Mygdonian general, who was reluctant to believe that the bloody giant in gory mail and the battle-armored woman were his saviors.

Tempus soon convinced him, over Cime's objections, that he was in friendly hands that would soon return him to his rightful home in far Mygdonia.

Crit appeared, soon after women had begun to weep in the seraglio beyond, to ask if there was anything that Tempus needed, any instructions as to the disposition of the women, or anything else that Crit should know. He gave the boy into Critias's custody, saying: "Guard him well; he's special. As for those women, let Cime make sure that they're all harmless—no witches hiding in among them—then let the men consider them as spoils. Speaking of which, find Bashir, and start dividing what we've got here. Have you seen Grillo? Niko?"

Crit said laconically, "Both. They'll live. And Randal, too, I'd bet, though now it's over, he's got an uneasy stomach that he says some krrf might cure." Crit was looking straight at Cime, an odd expression on his face: "My lady? Shall we obey our orders?" He bowed a mock and sweeping bow and Cime brushed haughtily past him, so that Tempus knew they were no longer quite such close friends as they'd been before.

She called back instructions, telling Tempus what words

would wake the Froth Daughter, and: "Since she's about to join you, I'll be bidding you goodbye. Don't bother to kiss me a fond farewell, my brother. I've no doubt we'll meet again. Regards from Aškelon to you and Jihan. And do be careful, if you can."

"Not so fast, sister. You've taken coin from me and not yet given satisfaction. You're not going anywhere without my leave, and I won't give it."

She glared at him, stuck out her tongue, made a handsign that was fit more for a Stepson than a woman, and stalked away with Critias, his smirk ill-hidden in her wake.

Then he went to the Froth Daughter, sleeping on her bed, and leaned down close and, before he spoke the words to wake her, kissed her flushed and lovely lips. Sitting back, her cool hand in his, he said them. Her eyelids fluttered. He was relieved: It was not beyond his sister to tell him wrong, to give him words to say which would hurt, not wake, her rival.

But Jihan's eyes came open, blinked. She stretched, pulling her hand from his. She rubbed her eyes; she sat up, frowning, demanding: "What's this with you and the widow Maldives? I'm only gone a few days and you have some petty twit to hump instead? How can you debase our union so? And what, pray, are you doing here? Where's Datan? You haven't done that poor man harm, I hope. He's told me all about the grudge you bear. . . ."

During the ensuing argument, he shouted: "And what about my horses? You *stole* them! *Trôs* horses! You foolish amateur at womanhood, you've not a brain in that beautiful head," and many more things he shouldn't have, until he realized that only one resolution to their argument was possible; and whirled her round and stripped her down, and, tired as he was, took time to have her on that bed she wouldn't believe she'd slept upon for weeks, not days.

\*     \*     \*

Despite the biers being set and the funerary games to come, Niko had been glad to leave the captured citadel early. He wanted only to reclaim his sable horse from the Successor-guarded cave where he had left it and to be rid of Randal, whom Tempus had decreed he must escort safely back to Tyse, though Niko suspected that the Tysian Hazard didn't need any Stepson's help. During the battle, when he and Ari had used up the last of their blossoms and stars and were pinned down in a stairwell by three gigantic, drooling fiends with whirlpool eyes, Randal had changed from man to towering, fiend-eating beast and devoured an enemy to whom poisoned blossoms were mere irritations. Niko, sword drawn, crossbow bolts expended, had been ready to move in and take what wounds he must to engage them with his dream-forged sword. But Randal had beaten him to it. Randal had, like as not, saved them. And Randal, throughout the entire battle, had been steady on Niko's right, so that never during the protracted fighting had Niko needed to worry about his back or even think about what might be coming up behind him.

The slight, long-necked, large-eared mageling had proved his worth in Niko's eyes, even put Stealth in his debt. But explaining that to other Stepsons would be perceived as boasting or some excuse for having accepted a sorcerer on his right; he didn't try it. The Stepsons in his unit had seen what kind of fighter Randal was; the rest would hear it from men whom, unlike Niko, they could believe.

For his part, he wanted to be quit of Randal, and wished he didn't feel that way. So when they'd brought their unit through without a casualty or incapacitating wound and stood in Datan's sanctum after Crit had counted heads and the Riddler himself given out commendations, Niko had made sure that Randal knew he was entitled to a Stepson's share of spoils.

"I want nothing, Stealth; I'm pleased to have been of

service." Randal had just come back from conferring, head to head, with Tempus, and Niko saw a smile in the mageling's eyes. "Feeling better, fighter? You ought to be. Though Roxane's not been found, Cime, Bashir, myself and your commander all agree: the witch's hold . . . *power*, that is . . . is broken. You're—*we're* free of her and Datan and all the rest."

"So? Why tell me? Look here, Randal, you saved my life. Take something. It's not fitting if you don't." And Stealth had looked around him, spied the magician's globe which lay tumbled off its golden stand and picked it up. A moment's examination confirmed Niko's first impression: the globe was studded with precious stones and marked with arcane glyphs, its diameter such that it fit nicely under his arm.

He'd brought it back and held it out: "Here. This globe's for you. My share and yours will more than cover what it's worth, and I want to call us even. You'll make good use of this, I own."

"Oh, my Niko. I couldn't. . . ." the mage murmured, his astounded countenance confirming that this was just the sort of spoils to put a gleam in an enchanter's eye.

"You'd better. Or I'll tear you limb from limb." He'd tossed the globe and Randal was at pains to catch it before it hit the floor and smashed.

So he'd come out even—not beholden to some Hazard of the mageguild or stuck with a right-side partner he didn't want or need. His men had fared well, luckier than some. There were six biers to be lit and seven seriously wounded who'd need litters to be carried down or have to stay awhile in the citadel, which was undergoing intense and fervid purification to purge it of all traces of evil. Niko could see the smoke and hear the chanting of Bashir's Successors and even see Enlil's sanctifying glow upon the remaining towers as he and Randal took their leave.

Tempus had given him a fond and personal farewell,

singled him out for commendation, a thing which made him proud. But when they'd walked atop the ramparts talking, man to man like equals, about what the victory could come to mean with Bashir in control of Wizardwall so that the war was now a war of men—Mygdonia against Imperial Ranke, soldier to soldier, priest to priest, lowly mage to lowly mage—his sister had come out to join them. Niko had fallen silent, remembering the time she'd grabbed him by the belt at the Vulgar Unicorn and offered him her favors. She made him even more uncomfortable this day, telling him while Tempus listened that the dream lord loved him and coveted his allegiance, and that any time he wished he could call on Aškelon for help or counsel through his dreams.

And the Riddler had said nothing, staring off over a mountainside of frostbitten grass and dead, brown clover, his tiny kill-smile pulling at the corners of his mouth.

Niko had objected heatedly that special favors from entelechies in higher spheres were something he didn't crave and offered back the cuirass, sword and dirk.

"You'd best keep them, fighter. You still need all the help you can get," she'd replied.

He'd been impolite: "I'm not used to taking orders from a woman. And if I need a patron, I have Enlil to call on, as befits a Stepson. So you just tell your unholy boyfriend 'no,' next time you see him: I want no part of him . . . or you."

Then Tempus had turned about, and taken Stealth aside, telling him to go on ahead and to forget about what she'd said, but: "Keep the panoply. We *all* need what help we can get."

So, under orders, he'd done as he'd been bid and brought Randal, one Trôs horse, and those men he'd led upcountry back to Tyse—all but the Successors, who stayed there in the high peaks with Bashir.

And Bashir had wished him life and offered him a home

with them, which Niko appreciated but declined. He'd loved Bashir, loved him still, but his friend was too much the instrument of his god. In their younger days it hadn't been like that, but then Bashir's father had still lived. Bashir had ridden down as far as the cave with him, though, and they'd embraced and talked about the future:

"You are still going west to Bandara?" Bashir had asked, his wide brow knit with worry lines and flat face full of care.

"I'm not sure. The fighting made me think I might be better off solving my problems on my own—no gods, no adepts, no special help . . . just me. That's it in the end, I've come to think: just you. That's all any of us have got."

Bashir had tsk'd mournfully: "Shrivel me, Niko, if you weren't so stubbornly agnostic, you'd make a formidable warrior-priest."

"No thanks. Gods have bloody hands. I'm reverent from a distance. I don't want to be any closer to the gods than death will bring me, and for that companionship, I'm content to wait."

So they'd parted on a note of honesty, each wishing the other was different than he'd become.

But the sable horse was just exactly right—perfect, Niko thought. With all the responsibility of leading men in battle, he'd not had time to revel in just how good was this horse he had. Even the shadow cast over the gift by its source had been banished by the sunny days through which he rode it down to Tyse, a dozen fighters at his back. Tempus had spoken of breeding the reclaimed Trôs horses and both the sables during the coming winter quartering: a stud farm could be purchased by Stealth and his commander; they'd buy a dozen mares and charge no stud fee to Stepsons. Both the Riddler and Niko were eager to see if the sables would breed true; the sable mare they'd certainly breed back to Niko's stallion, and thus fix the pure Askelonian line. And Niko's mare, once she threw her Trôs foal, would be immediately bred to his new mount; he could hardly wait for them to meet.

After parting company with Randal at the mageguild, he'd thought to go straight to the Outbridge barracks and be reunited with his sorrel mare, but Ari and the others wanted to stop by Peace Falls and be the first to recount their exploits to admiring girls at Brother Bomba's, so they rode down to Commerce Avenue instead.

Passing by the mercenaries' hostel, its back doors open wide, made Niko think of Cybele and the Peace River house in which she'd died. He'd learned long since to accept lost loved ones. Death came where and when it willed. But a part of him felt that somehow the sweet young girl he'd tried to help had died because of him.

In Brother Bomba's, its proprietress was effusive in her welcome, near beside her stately self with joy to hear that the Riddler's force had triumphed, and all but two Stepsons would be coming home—the others dead were Grillo's specials and Successors, men she didn't know or care about.

It wasn't until Niko's belly was full of food and wine and his head was pleasantly spinning from the pulcis mixture laced with krrf Madame Bomba pressed on him "to remind you of our business deal, and, of course, because you're my favorite Stepson," that he remembered what Randal had said: *Feeling better, fighter?*

The words danced in his memory while a girl Madame Bomba sicced on him tried to lure him upstairs to give him a "hero's" welcome, so that as he thought back over all the fighting he tried to determine just when he'd regained that particular balance between apprehension and acuity that Niko called his *maat*. Perhaps about the time they'd fought the giant fiends, he guessed, but like all things which really matter to a man, the moment he'd reclaimed his equilibrium had passed away unnoticed: It was so natural to Niko to proceed with perspicuity and balance, once it returned it was as if he'd never been without it.

Leaving Bomba's without the cadre, ponying Tempus' extra Trôs behind his sable horse, he rode due west toward Outbridge, part drunk, part drugged, but with most of him turned inward, reclaiming his rest-place. Where his mind went then, no agonized spirits met him, no ghosts loitered nor specters resided: just peace and a safe, green field for contemplation met him.

Riding thus, he heard his name called: once, then again.

He pulled his sable to a halt and looked around, then listened. He knew that voice. He called out: "Cybele? Cybele?" and waited for an answer. But none came.

Shaking his head, he cursed what must have been too many drugs he'd ingested during the revelry back at Bomba's, then urged the sable into a lope. He was on the outskirts of the Outbridge quarter, where Grillo kept a house and others of high station had sculpted hedges and well-guarded, walled estates. It must have been an illusion, he decided, part guilt and part wishful thinking.

Yet when he rode through sentried gates at the Outbridge barracks, Cybele's fate still rankled. Refusing to think about her didn't help his mood. Both krrf and pulcis have a down-side, and Niko never had been much of a drinker.

In the inner court, he had to fend off a crowd of anxious, then ebullient, stay-at-homes who wanted word of the Stepsons' faring in the battle, and find stable room for Tempus' precious Trôs and his new sable; then take time for a reunion with his mare.

He was stroking her, inside her stall, letting her rub her head against his hip and whicker while he scratched the spot where neck met chest so that she closed her eyes and sighed, when he heard it again: "Niko? Niko?"

His hackles rose; he turned and leaned out over the stall's half-door, looking left, then right. A girl stood there, comely, young, yet her face in the darkened stable corridor was shadowed.

For an instant he thought that it must be the waif he'd run to ground when he first crossed the Nisibisi border, but then she called out, soft and low, "Oh, Niko, I'm so glad I found you," and ran toward him.

"Cybele? Cybele? But how? What? . . . Tempus said—" He vaulted over the stall's door.

"Hush, hush, my lord. Don't ask me any questions." Her arms were about him, her soft blond hair in his nose, and she wanted—so she said—to lie with him just one more time in fond embrace before she took her leave forever.

She wouldn't answer any questions; she kissed them from his lips. She made him promise not to say a word to anyone, especially not to Tempus, about this final tryst: "You must not say you've seen me. Your commander and I are enemies, he thinks, though some day he may reconsider. Now, promise me."

"I . . . I promise." He had her in his arms and all he could think of was the bed of straw that awaited in the hayloft.

Roxane flew north on eagle's wings; Niko slept soundly, far below and far behind her. It had been a risky move she'd made, for reasons barely understood, to take again the Cybele form and bed him one more time. But when Datan had gone to his reward, the string she'd latched onto that the archmage tied so long before was snapped like twine; her hold on the fighter war-named Stealth was broken.

But his on her, it seemed, had not been. To break it clean and start anew, she'd had first to face the fact that it was there; then face, straight-on, all she'd done and lost because she'd fallen in love with a petty mortal and not been wise enough to know it. If anything had won the day on Wizardwall and lost the war for magic, it had been her feelings for a youth who didn't even know her.

So she'd flown south, not north, to lie with him in carnal love and try to overcome her feelings. Failing that, she'd hoped to convince herself in some way that saving him was worth it.

But Niko was what Niko was—no more, no latent mage or superman; she left no quieter of heart than when she'd arrived. She had to leave. He loved Cybele, not Roxane. Too many forces worked against her here: the Cybele form was known, notorious; he had friends among the mage-guild; the Riddler considered himself young Stealth's protector; and even Aškelon coveted the child's allegiance. She'd hoped to find out why, what the fuss *was* over this resoundingly mortal boy. She hadn't. Nor had she banished love with another dose of it, as she'd hoped. In his mind, which she'd so long inhabited, she could find naught to hate.

Below, the pastoral fires of evening lit; the purple sky ahead was glorious. In Mygdonia she'd settle, build a following, a power base, and wait for Shamshi to come home. She'd insinuate herself into the Mygdonian court: they were sore in need of mages, and she knew just how to do it.

But she couldn't outfly her regret, one she'd never thought she'd have: for once in a long and powerful life, Roxane wished that she were mortal, inconsequential, feather-headed and girlish with modest wants . . . in fact, she wished she could be Cybele. But live a life with Niko as a wench? Age? Lose his favor to others? And for what?

An eagle's cry rang out across the steppes, and echoed.

She banished all thought of Niko then, sent it out with her hunting call.

She would remember him fondly; have him later. She was, after all, Death's Queen: she was eternal: she was Roxane.

\*    \*    \*

A week after coming down off Wizardwall, Tempus was still plagued with repercussions from his "victory."

War with Lacan Ajami's Mygdonian Alliance was now winnable; on this everyone, from Grillo to Bashir, agreed. On nothing else could Tempus reach a consensus: not on where the Stepsons would best be fielded next, or whether Successors or specials should continue to be integrated into his shock troops, nor even if Tyse was a suitable permanent base for his Sacred Banders, though a manifestation of Abarsis on bier day in the high peaks had convinced the fighters themselves of that.

The problems were political, and as far as politics were concerned, Tempus tended to agree with Critias: they'd be better off without them and those who acted selfishly, cloaked in this or that "political necessity."

His cadre would do what he ordered, and, finally disgusted with territorial wrangling from Grillo's camp and purportedly god-prompted advice from Bashir's, he ordered it to settle in and begin training up for an undisclosed venture.

These problems he was having with men unable to consider themselves less than "co-commanders," his sister Cime proclaimed, were of his own making: he just wasn't capable of being any less than completely and autocratically in control.

If this were true, he would have ridden both his sister and Jihan out of town tarred and feathered on matching rails, or lashed them to rafts and let Peace River wash them out of his hair, he retorted one night. He wasn't used to being henpecked, and those hens he had were dauntingly powerful, the pecking order itself their main concern.

He reminded himself that women were divisive, spent as much time as he could steal with his sable Aškelonian mare, and fended off his sister's advances as best he might. In all these years, he'd never succumbed to her. But riding alone out behind the Outbridge station, he admitted that he wasn't going to be able to hold out much longer. The night before, at dinner in his quarters, they had been alone, and Cime had spoken bitterly of the years she'd scoured a world quite like this one, but subtly different (a world a plane away), of sorcerers, until Aškelon alone had remained:

"And you know how I botched that up, brother." She'd sighed and shifted so that she lay flat on her cushions with her head on his lap. "If I'd know that being cured of my curse would mean I'd have to subject myself to interminable happiness and unending boredom in the dream lord's realm, I'd have finished him on the beach that day. Then there would be no Froth Daughter to trouble you, or dreams of mortality at the sour price of humbling yourself to Aškelon. Believe, brother, no afterlife is sweet enough to be worth bending your knee and bowing this," she reached up and ran a finger through his hair, then down across his lips, "glorious head to the entelechy of banality. Hug your strife close, dear one, and battle on. It suits you. Life on the golden streets and the crystal quays of that archipelago would drive you mad, if life it is. Now, come here and let's take the sport we've earned; you've paid me, here I am. . . ."

He'd pulled away only when his hand in hers lay on her breast, thinking there must be a trick here somewhere; perhaps she thought incest would keep Aškelon at bay. He used the thought of it to keep her from seducing him; though their mothers were different, the chance remained, despite the legend that a god of war had sired him, that their fathers were the same.

He'd said: "You think to use me as a shield against the dream lord? Think again, Cime. I'll keep you owing until *I* decide it's time."

And she'd gone off looking for a Stepson or some other to console her and make him jealous. Watching her, whose flesh called him like no other woman's, but whose soul—in spite of Aškelon's promise of salvation to come—seemed more damned even than his own, he'd felt despair. They'd never solve it. That was the page and line of their shared and equal curse.

He'd found solace with the Froth Daughter, who was livid with jealousy and rage: "Bad enough she stole my destined husband, now she'll have you too, and I, who am innocent of any wrongdoing whatsoever, will be left all alone with only soldiers! Riddler, tend me well, or my father will hear this whole sordid tale!"

Between the two of them, he was miserable, and his sable mare, who'd fallen in love with Abarsis' Trôs horse and pranced around the paddock with her tail straight up for him in immodest display of heat, but ignored Niko's sable stallion as if he were a gelding or a mule, was making matters worse.

He had just decided to send Jihan with Shamshi, over what would doubtless be Grillo's most vehement objections, up to Mygdon, and was reining her around to find the Froth Daughter and make final his decree, when a wind whipped up and the day (which had been mild and gently fading) went dark in his vicinity.

His horse stopped still, shivering. He slid down and, feet firmly on the ground, fist upon his swordhilt, looked all around: "All right. What now? Who or what wants a word with me?" Somewhere there must be a land where Nature ruled completely, where things like day and night and life and death could be counted upon to proceed in an orderly, not arbitrary, fashion. But in this world his curse had consigned him to, beyond the truism that all things were happening by strife and necessity, nothing could be said for certain—not that day would come or night would follow, or that sleep would ever be his, though lately war had tired him more than once it had.

There were bushes scattered about, their edges obfuscated, and trees off farther in the murky dark, not night or day but dusky like a natural setting or rising of the sun. It was his favorite time when it came naturally. Right now, out of sequence, it brought back all the disgust and revulsion he felt toward manipulations of the natural order he'd studied so diligently in his youth. But this time, not even his despite was pure, for he'd consorted willingly with mages, broken a rule he'd obeyed for centuries. A part of his mind told him he deserved this, whatever it should turn out to be.

What it turned out to be was Aškelon, the very lord of dreams, who came riding over gently swelling ground, much more vital and substantially supernal than he'd been when last they met.

The entelechy wore a simple cloak of no color as if his mantle had been woven from the peculiar light which swathed them both. The horse he rode was like the sable Tempus held; the two beasts exchanged familiar greetings, and the lord of dream and shadow raised a hand to Tempus as if it were perfectly natural that Aškelon would manifest, his thick black and silver hair waving in a soft breeze, his cloudspun eyes fierce and too near at hand for the distance yet between them.

"Greetings, Ash," he said when the entelechy dismounted.

"Riddler. Blessings on thee and thine." The dream lord extended a hand and Tempus had to shake it; when he let it go he felt more peaceful, as if even the mad cosmos he lived in had shed disorder and all his troubles bled away.

It was a spell, he thought, and shook it from him, saying carefully: "You look well."

"And you look tired. Have you thought about my offer?"

"My answer is still the same."

"In that case, immortal sufferer, let us lessen at least one of your burdens. Your sister's here yet, I must assume."

Leading their horses, they walked toward the barracks. "Still here, yes. She's not anxious to go back there."

"Are you telling me you'll interfere with a pact solemnly undertaken? She has a year to spend with me. It was for your sake, and not hers, I gave her leave to visit and lend her particular sort of aid."

"For me? I didn't know you cared so much. Or was it for young Nikodemos? That soul, I'll fight to keep unfettered. He's told me he wants no part of dispensations from any higher plane or sphere or what-have-you. Is that clear?"

"Sufficiently, for now. And yes, I covet Niko's fealty. But you yourself know that a man cannot be brought to high estate against his will."

"He wills it not."

"You said that."

"That's right. I did. I'm saying it again."

"I could grant you sleep, one night's rest in thousands of sleepless nights. I'd just like to talk to him."

"Absolutely not."

The dream lord sighed. "Whatever you wish. But Cime comes back with me."

"She's taken coin from my hand and not yet given service."

The dream lord smiled. "She would try that. We'll have her give it back. Release her from her bond. Unless, that is, you want the *two* of them—Cime *and* Jihan—to try to deal with. I wouldn't, but the choice is up to you."

"She's my sister. I can't consign her to—"

Aškelon eyed him sidelong: "Consider it medicine for her ills. Without my help, she'll languish with that curse forever. She's never quite grown up. Children often resist medicine."

Tempus thought that over. "I'll get back my coin and leave the two of you alone. The rest is up to you."

"Good." He smiled and a break came in the dusky sky; sunrays burst on through. Then the dimness blew away and they walked in bright, pure sunshine. "A word of

warning: that boy you have, Ajami's so-called son, is half
a wizard. Remember Abarsis, and be careful with him.
What he becomes is partly up to you, Riddler."

"Up to his father, or the man who claims to be so.
You're telling me that Adrastus doesn't know?"

"Suspects, sleepless one. Suspects. By Mygdonian law,
he'd have to slay his wife as an adulteress and put the boy
to death. . . . So you see, as human matters are, it's delicate.
It needs a hand like yours to—"

"I have no patience with children. He goes to Mygdon;
that is that."

"As you wish, again. Now, take me to your sister. And
let's try to avoid meeting Jihan, if we can."

Tempus grinned: at least they had something more than
overlong existence in common; even Aškelon feared the
Froth Daughter's righteous wrath.

They found Cime cuddled up with Straton in his quarters;
Critias was pacing back and forth outside.

"She's in there with him, says she'll heal his eyesight,
but Strat's not up to fending off . . ." Crit paused, looked
up for the first time, saw Aškelon and made a warding
sign. His hand dug in his belt pouch, and Tempus, who
knew his first officer quite well, knew Crit was fingering
his good luck charms. "Well," he finished lamely, "she's
. . . more a woman than any of us quite know how to
handle, my lords. . . ." He raked his hair with spread
fingers: "Going in? You'd better knock first."

Tempus did that.

Straton came to the door, flushed and disheveled: "Your
sister. Yes, commander . . . right this way. I've got to go
find Crit at any rate. She was seeing if she might alleviate
this blurriness I see close-up or very far away—"

"It's fine, Straton. Thank you. Crit's right outside."

Then Strat had hurried past them, and Tempus stepped
in first.

She was lacing up the Ilsig doeskins she yet affected,

breathing heavily, smiling just a bit. "Now, brother, let's not argue. A woman spurned takes comfort where and when . . . she . . ." Seeing Aškelon, she scrambled up, her hands before her.

"I'll take that gold Imperial I gave you," Tempus said quite low.

"You beast! You wouldn't! Oh please. . . ." Then she seemed to quiver and to blink away the extra brightness in her eyes. "Here." She fumbled in her belt and slapped the coin into his outstretched palm. "Satisfied? Stay with your storm-sprung slut. And may you soon have need of me again. Now, go! Get out of here, traitor! Leave, and leave me to my fate, as you always do and ever have done. It's a lucky thing, after all, that you don't sleep, for all the wrongs you've done would surely make your dreams a horror—"

"Silence best becomes you," Aškelon interrupted and, amazingly, Cime shut her mouth.

"Good fortune, Riddler," Aškelon wished him. "As you said so long ago: 'War is common and right is strife.' War rightly, and may your Stepsons flourish, and your might prevail."

Then, in an eyeblink, both the dream lord and Tempus' sister were no more.

Alone, he sat down on Straton's unmade bunk to reconsider matters in the light of what had just transpired. With Cime gone, Jihan was not a major problem—his Stepsons weren't thrilled to have her bunking in among them, but whatever he did was accepted without question by Sacred Banders, and the others took their cue from how the pairs behaved. Perhaps Grillo was right in wanting to keep Shamshi as collateral until Adrastus came through with all the aid he'd promised. He'd keep Jihan close at hand (the boy was fond of her and she of him), and they'd confer on what to do about the child.

When he came out of there, a real dusk was just

beginning, and Crit was loitering by the threshold: "Everything all right, Commander?"

"Perfect, Critias. And with you?"

"Strat's vision—he says it's better." Crit's cynical grin flashed. "I didn't think that was really what she meant to do with him. . . ."

"I know." Tempus, as well as Crit, felt uncomfortable.

"Cime?" Crit asked, peering beyond Tempus, into the shadowed, empty room. "The dream lord?"

"Gone where dreams go and waking men can never follow, let's hope."

"Let's," Critias agreed.